What the critics are saying...

ഔ

5 cups of coffee! "Ari is a wonderful heroine, an unusual woman for her era with education, varied skills and a fierce will. Robert is a heart-stealing swash-buckling hero, part Native American but also scion of English nobility. In Ari he has more than met his match...Captured from the exciting opening scene, I had to read just one more page, one more chapter, staying up much later than I had planned. I thoroughly recommend this excellent historical romance." ~ *Coffee Time Romance*

5 Spies out of 5! "Victoria Dark has a wonderful way of using words to make her story come alive. The dialogue and description carry you away to this time period making you think the characters are not fictional... You'll fall in love with Fox just like Ari did." ~ *Gotta Write Network*

4 angels! "Two people who don't dare love or trust, find themselves in an impossible situation... Dangerous to Love is a romantic, historical novel at its best. Victoria Dark has created characters that are three dimensional and reach out to the reader. This is the type of novel that once you start the first paragraph, you'll stay up till the wee hours of the morning to finish it." ~ *Fallen Angels Reviews*

"If you like a story that is full of deceit, treachery, and secrets at every turn, then you won't want to miss reading DANGEROUS TO LOVE. WARNING—Be prepared to experience the full thrust of Fox and Ari's heated entanglements. Victoria Dark gives her readers an extremely intriguing tale from page one to her very climatic ending." ~ *Romance Junkies Reviews*

"Dangerous to Love was well written, witty, and I just plain liked it." ~ *Joyfully Reviewed*

"Dangerous to Love was a joy to read. The suspense was used to the benefit of the story and kept you guessing as the plot twisted and turned. Fox and Ari were both mistaken in how the other was thinking leading to a lot of humorous situations. In fact humor was in many of the scenes, keeping you glued to the pages. Fox and Ari were made for each other. Too bad it takes them so long to realize this. Victoria Dark has written a delightfully humourous, romantically sexy and wonderfully suspenseful novel with Dangerous to Love." ~ *Ecataromance reviews*

Dangerous
TO LOVE

VICTORIA
DARK

Cerridwen Press

A Cerridwen Press Publication

www.cerridwenpress.com

Dangerous to Love

ISBN 9781419956041
ALL RIGHTS RESERVED.
Dangerous To Love Copyright © 2006 Victoria Dark
Edited by Marty Klopfenstein
Cover art by Syneca

Electronic book Publication March 2006
Trade paperback Publication March 2007

Cerridwen Press is an imprint of Ellora's Cave Publishing, Inc.®

About the Author

෨

Victoria Dark is women's fiction and special projects editor for a hardcover publisher, but writing stories is what she loves most. After her first short story was published by a popular mystery magazine, Victoria began seriously pursuing a writing career. Since then, along with many short fiction pieces andarticles, she has published several romance novels, which include contemporary, historical, historical humor, and historical suspense.

When not reading, writing, or editing, she is busy helping to run her and her favorite cowboy's "organic" cow farm. All feed is natural grain or hay, with no steroids and no growth hormones. And she says the stuff she scrapes off the soles of her boots is about as organic as you can get.

Victoria Dark welcomes comments from readers. You can find her website and email address on her author bio page at www.cerridwenpress.com.

DANGEROUS TO LOVE

᳇

Dedication

❦

To Laura E Reagan, a gifted writer who has given freely of her advice and support,

and to Marty Klopfenstein, a fantastic editor, who was a blast to work with on this project.

Chapter One

The Devon Coast, 1809

Dartmouth Harbor

ๆ

One shot—she'd checked her priming carefully.

One shot—there'd be no time for more.

One shot. Through Lord Grandquest's black heart. Then…

And then…

And then…*what?*

Ari shifted the heavy pistol hidden beneath her cloak from one strong hand to the other as she considered the question. The jib boom of a tall ship angled above her. Other ships shouldered the embarcadero, or rode at anchor on the gray-brown water of Dartmouth Harbor. A small, bare forest of masts and yards rose into an azure sky, and a blustery wind keened through the high rigging and rattled pulleys against the spars.

Her gaze moved along the line of ships at anchor, lingering on the deep ocean vessels. Grandquest's ship was a three-masted square-rigger. Among these squat East India men, it should look like a falcon among fat chickens.

And after she'd found Grandquest and paid him back for his treachery, what then?

Why then some English magistrate would kindly arrange her future for her, she realized. A very short, dramatic future, to be sure—a brisk dance at the end of a stout rope. *Mon Dieu,* one could not shoot an English earl without *some* repercussions.

Well, not *in* England, anyway.

Although the hour was early and despite the cold wind slicing down from the north, Dartmouth's waterfront was alive with activity. The elite of the merchant class, dressed in old-fashioned frockcoats with shiny brass buttons and gold braiding, moved amid stacks of goods, haggling amongst themselves, as their harried-looking clerks rushed about and shuffled manifests, trying to keep up with the bargaining.

A half-dozen children in ragged clothing played in a nearby gutter. Running, laughing and shrieking, they seemed unmindful of the cold and the filth, and the stench of human refuse, which mingled with stench of long-dead fish.

Stevedores grunted, loading or unloading cargoes to rude orders shouted by gutter-mouthed second mates.

Adding to the cacophony, vendors with pushcarts moved through the crush, singing out their wares—*"Mulled wine, a ha'pence, a ha'pence, a ha'pence!" "Pasties, pasties, pasties!"* and *"'Ot an' spiced, 'ot an' spiced ale!"*—while red-skirted doxies hawked other goods. All were doing a brisk trade.

A gust of wind snatched at the hood of her shabby cloak, and Ari caught it and tugged it lower to shield her face. What would happen after she'd shot Grandquest? She considered the question and realized it didn't matter a whit. Her future did not show a great deal of promise in any event. She was alone on the Dartmouth waterfront. Dressed in rags. Penniless. Homeless, after the treacherous work against them last night. And, without a doubt, now wanted by the Crown as a French spy. Even if she should forego the pleasure of shooting Lord Grandquest, a noose had been around her neck from the moment the Devonshire Militia had burst through the door of the cottage last night.

That was, of course, if she wasn't merely shot down on sight.

Just as Grandquest had shot Dolpho... *No! Don't think about that! You will only start sniveling, and what good will* that *do now?*

But she had left him, still and alone in the damned English rain… How could she have just left him?

Grief clawed at her chest like a living thing. Her breath would go neither in nor out past the knot in her throat, and hot, stinging tears blurred her vision. Ari crammed her fist against her mouth and took shelter between two high stacks of wooden crates waiting to be loaded onto ships. It was too late for tears. She had relished every moment of their adventure—the plotting, the intrigue. Dolpho had wanted her to go back to London, saying things were growing too dangerous, but she had refused to hear of it—she'd been having the time of her life.

And so Dolpho had paid with his.

If she had left when he'd asked, if he hadn't had to help her escape when the militia came, he could have just put his heels to the horse and ridden into the woods…

Ari angrily wiped her eyes with the back of her hand. Dolpho wasn't the first man Grandquest had murdered. And the bastard would kill again, if she didn't stop him. She was the only one who could. The only one who *knew* the truth, knew him for the murderer he was.

Pushing away from her shelter, she made her way a little further along the quays, but stopped short, her heart thumping harder as she saw the sleek town coach drawn up in the alley between two warehouses. The Grandquest coat of arms crowned by strawberry leaves was emblazoned on its door. A livery-clad footman and coachman stood beside it, stamping their feet to stay warm in the cold morning air, their breath puffing out like fog.

If the Grandquest coach was here, so, too, must be the earl. Just as Dolpho had said he would be.

Looking over head, she found a golden jib boom jutting into the air above her. The figurehead beneath was carved by a master's hand, a lifelike figure depicting an American Indian woman, her arms raised as if in supplication. Even before she looked at the nameplate, she knew she'd found it, *The Midnight*

Dancer — Dolpho had described the ship and its figurehead in detail, and he'd also told her of the earl's unusual past.

Pulling the hood of her cloak lower, Ari made her way onto the gangplank.

"Hold, there!" The ship's officer of the watch stepped onto the plank, barring her way.

Merde! Why hadn't she anticipated this? Ari drew in a deep breath and shifted her weight to one foot — the one with the slipper — wriggling the toes of her bare foot to try to get the feeling back into them. Her other slipper had been lost as she and Dolpho cut a hole in the cottage's thatched roof and scrambled through as the Devonshire Militia broke down their front door. "I have... Oi 'ave somethin' fer yer master. The earl. 'E left it yesterday. Or, mayhap, were last night. So 'ard to tell, deary, with the shutters all closed." Ari winked.

The young man, who could have been no more than eighteen, went red to the roots of his light, baby-fine hair. Nevertheless, he resolutely blocked her way. "I'll give it to him for you, ma'am."

"You could not. Oi mean, it be somethin' of a...ah...personal nature." Ari let her hood slip back, just a little, so the young man could see her face. When his eyes rounded, she gave him a coaxing smile — a smile she'd practiced in the salons of Vienna as she'd made her entrance into society. She'd used it to charm archdukes and generals.

She read the uncertainty in the young man's eyes. He shot a quick glance at the tall man on the quarterdeck — the earl! Dolpho had pointed Grandquest out once in London as he'd helped a lady out of a coach in front of a Drury Lane theater.

Swallowing a sudden lump in her throat, Ari's grip on the pistol tightened. "There 'e is!" She pushed past the young officer. "Oi'll be naught but a moment givin' it to 'im, lovey. Naught but a moment." Resolutely ignoring his stuttered protest, Ari held her breath, but the young man didn't try to stop her again.

Just a few more steps, twenty…now ten. The white-scrubbed deck seemed to sway beneath her and her heart beat so, she thought she must faint. Grandquest had his back to her as he spoke with another man, from his dress and bearing, perhaps the captain of this vessel. Staring at the earl's wide shoulders, she willed her feet to move on. In a moment she would be so close she could not miss.

She must not miss — there would only be this one chance.

Grandquest turned suddenly, as if sensing her behind him. Ari found herself staring into a pair of cold, gray eyes, deep-set beneath dark brows that curved like an eagle's wings.

"You need something, madam?" He frowned, moonstone-gray eyes looking her over, taking in the ragged cloak.

Using both thumbs to cock it, Ari brought up her gun.

Overhead, seabirds whirled and cried, or fussed as they perched on the yards. The wind in the rigging piped a sailor's chantey. It caught her hood and whipped it back and her hair floated out. Her cloak flapped apart, for she could not hold it. She needed both hands to help level the heavy gun. Beneath the cloak, she wore only a nightgown, for she'd been abed when the militia had come pounding on the door. Ari shivered as the cold sliced through her as if she wore nothing at all.

And so did Grandquest's gaze.

Robert Travellion Fox Grandquest, seventh Earl Grandquest, studied the young woman before him, her hair a deep auburn flame whipped by the wind. God's truth but she was a beauty, tall and exquisitely formed. The rag she wore hid little. Was it a night rail? It was torn at the neckline and her nipples were visible through the thin lawn fabric. The wind molded the garment to her, outlining legs as long as a man's dreams.

Fox frowned as he studied the rusty red stain over her thigh and realized it was dried blood. A small, round hole centered the stain.

This grew stranger and stranger.

Bright spots of color burned on the girl's pale cheeks, hinting at fever. But her eyes—thick-lashed eyes, the same cerulean blue of the sky—were clear and filled with purpose.

She meant to kill him.

And from the way she held the pistol, she knew what she was about.

But why?

Ari was aware that all work on board the ship had ceased as sailors and stevedores gathered around them. The big, red-haired man with whom Grandquest had been speaking edged away from the earl and to the side.

Grandquest gave an infinitesimal shake of his head, directed at someone behind her, and she realized she'd left herself vulnerable from behind—where were her wits?

Keeping the long barrel pointing at the earl's heart, she carefully moved until she felt the taffrail at her back. Long moments passed as she searched the earl's eyes, looking for guilt or remorse.

"I take it, madam, that you mean to shoot me," he said as slow seconds ticked by.

His tone made her grit her teeth. He might have been discussing the weather—had the man no fear?

"Sir, you do not mistake my intention."

Ari hadn't expected this, oh, no. She had steeled herself against his begging and pleading with her to spare his life. Instead, the earl seemed completely at his ease. Darkly handsome. Superbly masculine. He was looking at her not as a man looks at his executioner, but as a man looks at...at a desirable *woman*. *Merde*, no wonder Dolpho had labeled this Grandquest the most dangerous man in England.

Appearing completely at his ease, Grandquest propped one booted foot on a keg and rested his forearm on his knee. Except for the seabirds overhead and her cloak, which flapped in the wind, all action on board the ship was frozen. More long seconds passed.

"Then, madam," he drawled, "get on with it, but, pray, do not bore me to death."

Her incredible eyes widened in disbelief and the fever roses staining her cheeks flushed cherry red. "Your pardon, My Lord. I was but allowing you time to make your peace with God. I thought, in your case, it might take a while."

Low laughter rippled through the rough sailors gathered around them and they shifted closer.

As Ari awaited his response, Grandquest's chiseled mouth softened in the briefest of smiles and a quicksilver flash lit his thick-lashed gray eyes, making her angrier, still. What manner of devil was this? A man who could smile at his executioner?

"That is most considerate of you. And, no doubt, my ragged soul should be blown to hell." His tone softened, "But if you do the deed, you'll hang. Now, wouldn't it be a pity if rope burns should mar such a lovely neck as yours, and over such a worthless hide as mine?"

Ari straightened, squaring her shoulders. "I will not hang."

Something cold snaked through his stomach as Fox read the glance she flicked over the side at the deep, gray waters of the harbor.

She continued, "I have no illusions of escaping, but that is not important, Lord Grandquest. I ask only the pleasure of finding *you* in hell when I get there."

He shook his head slowly. "Such venom in one so young... What have I done to make you hate me so?"

"What have you done?" Her wonderful eyes were blue fire as she glared at him. "It is no wonder that you can not make peace for your soul if your sins are so quickly forgotten!"

Fox flinched under her tone. She'd expected him to know why she was here and why she was holding the gun. Was it because of Peterson? This girl spoke with a French accent and Peterson's wife was an émigré. His demons raised their heads and smiled at him. Yes, if this was Peterson's wife, he deserved her hate.

"No, not forgotten." Fox shook his head to banish the ghost of a handsome young man laying dead in the filth of a London alley. "Never forgotten. But there are so many stains on my soul, you see, I would know by which I hurt you?"

"Then, Milord, you will die not knowing—"

"At least," he interjected, sensing her gathering her resolve and wanting to keep her talking, "tell me by what name I should greet you when you join me in those...*warmer* regions?"

"What name?" Ari blinked, realizing the opportunity he offered. She could tell him a false identity, if she could but think of one. Then her family's name would be protected.

But what name?

She had posed as Dolpho's mistress in London. "Tess LeBlanc" had gone to America when Dolpho had grown tired of the actress, or so they had put about.

She had been Mademoiselle le Comtesse in St. Cyr. To *Grandpere*, she'd been Arielle.

She had been Ari to Dolpho... *Oh, Dolpho, I'm so sorry I left you cold and alone. I should have stayed. I should have. But I promised you that I would find this man!*

The tall man at the end of her gun watched her closely. She couldn't tell him the truth. The Benoits were thought mad as it was. She wouldn't add *murderers* and more scandal. Better to leave her identity a mystery.

Lowering her chin, she promised him darkly, "I shall tell you my name when I get there."

Fox focused on the very dangerous young woman before him, waiting, praying for her attention to slip, so he could safely disarm her. But the heavy pistol had never wavered—were those slender wrists made of iron?

Then he sensed it. Beneath the thick, sable lashes, the pupils of her blue eyes widened. Looking into them was much like looking into the bore of the gun aimed unerringly at his heart.

The knuckle of her forefinger grew white.

Ari squeezed. Then squeezed harder. But the gun was old, the mechanism stiff. It had taken both thumbs for her to cock it. Now that the moment was hers, the trigger refused to work.

Suddenly, her wrist and the pistol barrel were caught in an iron-hard grip. She struggled to regain control of the gun, but Grandquest turned it harmlessly upward. Enraged, she punched the earl with all the force she could muster, the blow landing squarely on his chin.

Fox's head snapped back from the blow. Before he could recover, she threw herself sideways, twisting, pulling, surprising him and almost throwing him off balance with the abrupt shift in her weight.

"Damn, you little hellion!"

But she wasn't little. She was tall and strong. And those wrists were made of iron, he decided grimly. It suddenly occurred to him that he was fighting for his life.

Dieu! She'd been a fool. If she hadn't hesitated, the man who'd killed Dolpho would now be dead — the same man who'd killed so many others, the man who was going to cost England the war with Napoleon!

As she felt the pistol slipping from her grasp, panic gave her a surge of new strength. Throwing her weight in the opposite direction, she twisted and pulled, one hand on the barrel, the other still clamped around the butt. Abruptly folding her legs beneath her, she swung on the gun like a trapeze, pulling with her whole weight.

Yes! His grip was slipping — she felt it.

Then all the world exploded.

The seabirds perched in the high rigging flapped away in alarm. The ring of rough men jostled each other, crowding closer, the better to see the tragedy.

Fox Grandquest looked down, stunned, at the woman lying on the deck at his feet. One shapely leg was exposed, and her hand was curled beside her cheek as though she was a sleeping child. The wind whipped a strand of her glorious hair around his polished boot—the deep auburn curls clashed madly with the crimson stain spreading over the white oak deck.

She looked so young in death. Damnation, she could not be twenty.

Kneeling beside her, he swore at the needless waste of her life.

"Milord? I'm sorry, Milord." Young Graham Conners pushed forward through the knot of men. "I—I had the watch, you see, I—that is, she said she had something she must give you. I didn't think—"

"Aye, lad. Ye didna' think," Captain McMasters cut the young man off. "Ye'll present yerself in my cabin at eight bells. I'll pronounce yer punishment then. Now, back to yer post wit' yer."

Graham popped tall. "Aye-aye, sir."

Fox winced. Graham was the youngest and most inexperienced of his hand-picked crew. The earl wished the lad had not appeared quite so military in his response. Merchant vessels didn't maintain such precise manners.

Looking back at the young woman lying still on the deck, Fox grimly took the point of her chin in his fingers and turned her head, exposing the wound. Expecting a gruesome pulp, he was surprised. Instead of shattering her skull, the pistol ball had parted her hair from temple to crown.

Something faint and warm touched the back of his hand, and he tensed. As he reached for the pulse at her throat, a soft hand caught his large one.

"Dolpho?"

A tear slipped from the corner of her eye, and her eyes opened.

Ari found a dark head above her, silhouetted against England's cold October sun. *"Dolpho?"*

She was suddenly in Fox's arms, her cheek pressed against his chest.

"Oh, Dolpho, how did you find me? *Cher bon Dieu,* I saw you die!"

Chapter Two

ဆာ

Someone was cheerfully beating a rather large kettle drum in her head. Unable to make the pain stop, Ari opened her eyelids a crack. A bright ray of sunlight fell across them like a saber. Moaning, she snapped her eyes closed.

Mon Dieu, a mistake that.

Carefully, she turned her head, seeking the dark place where she'd been hiding from the pain in her head, but the little fires burning inside her skull grew hotter with every movement.

What had happened to her?

She tried hard to remember, but all was a blank slate.

A *boom, boom, boom* added throbbing rhythm to her pain. Slowly, she became aware that the source wasn't a cannon, as she had first thought, but something nearby. Peeking, she spied the ornate clock sitting on a carved marble mantle. Surely this was no ordinary clock! The devil's device was loud as a gong.

Wincing, Ari touched her throbbing head and found it swathed in a turban-like bandage. Ah, she'd been in some accident. That explained much. Had her mare thrown her again?

She groped for the bell pull. Better to find out than to wonder.

The pull was not at the side of the bedpost.

Curiosity forced her eyes open and ice-pink satin greeted them. The pink satin canopy and coverlet were strange, indeed. Which room in the château could this be? Why hadn't *Grandpere* had her placed in her own room?

Ari closed her eyes again and breathed deeply, trying to clear her head. When she felt up to the task, she propped up on an elbow and made a more thorough inspection of her surroundings. The room was in deep shadow, but she had the impression of elegance — high ceilings, painted moldings, and gilt-framed paintings. There was no room in *Château Nuage* so elegant.

Where was she? And how — *Mon Dieu*, it hurt to think. She decided not to try, and eased herself back on the pillows, closing her eyes. *Tick, tick, tick* ricocheted inside her head, surely making dents in her brain as it did.

Pulling the coverlet and a feather pillow over her ears, she tried to ignore it and sought to find the sweet oblivion of sleep.

The pain grew worse.

Merde, was there no servant about who could deal with this *horologe diable* – this devil's clock?

Pulling another pillow atop the one already covering her head, she determined to ignore the timepiece. But she became aware of other things, which niggled at her. Her mouth was horribly dry, and much of her body hurt, not just her head. The hot pain in her neck and down her back seemed to be connected to her head somehow. In addition, there was pain in her thigh that felt as though something gnawed on it. She gently explored the area and found her thigh bandaged.

Her head and her thigh?

And where was she?

The question of where she could be, once having presented itself, refused to let her lie still. Sighing, she pushed the pillows off her head and sat up slowly. After she waited for the room to stop spinning, she stood none too steadily and found she was weak as a kitten. Nausea rose in her throat and the pain in her head seemed to double. Closing her eyes, she held onto the tall bedpost. She should lie back down, she knew. She should. But there was that damned clock…

Drawing a steadying breath, she moved carefully, biting pain in her thigh with each step, as she made her way to the wide door at the side of the room. *Merde.* It had been a mistake to get out of bed. Her thigh ached twice as much as before, and there was now a ringing in her ears, in addition to the gong clock. No, it had not been wise to get out of bed. It was the preferred place to be when one fainted, as she suspected she was soon to do.

But she'd put too much effort into getting up to give up and go back now. Not if it meant enduring that hellish timepiece.

After traveling a small eternity, she grasped the curved handle of the door and frowned as it moved beneath her hand. She stepped back as it was opened by a short, round housemaid.

This was luck, since a maid was just whom she was in search of. Ari said, in French, "The clock. Remove it, please. It hurts my head."

The maid's small eyes rounded. Dropping the workbasket she'd been carrying, she put plump hands to her apple-round cheeks and screamed — a full-throated, high-pitched outpouring of feminine distress.

Ari clasped her head in her hands, certain the onslaught of sound would split it into two parts.

"You do not have to take it far. Just out of the room, *s'il vous plait*."

The maid screamed again, threw her apron over her head, and bolted. Unfortunately, with her vision thus impaired, her foot hooked the handle of the fallen workbasket and the woman measured her length on the marble floor.

Suddenly, the hallway was crowded. Footmen and maids stared at the woman screeching and crying and pleading to be spared whatever horrific end the *French Fiend* had in mind.

Pressing her hands over her ears, Ari closed her eyes and wished them all to perdition.

"Cor, but she's a tall 'un," breathed a footman.

Hearing the comment, Ari's eyes flew open. "You are English? We are in England?" she asked, uncertainly. Then answered her own question. "But of course we are. We are speaking English, are we not?"

Memory returned like a plunge into icy water.

She wasn't at *Château Nuage*. *Grandpere* was dead — a suspicious fall down the stairs the morning after a battalion of Bonaparte's soldiers marched up Mount St. Cyr. The general in command had declared, since there was no direct male heir — discounting Ari's claim as invalid under French law — the château and all properties connected with the title were forfeit to the Empire.

Her cousin, Dolpho, dealt with the general with the point of his sword, then she and Dolpho fled to England. Dolpho planned to join some English battalion bound for the Peninsula and fight against Napoleon. But once here, her cousin instead chose to help defeat the little Corsican in more subtle ways — by working for British Intelligence. Their quest to ferret out the leader of a spy ring had brought them to a wild stretch of coast, near Dartmouth…and then *something* had happened.

Something very bad.

What?

Ari frowned, trying to draw further memories past the pain in her head.

She found only confusion.

"What's this about?"

The voice, deep and rich, drew the attention of the small crowd. The knot of servants parted, and she found herself looking up into a pair of startling gray eyes, deep set beneath brows that curved like an eagle's wings.

New memories rocked her back on her heels. Rain, cold rain. Dolpho, his face contorted in pain, his blood flowing warm between her fingers. Dolpho, begging her to find this bastard… Obviously, she had found him.

Just as obviously, she had failed to see him dead.

She rubbed her throbbing temples, trying hard to think, to remember more. But pain was a red haze fogging her brain, taking her strength.

Fox Grandquest was taken aback to see his unusual houseguest up and about. Bringing her here might have been a mistake. But then, he'd really had no choice, had he? He could hardly have turned her over to the authorities until he learned what she knew. "Going out for a morning stroll, are you?"

She frowned up at him, rubbing her temples. "*Mon Dieu,* but you have a loud voice."

She dared to complain about his tone? He shook his head. "I will own I'm surprised you're up so soon. But then again, even from our short acquaintance, I suppose I shouldn't be too surprised at anything you do."

"Sir, I have no memory of our having been introduced." Ari lifted her chin, though it cost her an effort, and stared at him. He could only kill her once. She would be damned if she let him know he intimidated her. Think, think—what had happened after she left Dolpho?

One dark brow rose, and Grandquest smiled. "I will allow it wasn't a formal introduction."

His hair was like a blackbird's wing—so dark, it seemed to absorb the light. A lock fell across his forehead. A frown was etched between his dark brows. A definite hook, his nose was offset, as if it had been broken at least once. The tea-stained color of his skin was unusual.

However, it was his eyes that held her. Narrowed. Assessing. Cold as moonstones. And as hard.

Blackness formed a puddle at her feet, but pride compelled her to remain upright. The blackness rose, lapping at her knees. Deepening to her thighs. Buzzing filled her head. He was speaking again, but his words were indistinct as the world behind him spun crazily. Still, sheer power of will kept her standing.

"Attacked me, she did." The maid drew the earl's attention. Two stout footmen had helped the woman to her feet. "I just popped down to the sewing room to fetch more mending, to occupy me as I sat and, when I opened the door, she pounced on me," Littleburn insisted. "Started a babbling in some heathen language and threw me poor old bones down on the floor."

Fox turned back to his unusual houseguest. "Is this—*damnation!*"

He caught the girl as she fell.

Muttering obscenities, he hooked an arm beneath her knees and lifted the young woman and looked around, scowling, reminding his staff of duties left unattended.

"Mrs. Coventree, come with me," he ordered his housekeeper. "Bring a maid—one not so pudding-hearted as Littleburn. How could this woman have overpowered anyone? She has one foot in the grave."

* * * * *

Ari dared a peep through the thick screen of her lashes at the tall man at the far end of the long bedroom. The earl was speaking in subdued tones with another man, one who called himself a doctor.

Doctor? *Ha!* Dr. Keiss, who had taught her much about medicine, would not have let this supercilious oaf hold his coat. Doctor, indeed. Dr. Kilpatrick had done nothing to improve her condition. Instead, he'd driven her nearly mad with his probing and questions, when she wanted only for the pain in her head to ease.

She'd given the doctor no answers. Nor had she answered Grandquest's questions. Some instinct for self-preservation warned her that the earl's curiosity about her might be what had kept her alive. So far.

She was having trouble accepting what he'd told her before the doctor arrived—not that she'd tried to shoot him, but that she'd shot herself, instead. *Mon Dieu*, that would have been beyond careless!

Ari sighed. She needed to think, to remember exactly what had happened, and she needed time to garner her strength, so she could escape. Whatever Grandquest was planning for her, she was certain it would not be pleasant.

The word *amnesia* floated to her, and she felt a tingle of excitement as she peeped through her lashes again. Revising her opinion of the doctor slightly, she decided he might not be totally useless. It was kind of him to gift her with amnesia. A memory loss caused by her head wound would perfectly account for her having answered their every question with "I do not know."

There'd been a groom at the château who had been kicked in the head by a horse. When the groom returned to consciousness days later, he didn't know who he was, or where he was. Indeed, the poor man was never the same, but spent every day after he recovered his physical strength methodically cleaning the tack. Like an automaton, a deep, crescent-shaped indention in his forehead, he'd go over each piece and then start over where he began, even re-polishing those pieces not yet used.

Grandquest wanted answers. Now that she was awake, he would no doubt employ certain persuasive questioning techniques to get them. Ari's stomach knotted as she imagined the shackles and beatings that were to come. But if she could convince the earl that she truly could not remember, it might buy her some time. Time to recover. Time to escape.

What did she have to lose?

She wondered if she should try to mimic the groom's weak-minded behavior? But no, she had shown too much of herself to pull off such a hummer—as Dolpho's friend, Stubby, would term it.

Stubby! He was the answer—why hadn't she thought of him sooner? If she could get to Stubby—Harold Stubbins, Viscount Lynching—he would help her escape, then hide her from Grandquest and from the authorities.

Ari sensed the earl was standing by the bedside. Touching her bandaged head, she moaned softly.

Dr. Kilpatrick stood on the other side of the bed. He bent over and lifted first one of her eyelids, and then the other, just as he'd done earlier a dozen times.

"Enough," Ari pleaded after the doctor had lifted each three more times. "You can not know what that feels like."

The draperies had been opened, and light streamed in the room. It hurt even to see the light through her closed lids.

Kilpatrick said coolly, "I am aware that there must be some pain."

"Aware that there must... *Mon Dieu*, you are *most* sensitive."

"You don't remember his lordship?" He had asked this question twice already.

Ari said nothing. Perhaps, if she held very still, they would all just go away.

"Madam, answer me," the supercilious voice insisted.

She sighed. "*Non*. No."

"What is your first memory?"

She wondered how she should answer? What would be her answer had she really suffered a loss of memory? "I think I remember being carried in someone's arms. I cannot be certain. Everything hurts when I try to think."

This last was the truth.

"You don't remember encountering Lord Grandquest in Dartmouth?"

"I don't remember ever being in Dartmouth," she whispered hoarsely. That was also the truth. "Who is this Grandquest?"

"The same gentleman you met in the hallway a short time ago," the doctor said.

"What hallway?" Ari turned to the tall man at the other side of the bed. His gray eyes were shadowed by deep concern—she wanted to snort in disdain. All his concern was for the doctor's benefit, of course.

She asked weakly, "And you are?"

"I am Fox Grandquest."

"I am sorry. I do not remember meeting you," Ari said, letting her voice quaver just a little.

"Don't let it frighten you. You will remember. It will take time. That is all."

The doctor inserted, "Actually, your lordship, from what I've read of memory loss due to head injury, it is usually the case for the most recent memories to be affected until the trauma has healed."

Returning his attention to Ari, Kilpatrick asked, "How many fingers do you see?" He held his hand up, three fingers displayed.

"Three."

"And now?" He changed the number.

"Two." Ari clasped her head as she was seized by a fit of coughing. After it passed, her exhaustion was quite real.

"Now, how —"

"I think that can wait." Fox picked up the glass of water and a vial from the bedside table. He counted the drops as he added laudanum to the water and sat on the edge of the bed and raised her, so she could drink easily.

"*Merci*," the young woman whispered when she'd finished and he laid her back on the pillows.

The doctor cleared his throat. "Well, yes. I suppose a little painkiller was in order. We'll change the dressing on her thigh, bleed her, and then let her rest."

Ari glared at the doctor. "*Monsieur*, I will be most grateful to be left to rest. But you will not bleed me, and kindly do not speak of me as if I am not here."

The housekeeper, who'd been hovering uncertainly behind the doctor, covered her mouth with a plump hand and went into a wheezing fit.

The little maid beside the housekeeper turned her back and began polishing a small table with the tail of her apron, her thin shoulders shaking like a *blanche mongé*.

"Your pardon, Milady," drawled Kilpatrick, obviously intending his use of the term to be sarcastic.

Grandquest watched as the woman's incredible blue eyes opened and raked the doctor with disdain.

"Pardon is granted, sir, but, please, do not let it happen again."

As she tried to suppress her mirth, the housekeeper's face contorted and chuckles escaped in spite of her best efforts, her ample bosom quivering like pudding. Guffawing, the little maid bolted from the room.

Fox followed, striding from the bedchamber. As he closed the door behind him, his laughter erupted, rolling like thunder down long halls—and quite frightening any servant who heard the strange sound.

Ever since he'd inherited the title and Stonerose Manor several months prior, no one had heard his lordship laugh. Indeed, they didn't know he knew how.

After his amusement died to a smile, Fox started for the study and the two men he'd left hidden there. His mind, however, was still on his unusual houseguest. She was easily the most fascinating woman he'd ever encountered.

He sobered as he remembered those very blue eyes, boring into him over the long barrel of her pistol, and her promise to see him in hell when she got there.

The most fascinating, certainly.

And, without a doubt, the most dangerous.

* * * * *

After carefully locking the study door, Fox swung a floor-to-ceiling bookcase forward on well-oiled hinges. "You can come out."

Two men emerged from the hidden space, blinking as their eyes adjusted to the light. They were dressed in the woolen trousers, coats, and caps of common laborers. Looking their costumes over, Fox shook his head. Luckily they hadn't been caught and forced to bluff it out. They looked like a pair of cats dressed in feathers.

Fox had known them since he'd been a ten-year-old cabin boy on the merchant vessel *Grace Hampton*, where he'd found himself after running away to sea. Benjamin Higgins and Toby Anderson, then both peach-cheeked lads of sixteen, had been out drinking at the wrong end of Boston when they'd been recruited as able seamen by the energetic application of a belaying pin. A year later, when they sailed back into Boston harbor, they'd all jumped ship and had helped Fox find his real father, a quest that had ended in Baltimore, where Jules Fox had welcomed the natural son he'd never known existed.

"Sorry for the interruption." Fox gestured to wing-backed chairs of rich Moroccan leather drawn up before the crackling fire. As the two men made themselves comfortable, he explained about the woman upstairs and what had happened on his ship. "She tried to put a hole through you, and you brought the chit here. Are you daft, man?" Ben eyed Fox incredulously.

"Crazy as a loon, no doubt, else would I be involved in high treason?"

"You'll have your throat cut in your sleep," Toby predicted. Stretching his scuffed boots toward the crackling blaze, he added, "Damned cold in that hidey-hole, Fox, damned cold."

One side of his mouth curved upward as he took the hint and splashed brandy into glasses. He selected one for himself and propped a shoulder against the elegant, white marble mantle. Swirling the dark liquid, he watched the firelight play through it.

"I saw no choice but to bring her here," he said slowly. "Should I have turned her over to the authorities? She might have talked in her delirium, and there is no way to know what might have been given away. I don't know what she knows about our activities. More importantly, who else might know."

There was another reason, he admitted to himself. With her wounds, she might not have survived if thrown into some dank prison. Infection, pneumonia—something would have taken her. He didn't want another death on his conscience. As he'd told her over the long barrel of her gun, his sins were not forgotten.

You're growing soft, Grandquest, he told himself. In his business, growing soft was usually a prelude to growing dead.

Frowning, Fox sipped his brandy. "So, what did you learn?"

"Our French friend was waiting off Goat's Head by the dark of the moon—a sloop, just as you predicted." Toby drained his glass and helped himself to more.

Ben propped his elbows on his knees. "We were up on a knoll, hidden in the trees, where we had a view of the creek and of the beach below the bluff. A bobbing lantern showed that the smugglers had rowed out to meet the Frenchies—not that we could see much else. Black as a banker's heart, it was. Before they got about their business, a bloody great squadron of Devonshire's best started beating about through the bushes. The poor coves waiting on that little spit of beach flew like partridges, all which ways."

Fox straightened, frowning. "Did the militia capture the smugglers?"

"No. I don't think they saw them. The lantern in the boat was doused and the French ship sat silent. As I said, the men waiting on the beach fled in various directions. I plain don't think they saw 'em," Ben said. "As to how they was missed, I won't venture to guess. It got so thick with horses and men, Toby and I were obliged to climb a tree. Lucky, there was a big oak at hand. The limbs were wide and made for a comfortable seat."

"Speak for yourself. I had a knot up my arse."

"You always got some'ot up your arse—usually your head," Ben chortled.

"The militia?" Fox directed them back to the matter at hand.

Toby glared at Ben. "Yes, well, the bloody sods decided to use our tree, mind you, as a rendezvous point, so we were well an' truly stuck. We got our ears full, however. Long and short of it is, someone had tipped 'em to a nest of French spies, holed up in a cottage down the coast a bit—though what spies would have been doing there, I wish you'd tell me. The militia'd donned their brass buttons and went riding in to do the glorious. So, they missed the smugglers while chasing other birds."

"They must have met with more than they'd bargained for," Ben said. "A couple had lanterns, looking for tracks I suppose. By the light, I saw two with arms caught up in slings and another with a cut on his head and a swollen eye. A couple more looked bruised and battered."

"I heard a young corporal talking about fighting off five men. He was the one with the swollen eye. But I think all his talk was just plain bragging. I don't think they knew the right of it," Toby asserted. "The poor sods had probably pounded each other in the dark.

"We overheard talk of one great capture, though. A woman who threatened them with a frying pan. It had evidently been a great disappointment when she proved to be a cook, and not one of Boney's spies. Ben and I almost fell out of the tree, laughing."

"A squad of dunces," Ben agreed.

Fox unconsciously tested his jaw, moving it from side to side. It was still tender from the sock on the chin he'd taken. "Were there any other women at the cottage?" Maybe a tall woman with a flame of deep auburn hair? It would explain much about his unusual guest, though not why she'd tried to shoot him.

Toby sat straighter. "Hey, I see what you're thinking. Ben and I were wondering what happened to the Italian's wife."

Fox looked from one to the other.

Ben nodded. "So we were. Little Braxton's the nearest village, six miles inland. We did a bit of checking there the next morning, after the soldiers departed and we could finally climb down from our tree. I found the officer in charge of the squad, a Captain Phips, at a tavern near his headquarters. Unfortunately, as he took a glass of beer, he wouldn't be drawn into casual conversation about the business. Right unsociable, he was. I think he was a bit embarrassed that all his rabbits got away.

"Anyway, a talk with the greengrocer proved more informative. The cottage was rented to an Italian émigré and his wife, though the grocer had never seen the wife. She supposedly spoke only Italian, and, anyway, the cook did all the shopping."

Toby added, "We did think to ask the grocer how much food they bought of a week. He described enough to keep a man and his wife and a servant, but not the nest of French pigeons the militia supposedly flushed. I think we'd have answers aplenty if we could find that cook."

Fox drained his glass. "Yes. The cook might identify the woman upstairs and tell us what was really going on." He looked into the fire for a moment, testing the pieces. They seemed to fall into place. All but one—why had she attacked him? And with such thorough hate?

Toby eyed him narrowly. "I know you're as close-mouthed as a clam, Fox Grandquest, but I have to wonder just who is this Dandelion you're trying to snaffle? And why you're so anxious to nab him?"

Fox shrugged and smiled sardonically. "No information is secret in Whitehall these days, not even, it seems, in the Privy Council. This Dandelion, as he styles himself, is the keystone of the spy ring. This man could turn the tide of the war in favor of the French."

"But that doesn't say why *you're* so set on doing the Brits' work for them. Seems to me, the more the Brits and Frenchies fight, the less likely they are to turn their greedy eyes to the American side of the Atlantic."

"Call it a debt," Fox said, all too aware he'd never intended to embroil himself in Britain's struggle against Bonaparte. Having lived most of his life in America, he'd always thought of himself as an American, and it was to that country he was loyal.

But some debts had to be repaid.

He changed the subject. "I received orders via Sir Leonard this morning to return to Whitehall. I could be gone as much as a fortnight, so the business with the cook will have to wait until I get back." He set his glass on the mantel and turned, regarding his friends solemnly. "I think you'd better go to the inn in Dartmouth where you left your things, and come back again when you've had a bath and change of clothes. To the front door, this time. You'll be my old friends from America, here for an extended visit. That way you can keep watch on the woman upstairs while I'm gone."

Ben straightened. "Now that'll put a fat fly in the soup. Once we're linked to you, we'll be no good for doing nefarious stuff."

"Right, ho," Toby concurred.

Which was exactly why he'd asked them to do it. Fox let out an eloquent sigh. "You're ruined anyway," he told them bluntly. "You have no idea what a closed society an English village is. Two strangers asking questions must have raised eyebrows all along the high street. You, Ben, trying to get information from a militia captain—lucky you weren't shot."

"We're not total flats." Ben looked aggrieved. "Except for the captain, everyone in the village was talking about the business. They could talk of nothing else. It was likely the most excitement they'd seen since the Spanish Armada sailed into the Channel."

Fox ignored their sullen looks. Dandelion, as Toby had pointed out, was of no concern to the United States. He should never have involved them. Although having them watch a certain section of coast had seemed an innocuous enough task.

"You're really going to have us be nursemaids?" Toby asked.

"Don't underestimate her." Fox remembered those cerulean blue eyes as he'd fought with her for control of the gun. Eyes filled with fire and determination. He'd no doubt she would have sent him to hell if she could have.

She'd given it a damned fine try.

Ben said, "You don't believe she's no memory, then?"

"I don't know," Fox said honestly. "Even if she has lost her memory, Dr. Kilpatrick assures me there's every chance she'll get it back as her concussion heals."

"And if she doesn't?" Ben asked.

"Then, when I get back from London, we'll find that cook. The mystery won't take long to solve. With her accent, her unusual height and looks, she should be the easiest woman in England to identify."

Chapter Three

ೋ

Ari gazed at the winter wood, a gray and uninviting scene. Although it was well into October, a scattering of yellow leaves still clung to the beech and ash trees, specks of tattered color, which only emphasized the dreariness of the day. Whipped by a breeze with a hint of ice in it, a fine, cold mist chilled her cheeks. The breeze glanced off the wall below her, ricocheting upward, belling the skirt of her borrowed dress and chilling her bare legs and feet.

Standing on the six-inch ledge outside her bedroom window, she planned her route of escape.

Though barren of blossoms at this time of year, rose bushes were laid out in neat beds thirty feet below. It looked a nasty drop. Grooves formed by the mortar spaces between the square cut, rose-colored stones offered a way down, but the climb would be difficult. She had certainly made more perilous descents while growing up at *Château Nuage*. Boredom due to their isolation had given her and Dolpho a mad thirst for adventure—which they'd indulged at every opportunity. As a result, rock climbing was only one of her less than ladylike skills.

Unfortunately, her wounds still weren't healed completely. Stiff and weak, her leg was probably not up to the strain of such a descent. The stitches in her scalp had been removed that very morning. When she'd inspected her scalp in the mirror, the long streak where the pistol ball had parted her hair looked pink and fully healed, though it was still tender to the touch.

The terrible headache was gone; however, she suffered from dizziness whenever she became fatigued. It would prove unfortunate if she should suffer such an episode while climbing down the wall. Indeed, she'd ventured out on the ledge as much to test her equilibrium as to consider her options.

She counted herself lucky Lord Grandquest had been away a fortnight and she had escaped further questioning. She would be gone before the earl returned.

Thick, green ivy grew over the adjoining wing, a thirty-foot lateral journey along the narrow ledge. Ari studied the thick growth with a judicious eye, wondering if it would offer an easier descent than the wall. At the thinner growth on the edges, the vines seemed to hug the stonework too tightly, leaving little or no purchase for fingers and toes. Perhaps, though, where it grew thicker and climbed over itself, it would offer a better hold.

Back against the wall, Ari inched carefully along the ledge to get a better look. She'd gone no more than ten feet when a loud knock drifted out the open window from her bedroom door.

It couldn't be Bailey, the maid who served her. She'd told the girl to leave her undisturbed.

The knocking sounded again, louder and more insistent. "Milady? Are you in there?"

She recognized Ben Higgins' voice. He was one of his lordship's watchdogs. *Damn.*

With the rough stones brushing the back of her head as she arched her back for balance, her hands flat against the stonework, Ari slid along the ledge as quickly as she dared. When her fingers touched the window casing, she turned. But as she did, her bare foot found a spot of slick, green moss. Her foot shot out.

Tilting backward, Ari frantically windmilled her arms, then caught the chest-high sill and hugged it. Her heart beat in her throat, making it difficult to breathe.

"Milady?"

Ari glared at the door, wishing a pox on the man behind it. The handle rattled. The key, which she'd left in the lock, fell to the floor. She realized Ben had pushed it out by inserting a key from the other side. The nerve! He was going to unlock *her* door!

"*Sacre bleu*, but this is *too* much." As she hoisted herself through the window, Ari loosed a string of French expletives that would have made a Calais fishwife blush. Still muttering, she jammed her feet into her shoes, which were borrowed and pinched her toes, souring her mood even more.

Arms crossed over her chest, she waited by the door as it slowly opened. When Ben Higgins eased his long face around the corner, she pinned him with a darkling look. "You, sir, are not a gentleman. Gaining entry to a lady's chamber uninvited." She stomped her foot, wincing as the hard shoe pinched her toes.

He flushed guiltily and pulled the key from the lock. "But, Milady, I didn't. I mean, when you wouldn't open the door—"

"I didn't answer because I wished only to be left alone. To have a little peace. But you thought to take advantage of me. I see how it is, Sirrah. I am alone, so all alone. And there is no one I can trust. No one I can turn to."

"Begging your pardon, Milady, I was only concerned—"

Ari snatched the key from his hand.

"Ho, now. You can't have that, Milady."

"Oh, but why not?" She dropped it into her bodice and clasped her hands at her breast in a pose of martyred innocence. "I thought you a gentleman, but you, sir, are a rogue and…and a blackguard!" Ari sniffed convincingly as she felt a tear slip from the corner of her eye. She congratulated herself on her performance. Dolpho really should have allowed her to tread the boards, as she'd longed to do when they'd been in London. She would have been the toast of the Drury Lane.

Thinking of Dolpho caused another tear to chase the first. His loss was still raw. Never had she felt so alone.

"But my key!"

Ari gasped and took a dramatic step backward. "So, you admit it!"

"Admit what?" Toby Anderson asked, striding down the hall toward them.

"Milady thinks I was up to no good just because I was unlocking her door," Ben explained. "She took the key."

"Were you up to no good, Ben?" Toby looked Ari over and smiled like a cat eyeing a bowl of cream. "By God, can't say I blame you."

"You are no gentleman!" Ari took a small step closer to Ben, like a child seeking protection from a bully. Because she stood half-a-head taller than him, it made playing the role of fragile flower something of a challenge, but one she thought she pulled over brilliantly, nonetheless.

Ben glared at his friend and patted Ari's hand. "I'm most contrite for having offended your sensibilities, Milady."

Toby snorted.

Ari ignored the rudeness and gave Ben a small, tremulous smile. Ben's infatuation was written plainly on his long face as he gazed at her adoringly. He'd assured her he believed her story of memory loss. She'd been able to engage his sympathy, gaining his trust and manipulating him in small ways, like the matter of getting the key. But her conscience pricked. He really wasn't a bad sort. Would Grandquest exact a terrible revenge on him if she could use him in some way to escape?

She firmly pushed the thought aside. Grandquest would certainly deal roughly with her should she still be here when he returned. If the opportunity presented itself, she must use Ben—or the devil, himself—to gain her freedom. She dared not let any chance pass her by.

Glancing at Toby, Ari saw the look in his eyes and knew that he, as usual, was having none of her act. During the past two weeks, Toby had believed nothing she said and had actively worked to erode Ben's growing faith in her.

"I am sorry I doubted you," Ari said to Ben, casting a fearful glance at Toby. "This one makes me so nervous. His eyes always devour me so. *Mon Dieu*, I feel so vulnerable with no one to protect me."

"You have me, Milady." Ben patted her hand reassuringly.

Toby shook his head. "Let's have the key back."

"No! I think you are a very bad man. How could I ever sleep knowing such as you could come in at any time, *Monsieur* Toady?"

Ben snickered.

Toby glared. "That's Toby. Now let me have the key."

Ari caught Ben's hand, moving even closer to him as she watched Toby fearfully. "Must I?"

"Now, Toady. Let the lady keep the key if it makes her feel better. After all, Fox will be back tonight, and he's bringing—"

"To-by," he said, cutting Ben off. "And you've a loose tongue."

Ari felt as though she'd swallowed a cannonball. Lord Grandquest here, tonight? She should have climbed down the wall last night, she realized. Instead, she'd tried to interest the footman who kept vigil outside her door each night in some hot cocoa laced generously with laudanum. Unfortunately, the fellow would have none of it.

"Ben?" She blinked in pretty confusion. "Who is he bringing?"

"No one. Now, never mind that. It's nothing to concern your pretty head about," Ben assured her.

Ari eyed the hand she was clasping. With only the greatest difficulty did she fight down an urge to bite it. *Pretty head, indeed.*

She dropped his hand and sighed dramatically, closing her eyes. "Oh my, I fear all this controversy has exhausted me so. I still tire so easily. I think I must rest."

Ari pointedly ignored the other man as she moved to close her door.

Toby stopped it with his boot, his smile piratical. "One moment." He retrieved the key from the Aubusson rug.

Realizing it was the one pushed out of the lock as Ben had tried to open her door, Ari ground her teeth in frustration. *Merde.* She'd only exchanged one key for another.

Smiling smugly, Toby placed the door key in the pocket of his green-striped waistcoat. "A pity you're feeling not quite the thing, Milady. I came up to tell you that luncheon is ready."

Ari considered her dwindling options. She needed to learn when Grandquest would arrive, and whom he was bringing with him. A constable? A magistrate? A man in a black mask who liked his irons heated red-hot?

It was time for bolder measures. Just what those measures would be, she wasn't quite certain. But there would be more opportunities downstairs for her than shut away in her bedchamber. Unless she was willing to test her injured leg on the wall.

"Perhaps food is just what I need to set me to rights," Ari said. Turning to Ben, she gave him her best smile and laid her fingers on his sleeve. "With your strong arm to lean on in case I become too fatigued, I shall try to go downstairs to luncheon."

* * * * *

Ari tossed her heavy braid over her shoulder and took the iron poker from the rack. She probed at the half-burned logs, moving them closer together to intensify the heat. Red coals glowed between them before a tiny blue blaze sprang to life.

"I say, allow me." Ben reached to take the poker from her.

"No, no." Ari shifted the instrument to her other hand and jabbed at the foremost log, as if putting a fine adjustment on her work. "I mean, I am enjoying this. There is something about a fire… I find it so relaxing. Why don't you set up the chessboard? Remember, you promised me a game. 'Twill help while away our afternoon."

"Right you are. A game of chess is just the ticket." Ben moved to a small side table and, his back to her, began setting chessmen on their proper squares. "Though I wouldn't want you to tax yourself. Too much strain on the female intellect can lead to nervous disorders and megrims. Anyway, I'm quite an accomplished player, so you mustn't give it a thought if you're not up to the challenge."

As he talked on, Ari eyed a spot on the back of his head where his brown hair was thinning. She hefted the poker, testing its weight.

It did seem a bit much. She wished only to render the man unconscious, not brain him.

The sense of urgency she'd been feeling had grown until it was an alarm ringing as loud as the bells of London's St. Mary LeBow. It urged her to take action now while it was just she and Ben.

The abominable Toby had disappeared after lunch. Probably having his way with one of the housemaids, Ari surmised.

This was the time of day the grooms exercised his lordship's riding horses. When she'd pumped the lad for information, the manor's ten-year-old bootblack avowed his lordship had a stable of "prime 'uns".

After she'd dealt with Ben, she would fly to the paddocks and relieve a groom of his chore and make her way to London and find Stubby. Stubby would help her, she told herself.

All she need do was give Ben the lightest of taps…

Steeling her resolve, Ari gave the logs a final poke and turned, lifting the poker as she did.

"*Madre de Dios!*" It clattered as it fell to the polished floor.

Fox Grandquest stood in the doorway. "First English, then French, and now Spanish. Your education in languages seems extensive. I wonder—does it include Italian, too?"

Ari made no reply. She was unable to speak past the knot of fear in her throat. Grandquest closed the door of the study, and

Ari thought there was something ominous in the action. And in his size. She stared as he moved toward her, like a mouse mesmerized by an adder, knowing the danger but unable to look away.

The tassels on his mud-splattered Hessians danced as he walked. The way his tanned, doeskin breeches fit his muscular thighs and lean hips was positively indecent, leaving little about his form to the imagination. And surely, buckram padding beneath his cutaway coat of dark blue superfine was responsible for the breadth of those shoulders. She hadn't remembered the man being so large.

She had remembered his eyes, deep-set beneath curving brows and shadowed by thick black lashes. Light gray and assessing. He studied her as though she was that mouse, and he, the adder, was sizing her up for a meal.

"I say, Fox!" Ben exclaimed.

So intent on Lord Grandquest was Ari that she had forgotten Ben was in the room. She jumped as though goosed.

Ben pumped the earl's hand in greeting. "Good to have you back. But where's the cook? Wasn't she in Little Braxton?"

"The cook?" Ari questioned. A cook from Little Braxton? She clenched her hands in the folds of her skirt to hide their trembling. Surely not the cook from the cottage. Not bread-like-a-brick Hilda. Why would Grandquest bring Hilda here?

To positively identify her, of course. He would wish to be certain whom he was about to do away with. One liked to keep these things tidy.

Lord Grandquest's gray gaze found her again. She stammered, "But you've a wonderful cook, already. Why, the salmon we lunched on was magnificent. The dill sauce, perfection—"

Lord Grandquest smiled—something so unexpected, Ari took half a step back.

It was a beautiful smile, she thought abstractly. His teeth were even and startlingly white against the bronze of his skin.

"You remember me, then?" he asked, abandoning Ben and moving to Ari.

His tall form radiated power and energy. It was as though the very air vibrated between them, charged like the atmosphere before a summer storm. Ari rather wanted to take another step back, but a glance behind her showed there was nowhere to go but into the fireplace amid the glowing coals.

She shook her head. "Yes. I mean, *no*. I mean, Ben called you Fox. Therefore, you could be no one but the earl. The earl's name—your name—*is* Fox, is it not?" she finished breathlessly. *Mon Dieu,* this was no time for her wits to go begging. She was supposed to have amnesia. And if that was the case, should she even know him?

"Have you remembered nothing?" he asked softly. "A name? A family?" He reached into the folds of her skirt, gently caught her left hand and held it up. He touched the gold band circling her ring finger. "A husband?" He searched her eyes.

Ari had forgotten about the wedding band. She and Dolpho had posed as man and wife while renting the cottage.

"You know who I am?" she challenged, trembling.

"No. Nothing certain. Only who you might be. You've remembered nothing at all, then?" Fox asked, examining the hand he still held. It wasn't as soft and white as warm dough, like the hands of the society women he knew. Her nails were short and neat. The pads of her fingers were lightly callused. Hers were capable hands. He remembered the strength in those fingers as he'd tried to break her grip on the gun.

Something shadowed the earl's fine eyes. If she did not know better, she would have thought it regret. Ari pulled her hand free. She gave a small, negative shake of her head then dropped her gaze to the folds of his cravat.

"Don't let it upset you. I have found someone who might help."

Ari marveled at the sincerity of his tone. She could almost believe she had his sympathy. *Dieu*, and she had thought herself a talented thespian.

"You did bring the cook, then?" Ben asked.

Grandquest moved to the bell pull and tugged it. Ari found she could breathe much easier with some distance between them.

"I sent my coach into Little Braxton for the woman while I rode on ahead."

"Did you hear that, Milady? You'll soon have your answers." Ben told her enthusiastically.

Ari dredged up a weak smile. Her mind, however, was on the wide French windows. She was wondering, if she flung them wide and made a desperate dash, just how far she might get.

"Milady?" Fox cocked an inquiring brow.

"It's how the servants address her." Ben shrugged. "And we have to call her something, don't we?"

Ben had a point, Fox conceded, though he would not have chosen *lady*—which was a title either inherited or gained through marriage, and not merely an address of respect. Besides, no lady would venture onto the Dartmouth waterfront alone, or, for that matter, try to shoot a peer of the realm.

Looking back at the woman in question, Fox decided that, despite her having done both, lady suited her. Her shoulders were squared, her back, ramrod straight. That sack of a dress she was wearing might have been the purple and ermine; that ugly, white mobcap, a tiara. Looking more closely, Fox recognized the gray garment as some housemaid's patched dress, to which a foot-long ruffle had been added, making it longer. But even so ill-clothed, she possessed innate dignity.

He realized with some surprise that she was studying him as though taking his measure, much as he'd just studied her.

"I was about to offer Milady some instruction on the finer points of chess," Ben said. "By the way, Toby's about that certain business you mentioned in your letter."

45

"Is he? Good. Pray continue with your game."

She gracefully seated herself in the lyre-backed chair Ben held for her. Her thick braid ran over her shoulder and disappeared beneath the table. Fox remembered how her hair had looked aboard *The Dancer*, floating out on the wind like a glorious, dark auburn flame. The heat he felt increased dramatically.

Damn, but this wouldn't do. He dared not forget how earnestly she'd tried to shoot him. She might still be planning his demise.

A footman answered his summons, and Fox ordered a cold lunch and a hot bath brought to his bedchamber. He then excused himself and left the chess players to their game.

After the earl had gone, Ari stared at the carved moldings trimmed in gilt and the shiny, curved brass handles of the closed doors, trying very hard to figure out what had just happened.

"The pawns can move only straight forward. Two spaces for the first move, if you like, but only one, thereafter," Ben explained. "Do you understand?"

"What? Oh, yes." She drummed her fingers on the table. The earl had left her here, just as if she was an ordinary houseguest and he was an ordinary host.

Ben continued, "Now, the rooks can only move in a straight line, either horizontal or vertical."

Ari glared at him, but he failed to notice. *Mon Dieu,* she was so nervous she was coming out of her skin. She needed quiet, to think and plan. "I seem to recall how each piece moves. Perhaps we can just play?"

Ben gave her a doubtful look. "'Tis complicated, y'know."

"We could try, *s'il vous plait*? You go first, and I will watch how you go on. You can correct me if I make a misstep." Ari managed a convincing smile. Her mind, however, was fully occupied with a deeper game. The one Lord Grandquest was playing.

Ben moved his king's bishop's pawn to king's bishop six. "The pawns are the key to the game, y'see. Frontline defense, like infantry soldiers."

Ari absently nodded and moved her king's pawn to king three. She had feared what would happen if she wasn't able to escape before the earl returned. But he had returned. To her surprise, she wasn't now strapped to a rack, or chained in some sub-cellar while a man in a leather hood pumped at a bellows and shoved iron rods into a forge of glowing coals.

Well, of course not. Ari gave a slight shake of her head as she realized her error. When it came to doing away with her, the earl would be more subtle. He might be a villain and a blackguard, but he did, after all, have a position to maintain. He couldn't have the county gossiping about how houseguests at his manor were apt to be misplaced, or have his servants reporting how screams issued from the bowels of the house in the night.

Tsk-tsking, Ben shook his long head dolefully. "I see you have much to learn. You always want to leave your king protected." He moved his king's knight's pawn to king's knight five. "Do you see how I'm forming my pawns into a saw-toothed line for defense?"

Ari stared sightlessly. No, the earl would not do away with her at Stonerose. She imagined a more likely scenario, the earl bundling her into his coach, perhaps, on the pretext of having found her family. No doubt, with a driver who might be counted on to be discreet and the Abominable Toby as watchdog. She would find herself taken to some isolated place, a fisherman's shack or a ruined tower in the remains of a Norman castle. There — unconsciously punctuating her thoughts, Ari moved her queen diagonally to Ben's king's rook five — *finis!*

"There has to be something wrong with that." Ben blinked at the board.

Yes, she admitted reluctantly. There was something wrong. A huge hole she'd tried vainly to ignore, but through which doubts persisted in crawling. Why had the earl taken care of her, and very good care at that? She understood that he would not have wanted to involve the authorities when she'd tried to shoot him, and so had removed her from Dartmouth. He might want to be certain of her identity and of whom else might know about his activities before he did away with her. But why bring her to Stonerose—why not bring her some place more secluded, where her eventual disappearance wouldn't lead to awkward questions? When he'd found out what he wished to know, he could have done away with her more easily.

Grandquest had instead taken her in and allowed her to recover. He'd even had a doctor treat her wounds—though calling Kilpatrick a doctor was a disparagement of the word, she thought. The Austrian doctor who had taught her what she knew of healing would have applied the toe of his boot to Kilpatrick's rear at his incompetence.

But Grandquest had meant well, nonetheless. Now that she considered Grandquest's actions more closely, there was much about them that didn't make sense. If he was Dandelion, was he up to some elaborate ruse?

Ari blinked, suddenly aware that Ben was staring at her as if she'd sprouted another head. Looking back at the board, she realized why.

She'd placed him in checkmate in two moves.

* * * * *

Fox tried to read what he'd written, a coded message to President Jefferson couched in the form of a ship's manifest, but the words danced and blurred in the flickering light from the brace of candles. He dropped the paper onto the sandalwood desk and rubbed his temples. He'd spent last night at a posting inn on a lumpy mattress and arose in the small hours before dawn to ride on over mud-choked roads. But it was more than fatigue that troubled him.

It was the ghosts. His brother, Darien, was the first. The gift of the black stallion, a prime piece of horseflesh, was to have been a peace offering, a way to bridge the gap between him and his brother. Darien had been the last of his siblings, save for Anne. All the others contrived to die before they were much past middle age. He had no idea Darien would try to ride the brute of a stallion while too drunk to sit the saddle.

Peterson's ghost was not far behind—Peterson, who had married the just the month before and talked incessantly about his beautiful, red-haired wife. Peterson trusted him...

Restless, Fox shoved away from the desk. Opening the tall French windows, he stepped out onto the balcony into the still, winter's night. He wore no coat and his shirt was open down the front, but he welcomed the sting of the cold air. Inhaling deeply, he savored the crispness of the night. The smell of wood smoke issuing from the manor's chimneys brought unexpected memories.

Once that smell had taunted him, representing everything warm and comfortable. Everything that was out of reach. His brother Henry, the third earl, had called him a *cuckhold's bastard* and banished him to the unheated room above the stables. A boy of eight, Fox was hurt and confused by his brother's hatred. Lost and alone, he often stood in the stable yard, teased by the sweet smell of wood smoke issuing from the manor and dreaming of warmth and a full belly.

Of all the large Grandquest's brood, only his older sister Anne cared. She defied Henry by sneaking him food, warm clothes, hugs. She made his life bearable. It was Anne who told him why Henry treated him badly—the truth everyone else had always known, that her and Henry's father wasn't Fox's real father. The general, a sophisticated man, hadn't really cared, having nine children by his first two wives and honest heirs aplenty.

When Anne married and left Stonerose, she tried to convince Henry to let Fox go with her and her new husband. Henry refused. Soon after, Fox ran away to sea, swearing never to return to England. He would have held to his promise to never return if President Jefferson had not asked him to, gathering intelligence that might help America avoid war with Britain. He'd never wanted the title, but Darien had died without an heir and the earldom had provided entrée into Whitehall and a post in the foreign office that was an invaluable source of intelligence. At Stonerose, it surprised him when his tenants started asking his advice about their crops or seeking loans for new plows and seed. The earldom, which Fox had at first viewed only as a tool in his mission, had rapidly become a trust.

Somewhere below the hill, an owl hooted, its calls echoing eerily through the still night wood. Fox smiled, remembering how his father—his true father, American Jules Fox and not the English general, Samuel Grandquest—had taken him to America's Northwest Territories. There his father had introduced him to his grandmother, Owl Woman, a respected medicine woman among the Shawnee. Fox knew his cousin, The Prophet, would probably say this owl was Owl Woman's spirit bringing him a message, or a warning. But a warning about what?

He leaned on the railing, the stonework cold beneath his forearms through the lawn of his shirt, and thought about the auburn-haired woman. Indeed, there was much to be warned about where she was concerned. He still didn't know if she had in truth lost her memory, or if she was playing a deep game, watching for an opportunity to do him in? He had to find out, before his sister Anne arrived to act as chaperon for her.

The woman was certainly an enigma. He'd been disappointed when she had stayed in her room and hadn't put in an appearance at tea or supper. Perhaps talking with her again would unravel the mystery that still surrounded her—a mystery he'd spent much of the last two weeks trying to solve.

The investigator he'd sent to Little Braxton had interviewed several militiamen and brought back conflicting reports. Some claimed there were several men who escaped; some said only two; and one young corporal claimed to have seen a woman's ghost.

The most troubling information the investigator unearthed was that Captain Phips believed he'd been acting on a letter from none other than Fox, himself. A letter Fox had certainly never written. It had been stamped with Fox's own crest, a lion and a griffin holding a posy between them. The seal was an artful forgery.

Fox sensed Dandelion's fine hand at work, but to what purpose? What threat had the Italian in the cottage posed to the French agent?

Fox straightened as he spotted the bobbing light of a coach lantern winking through the trees where the road to the manor wound atop the far ridge. A faint clink-clink of harness and the crunch of coach wheels on gravel came to him through the still night.

If she was the Italian's wife, he'd soon know. The cook that had worked for the couple should be in the coach. But she was more likely the émigré to whom Randolph Peterson had been wed.

Both had reason to wish him dead.

Toby had returned from Dartmouth with news that *The Dancer* was rigged with new canvas and cable and the spars lost in a storm during its last voyage had all been replaced. The ship would soon be through taking on cargo to sail to the West Indies. Fox needed to finish committing what he'd learned in Whitehall to paper. Then he would ride down to Dartmouth on the pretext of making a final inspection of the ship, and give the message to McMasters.

As Fox turned to go back inside, a shadow amid deeper shadows high up on the wall of the manor caught his attention. The moon had not yet risen, and all was dark on that section of wall. There were no balconies there and no growth of ivy.

He studied the area carefully. When the shadow didn't move, he decided it was nothing.

* * * * *

Ari gritted her teeth and waited until the earl disappeared inside, then flexed her stiff fingers and carefully felt out a new fingerhold between the stones of the wall. When she found one, she hoisted herself high enough to put a knee on the narrow ledge. After she had both knees on it, she threw the pillowcase containing her shoes, stockings, and the food she'd managed to gather for her escape through the window of her bedroom, and then climbed in after it, muttering imprecations all the while.

It had been a close thing, she thought grimly. Ari angrily hobbled to the armoire, her injured leg protesting each step. Jerking the door wide, she tossed the pillowcase into the bottom of it and flung her cape in over the bundle. She then threw herself atop the satin coverlet and winced as her injured leg protested the action.

Seeing the faint candlelight striking the stonework of the balcony, she'd debated whether or not she should wait until all the house was firmly asleep. She'd decided she must chance it before the moon rose. How could she have guessed Grandquest would make an appearance on that balcony?

Not daring to move, she'd hung on the wall for what had surely been hours as she'd waited for the earl to go back inside. Her fingers had grown stiff and weak from the strain, and her leg had begun trembling beneath her weight. When he'd finally quit the balcony, she'd had no choice but to make the short climb back into the bedroom. She could not have managed the far longer climb down the wall.

Ari closed her eyes and the image of the earl on the balcony returned to her. His face was hidden in shadow, but candlelight spilling through the open doors behind him limned his tall form. There had been something about Grandquest as he stood there, looking off into the night. Vulnerable was the word that came to Ari's mind.

Vulnerable? *Ha!* She was indeed in trouble if she was so addle-pated as to believe Fox Grandquest vulnerable! The last coals of the fire glowed faintly. Looking into them, Ari knew she dared not wait to find out whether Lord Grandquest was guilty or not. If he was guilty, she would be his next victim. If he was not guilty, he would turn her over as a spy when he discovered who she was. She must leave, as soon as she could. To that end, when she was rested and warmed, she would have another try at the wall...

An imperative knock at her door startled her, and she reluctantly got out of bed.

She opened the door, and found the earl, a brace of candles in one hand, a long-barreled pistol in the other.

The pistol looked rather sinister, Ari decided.

In the light of the candles and hall sconces, she noticed fatigue etched in the lines of his face and the tight line of his mouth. The set of his jaw, however, showed determination.

About what was he determined? Dangerous possibilities offered themselves to her imagination.

"Milord, what is it? What do you want?"

"A moment of your time." He didn't wait to be invited in, but stepped past her. "Close the door, please."

Her heart beating wildly, Ari wondered what this was about. Surely, his aim was not to try to seduce her. Why would he have brought the gun? Looking at the old weapon, she wondered if she'd been too quick to doubt that he was the villain who'd shot Dolpho. Had he now come to finish her?

Setting the candles on the bedside table, he turned. The candlelight splashed sideways across his strong features and the stark play of light and dark painted deep shadows and stark angles on his face.

It is like looking at Satan, himself, Ari thought as she reluctantly closed the door.

His gaze moved over her. Realizing how disheveled she must look with her hair tumbling about her shoulders, Ari put a hand to her curls to smooth them. The movement drew his attention and his eyes became the color of old pewter.

Crossing her arms protectively at her waist, Ari prompted, "You wished to speak with me?"

"Yes." Grandquest smiled. He had come here to talk. To surprise her with a test. But the candlelight splashed highlights of burgundy over her hair, and her lips looked like moist, crushed strawberries. Wondering how they would taste distracted him from his goal. Watching her closely, he held up the pistol, the barrel pointing upward. She eyed it as though he held a snake. When he thrust it out to her, she took an abrupt step backward.

"My lord?"

"This is yours. Take it. Holding it may jog your memory. Perhaps, all will become clear."

Meeting his gaze levelly, she took it from his grasp. It weighed a full stone and more.

He knew most women would have been dismayed at the weight and awkwardness of the thing, but not this auburn-haired Valkyrie. She grasped the barrel and curled her fingers around the butt, slipping one into the trigger guard as though she was accustomed to handling such weapons.

"What would you have me do with it?" Her voice was velvet, soft and throaty, and there was a gleam in her eyes, until her thick lashes lowered, hiding their expression.

"Tell me all you can about it." Fox moved to a cheval glass in the middle of the bedchamber, presenting her with his back. The cap she'd been wearing that afternoon hung on one of the posts and he lifted a satin ribbon.

"This is the pistol I pointed at you in Dartmouth?"

"Yes."

"I cannot tell you a great deal." She said after several moments had passed. "It is old. Awkward and heavy, it has no balance. It seems a poor choice for me to have used if I was so very set on seeing you dead, My Lord. The ramrod is slightly bent.

"And this gun is loaded."

54

Silence followed her last remark. As Fox waited, it thickened, broken only by a candle flame spluttering in wax. Then he heard what he'd been waiting for, the heavy metallic click of the cock being thumbed back.

Chapter Four

ℭ

The ribbon slipped from his fingers. Disappointment draped a heavy mantle over him as Fox waited for the *click* of the falling hammer. He had no fear of being shot. The gun wouldn't fire. He'd loaded it, but the powder he'd used lacked niter. Charcoal and sulfur alone would not explode.

When no click sounded, he turned and found her sitting on the edge of the bed, leaning close to the candlelight, absorbed in examining the pistol closely. The long barrel was pointed harmlessly toward the windows as she studied the mechanism.

As the tension eased from his body, he asked, "Did you find something interesting?"

"Indeed, My lord—"

"Fox, please."

"Fox." She glanced up at him as he moved nearer. "This cock has been repaired at some time. I see where a new piece was added, and that of a softer metal, which has worn out of round. It would be almost impossible to fire this weapon." She raised her brows. "If I was serious about shooting you, I should have used a better gun."

"Aye. You were serious."

Ari decided she had only thought him unsettling before. As he slowly smiled, she was completely aware of the breadth of his shoulders in his well-tailored coat, and of the rest of his form—his knit pantaloons left little to the imagination.

"I'm happy you didn't." Taking the gun from her, Fox held her gaze, as though he wanted to say more. At length, he nodded. "I bid you good night."

After she'd locked the door behind him, Ari donned her nightgown and crawled back into bed, smiling to herself. So, the earl had put her to a test—one she had seen through. She must be on her guard for more.

He really wasn't at all what she had expected. Oh, he was a dangerous man, to be sure. Remembering how his gaze seemed to reach into her and warm her from the inside out, she didn't doubt that for a moment. But a murderer? The man who'd shot Dolpho?

There'd been concern in those deep-set gray eyes. And shadows. Remembering his gaze, a small flutter flitted through her stomach and she drew a deep breath.

She was no longer certain he was the cold-blooded killer she'd thought he was. If he was, surely it would show. She would sense it.

And what do *you* know of killers? They do not wear a sign. He might be the worst fiend in creation, how would you know?

The thought trailed away as Ari's gaze probed into the shadows in the corners, the fine hair prickling at the back of her neck. She felt as if she was being watched.

Telling herself it was only her imagination, she got up and pulled the bed curtains then slid back beneath the covers and drew them up under her chin. She was so tired, it was hard to think. Tomorrow. Tomorrow would provide another opportunity to escape.

Or, perhaps she should just stay here and see what happened?

One thing was certain, she would write Stubby a letter, telling him where she was and bribe a servant to post it in the nearest village. She'd been working to gain the confidence of the little maid who saw to her needs. Then, after Stubby came—

Someone sneezed—someone very near.

Ari sat bolt upright, staring into the darkness of the room.

* * * * *

Sunlight splashed the carpet with golden pools of light as Ari searched the bedroom wall. Running her hands over the carved gilt frame of a landscape painting, she wondered vaguely why every artist seemed to think a good work should be brown, when the world was filled with color?

Sliding her fingers across the gold-flocked wallpaper, she continued her search. After the sneeze last night, she had examined this wall, finding nothing by candlelight. Now, she discovered what she'd suspected. Hidden near the corner of the room, in the angle of one of the painted moldings that divided the wall into rectangular sections, was a small hole no bigger than her fingertip.

She put her eye to it and saw not total blackness, but a faint glimmer of light and a space easily large enough for a man.

A fist-sized knot formed in her stomach as the use for the space became clear. She hugged herself as she imagined how many times she might have been observed when she thought herself alone. Dressing. Sleeping. Perhaps, even when she'd put the laudanum in the pot with the cocoa. Or when she'd shed shoes and stockings and crawled out the window on the ledge.

Was this why Toady refused to believe her charade? The swine. She could well believe him the culprit who'd been watching her.

Realizing she had not had the feeling of being watched before last night gave her pause. Not before Grandquest returned to Stonerose. Had it been the earl?

But no, he'd been with her shortly before that damnable sneeze. She'd wanted nothing more than to hide under the covers, but she bound up her heart, tossed them off, and lit a candle. Holding it aloft, she'd searched the room's shadowy corners.

All were empty.

A knock sounded at the door, interrupting her thoughts. Expecting the maid with her breakfast, Ari called, "Entrée." Moving to the fireplace, she held out her hands to the blaze.

"You're shivering. Have you no shawl?"

The deep, distinctive voice reverberated down her spine. She didn't turn. Was this the voice of a killer? The man who shot Dolpho in cold blood? Again her instincts told her, "*No.*"

Her throat was dry and she swallowed before she spoke. "No, My Lord. I have no shawl. I have little of my own. A torn nightgown, one ruined slipper, and a disreputable looking cloak are the sum total of my worldly possessions. No family I can name to send to for help. I am alone."

And he must know how it feels. When he'd been on the balcony last night, there had been something vulnerable in the way he leaned on the stone railing, gazing out into the darkness. Like Atlas, bending under the weight of the world. He'd thought himself unobserved, and had let down his façade.

But she'd seen. And she knew that feeling. It was the feeling of being utterly alone.

No, no, no. This would never do! She mustn't allow herself to feel empathy for the earl. Was she going to have her opinion turned by a handsome face? By what she had imagined she'd read in the tired set of his shoulders? She would not allow herself to be a stupid, malleable cow like those simpering twits at Almacks.

Thus having firmed up her defenses, turning, she wondered why her pulse leapt as she met his gaze. Those eyes, they were wicked and gentle at the same time. But, *Mon Dieu*, he was just a man, for all that. A superb man—oh yes, *superb* was the word. A pleasure to look at, *oui*, to be sure. A cutaway coat of blue superfine covered his wide shoulders without a wrinkle and his buff pantaloons followed every line of muscle in his thighs, every mound—

Yanking her eyes back to his throat, she firmly resisted dwelling on *that*.

His throat had interesting points, also. Instead of the elaborate cravat that Dolpho had always affected, the earl's collar was open, his cravat unstarched and flowing. With those eyes, that build, and darkly handsome face, he was a superbly masculine. Also, he was easily the most compelling man she'd ever met.

And as his gaze moved over her, mockingly at first, as though mimicking her perusal of his better points, she felt a dangerous thrumming in her veins. When his look darkened, moving over her breasts, then moving slowly back to her face and eyes, she knew she was in serious trouble. There was a fluttering under her diaphragm that seemed to make her limbs weak. Nodcock, desiring this man was the stupidest thing she might do. She had no proof that he had not killed Dolpho. Only a gut feeling—how could she trust that, when she'd just found she was as weak to temptation as any of Eve's children?

Ari drew in a deep breath determined to calm her racing pulse. Desiring a man, even imagining herself in love, wasn't new to her experience. Having a man desire her wasn't new to her experience, either. She'd discovered the power she wielded over the male gender at the age of sixteen, when she'd had her season in Vienna.

A more bitter discovery was, although men flocked around her vying for her smiles, the only offer she'd received was for a *carte blanche* — her mother had been an American baker's daughter. In any noble society, that low birth made Ari undesirable as a wife, however desirable the men might find her for their beds.

Worse still, she was one of *the Mad Benoits*. The supposed taint of madness in her blood was more damning than the taint of shop.

She was certain Grandquest, had she met him socially, would have acted no differently than those young Viennese nobles.

"I've been remiss," he said at length, his voice a deep caress. Going to the newly made bed, he whipped the satin coverlet from it. Bringing it to where she stood by the fire, he wrapped it around her shoulders.

Ari caught the edges as he brought them together. As he released it, his fingers grazed her chin, and she shivered. How did he cast a spell over her so easily? Her breath caught in her throat as his gaze moved to her lips. She held still, knowing she should move…just turn away and the moment would be broken.

She didn't move. *Oh, oui, you are Eve's child! You cannot resist!*

As she watched, his gray eyes darkened to the color of storm clouds. Grandquest slid his hand around her neck. Her sensitive skin leapt to life beneath his fingers. He lifted the heavy fall of hair trapped beneath the makeshift cloak and let it slide through his fingers, watching it and caught a lock and inhaled its scent.

It was a completely intimate gesture.

It set her blood aflame.

"Lavender?" His voice was soft gravel.

Ari wet her lips. "The soap Mrs. Coventree gave me is scented with lavender." The words were little more than a whisper, and she cleared her throat. She wished her voice was steadier.

"I came to ask if you would care to come down to…breakfast."

Breakfast…*breakfast?* She blinked. His mouth said *breakfast* but his tone invited her to a more hedonistic feast.

He continued in the same husky tone, "Afterward, I'll have Mrs. Coventree see about proper clothes. I believe my sister-in-law, the dowager countess, left several trunks stored in the attic. I'm certain Mrs. Coventree can help you alter some things to fit you. Also, my sister, Anne, has accepted my invitation to come for an extended visit. When she arrives, she may be of help. Although it is a little belated, I hope she will act as chaperon."

"Who?"

"Anne." His eyes glinted. "My sister."

Merde! He made her into a brainless twit with no more than his nearness and a few intense glances. She wanted to step back, but to do that would be to give him the victory in their little duel.

"Thank you. I would like to join you for breakfast. However, I must decline your kind offer of clothing. You have been too generous already."

"Nonsense."

The one word brooked no argument. He was a man used to getting his way.

Heat pooled in her center.

"Now, if you are ready to break your fast?" He offered his arm.

"One moment." Ari determined to gain some control over the situation. To let this man play her emotions like a fiddle was madness — Benoit madness? Oh, no, she would not be like her poor grandfather, who in his youth had been so besotted by one of the Hapsburg princesses, he'd scaled the walls of Hofberg, the Hapsburgs' winter palace, and persuaded her to elope.

Ari dropped her gaze and worried her bottom lip, aware she had Grandquest's full attention. When the pause had gathered just enough drama to suit her purpose, she sighed. "I do not know what to do. Last night, I did not sleep well."

"I'm sorry to hear it. Perhaps a sleeping draught would help. I'll ask the doctor — "

"No, you do not understand." She met the earl's eyes briefly and looked away, fluttering a hand. "After you left, I...I had the strangest feeling of being watched. Although I knew I was alone in the room, the feeling would not go away. This morning, I discovered this." She stepped to the wall near the corner of the room and pointed to the small, round hole, watching Lord Grandquest's reactions closely.

His face suddenly blank, he moved and inspected the hole, bending and putting an eye to it, just as she had. "I didn't know about this."

"But you seem not to be surprised."

"I'm not." He straightened, his expression enigmatic. "This house is riddled with passages and peepholes, though I've put a lock on the door leading to a tunnel which goes to the creek. The gentleman who built the house in the early part of the last century realized a good deal of his income from smuggling—until he was hanged and his estate was forfeited to the Crown. When my grandfather was ennobled as the first Earl Grandquest, the estate was awarded to him."

"Who was watching me?" Ari asked.

His cool gray eyes never left hers, but the thick lashes drooped, shielding their expression. "It isn't likely anyone was watching you."

"Lord Grandquest—" She had been about to inform him that the *no one* who was watching had sneezed, but he stopped her with an upraised hand.

"I am certain it was your imagination."

Ari clamped her teeth together. His expression was as bland as unsalted porridge. Had it been Grandquest? It might have been. Still somehow, she didn't think so. He didn't seem the type to peep into a lady's bedroom...more likely to stride through the door, feeling certain of his welcome. "Of course, my imagination," she said dryly. Grandquest had left the bedroom door open, as propriety demanded. The young maid, Bailey, entered through it, carrying a tray with covered dishes.

"Pardon, Milady. I have your breakfast."

"Milady was just going to accompany me down to the breakfast room. You may take the tray away."

As he offered his arm, Ari realized it was the first time he'd used the title that had become her name. So, a little victory. Perhaps, he did believe she had lost her memory.

Or, perhaps, he wished her to think he believed her to make her lower her guard...

"Wait, please, Bailey." Ari stopped the girl as she turned to leave. "You may put the tray on the little table by the chair. I would like help with my hair, *s'il vous plaît?*

"Lord Grandquest, if you would be so kind as to wait in the hall?" She made the request in the tone of one accustomed to having polite requests instantly obeyed and was pleased to see one of his dark brows rise.

"Of course." Gray eyes gleaming, he bowed slightly and left.

Ari watched until the door was closed behind him, then draped the coverlet over a chair and flashed the maid a smile. "You may eat the breakfast you have brought while I comb my hair. I am certain the cook cannot be feeding you enough. You have room for a few pounds."

"No, Milady. I mean, yes, Milady. Oh, I should help you with your wonderful hair, Milady. Mrs. Coventree would be mad as a wet hen if I were to —"

"Nonsense." Ari looked around the room and spotted the laudanum bottle on the bedside table. She picked it up and popped out the cork stopper. "This should do nicely."

"Do, Milady?"

"Eat. *Dieu.* You are likely to blow away in the first good winter wind. Eat."

With a doubtful look, the maid sat and lifted the cover on a steaming bowl of porridge and dipped a spoon into it.

Ari moved to the corner with the peephole and stuck the cork firmly into it. Pulling off one of her shoes, she used the heel as a hammer, driving the cork in tightly.

Standing back, she admired her work. "Ah. Now I feel better. When 'no one' comes back, he will see nothing."

Fox was waiting by the door of the breakfast room when he heard her footsteps in the hall, her slight limp evident in the rhythm of her footfalls. He'd been very near going in to check on her, thinking the girl had bolted.

When she appeared, her deep auburn hair had been caught back in a blue ribbon, with a few short wisps left to curl at her temples and cheeks. He had the urge to touch the silk of it again, to wind his fingers through it and lift the tumble, testing its weight. How did just the sight of her arouse him so easily? He wasn't a green boy.

She reached to take his arm, as one accustomed to accepting gallantries as her due. Suppressing a bemused smile, he escorted her to the table. "What was that hammering?"

"Hammering?"

Turning to look up at him, she arched a thin, winged brow, her very blue eyes, dancing merrily. He'd never seen more unusual or more beautiful. They seemed to be lighted from within.

She shrugged. "It must have been your imagination, Lord Grandquest."

"My word. You get more lovely by the day," Ben said, rising abruptly, as though just remembering his manners. His chair was tilted back precariously, and as he whipped about to steady it, his coat sleeve upset his coffee cup and the hot liquid ran over the finely polished wood table.

"Thank you, Ben," Ari said demurely, taking no notice of his clumsiness. "You are always the gallant."

As he gazed at her, turning red, she felt a prick of remorse for having tried to bash him with the heavy poker. It would have been like kicking poor, sweet André, a faithful St. Bernard she'd had as a girl. The dog had followed her everywhere and was a great nuisance, but he had looked at her with the same soulful adoration as was now in Ben's eyes.

"Ben, you're a total flat." Toby stood and lifted his newspaper out of harm's way as coffee pooled around his plate. A footman leapt to mop up the mess with Toby's napkin. But instead of absorbing the liquid, it swept it before it, and coffee dribbled off the table onto the toe of Toby's boot. Muttering imprecations, he took a quick step back and looked in disgust at the ruined shine.

"A total flat."

"I ain't the one with coffee on my boot."

As Toby glared at Ben, Ari smothered a smile. "Ben has a point, *Monsieur* Toady."

Ben laughed. Toby scowled and muttered something about French whores.

"Here now. There's a lady present," Ben exclaimed, his cheeks turning red.

Toby looked straight at Ari. "Where? I see no lady."

Beside her, Grandquest tensed. Ari felt the muscles of his arm bunch under her hand.

"I think an apology is in order." The earl frowned at Toby.

"Please. Let there be no dissension between you because of me." Not waiting for an answer, she turned to Toby, her back ramrod straight, her chin lifted. "*Monsieur*, I await your apology, but you are correct in one thing. I do not know if I own the right to be called 'lady,' the term being a title and not merely a polite means of address. I know nothing about myself." Lying to these people, some of whom she was coming to know and like, was becoming increasingly difficult. "I do know that your crude speech offends my sensibilities."

"Here now. Only a total flat would fail to see you're a lady." Ben shot a glare at Toby. "Your education, your manners, Milady, and your genteel nature all tell the tale."

Though it was hardly a mark of gentility to be prowling the Dartmouth waterfront in a nightgown, or trying to shoot a peer of the realm, Ari didn't quibble with Ben's assessment of her character. She gave him a grateful smile. "Perhaps, I'm but a humble governess. Or a teacher."

"Or a rich man's mistress." Toby suggested, with a leering glance at her figure.

"That's quite enough, Toby." Grandquest spoke with deadly calm.

Glaring at him, Toby threw the newspaper onto the table. "I've lost my appetite. I don't expect Ben to be too fast on the uptake, but, Fox, you seem to have forgotten that this is the woman who tried to blow your head off. "

Toby strode to the door and paused. "I'll find the cook who arrived last night and wait in the study for you and...*Milady*. It is about time we put an end to this nonsense once and for all."

Cook? Ari felt a knot of dread forming in her chest. Bread-like-a-brick Hilda was here already? The game was almost over, then. Very soon, she would be exposed — *mérde!*

Turning to Fox, she looked into his eyes and looked away and tried to speak past the knot of fear in her throat. "Your lordship, I..."

"Now, look at how the oaf has upset her! Excuse me, Milady." Standing, Ben threw his napkin onto his plate and curled his hand into a fist. "I'll just have a word with that nodcock about his manners."

"No, Ben. You must not." Ari shook her head. "Toby is only concerned for his friend. I think I would mistrust, also, were our situations reversed."

"Always the lady." Ben bowed. "I'll make it a gentle word then. No blood drawn. Some slight swelling, maybe..."

As Ben quit the room, Ari met Grandquest's curious gaze. Swallowing hard, she said, "When I tried to blow your head off..." Would she never remember just what had happened? She knitted her fingers, trying to get past the fog in her memory.

"No." The earl looked from the beautiful young woman to the footman, who had finished wiping up the coffee and returned to his post by the sideboard. The man might have been carved of wood, so still was he, and he was obviously absorbing every word. Fox nodded, and the man left, closing the door behind him.

"I did not try to kill you?" Ari blinked. "Lord Grandquest, I am confused…"

"You did most assuredly try to kill me. But you didn't try to 'blow my head off'. The chest presents a much larger target, and that's the target you wisely chose." He smiled sardonically.

Ari put icy fingers to her temples and massaged. "This grows bizarre."

"Do you remember it?" He watched her closely.

"*Non!* No." She did not remember their encounter in Dartmouth. That was no lie. But she knew that was not exactly what he meant, either. Shaking her head, she asked herself what was the point? He had found the cook from the cottage. Soon, she would be identified as the woman who had lived there. If she was wrong and the earl was indeed the French spy whom she and Dolpho had been trying to trap, she would soon be dead.

If, as she was coming to think, Grandquest was not Dandelion, then he would believe that she was a French agent and turn her over to the authorities.

The end would be the same.

She should have risked the wall last night…

"Knowing you tried to take my life upsets you?" he asked, his voice deep and soft.

Mon Dieu, what did he expect her to say?

"Yes."

Taking her hand, Fox found her fingers were cold. He touched the gold band circling her ring finger. "What if I told you that, if I'm right about who you are, I believe your actions justified? That I hold you blameless?"

"You are confusing me."

He folded her cold hand in both his own. The look in her eyes was that of a lost child. Remorse swept over him as she closed her eyes and trembled visibly.

Remorse, and something else. Something warm and needful.

What was it about this woman that called to him, made him completely aware that he was a man? Fox pulled her into his arms and felt her breasts pressing against his chest. Melting against him, she buried her face in his coat, her head just beneath his chin. Stroking her glorious hair, he inhaled deeply of her scent of lavender.

And he felt just like a thief.

"Forgive me," he murmured.

Ari raised her head and was captured by the look darkening his eyes. "Why?"

"Because I don't want you to remember. When you do regain your memory, you'll...remember why you hate me. Bloody hell." He cupped her face. "Do you know what you do to a man?"

Rioting sensations coursed through her as she waited, willing him to get on with it. His eyes were polished pewter, now shaded by his thick lashes. His features were tense. When he slowly lowered his lips and touched hers, tentatively, as though she were incredibly fragile, that light touch took her breath and filled her with rushing liquid heat.

And pleasure. She wanted more. She thought she'd been kissed before, but realized now she'd been wrong.

Ari tilted her head back, inviting him to deepen the contact. In response, Fox slanted his mouth across hers, flicking her lips with his tongue and plunged his tongue deep inside her mouth, exploring it. Heat flooded her and her breasts tingled madly, and the sensations echoed in her abdomen and between her thighs. His penis was hot and hard against her belly, and she pressed tighter against him, enjoying the feel of it. Twining her arms around the strong column of his neck, she rose on her tiptoes, telling him by her actions she wanted more.

He broke the kiss, his hands around her rib cage setting her away from him.

"Bloody hell," she whispered when she'd regained her breath.

"Yes, bloody hell." He sighed roughly, shaking his head. "I had no right."

"No right?"

"No." His tone was grim. Pulling her against him, again, he tucked her head beneath his chin and stroked her hair. "You'll understand soon enough. For pity's sake, woman, hold still," he said as she wiggled to be free of his arms.

Deciding it was wise to hold still, Ari rested her cheek against his chest, enjoying the echoes of sensation awash through her body, and wishing she could have met him under different circumstances.

But there were no better circumstances for her, she reminded herself, regaining control with the thought. Had she learned nothing in Vienna?

"Come," Fox said when he felt the evidence of his desire had faded away sufficiently. He took her arm and opened the door. "Let us get on with this."

Ari held back when he would have guided her through the portal. "Where are you taking me?"

"It's time to find out who you are. For good or bad."

"I…I am not certain I want to know." Ari followed, compelled to do so by his grip on her arm. She did briefly think of breaking and running, but decided she could never outrun him with her wounded leg, and it would be wholly humiliating to be caught.

He muttered, "Nor am I."

She planted her feet outside the study. "Lord Grandquest, I must—"

"Courage." Fox knocked lightly.

Creaking ominously, the door slowly opened. Ari eyed it as though it was the gateway to hell. And, adding to the impression, the odious Toby appeared in the doorway.

Toby made a mocking bow, ushering her in. "There's someone here anxious to become reacquainted with you, *Milady*."

Clamping her teeth together when they started to chatter, Ari raised her chin and swept past him. So, she was to be exposed...she would not give this one the pleasure of seeing her quail and quake, no matter her discomfort at the prospect of being hanged.

Her attention was immediately claimed by the woman by the marble fireplace. It was indeed bread-like-a-brick Hilda. Ari wound her fingers together and waited for the worst as Toby introduced the earl to the woman.

The cook executed a stiff curtsy. "My lord."

"I understand you were employed as a cook by a certain couple near Little Braxton," the earl said.

"Yes, Milord." Hilda bobbed her head.

Ari recognized her own powder blue capelet around Hilda's slightly stooped shoulders, and her favorite brooch pinned at the collar held it together. This is beyond enough! She is wearing my things! The brooch wasn't an expensive piece, but still, it was the principle, Ari thought, incensed. Further inspection showed the woman was clutching one of the lace-edged handkerchiefs that Dolpho had given Ari for her birthday. Oh, that was beyond enough.

But what was most unforgivable was the sight of her own butter-soft kid shoes on the cook's feet, when Ari stood with her feet screaming for release from her borrowed too-short, too-hard shoes.

No doubt, Hilda would have been wearing her dresses, too, if the cook had not been broader in the derrière.

"Can you identify this lady?" Grandquest continued.

"So, this is the poor dear what's lost her wits." Hilda *tsk-tsked* sympathetically, but there was a triumphant gleam in her eyes.

Ari decided she would have her shoes back. If she was to be arrested, she would go to jail in comfortable shoes!

"Tell the earl what he wishes to know," Ari said through clenched teeth. She had the pleasure of seeing the cook's eyes round in surprise. Dolpho had told Hilda that Ari spoke only Italian, and the woman had never heard her speak English before. No doubt, Ari decided, the cook was now repenting all the nasty things she'd muttered about "bloody furriners" when she thought Ari didn't understand.

But if Hilda was nonplussed, she quickly recovered and shot Ari a sly look.

Clenching her fists, Ari thought she must scream if the woman did not get on with it.

Chapter Five

🔊

Shaking her head, Hilda said stoutly, "No, My Lord. I ain't never clapped me eyes on this poor lass a'fore. Poor mite. Looks like a beggar lass, iff'n you ask me."

Stunned, it took Ari several seconds to comprehend that the cook had not given her away.

Realizing she stood with her mouth open, she snapped it closed.

Grandquest expelled a long breath. Whether in disappointment, or relief, Ari couldn't tell. His expression gave nothing away.

Toby's face, however, was wreathed in disbelief.

"What? You described this woman to me perfectly not ten minutes before she entered the room—foreign, tall, with red hair. Now you're telling us you've not seen her before?"

"The woman at the cottage had hair dyed henna red, sir, to be sure. Not a true redhead, like this poor lass. And the woman you're speakin' of was an I-talian, you know. I ain't never knowed of an I-talian with red hair. Didn't speak a word of the king's English, neither."

"Do you speak Italian?" Toby demanded of Ari.

"Maybe a little," Ari admitted, clasping her hands together to hide their trembling.

"It don't matter none, sir. She still ain't the I-talian's wife." Hilda fingered the brooch at her throat as she smiled at Ari.

Understanding dawned. Why, the crafty witch! She had helped herself to her and Dolpho's things, no doubt selling all that was of no personal use. If the cook didn't identify her, she could not point a finger and call her "thief"!

Pain shot through her cramped toes, and she glanced longingly at her own comfortable shoes on the woman's feet. *Mon Dieu*, having them would almost be worth admitting the truth.

"Thank you for your time, madam," Grandquest told Hilda, dismissing her. She dropped another stiff curtsy.

Strong fingers cupped Ari's elbow. She shivered at the contact. Looking up at him, she found Grandquest watching her closely. The look in his eyes made her remember the feel of her breasts crushed against his chest, his manhood burning against her, his lips moving over hers.

She shivered again.

"Are you all right?"

"No," she said honestly, with a final glance at her longed-for shoes as Hilda hurried from the room. "I am very disappointed."

Realizing by the expressions on Toby's and Ben's faces that they found her answer odd, she added quickly, "I had hoped to have a name by which to call myself." *And my owned damned shoes!*

"You wouldn't have wanted to be named as a French spy," Ben said.

She blinked at him. *Mérde, having her toes free of these iron traps would almost be worth it.*

"Were this Italian and his wife French spies?" she asked ingenuously. Inwardly she was hungry for information. What had happened to Dolpho's body? What was being said of them? Did no one think that they'd been falsely accused?

"By all accounts, they were," Toby cut in, looking uncomfortable. "I'd, ah...like to make that apology, now, if I may...Milady." The word seemed to affect him like biting into a green plum.

Turning to face him, Ari raised an eyebrow in disbelief. "Indeed?"

"Yes. See, we've long known who the Italian was. A young prince of a very minor state on Italy's frontier with France. It was well known that the prince wasn't married, you see. However, he did have a reputation as a rakehell. I believed you to be the actress he'd been keeping as his—well, you understand what I believed. I offer most humble apologies for my assumption."

"About time, too." Ben glowered at his friend.

They had *long known* who the Italian was? A slow cold feeling washed over Ari as she considered the implications.

Flicking a dismissive glance at Ben, Toby added, "That doesn't mean I'm nodcock enough to trust you, you understand? You did try right keenly to put a hole in Fox, here. For all I know, you're an escaped Bedlamite who'll murder us all without cause. But you aren't the prince's...woman of loose morals—as far as we know—and as for treating you as one, I apologize."

A slow smile curved her lips. "In that case, I accept your apology, *Monsieur* Toady," she said demurely. "And let me assure you, sir, that I will not murder you in your sleep...without cause."

"I..." Toby's mouth opened and closed several times.

Ben chortled, "Stop flapping your yapper. You look like nothing so much as a beached trout."

Grandquest chuckled softly. "Give way, Toby. Here." He pulled his wallet from the inner pocket of his coat and gave Toby several banknotes. "Please see that the cook is recompensed. Doing so will allow you to make a graceful exit before our firebrand skewers you again."

Toby nodded and, with a disgruntled glance at Ari, left.

"I'll have the coach brought 'round and see the cook on her way," Ben said. "I can't believe he ever entertained the notion that you, Milady, were Prince Dragonetti's consort. I certainly never did." He followed Toby from the room.

Ari sat down in one of the leather chairs drawn up before the fire and stretched her cold fingers toward the blaze, feeling numbed by all that had transpired. Hilda had come and gone and still she was free—life's turns were indeed unpredictable!

Grandquest moved nearer, placing his hand on the back of her chair. He did not touch her, yet she was completely aware of him. She was alone with the earl. Again. That was not a good thing to be.

He was a dangerous man to be alone with.

Trying to rein in her wayward emotions, she said softly, "Tell me of this Italian prince and the red-haired woman."

"What would you want to know?"

"What happened to them?" Just what were the rumors flying about? Even in this remote place, surely the countryside was alive with the news of the *spy*, who'd been killed and the other who had escaped.

"Acting on information received, apparently from someone highly placed, the militia raided the couple's cottage. The pair escaped into the night. A storm washed away any tracks, but we know at least one of the pair was shot."

Staring into the fire, Ari bit the inside of her lip, using the pain to keep the tears at bay. Poor Dolpho. What had happened to his body? Was it still out there? Was he still alone? Had he been found, his head been severed and stuck on a pike outside some city gate? Or had his body been strung up from some gallows and left to twist in the wind as it rotted? These English had such genteel customs.

She swallowed. "Killed?" With an effort, she kept her voice steady, but couldn't trust it beyond the one-word question.

"There is no way of knowing."

"You said one was wounded—"

"A neckcloth was found. Despite the washing rain, it showed signs of having been soaked through with blood."

"A neckcloth? That is all? Not his body?" Realizing her mistake, she added hastily, "Or her body?"

"Only the neckcloth," Fox said.

Dolpho's body was not found? Something inside her sang to know her dearest friend and cousin had not been mutilated and dishonored in death.

But what had happened to his body?

The flames of the fire blurred, and she blinked the moisture from her eyes, her mind shying away from possible answers. It did not bear thinking on.

Dolpho, I will find the man responsible, she thought.

She remembered making very nearly the same vow as she knelt beside him in the rain.

They'd escaped from their cottage by cutting through the thatched roof, just as the Devonshire Militia was breaking down the front door. A hellish storm roiling the nearby Channel drenched them in the first instant they were outside. In a flare of lightning, Dolpho spotted a mounted lieutenant from the edge of the roof and dropped onto him, knocking him off his horse. Other men left to guard the mounts tried to stop him, but Ari had grabbed a heavy stick of kindling as she passed the woodpile, and she used it to good effect, whacking anything that moved. In the dark and the drenching rain, the soldiers were confused and fighting each other.

Leaping onto that lieutenant's horse, Dolpho reached down and pulled her up behind him. They had escaped, galloping down the narrow, tree-lined lane.

Or, they had almost gotten away. A little way down the road, a tall man stepped from behind a tree. She remembered how odd his hat had looked, a gentleman's high-crowned beaver, squaring the top of an oilskin jacket.

As she had wondered why a gentleman would be out in the storm, he brought up a rifle and fired. Dolpho would have been knocked from the horse, but that she'd been behind him. By an effort of will, Ari held him on the animal and managed to rein it into the thick bracken and undergrowth on the side of the road, putting her heels to its flanks. Putting a half-mile behind them, they made it to a clifftop road edging the Channel, when her strength gave out and he slipped from the horse.

She was on her knees beside him in an instant, shielding him from the breaking storm with her body as she frantically loosened his cravat. "*Mon Dieu*, Dolpho, are you trying to break your neck?"

She packed the neckcloth into the deep hole in his shoulder, and his warm blood, seeping between her fingers, had chilled her far more than the cold rain seeping through the old cloak she'd snatched from a kitchen peg.

Too much blood. There was too much blood.

"*Go on!*" he ordered.

"And leave you to…to drown in this rain?"

He shook his head, the movements exaggerated in the lightning flashes. "How I hate this damned English rain… It will be snowing now in St. Cyr, the high passes already too deep to cross…" He wiped at his face. "*Grandquest*. Dartmouth, this road will take you. Find Grandquest—"

"Grandquest." The tall man sighting down the rifle barrel flashed in her mind's eye. "You recognized him, then? It was the earl?"

Dolpho shook his head wildly. He'd caught her hands, trying to push them away from his shoulder. "*Find Grandquest.*"

"*Non!* Only let me stop this little bleeding, this tiny bleeding…"

Arching upward, he face twisted in pain, he groaned from deep in his chest, and he went still, his breath leaving his chest in a gust, which she heard above the pounding rain.

"Dolpho?"

"*Dolpho!*"

Her cousin had not answered.

Now, blinking at the fire, she replayed it all in her mind, and she wasn't certain what he'd meant. He might have been telling her to go to Grandquest for protection. Could that have been the case?

Or, since she'd been acquainted with Grandquest, did she just prefer not to believe he was the man behind the gun?

Ari grew colder, despite her hands outstretched to the flames.

"Toby thought I was this woman. Tall, with red hair. I see how he drew the conclusion."

"Pallas."

The earl's voice was low and warm and intimate. It vibrated down her spine and set sweet confusion to swirling in her head.

"I beg your pardon?" She blinked at him.

"Pallas Athena. You do need a name. What do you think of it?"

"Pallas," Ari said softly. "The goddess of wisdom. A strange name for someone with no memory."

"Also goddess of war." He smiled enigmatically. "I assure you it is fitting. And Pallas Athena sprang to life full-grown, dressed in armor and ready for battle, as you seem to have done."

"My lord, you have me at a disadvantage." She turned back to the fire. Ari again wished she could remember their encounter in Dartmouth. That remained a mystery.

"Fox." He was pleased with his inspiration. Until she remembered her own name, Pallas was more than fitting for this woman, who had fought with such fury.

And when she remembered her own name?

The declaration she'd made aboard *The Dancer* came back to him—"*I ask only the pleasure of seeing you in hell when I get there.*"

She had meant every syllable.

If she did remember, he'd deal with it then, he decided. He offered his elbow. "Come. Let us see about that breakfast we never got around to eating."

"Yes." She rose, accepting the arm he offered. "Will you tell me about your sister, Lady Anne?"

"I think you'll like her. She has great courage. Just as you do."

If he was honest with himself, he'd admit the truth, Fox acknowledged as he gazed at the woman beside him. He'd tell her who she was. With the woman from the cottage eliminated, he was almost certain of her real identity.

When she remembered the man who'd placed that wedding ring on her finger, she would remember why she hated him, Fox knew.

And he also knew he deserved her hate.

But until she remembered, he would do all in his power to make her life comfortable and to see her fully returned to health. It was the least he could do.

And, maybe, taking care of Peterson's widow would lay one of his ghosts to rest.

* * * * *

"You must be mad!"

"Of late, that assessment is the popular one," Fox told his sister. Her hands on her hips, she glared at him and began pacing the parlor. Hiding his smile in his teacup, he sipped his Earl Grey as he watched her.

"You would place me and a mere child like Geoffrey in danger, having me play chaperon to this murderess you've foolishly ensconced beneath your roof? I think not, Fox. Indeed, I can't fathom what maggot has gotten into your head. You should have told me of this in your letter." As she punctuated her tirade with gestures, she looked like she was conducting an orchestra in one of Beethoven's more energetic compositions.

Short and plump, with wheat-colored hair and a complexion that was a bit too ruddy for beauty, Lady Anne in no way resembled Fox, with his height and dark coloring. In truth, though she was his half-sister by law, they weren't related at all. Everyone knew his American mother had been pregnant when she had married the earl.

Still, Anne had been sister, mother, and teacher to him after his own mother died. Remembering his sister's kindness, which was all that had made his youth bearable, her vehement stand against Pallas surprised him.

"She isn't a murderess, Anne. After all, she only tried to do away with me, no one else. Since she failed, I think it would be rather poor spirited to hold that against her."

"*Poor spirit—*" Anne stopped pacing the parlor and whirled to face him, her eyes flashing. "Now, I know you are having me on."

"Just a little," he chuckled. "There's more to the story than you know, of course."

"Nor do I care to know more."

"Now, Anne, you can't mean to tell me you're condemning the girl out of hand."

"Fox, you've stayed in the wilds of America too long. You've lost sight of how things are done in a proper society. Any woman who would act like this guttersnipe you've described has placed herself beyond the pale. Even if she wasn't dangerous, which she most certainly has shown herself to be, I would not sully my hands with her."

His normally gentle sister's attitude angered him. Was this what Pallas would face everywhere?

"I never thought you would turn into a high stickler—one of those bitter, old society cows who take no pleasure whatsoever in life and are bound to see that no one else does, either. Pallas is far from a guttersnipe. More of an avenging angel, if you would know the truth. Yet, I will accept your decision—"

"Good," Anne snapped.

" —if you can but tell me that, had you the opportunity to shoot the cutthroats who murdered your husband and older son, you would not seek vengeance."

Anne's eyes widened with hurt. "Foul. Oh, foul." She sat down on a lyre-backed chair and hugged herself, compressing the rows of ruffles and making her too-ample bosom look even larger than it was. "You cannot compare the two things. I was robbed of Bobby and John by the lowest dregs of humanity, footpads who killed them for their coin. And I would indeed send the bastards to hell if I had the opportunity! I curse them every day of my life.

"You cannot compare that to a wild woman trying to murder a peer of the realm. 'Tis not the same thing at all."

Fox spared her a sardonic look. He said quietly, "To my great shame, I must own that what Pallas attempted should be counted as exactly the same thing. She was justified in wanting me dead."

"You speak in riddles."

He hesitated, then finished his tea and placed the cup and saucer on a low table. Straightening, he met his sister's perplexed gaze. "The girl's husband is dead, and I am responsible."

The words hung in the air between them.

It was the first time he'd said it aloud. Admitting the truth did nothing to ease the knot of guilt rubbing at his conscience. Indeed, it seemed to tighten it. Had he not broken his word, the man Pallas loved would still be alive.

"In case you are wondering at my silence, I am awaiting your explanation." Anne folded her hands in her lap.

"I guessed you would want details. Yet there is much I am not at liberty to tell you."

"Because of your post in Whitehall?"

Fox made no answer, letting her assume that was the case.

However, he knew it was because he had chosen to serve America first, the land where he'd spent the greater part of his life, that Randolph Peterson had died.

"Then just the meat of it, if you please."

"Have you ever been forced to choose between duty and honor?" Glancing at his sister, who obviously hadn't a clue what he was talking about, Fox went on, "A young friend of mine, a clerk in the Foreign Office, sent me a note saying he had information as to the identity of the spy in Whitehall who has been leaking information to the French. He asked that I meet him at a certain pub within the hour. He also said he was in fear of his life and depending on me to help him. I sent him a reply agreeing. Then…duty unexpectedly called me elsewhere. Only for a short time. I saw no harm in the short delay."

He sighed. For what seemed like eons he'd been playing his part, every moment spent in London he was balanced on a knife's edge. And he had slipped. He'd allowed himself to be diverted by a clever ploy. Dandelion must have known that Peterson had contacted him.

"I was a half-hour late for the meeting. Peterson lay dead in the alley, my note in his hand. Though there seems to be no way to confirm it, until I find someone who can identify her, I have no doubt Pallas was Peterson's wife, the daughter of a French émigré and an Irish woman."

Anne stared, wide-eyed. "Oh, my."

"Because of my note, I was under suspicion. And because of my title and position, I was cleared, though I had no alibi. I was not at liberty to reveal my whereabouts when the deed was taking place. So, it follows that Pallas would believe me guilty of the crime. You see, I am guilty in a sense. Had I been at the meeting place on time, I would have prevented the man's death."

Anne said, "You seem to be taking the responsibility for this unfortunate event completely onto yourself. Surely, the girl's family would be better suited to care for her."

"She is an orphan. Completely alone. I've been making inquiries after someone who can identify her. So far, without luck."

A creak of floorboards beyond the door caught Fox's attention.

Anne shook her head, her curls bouncing. "You must not borrow blame—where are you going?"

He put a finger to his lips as he moved noiselessly to the door and jerked it wide.

His lovely houseguest, who'd obviously been crouching with an ear to the keyhole, lost her balance and fell into the parlor in a flurry of powder blue velvet, white petticoats, spools of thread, and deep auburn curls.

Ari found herself on the floor, the skirt of her new dress twisted about her calves. Scissors, thimbles, and scraps of material were scattered around. "*Du mien Gute,*" she muttered in German, and, sitting up, she threw the rest of her sewing supplies aside in disgust. She straightened her skirt with as much dignity as she could muster, covering her ankles and lay back on the floor, staring up at the earl's mocking face. Viewing him upside down, he seemed to tower a great height above her.

"My Lord," she said, crossing her arms over her middle and assuming a relaxed attitude.

One dark, curved brow rose. She fancied she saw his lips twitch.

Fox glanced at someone beyond her range of vision. "Anne, I would like to make you known to Pallas. Pallas, this lovely lady is my sister, Anne, Lady Brickingham."

Chapter Six

ප

"Lady Brickingham," Ari acknowledged, tilting her head back and viewing the lady upside down. Fox's sister sat forward on a chair, her fingers over her mouth and eyes rounded in genteel surprise—the epitome of proper English womanhood, even viewed from this angle. "I beg your pardon, but I find it difficult to execute a proper curtsy at the moment."

Lady Anne's fuchsia day dress was an unfortunate choice, Ari decided. Fox's sister would be pretty, if her coloring wasn't at war with the vivid fuchsia—a war which the fuchsia easily won, taking no prisoners. Ah, well, Lady Anne might claim a superior bloodline, but that did not give her a superior sense of style.

So, the lady did not want to "sully her hands". It was better to know where one stood at the onset in these matters. Lady Anne's feelings of distaste were stronger than Ari had run into before, but they were not new to her experience. Ari's father had followed his friend, Lafayette, to the American colonies to fight with Washington's army. There, he had fallen in love with a Philadelphia baker's daughter and made her his wife—much to the amusement of Europe's aristocracy. Ari sighed. It seemed all her life she'd been caught between two worlds, not of the working class and not quite of the nobility. Tolerated by both and accepted by neither.

A familiar bitterness tightened her chest.

"Allow me." Fox offered his hand to help her up.

She frowned. "My lord, I am still thinking about how best to go on."

His buckled shoe was by her head. Her gaze was drawn up to what appeared, from her position on the floor, to be a mile of tan-colored knit pantaloons. It outlined a well-developed calf and stretched over the heavy muscles of the earl's upper thigh. Though she firmly told herself not to glance any higher, curiosity compelled her gaze to the bulge at the apex of his legs.

Seeing what was there from this position was a revelation. Indeed, it was obvious that the statue of a Greek discus thrower in the earl's library was wholly inaccurate. The walnuts and little *thumb* peeping from stone pubic curls weren't at all to scale. *Mais*, the sculptor had taken artistic license, she supposed.

Or perhaps not. Perhaps, just as women were endowed with different size breasts, men were equipped in various sizes...?

Her gaze moved to Fox's face and she found his gray eyes gleaming beneath half-lowered lids.

Heat flooded her cheeks.

And her body.

Lady Anne asked, "What caused you to stumble? There's no rug on which to trip. Did you slip?"

Grateful for the diversion, Ari looked behind her again and hoped Fox's sister would think the red in her cheeks due to embarrassment at the fall. "I did not trip, Lady Anne, I was listening at the keyhole."

"Oh." Anne's eyes rounded more, and she darted a look at her brother. "I...see."

Ari continued, "When Fox opened the door, I lost my balance, you see, and tumbled inside."

"Do you often put your ear to keyholes?" There was something suspiciously like a chuckle in Fox's voice.

"I—" Just before a confession slipped out, Ari remembered she was supposed to have a memory loss. *Nodcock, where are your wits?* "I do not think so. You see, it was an awkward position. I am rather tall and keyholes are so low. Bending to it was most uncomfortable." Schooling her features into a bland expression, Ari met his gaze innocently.

"I see." The earl's lips twitched.

Ari peered behind her again. "You must allow, Lady Anne, my listening might have saved us both from a great deal of bother. You see, having received Fox's summons to join you, I was hurrying to the parlor when I heard the tone of your voice. You seemed distressed. I had no wish to inflict my acquaintance on you if you disliked the notion, so I sought to learn more of what was being discussed before I entered.

"But here I landed, instead. Had Fox not jerked the door open, I could have gone quietly upstairs and sent my regrets, this unpleasantness for you avoided. I am sorry."

"Sorry? For listening at the keyhole, or getting caught?" Anne asked.

"For getting caught, of course. If I had been sorry for listening, I should not have done it."

Fox burst out in laughter. Anne looked at her brother, her brows raised in disbelief. "Is she always so…"

"Refreshingly original?"

"That is one way to put it, I suppose." Anne snapped open her fan, and applied it vigorously.

Fox chuckled. "Pallas seems to have as little regard for society's dictates as I do. And as you do, also, if you'll admit the truth, Anne."

To Ari, Fox said, "I am sorry to have spoiled your *keyhole diplomacy*."

"What's done is done." Ari shrugged again, although she feared the effect lost in her present position. "You should not tax your sister so, Fox. She does not wish to know me, and my acquaintance has been thrust upon her. Now, she is trying to think of how to delicately remove herself from this situation. Perhaps you have an idea for her? How she might extricate herself?"

"Nonsense. She's been at Hornsgate Abbey with her pan-faced in-laws until they've drained all joy of life from her. I apologize for her rigid disregard for what is right in favor of what is *'acceptable behavior'*."

"*Non.* You really do not allow for how unbending society is and how merciless it is to one who falls out of favor. You should have told her the whole before she came. It was too bad of you to risk her reputation and position in society over this inconsequential personage."

"Enough." Anne laughed. "There is no need to do it up quite so brown, young lady. Fox, do help her up. I would have a better look at the person who dares tweak my whiskers so mercilessly."

"It will be my pleasure." One winged brow lifted as he gazed again at Ari. "Have you decided?"

"About what?"

"About…it?"

His voice was dark honey, rich with undertones that pooled in a warm place deep inside her. The look in his eyes disturbed and excited her and said he knew exactly what she'd been looking at.

Mérde!

"Not completely." Arching a challenging brow, Ari sat upright and held her arms out. "Perhaps if you just got behind and gave a little lift?"

He did as she asked, lifting her easily. He then steadied her, and his hands on her ribs filled her with warm tingles that seemed to permeate her torso and sparkle like Chinese rockets in her middle. She quickly stepped away, putting distance between them. It would never do to let this one play her emotions like a fiddle—she had already learned he did it too well. This weakness she sensed in herself was why she had wisely avoided the earl as much as possible over the last several days. Oh, she was Eve's daughter, to be sure! And there was something dangerous about this man that drew her to him—an intriguing mix of raw power and civilized manners.

But, as she'd thought many times, it was his eyes that captured her and drew her into his spell, those beautiful, deep-set eyes. She wondered at the shadows in them. And the hidden depths.

The earl offered his arm. Giving him an easy smile—she'd not let him think he discomfited her!—she laid her hand on his sleeve and allowed him to lead her the short distance to his sister.

Lady Anne placed her *pince nez* on her nose and looked Ari up and down, like a goodwife eyeing a three-day-old eel in a fishmonger's shop.

Ari cocked a brow and met Anne's gaze steadily. "Let me know when you are quite done. I wish to sit down before these dreadful shoes I am wearing do me a permanent injury."

Lady Anne let the eyeglasses dangle from a pink ribbon pinned to her generous bosom—which had a plethora of brooches adorning it. She clasped her hands before her dramatically, her eyes wide and twinkling as she shot her brother a glance. "She frightens me, Fox. At Hornsgate, I am accounted the veriest dragon, but this girl isn't cowed by my tactics at all. What am I to do? She matches me tit for tat."

"I am at a loss about what to do with either of you." Fox shrugged.

Ari caught the gleam of humor in Lady Anne's eyes and felt herself relax. "I do beg your pardon," she said meekly. "I will endeavor to be more pudding-hearted in the future, if that will put you more at your ease, Lady Anne."

"Just plain *Anne*, if you please." She patted the seat of a nearby chair and Ari obligingly sat down. "I only trot out my title when I'm trying to impress someone. I must say, it seems a wasted effort where you are concerned, my dear. Tell me, is it true you remember nothing of who you are or where you came from?"

Ari glanced at Fox and found him watching her closely. Biting her lip, she shook her head and sighed. Lying was wearing heavily on her conscience, and whenever she looked into the earl's eyes, she had an urge to unburden herself completely. She wondered how she could have ever thought this man a murder and a spy.

However, if she were to reclaim her true identity, she would be inviting arrest and hanging. And it would be better for Fox if he could rightly claim he didn't know she was wanted by the Crown.

Cher bon Dieu, was there was no way out of this tangle?

"A pity. From your cheeky manner, which I find quite refreshing compared to all the simpering misses in society nowadays, I would guess you to be at the least an archduchess. Fox, would you know if any country is missing one?" At his blank look, Anne said, "An archduchess, brother. Do think about it while you ring for tea, won't you? There's a good lad."

Lady Anne waved him away with her hand and refocused her attention on Ari. "Now, what was I thinking of? Oh, I must know where you found that lovely day dress. It reeks of Paris." She wrinkled her nose. "But that, of course, is quite impossible. The war is so inconvenient. Those military-style cuffs and frogging quite make the style. Is that to be the rage this season? It will be too bad of you not to remember which *modiste* in Bond Street made it for you."

Ari looked down at the dress she'd created from two old velvet gowns she'd found stored in a trunk in the attic. She'd taken the one in best repair used it for the main body, adding an edging around the square neck, a foot to lengthen the body, and long cuffs to lengthen the sleeves, all in a darker shade of velvet. Braid work, buttons and frogging robbed from a third dress added a military flavor Ari thought suited her better than ruffles and lace.

Smiling, Ari shook her head. "Your pardon, Lady Anne. I find I am still too nonplussed over Fox being acclaimed 'a good lad' to answer."

* * * * *

It was time to go.

Ari paced before the fire in her bedroom, her stocking feet noiseless on the parquet floor. At tea, Lady Anne and Fox had talked of the Christmas holidays.

Ari had listened and smiled and nodded in all the right places, and imagined how it would be if she were really an accepted part of the earl's household. She was very much aware that she was not, though they generously included her in their plans.

It had grown to be too much. They made her yearn for things that could not be.

Her thoughts went to Ben and the abominable Toby and their fantastic tales of America. Both had taken their leave yesterday and now were aboard ship in Dartmouth, due to sail on the evening tide. Without Toby to fight with her, her only diversion from her unhappy musings during tea had been watching Anne's fourteen-year-old son, Geoffrey, droop his lower lip. He was unhappily home for an extended holiday after being sent down from Harrow for an incident involving an adder and the headmaster's wig.

After watching the boy engage in torturing a potted palm by heating an old cavalry saber to white-hot, then burning off one frond at a time as he pretended to be Robespierre interrogating an enemy of the revolution, Ari's sympathies were firmly with the adder.

What was she to do? She could not remain here at Stonerose. Even if her conscience would allow it, it was only a matter of time before word of her presence here reached the authorities.

A log in the fireplace broke into two pieces, startling her as it fell between the andirons with a *thump*. Sparks flew and a coal nearly rolled out onto the floor. She stepped toward the fireplace, reaching for the poker. "*Ouch!*" she cried as she stepped on something hard. Mumbling expletives, she hobbled to a nearby chair, sat, lifted her foot, and rubbed the arch. She spied a bottle cork on the floor and frowned. A glance at the peephole confirmed where it came from. *Sacre bleu*, this was the third time some jokester had knocked it back out from the inside. It was beyond too much.

A knock sounded at her door and she threw it an irritated glance. She expected her maid, whom she'd sent to fetch pen and paper. "Enter, please. It is unlocked and I am lamed."

Carrying a lap desk, Fox paused just inside the bedchamber, his hand on the knob.

Pallas sat with her foot in her hands, the shapely length of her calf exposed. A half-dozen deep auburn curls, so red they gleamed with burgundy highlights, cascaded from the knot atop her head and caressed her cheek and rioted over her shoulder as she bent forward, examining her foot. The blue velvet day dress she'd created was the perfect contrast for the ringlets. When she looked up, meeting his gaze, her eyes seemed aglow with a light from within, as though she was pleased to see him.

"My lord?"

She hastily stood and straightened her skirt and clasped her hands before her. Was she nervous? He hadn't failed to notice that she'd avoided being alone with him the last several days.

Since he'd kissed her.

Heat gathered in his groin at the memory.

And she was as interested in him as he was her. The way she'd looked over his *attributes* in the sitting room had shown him the same things were on her mind.

Heat became hardness, and he shifted the lap desk to cover his erection.

"You asked for writing materials?" His voice came out husky and he cleared his throat.

"I did. Thank you. There was no need for you to trouble yourself. Bailey could have brought them."

"Bailey?"

"The girl who acts as my maid." Ari removed a vase from a small table. "You may place it here, *s'il vous plaît.*"

"So Bailey might have done. But I was curious and so came in her stead. To whom do you plan to write?"

"I thought I might pen my autobiography."

As she moved to place the vase on the mantle, the silhouette of her breasts against the flames made his penis throb, and he held the desk against it, enjoying the pressure. "You might write an account of our meeting in Dartmouth. The story would be an instant success."

"Should I make that my bid for fame, My Lord, the only rub would be that I do not remember Dartmouth." This was still a blank spot in her mind. That at least was not a lie.

"That is a problem."

His eyes were heavy-lidded, their expression unreadable, but his voice played over her nerve ending like a rasp.

Ari clasped her hands and looked into the fire. "Littleburn and Bailey are helping me to alter another dress. I needed pen and paper to sketch out the design. And to make lists."

It was half the truth. She also would write Stubby that she was in urgent need of his help. Surely, it would not be too difficult to have the letter posted in the nearby village. If she was lucky, she might manage to be gone within a fortnight.

Ari worried her bottom lip. Why didn't the thought fill her with relief?

The reason when it burst forth in her mind stunned her. *Because she felt safe here.* Remarkable as that was, illogical as it was, she realized it was true.

If Grandquest did not kill Dolpho, the murderer was still out there, surely looking for her.

"So, you've convinced Littleburn you aren't intent on murdering her in her bed. Well done."

"I find I can be quite persuasive when I have no choice. You see, of all your staff, she is the only one with any talent for fancywork with a needle. Other than Thigpen, the second footman, that is."

"I've no doubt of your powers of persuasion." Fox frowned. "The second footman?"

"Oh, yes. In his youth, Thigpen was apprenticed to a tailor, but the poor tailor had a hard time collecting monies due him from his clients and eventually lost his shop."

After setting the lap desk on the table, the earl moved to the fireplace and stretched his hands to the blaze. "If you don't sew, why were you carrying a basket of needlework this afternoon? A footman is still searching pins out of the parlor rug."

Ari shrugged. "It looks ladylike to have some work at hand. And I do baste. Also, I tack." She moved to a small sofa, where parts of a disassembled walking dress of gray merino were spread out awaiting alterations. "If you please, My Lord—"

"Fox."

"Fox. Why have you really come?"

"I told myself it was to talk to you about Randolph Peterson—you must have heard what I told Anne as you were listening at the keyhole."

She nodded.

"It's time all the pieces I have are placed on the table so that you might try to fit them together." He paused, then shook his head. "Now, I find your husband is the last thing I want to discuss with you."

"I have no memory of a Randolph Peterson." She shrugged. "The name means nothing. Why discuss him?" It burdened her conscience to have the earl feel sympathy for her, that was not deserved, especially now that she knew why he had helped her and what debt he wrongly felt he owed her.

"Does the name Marie Angelique mean anything?"

"Nothing. Less than nothing. Is that who you think I am?" She picked up a cuff and began picking out the old threads. "I do not believe I am this person."

"Your mother's name was Rose O'Day. Your father was Jean-Michael LeClare. Both died when you were very young and you were brought up by your father's mother."

"Nothing and nothing. They are just names. Perhaps there is someone who can verify that I am this Angelique, or that I am not?"

"I have inquiries out. It is proving difficult. The grandmother has died. The girl has not been seen since the funeral."

"These people mean nothing to me," she repeated. "Now, if that is all, My Lord…?"

"There is more. Two of the medical experts I consulted in London said that your memory was unlikely to return. I did not tell you before because I didn't wish to upset you."

Ari drew in a deep breath and released it in a gust. "I am not the least upset. Why struggle against what cannot be changed? I think I will never remember these people because I do not believe I am this Angelique. The name feels wrong."

What truly felt wrong was to steal the name of this woman who had lost so much. Ari could not in good conscience do it.

"If I could be sure of that…" Fox took the cloth from her and clasped her hand. Her slender fingers looked pale and fragile against his longer brown ones as he studied them.

Her eyes were wary. And darkening. Again, hot need tickled his loins.

"If you could be sure of it, what?" Ari pulled her hand from his grasp and moved back to the fire, again putting distance between them. "What would it matter? It would not matter at all."

"Wouldn't it?" he asked softly, catching her chin and compelling her to look at him.

There it was again. That intensity in his moonstone gray eyes that drew her in.

Want.

She felt it, too. *Merde*, it consumed her when he looked at her so.

Then the implication of what he'd said hit her. "*Non!* Do not make me believe you could care for me. Or that it would matter!" Ari stiffened her spine and her resolve. To be drawn into this fantasy would be beyond madness. "You want me. Nothing more. There is no reason to pretend."

Fox touched her cheek, brushed his thumb across her bottom lip, smiling in satisfaction as her breath rasped in her throat. "Oh, there could be more. Never doubt it."

She placed her hand over his and held it against her cheek. "You want me. I want you, too. Feel me tremble? And I do think you might believe what you say." She smiled sadly. "But that does not make it true. You see, I listened at that keyhole for a very long time. The guilt you carry over Peterson's death is unearned, to my way of thinking. Men," she scoffed gently. "If the seasons change, then you think, being all-powerful, you must be responsible. You did not murder the poor man. Had you kept your appointment, nothing says you would have prevented his death, and you may have been murdered, too, but that is not the point."

She held his gaze, willing him to understand. "You want me, and your conscience scolds you because of this man's death, your desire for me seems to dishonor him, so you imagine there are other, nobler feelings involved as well as your desire. But there cannot be, and for the very same reason."

"Are you so sure?" he ground out.

"I am sure, because that is what my heart tells me."

"Your heart is wrong."

Ari took a small step away, once again putting distance between them. "I cannot breathe when you are so close."

"Good." Stepping nearer again, Fox smiled darkly and placed his fingers on her lips, exploring them. "You truly don't think that you are this woman?"

"Pray, do not do that." Her voice was ragged.

"Why?" Holding her gaze, Fox very deliberately cupped her face in his hands, then slid them down the slender column of her neck and over her shoulders. He wrapped his arms around her, folding her softness and warmth against him. "Why, when it feels so right?" He whispered into her glorious hair. It smelled of lavender, as he'd known it would. He kissed her topknot and rubbed his cheek against the curls, which cascaded from it.

Something new and fragile unfolded inside him as she tentatively wrapped her arms around his waist and hugged him, pressing her breasts more tightly against his diaphragm.

"Pallas."

As she lifted her head and looked up at him, his lips came down to meet hers. Kissing her, plunging his tongue deep into her mouth, tasting, savoring her sweetness, her heat, he knew this wasn't about guilt.

This was in spite of it.

She held still in his arms at first, before opening her mouth to grant him fuller access and meeting the thrust of his tongue with her own.

Lifting his head, Fox circled her waist with his arm, pulling her more tightly against him. Watching her reactions, he pressed his hard erection into the softness of her stomach, letting her feel his need. Then he pressed again, unable to deny himself the pleasure-pain of the action. Cupping the softness of her breast through the blue velvet of her gown, he unerringly found her nipple at its crest and stroked it with his thumb.

"*Bon Dieu!*" Ari caught his shoulders and held on weakly as her knees threatened to buckle. As she gasped and arched against him, he met her with another thrust, his need to be inside her suddenly white-hot.

Ari moaned as lightning arced through her core again and again, and her nipples were on fire. *Merde!* Her German baron in Vienna had not kissed her like this or moved against her so erotically. But even if he had, she knew, somehow, that she wouldn't have felt this wild yearning and sweet, painful heat.

"Is it always like this...this *madness*?" she asked raggedly.

Chapter Seven

ɛɔ

Ari, her blue eyes half closed, looked at him in passion-drugged wonder.

Fox lifted his head as the strangeness of the question penetrated his desire-fogged brain. He stroked her cheek with the back of his knuckles, the softness making him quake with need. She was almost like an innocent in her reactions. "What do you mean?" He dipped his head to trail kisses where his knuckles had just touched.

She shook her head slightly, pulling back. Her pupils were dark with passion. "I...I have never felt anything this—"

"Never? Have you no memory of being with a man?" Holding very still, his eyes gleamed like polished pewter. "Of making love to a man?"

"*Non.* No."

A possessiveness squeezed his chest and for a moment he buried his face in the loose curls at her neck.

She remembered no other man's touch.

She didn't remember ever making love.

He would be her first memory of joining with a man.

"Sweeting—"

Blushing red, she stiffened in his arms and tried to push him away.

"Ah, Sweeting." His breathing was as unsteady as his shaking hand as he smoothed a deep auburn curl from her cheek. He wanted to love her so well, he'd be the only man she ever wanted to remember. Pulling her back into his arms, Fox kissed a sensitive spot beneath her jaw and nipped the soft lobe of her ear, determined to do just that.

Sensation cascaded through her, and Ari was lost in wonder, treading water in dangerous seas. He murmured something she couldn't understand, his voice a rumble in her ear.

"What?" Her own voice sounded husky and far-off.

He drew back a little, his features taut. "I said put your arms around my neck, Sweeting."

Strangely, Ari felt like she wasn't really inside her body at all, but watching her actions from some distant, magical plane. As she twined her arms behind his head, Fox hooked an arm behind her knees, lifting her as though she was no more than a sack of feathers.

She loved his size and strength. She'd always felt large and awkward, but the way he carried her made her feel small and delicate.

But as he moved toward the bed, his purpose penetrated her passion-fogged mind. And what he would find if she let him make love to her — he would find out that she was not a widow!

"Non!"

"Damn. The door is open." Placing her on the counterpane, he gave her a deep, drugging kiss. "Don't move." He planted another kiss on her bruised lips. "Don't undress." He kissed her again, stealing the strength from her limbs. "I want to undress you." He moved away to the door.

He wants to undress me. Thrills chased themselves over her breasts and deep into her abdomen as she imagined his large hands peeling away her clothing.

And leaving her naked.

And then making love to her and —

She sat bolt upright. *"Non! No!"*

After closing the door, he turned, loosening his cravat. "What is wrong?" He removed the starched, white muslin from his throat and sat on the bed, tossing it aside.

Ari scrambled off the other side. "I was not thinking. I was…I was…"

"Being seduced. Come back to the bed. You'll like it." His voice was dark silk, his eyes, silver beneath half-lowered lids. A guilty twinge stabbed at his conscience. He knew who she was. He was responsible for her husband's death—even if she no longer blamed him, she would remember, eventually, and then—

Shoving the thought from his mind, he coaxed, "Come here."

"*Non*, no. I do not like being so out of control." She backed away.

Her hair was coming free of its pins and her lips were swollen and red, her eyes, dark with passion.

"You will," he promised, his voice soft as he started around the bed.

Ari turned, looked behind her, and saw there was no place to run. "Leave. Please."

"You don't want me to leave."

"No, that is true. But I need you to! If you do not leave now—if you will not…" He stopped inches from her and she kept her eyes firmly fixed on his chest.

Fox clenched his fists. Her eyes were bright with moisture. Her bottom lip trembled, and she bit it. What in Hades was wrong? What had happened?

Perhaps, she was afraid there would be consequences if they made love.

He took another step forward, his voice a deep rumble, as though he was soothing a skittish filly. "Don't be afraid. I'll take care that there's not a child. There are ways, if that is what is making you anxious—"

"Mon Dieu, a child?" Putting her hand to her mouth, Ari looked at him in horror. It was obvious she'd not even considered a child.

Taking another step toward her, Fox asked, "If not fear of pregnancy, what is upsetting you?" More than he wanted to make love to her, and he wanted to do that so badly he was on fire, he wanted to wrap her in his arms, comfort her, and find out what frightened her so.

"I will tell you what is upsetting me! It is that I keep telling you *leave* and you keeping advancing, refusing to go!" When she finally met his gaze, her bright blue eyes were blazing with accusation.

Stopping stock-still, Fox sucked in a harsh breath, clenching his fists. Then he turned on his heel and left, closing the door quietly behind him.

After he'd gone, Ari sat on the bed, staring at the door. What had she been thinking? How had things gotten so out of hand? Dolpho had said Fox Grandquest was the most dangerous man in England—Ha! Dolpho had not known the half of it. He had never had Fox approach him with that silvery look in his eyes melting his bones.

Suddenly, a picture of Fox stalking Dolpho around the bed, trying to persuade him to make love formed in her mind's eye and she was obliged to clamp both hands over her mouth to smother her laughter.

Not bloody likely, as Stubby would say.

Oh, mon Dieu, *Stubby! I need your help!*

As suddenly as the laughter had gripped her, it left, replaced by tears, which ran hotly down her cheeks.

Sniffling, standing on unsteady legs, she moved to the lap desk and opened it, quickly taking out pen, paper, sand, and ink. The faster she got word of her predicament to Stubby and enlisted his aid, the better off she would be.

She had to leave here, and soon. Fox Grandquest had the power to strip her of her will. If she made love to Fox, she would never want to leave.

And if she did make love to him, he would never want her to stay.

* * * * *

"I saw a ghost last night." Geoffrey lifted a spoonful of porridge and watched it plop back into his bowl.

"A ghost?" Anne rose and went around the breakfast table to where he sat. "Oh dear, did you have a nightmare? You look pale—did it keep you from sleeping?" She clapped a soft, pink hand to the boy's brow. "You may be fevered." She puckered her mouth as though trying to decide if this was so as she continued to test his forehead for warmth. "I'll have to see if Mrs. Coventree has some white willow bark in the stillroom. I should have guessed something was wrong when you weren't eating your porridge."

"I hate porridge." Obviously used to enduring such fever inspections, Geoffrey lifted another spoonful and watched from beneath her palm as it plopped.

"Excuse me," Anne said to no one in particular. "I must find Mrs. Coventree."

Ari met Fox's gaze questioningly as Anne hurried off.

Fox told her, "You must understand. Anne is somewhat overprotective of Geoffrey because she lost her husband and older son." He looked at the boy. "We have talked about this before, have we not?"

"Yes, uncle." Geoffry sighed and let another spoonful plop.

Ari said, "I heard about the tragedy. I was listening at the keyhole—remember?"

Fox's eyes glinted. "I had forgotten. I've been preoccupied thinking of other things that happened yesterday."

Her gaze snapped to his. Oh, no. He wouldn't be so ungentlemanly as to refer—oh yes, he is referring to that! *One and one are two—I will not blush like a silly schoolgirl.*

Ari shot him a darkling glance. Finding an avid gleam lighting his eyes, she quickly turned her attention to the eggs, which she'd been stirring about on her plate. *And two and two make four.* She only came down to breakfast to show Fox she was not going to cower in her room after what had happened between them. That she wasn't some silly blushing Miss—*four plus four is eight.*

Much to her dismay, she discovered it took an effort of will and much arithmetic to keep her cheeks from flaming every time she looked at him.

How did he always wear his clothes in a way that made her imagine him without them? It was not decent!

And why she should be the one who was uncomfortable, she hadn't the least idea! He was the one who had tried to seduce her. It seemed as though the least he could do would be to act a bit sheepish. But no. He was completely at his ease, while she was as nervous as a sparrow.

Echoes of sensations skittered over her nerve endings as she met his gaze, his eyes, shiny as pewter under his thick lashes.

Eight and eight are sixteen.

This was not at all fair!

Geoffrey held a spoon filled with porridge over the polished cherry table.

"Don't even think about it." Fox lifted a brow, the look he sent the boy as dark as his tone.

A flicker of interest crossed Geoffrey's face as he met his uncle's eyes. "Why?"

"Because I will thrash you."

Ari had no doubt that Fox meant every carefully enunciated word.

"Why?" Geoffrey asked again.

Rising, Fox put down his newspaper and pinned his nephew with a look that said he knew damned well *why*, then strode from the breakfast room.

Staring after Fox, Ari sensed Geoffrey had just had a narrow escape.

"All I asked is why." Geoffrey was petulant.

"And you already knew the answer," she told the lad. "He would thrash you because you are his nephew, and it is his duty. Your improper behavior reflects poorly on him. He is an earl, after all."

Geoffrey snorted. "I'm a viscount. Don't mean nothing. My mother still lays out my clothes and has me served porridge when I tell her I don't want it."

"Doesn't mean anything." Ari frowned, making a mental note to practice enunciating the contraction.

"Don't. Doesn't. Anything. Nothing. Don't matter which I use. I'll still be a viscount and Mother will still treat me like a babe in leading strings."

Blinking at him, Ari folded her hands, frowning in feigned confusion. "Pardon me, but I thought you act the way you do because you wished your mother to baby you. I see now I was wrong. Pray forgive me." She patted his hand. "If you are merely slow, no one will think less of you if you do not use proper English and table manners."

"I ain't—*I'm not* a slow top." He glared at her.

"Of course you aren't." She smiled patronizingly.

"I'm not."

She shrugged. "A man is judged by what a man does. If you act like a lack-wit, people will believe what you are telling them by your actions."

Sitting up straight and scrunching his mouth to one side, he seemed to consider this bit of wisdom. "I see what you mean. When the bullies at Harrow beat the snot out of me, it tells me they're bloody mean sods."

"That is terrible. How do they get away with that? Have you told the headmaster?"

The boy looked affronted. "I'm not a telltale."

Smiling, she said, "That is a very admirable trait, Geoffrey." It was in fact the first admirable trait she'd discovered the lad possessed. Unexpectedly, she felt sympathy for this overindulged child. His mother's coddling had not helped him learn to be socially adept. Quite the opposite, it seemed. She guessed he was lonely and didn't really know how to go on.

And she understood that feeling only too well.

What the boy needed was a friend.

Putting down her fork, she asked, "Earlier, you said you'd seen a ghost. I have never seen a ghost. What did it look like? What did you do? Was it scary?"

"Was it!" His face brightened. "It scared the muffins out of me!"

Ari arched a disapproving brow.

"I mean, it was horrifying. I had got up to find the privy, with only a candle to light my way. Suddenly he was in the hall, right before me. His hair was all shaggy and black, his eyes like black holes, and his skin, white like chalk. He was clutching his chest, and his shirt was all floating about him in tatters. He stared a hole through me, and then he disappeared, right into the wall."

"How horrible!"

"Was it ever," he agreed cheerfully. "I hope I see him again."

Geoffrey stood. "I have to leave now. Mother will be back any moment with something really horrible for me to drink."

"I understand," Ari sympathized. "You know, I feel in need of something to do. Would you like to play piquet later, after you have avoided your mother's nostrums?"

"Would I? I mean, I'd like that." He beamed.

She watched as he slipped through the French doors and disappeared into the frosty garden without coat or cap. She expected Lady Anne would be in hysterics if she caught sight of the boy.

Geoffrey's footprints stayed in the heavy frost. The garden was crisp and white, limbs and twigs glistening in the sun, the sky, crystalline and blue. Looking out at it, Ari was hit with a wave of longing for St. Cyr.

She imagined what the valley beneath the château must look like, all still and white. In the high Alpine country, the cold would be unrelenting. The whole world would be frozen and *Château Nuage* would be coated thickly with ice, its many turrets capped with white, like a gingerbread castle in a fairy tale. But for the occasional snap of an over-laden bough on the mountain, the silence would be as deep as the snowfall.

She and Dolpho had spent the long winter days playing chess and backgammon before the massive fireplace in the hall, or fencing, though to her ire he had always bested her with a foil.

Now St. Cyr was lost to her.

As was her cousin.

And this was not her home.

It was time to decide where to go from here and what to do. She had a small pouch of coins hidden away in their London flat and five hundred pounds in a London bank. That money from the sale of the D'Ambois jewels, with which she and Dolpho had managed to escape from St. Cyr.

If she used it to open a business, she could provide for herself and need never marry. Dolpho had often said she had a good sense of style. She could open a shop designing dresses and employing Littleburn and the second footman as seamstress and tailor. Independence for life had its appeal.

However, London was not her home. The thick coal smoke hanging like a pall over the city made her feel choked and the crowded streets seemed oppressive.

No place she'd been had seemed like home. Not even St. Cyr, though she missed its clean Alpine beauty.

But she could not stay here at Stonerose.

"I grow maudlin." Ari pushed her chair back. What she needed was fresh air and to feel the cold on her cheeks. She needed to simply forget the things being in Fox's arms made her feel. Even if she was not wanted as a spy, there was nothing but heartache if she gave in to the madness and made love to him.

She had long ago come to terms with the limits of her life — and that gave her freedom to live as she pleased, she reminded herself.

Once she was gone from here, once she had put distance between herself and the Earl Grandquest, she'd no longer be tormented by the need to hold him and give in to the fiery yearning he aroused so easily inside her.

* * * * *

"Here, kitty, kitty. Here, *meenoú*." Ari stood at the corner of the stables, looking over the paddock fence for the stable cat.

A boy pushed a wheelbarrow filled with manure and straw out of the gate toward the manure pile in the pasture. She could hear other lads talking and laughing inside the stable as they went about their morning routines of mucking out the looseboxes and feeding oats and hay.

At the end of the long paddock, Billy Freeman exercised a young black on a lunge rope, trotting the horse in a circle at the end of the tether. The groom was brother to Ari's maid, Bailey. Ari had been cultivating his acquaintance, hoping he might aid her if quick flight became necessary.

Assured that no one was paying her any attention, she again looked around for the cat. "Where are you, kitty, kitty?"

A sooty calico with a patch of orange on its nose peered around the corner of the stable door. After assessing the area, the cat darted across the open space and under the fence.

"There you are, *maman*. How are your little ones this morning?"

The cat stopped several feet away and regarded her warily. Ari knew from past efforts it would not be coaxed closer. When it picked up the scent of the meat she'd brought, it stretched and meowed avidly, twitching her whiskers in anticipation.

"*Shhh!* You will give me away." Ari glanced about her before bringing out a rough sack from beneath her old brown cloak. It held the food she'd gathered to carry with her the night she tried to climb down the wall. Thankfully, she was now certain such drastic measures as climbing the wall would no longer be necessary—since she was still unsure that she could perform such a climb.

A footman no longer kept vigil outside her door at night, and she could enjoy going outside the house without someone accompanying her. When she was ready to leave, it would be easy.

The thought did not cheer her.

"Here is some roast chicken. It smells a little old, but you will not mind that. Cats have strong stomachs, no? And here is bread. The bread is hard. If you do not want it, the sparrows will peck it up, I am certain." She put the food down. Sitting with its tail curled daintily around its feet, the cat waited until she backed several feet away, then darted forward. Seizing the large piece of chicken in its jaws, it streaked back under the fence and into the stable without a backward glance.

"You might have said, 'Thank you'," Ari called softly, smiling.

"Never expect gratitude from a woman," said a sardonic voice behind her.

Spinning around, Ari found a man lounging against the bole of the gnarled elm.

The most beautiful man she'd ever seen.

His features were strongly sculpted and even. High cheekbones ran to a lean square jaw, and his chiseled mouth held a mocking twist. Ebony brows sat above blacker eyes that held an impudent light. Both were at odds with his hair. Though the man looked to be no more than his late twenties, his hair was completely silver.

As though to call attention to it, he wore it loose, well past his shoulders. With his tea-stained complexion, much like the earl's, but deeper, and silvery hair, the man's looks were arresting.

Pushing away from the tree, he walked toward her. There was arrogance in his step and his expression both that belied his servant's dress.

"You frightened me. Do you always go about frightening innocent women?"

"From what I've heard of you, you wouldn't frighten if the devil, himself, came to tea. As for 'innocent' women..." He arched a derisive brow. "Women are perhaps born innocent, but they all possess the instincts of that pussy, who just ran off with your food without a backward glance. Soon as they develop breasts, they learn to use those instincts."

"You are impudent."

Walking around her, he made an arrogant inspection. "That's rich. The woman who held a gun on Fox Grandquest calls me impudent?" He laughed. "By God, I should have liked to have seen that little drama but I was away from the ship. The story goes that you were as cold and rock-steady about the business as a sergeant in the Marines. Were you? Or is it all a hum?"

Ari made no reply. She sensed this man was dangerous—almost as dangerous as Fox. The beautiful man shrugged. "I don't know if I quite believe that. But to hold Grandquest at gunpoint is something in itself. You either are a very foolish woman or you have bigger balls than most men I know."

"You are insufferably crude."

His black eyes gleaming wickedly, he bent close to her ear and whispered, "Some women like crude."

Before he could react, in one quick movement, Ari hooked her leg behind his, grabbed his shoulders, and threw him down into the winter-brown grass in a move the Greek wrestler, who'd taught her and Dolpho much about self-defense, had called a "hip toss".

Enjoying the disbelieving look on his face, she said coldly, "And some women do not."

To her surprise, he propped on up his elbows and laughed, his even white teeth flashing in the sun — Ari was reminded of the tales the sailors told of sharks on the ship she and Dolpho had taken from Cologne to London, after they'd fled from St. Cyr.

"No one has put me on my ass that easily in years. Well, not when I was sober. Well done. I'd like to know how you did that."

"Perhaps not so well done," Ari muttered, aware of the tall figure of the earl striding toward them.

Surprise on his usually unreadable features, Fox looked from the groom to Ari. "What is going on?"

"I am terrorizing your groom," she said, knowing he must have seen the whole thing. *Fool,* she chided herself. She did not want the earl to again start thinking of her as *dangerous,* just when she'd earned a modicum of trust from him. If she did not learn to control her temper, there would be two footmen posted outside her door each night and three by day, all armed to the teeth. Then how would she escape?

Fox arched a brow at the man scrambling to his feet. "Is this true, Julien?"

"I fear it is. I am quaking like a *blanche mongé.*" He brushed at the seat of his pants.

Looking from one man to the other, Ari thought it strange that a groom would not use the proper title when addressing a peer of the realm who was also his employer.

Then again, she decided, there was little subservient about this groom. He was certainly no ordinary servant.

She asked, "You said you were on Lord Grandquest's ship in Dartmouth. You sailed from America on it, then? Your speech is different from Toby's and Ben's. Are you from a different place in America?"

Julien looked taken aback. "She's not slow on the uptake, I see." He and the earl exchanged a look.

For no reason she could name, a finger of unease slid down her spine and reminded her of the old saying about curiosity and the cat. Feigning disinterest, she shrugged. "It is nothing to me, but I find I have an ear for languages and was curious about your accent."

"Baltimore is my home. We have what is called a *drawl*, with the vowels emphasized. Toby and Ben are from the old side of Boston, a place with its own distinct speech."

"Thank you for explaining." Ari wrapped her cloak tighter against the chill. The look in Fox's eyes made her uneasy. "I think I will return to the house. Anne has promised to help me search through more trunks. I hope to find a riding habit I might alter, if you do not object, My Lord, to my making use of your stables?"

"As long as someone accompanies you when you ride, I have no objection." His tone was reserved.

Julien added, "Yes, she can protect the grooms as they're inspecting the bridle paths."

Ignoring the comment and Julien's audacious gaze, she turned to leave, wondering just how much damage she had done.

"One moment. I will walk with you," Fox said.

"There is no need. I can find my way."

"I insist," he told her firmly. Turning to Julien, he added, "Get together an inventory of the tack we were going to look at this morning and bring it to my study."

"Yes, My lord." Julien doffed his cap and tugged his forelock respectfully, then quite spoiled the effect by winking at Ari.

As she and the earl walked across the brown lawn, silence hung heavily between them. The sun had thawed the frost and the grass was damp and spongy, except where rhododendrons and clipped yews created small patches of icy shade. The sunshine caught the rose-hued stones of the manor and winked in its many-paned windows. A pink rectangle, with little adornment and only a modest portico, it looked solid and lasting, even though not nearly so impressive as most country houses of the nobility.

Looking up, Ari wondered at the affinity she felt for this manor. Strange considering how little time she had been here and how she had arrived.

"What gave him away?"

Fox's question caught her off guard.

"What do you mean, My Lord?"

"You know well what I mean."

Ari felt like a butterfly caught in a spider's web. "About the groom, Julien? What gave him away is he is plainly not what he pretends." She decided being straightforward—to an extent— was her best course. "He is dressed as a groom, but he stands like a lord. If there is an ounce of subservience in him, I would be much surprised. And he never once addressed you with the respect your station demands. Obviously, he considers himself your equal." She sighed deeply. "And though his boots were old, they were excellently made and in good repair. Well-oiled." At Fox's questioning look, she added, "I find I notice footwear a great deal of late."

"What do you think of him?"

The question was asked casually, but she sensed that she had stumbled into somewhere she should not have. She decided to give the earl a plausible explanation why Julien didn't fit a groom's role. "It is common knowledge that you spent a great many years in the United States. I think this Julien, if that is even his name, is a friend of yours. Perhaps one who found himself in trouble. Debt? Or even a more serious crime. After looking into his eyes, I think that the latter is possible. He definitely has a criminal look about him."

"Your insights intrigue me. Pray go on."

She pursued her lips, as if deep in thought. "If he is in trouble, he might have hidden among the crew on your ship as it sailed to England, but dared not return to America with it. So, you employed him as a groom."

"Stable master. He is the best man with horses I've ever known."

"Ah, so I am right. It was probably some trouble over a woman. He does not think much of us, it seems. Not to worry. I shall not give him away. But if this Julien is going to play a deep game, he ought to learn his role," she said brightly, congratulating herself on her own performance. Perhaps she should go on stage instead of opening a *modiste's* shop.

As they rounded the corner of the manor, Ari suddenly found herself pinned against the wall, hands held in a grip of iron against the cold stones on either side of her head.

Fox's eyes glittered, his face inches away from her own. "And what role are you playing, Madam?"

Chapter Eight

෨

"Well?" Fox kept her wrists in a tight grip, pinioning her to the wall with his body. He made certain she didn't have the opportunity to knee his groin. He'd been played the fool enough by this girl. Now he was taking no chances. "I've seen Julien fight three Shawnee braves and never be taken down. You did it easily."

"He was insufferably rude." She shrugged, the action hampered by her arms being pinned. "I succeeded because I caught him by surprise. He did not expect it."

"Julien always expects the worst from women," Fox said dryly. Instead of struggling against his hold, as he'd expected, she held perfectly still. Her eyes, incredibly blue in the morning sunlight, stared up at him unblinkingly, drawing him in. The gentle scent of lavender urged all thought but her nearness from his mind.

No, he wouldn't let his lust for this woman blind him. Not again. Bright, charming, unique, with a zest for life he wished he could share—his attraction to her had made him forget that she could be dangerous.

And any woman who could best his half-brother was very dangerous, indeed.

"Who are you?"

"You told me I am this Marie Angelique Peterson. I told you that I do not think so. I feel nothing when I hear the names Marie Angelique or Dolpho Peterson."

The name was wrong, but it was one he'd heard before. "His name was 'Randolph'," Fox said slowly. "No one called him 'Dolpho'."

She went perfectly still, her face draining of color.

"What is it?" he demanded.

"Nothing. These English names confuse me."

As he stared into her eyes, something settled into place. "But it's not the first time you have used that name. After you were wounded aboard *The Dancer,* you thought I was this Dolpho. You told me that you saw me die. I thought it just confused babbling. But it was more, wasn't it?"

"No," she whispered, shaking her head. Suddenly, she struggled fiercely to free herself and sagged in defeat when he held her firmly. "No." Tremors shook her body, and tears pooled in her eyes, but didn't fall.

Fox brought her arms down between them and loosened his hold on her wrists. "I thought it your pet name for Randolph. You were right last night when you said I was deluding myself because my conscience was heavy with his death. It felt right to believe that you were the avenging widow. And it was vengeance you wanted, wasn't it? But not for Randolph Peterson."

He whispered gently, "For whom, then? Who was this Dolpho?"

Her teeth sinking into her lower lip, she shook her head. Drawing in a shaky breath, she said, "I would not hurt you now. Please believe me, Fox. It is impossible to imagine that I ever tried. Let me go. Let me leave here. You will never see or hear of me again."

"No," he said on an explosion of breath.

"Why?"

Rubbing the skin of her wrists where he feared he might have bruised them, Fox wondered the same thing. Why, indeed? It was foolish not to just let her go as she asked. If he did, he would be finished with the obligation he felt toward this woman.

Obligation? An inner voice scoffed. It wasn't obligation that had him spreading his feet apart to allow more room in his pants, just from being close enough to inhale her scent and feel her warmth. Obligation hadn't been anywhere near her bedchamber last night, though he had told himself when he went there it was to discuss Randolph Peterson and her past. Wanting her had been what was really on his mind.

As it was now.

Releasing her, Fox stepped back. "Who are you?"

The question was gently put, but it was still a demand.

Ari bit her lip again. His face, etched in hard planes and angles, looked cold as the stone wall on which she still leaned. His eyes held no compassion, though his tone was soothing. A tone a groom might use with a skittish filly being broken to rein. Fox was determined to have the truth, but she dared not tell him. The charge of spying was still hanging over her.

Shaking her head, she said, "I have no answers to give you."

"Then if you leave, where would you go?"

"Where?" There was a tightening in her chest, and she studied the toe of his tasseled Hessian, blinking moisture from her eyes. "Fox, I do not know. I can think of nowhere I belong. No one who will welcome me when I get there. Still, I cannot stay here."

"I will know who you are…and what you are," he told her quietly. "And who this Dolpho is…or was. Then, and only then, you may go."

The threat she heard in his words was all the more ominous for his soft tone. "I told you I have no answers for you. What if you never learn these things? Will you keep me here forever?"

Something glimmered in his moonstone gray eyes, briefly softening his tense features. Quickly gone. She wondered if she had imagined it.

He turned on his heel and disappeared around the corner of the manor house.

Dashing tears of frustration from her eyes, she watched her breath steam in the crisp air as she tried to gather her scattered emotions. Her wrists still tingled where he had rubbed them. Damn! How could he make her feel pleasure so intense it took her breath away, then coldly threaten her, as though no soft words or touches had ever passed between them?

Could all men separate their bodies from their minds so easily?

Had they no hearts?

Cold penetrating through her cloak made her push away from the wall and start toward the kitchen door, not wanting to chance bumping into Fox in the main hall. Two girls carrying baskets heaped with wet, steaming laundry to the clotheslines hidden in the yew hedges at the west wing looked at her strangely as they passed. Ari guessed her face showed her distress.

Growing too sure of herself had been her first mistake. Wanting to believe Fox's desire for her meant she could trust him was her second.

This encounter had been a much-needed shock, a lesson reminding her of just how precarious her position with him really was, and that she must not trust Fox, no matter what her heart and body said to the contrary.

Her letter to Stubby was written. She must find a way to post it. That failing, she would simply ride away from Stonerose, keeping to the woodland and wild stretches along the coast. Without money, winter, even mild southern English winter, would make such a journey difficult. But she would be free from Fox Grandquest before she did something truly foolish.

* * * * *

"Enter." Fox stacked the estate's receipts he'd been reading and put them to one side and rose as the door opened and a maid showed Julien into the study.

"You sent for me, My lord. I'm here as you ordered, My lord, with the inventory of the tack in your lordship's stables." The picture of obsequiousness, Julien bobbed his head repeatedly, twisting his cap in his hands. Only the laughter in his black eyes betrayed him.

The maid stood with the door handle in her hand, staring raptly at his brother. Girls, then women, had been wont to look at Julien in just that way ever since Fox first met him. Julien had been a lad of seven when Fox had arrived on their father's doorstep in Baltimore. Although only ten, Fox had felt decades older.

"Leave us," Fox told the maid.

Made aware that she had been standing with mouth agape, she blushed, curtsied, and disappeared.

As the door closed behind her, Fox said, "I won't have you making conquests among the staff."

Julien frowned and glanced at the closed door. "A man has needs."

"Slake them at the tavern in the village. There's a couple of serving wenches there who are to be had for a price."

"Pay?" Julien looked aghast. "Now see here, certain things are against my principles. I have never paid for a woman's charms." He tossed his battered wool cap onto the desk and a shadow crossed his handsome face. He propped on the edge of the polished surface, his gaze drifting far away. "Well, I've never crawled between a woman's legs knowing in advance there would be a price to pay for her favors."

"Pallas is right. You are crude." Fox wondered what Julien had said to her to make her so angry.

"Pallas? Is that what you're calling the pretty piece who put me on my ass? She hasn't regained her memory, has she?" Julien shook his head. "I'm still not certain how she did that neat little trick. Flipped my weight over her hip, somehow. Amazing." He smiled slowly. "It makes me wonder what other tricks she knows."

"Stay away from her." Fox found his hands clenched and willed himself to relax.

"Stay away from...why? She isn't among your staff."

"She's under my protection."

Julien cocked a dark brow, his look speculative. "You've made her your mistress? Staying in the house with your sister? Isn't that what you Brits call *bad form*?"

"That is not the type of protection I meant, and well you know it," Fox ground out. "After all these years, you still have the power to infuriate me after enduring five minutes of your company."

"You are avoiding my question. My, my. This could prove serious. Falling in love with an ordinary woman is the height of stupidity, best done when one can claim the inexperience of youth. Succumbing to this one's charms would rate Bedlam. I thought I felt the Earth tremble, and there is an ominous clarity in the air, don't you think? Do stick your head out of the window and see if the four horsemen of the Apocalypse are taking up positions at the compass points?" Julien laughed. "I may have to repent my wicked ways. Surely the Day of Judgment is at hand when the levelheaded Fox Grandquest does something so unwise as to fall in love—and with the woman who tried to blow his head off."

"She suggested that if you are going to play a deep game, you learn your role," Fox said dryly.

"Did she?" Julien frowned and plucked an ostrich quill with a golden nib from the holder on the desk. Studying the detailed engraving adorning the pen, he said, "I suppose I must heed advice from such a master of deep games. Or, rather, *mistress*."

Ignoring the jibe, Fox took the pen from his brother and returned it to the holder. "It's good advice. If she could see through you in a matter of minutes..." He left the sentence unfinished and shrugged.

Julien sobered and nodded. "The boys in the stables put my eccentricity down to my being an American. But speaking of deep games, have you discovered what game she's about?"

"I think she truly remembers little or nothing." Fox was convinced after their confrontation.

"You still have no idea of who she really is?"

Fox shrugged again. "Two women have reason to hate me, perhaps even hate me enough to want me dead."

Julien clicked his tongue disapprovingly. "Only two? You haven't been living right—all right, I desist." He held up his hands in mock surrender as Fox turned on him. "I'm aware of the two. Marie Angelique Peterson is one, and the Italian's redhead, the other. I was never clear what the latter might have against you."

"This." Fox opened a desk drawer and removed a folded sheet of paper. Sliding it across the rosewood desk to Julien, he said, "Note the seal and the signature."

Moving to the long windows, Fox parted the drapes and gazed out without seeing. It felt strange to hear Pallas referred to as another man's woman. She had been. There was no doubt, he reminded himself, wondering at the stab of jealousy he felt. Now, he knew to whom she had belonged. Dolpho. Rudolpho. Whether she remembered Prince Dragonetti or not, she had belonged to him. Had loved him. She loved him enough to try to kill the man she believed responsible for his death.

What would it be like to be loved like that by such a woman as Pallas?

When he realized the direction his thoughts were taking, he gave himself a mental shake. He couldn't afford the lovely distraction. As the two great powers in the world warred, America was in danger of being drawn into the fray. He'd come to England to help America avoid war. True, he had never guessed that he'd inherit the earldom or that his feelings of loyalty would be so thoroughly divided. Or that the job he had committed himself to would become so onerous. Still, he'd given his word to President Jefferson. And he must let nothing distract him from his duty.

Turning, Fox watched as Julien fitted the broken wax halves of the seal together and studied them.

"This is yours." He turned his attention to the contents of the letter and whistled softly. "You appear to have been up to a bit of villainy, using your position to set the militia onto these poor sods."

"Neither was captured, but there is reason to think the prince may have received a mortal wound. Of course, I didn't write the letter. The prince was working for Lord Blaine, the same as me. However, there was damning correspondence found in the cottage suggesting the prince was actually Dandelion, the double agent I've been after."

"Why do I get the feeling you don't believe this evidence?" Julien asked.

"I don't think he was playing a double game. Napoleon overran his kingdom when the prince was a lad, and the little Corsican put his cousin on the throne. The prince grew up in exile in St. Cyr, on the Austrian-French border, under the care of his maternal grandfather. When the French marched into St. Cyr, the prince again lost his home. He came to England and offered to use his contacts in Vienna and Paris to help defeat the French."

"Who do you believe wrote this, and how did he get your seal?"

"The real Dandelion. The fellow you're going to help me find. Copying the seal would have been a simple matter, using a plaster of paris cast of an authentic seal for a mold."

"Dandelion. I think there must be an obvious clue in that damned silly name. Who would choose it without a reason?" Julien returned the note.

Fox placed the letter back in the desk drawer and turned the key. "I've thought the same thing, but if there is a riddle that could be answered, it's well hidden."

Moving back to the window, Fox parted the drapes again. "Why didn't I see the truth of who she is sooner? With her intelligence and charm, it makes perfect sense. Pallas is more than a fit consort for a prince."

"Fit, indeed. I didn't get a peek at her form beneath that ugly cloak, but from what was open to my eager eyes, I'll allow that the prince was a lucky man. She is tall—God, I've been trying to imagine how long her legs are."

"Don't." Fox glared at him. "Don't demean her."

Julien smiled. "So she means nothing, does she? As to why you didn't see the truth sooner, that cook did swear that she wasn't the woman from the cottage. Why the cook did such a thing might bear looking into." He shrugged. "It's mere speculation on my part, of course, but after my brief encounter with the woman at the stable, I'd say the cook may have feared bones would be broken."

"Be serious. You're giving me a headache."

Julien grinned as if he'd won a prize at a fair, then his expression turned serious. Rotating the battered woolen cap in his hands, he looked at his brother. "It's not certain she was his mistress, you know. She is wearing a wedding ring. The two may have been secretly wed."

"It is possible." Fox didn't want to pursue what Pallas' relationship to the prince had been—if she was indeed the woman from the cottage. He believed now that she was. There had been pain in her eyes she couldn't disguise when he said the name *Dolpho*—a nickname suited more to the Italian Prince Rudolpho than to the Englishman Randolph Peterson.

Her pain must mean she was starting to remember the man she had loved.

Changing the subject, Fox said, "I'm expecting a letter from the minister who married the Petersons. When I get his description of the bride, it should help confirm Pallas' identity."

"It should, unless he describes a tall woman with an auburn flame of hair." Julien stood. "Now, to other matters. It's the dark of the moon tonight. The Frenchman is sure to be off Goat's Head, considering there could have been no exchange of information last time the ship was there, with the militia swarming over the area. Are you ready?"

Fox nodded. "Pray the wind stays from the north so there'll be no fog."

"And no surprises," Julien added, "like our smuggler friends had last time."

* * * * *

"Lovely. My word, you have a genius, my dear." Lady Anne beamed as Ari turned for her inspection. "You'll have all the ladies in the district wearing tiered skirts. Why, I shouldn't be surprised if the trend races to London. Do take a turn about the room and see how it feels when you dance. I once had a beautiful gown that pulled dreadfully whenever I placed my hand on my dance partner's shoulder. The top wrinkled in the most horrid fashion. In the withdrawing room, I discovered the silly seamstress had sewn part of the sleeve to the bodice."

"Lady Anne—"

"As I've told you repeatedly, just *Anne*, please. There should be no formality between friends."

"Anne, I do not think I shall be invited to accompany you to any holiday parties." Ari planned to leave Stonerose at the first opportunity. But even if she should stay, the local gentry weren't likely to include her in their Christmas celebrations.

"Nonsense," Anne answered firmly. "I shall let it be known that I shan't attend any party where you are not invited. More importantly, if I do not attend, neither will Fox."

"You would do that? You should not restrict your entertainments for me," Ari said sincerely. She had no wish for Anne to garner ill feelings on her account. It would weigh heavily on her conscience after she left.

"There will be no sacrifice, dear. Many of the neighbors have daughters they would see married to the Grandquest title. He is quite a catch, you know. Also, I have a greater position in society than anyone in the district, and I am regarded as a London hostess. If that isn't enough to sway opinion in your favor, I may soon become a patroness of Almacks. No mother who wants her daughter to receive an invitation to those assemble rooms will dare to throw aspersions your way." Her eyes glittered behind her *pince nez* as she smoothed the three ribbons she was about to sew.

Filled with too much emotion to speak, Ari watched as Anne tacked the ribbons together. She made it seem possible that Ari would be accepted, if grudgingly, by the local gentry. It had been a very long time since she attended a party or danced. She longed to forget her troubles for a time and just enjoy a party.

She put the thought firmly out of her head. If all went well, she would not be here.

But leaving without confiding in Anne would be hard. She was a joy. Never had Ari had a close female friend before, and knowing her, even this short while, filled Ari with a special warmth. She had spent time with her distant cousins, the Austrian princesses, but they had always remained remote. Especially Marie Louise, about whose hand, it was rumored, Napoleon had approached Emperor Francis II.

Swallowing hard, Ari found her voice at last. "I doubt it no longer. You are a veritable dragon."

"Am I not?" Smiling her pleasure at the epitaph, Anne knotted the thread.

"Thank you." Impulsively, Ari gave her a quick hug.

"Oh, *pish*." Anne squeezed back and stood up, looking slightly flustered. "Hold up your arms," she ordered and slipped the ribbons around the high waist, tying them beneath Ari's breasts. The ribbons matched the three colors of the gown. "These are just what was needed. They bring continuity to the whole. Now, do turn around again and let us see if the hem is right."

Ari did as she was bid. Moving to the peer glass, she studied her reflection, pleased with the way the gown had turned out. It fit her perfectly in the bodice, the pale coral satin complementing her complexion and her hair. Cream and peach tulle made up two tiers of the skirt. The third was the same coral satin as the bodice. A wide band had been added beneath the two layers of tulle, making it the proper length. Puffed sleeves just off her shoulders made her long neck appear graceful, and the deep neckline revealed enough bosom to draw male attention.

Imagining Fox's gaze upon her cleavage, the look that would warm his gray eyes, Ari felt her skin prickle.

Arret! Stop! You aren't some silly schoolgirl! If she kept imagining herself with Fox, she would only make herself miserable. Anne had just told Ari what a fine catch he was and how many in the neighborhood were aiming for a match.

He was above her touch.

And she would soon be gone.

Since their encounter yesterday, she knew she needed to get away from Stonerose as soon as possible. Until she could, she planned to keep her distance from him. The Earl Grandquest was no one's fool, and he was starting to question far too much. It was certain he suspected the truth, though, thanks to Hilda's perfidy, he had no proof. She needed to leave Stonerose before he found that proof, or before she gave herself away completely.

To avoid Fox's company, she'd pleaded a headache the day before and had not gone down to tea. At supper, a concerned Anne had flown into Ari's bedchamber and dosed her unmercifully with what Ari thought must have been a mixture of alum and quinine. An excellent brew to ward off the ague, Anne had assured her.

It was also an excellent choice to cure pretended illnesses, Ari could have told her.

Faced with Anne's determination to keep those about her in good health, Ari hadn't had sufficient nerve to plead another headache. Luckily, she need not have worried about being under Fox's scrutiny. He'd ridden out yesterday afternoon, citing business in Dartmouth, and hadn't yet returned.

"The gown seems fine." Putting on her *pince nez* again, Anne circled around her, making an inspection of her handiwork. "That severe coronet of braids takes away from it. I think with this gown you should wear your hair in a tumble of curls, instead. We'll need gloves. Perhaps a plume or two for your hair, dyed to match the dress, of course. You may borrow my topaz earrings and necklace. Oh, we need add a few brooches as well. *Hmmm.* And all the unmentionable necessities. And shoes. A shawl."

"Shoes…" Ari sighed dreamily, her toes aching their approbation. "Shoes would be glorious." She twisted the wedding ring she wore. "But I have no money, Anne. Do you think I might sell this for enough to pay for shoes?" *With enough left over to post a letter,* she added silently.

"Fox has a plump purse."

"I would rather not accept the earl's money." Perhaps she could go to Dartmouth with Anne on the pretext of shopping and just slip away. With her old brown cloak, she should go as unnoticed as she did before…

But to do so would upset Anne and she would worry. Ari couldn't do that to her new friend.

This was a tangle!

"Nonsense," Anne declared. "Fox has deep pockets, and you have none."

"No. I owe him too much as it is."

"He is the one who believes he owes you. Let him do this, and you will help him feel he's repaying you in some small part. You must not sell your wedding ring in any case. That will be the key to your social success." A mischievous smile twitched Anne's lips.

"The staff here has been kind and helpful, and I do not have a *sou* with which to tip them. I could sell my gun, I suppose, though it may not fetch much. It could not bring down a large earl at less than a yard," Ari added wryly

"What gun? What earl?" Anne asked, suddenly all interest. Her eyes rounded and she clapped her hands to her cheeks. "Oh, my. You don't mean *the gun*. My dear, do you still have it? This is too delicious. I must see it! Better still, let me buy it from you. I shall mount it above the fireplace in my drawing room in London. It will be the perfect conversation piece."

Ari smiled. "Then you shall have it. Your brother has it now. I will tell him to give it to you."

"But, I want to buy it. I insist. You have so little to sell, I could not take it without paying."

"*Non.* Consider it an early Christmas present. And if your conscience bothers you," Ari said, "you may gift me with hair pins, which I very much need. And perhaps a comb, but not an expensive one."

"Done. I shall tell Fox as soon as he arrives." Anne's expression lost some of its animation. "Which I hope is soon. He said he would be back for breakfast, and it is near luncheon. The weather has been passable. I wonder what has delayed him?"

The question was answered a few minutes later when Ari heard voices raised excitedly. Hurrying to the top of the stairs above the central hall, she looked down and found Fox standing just inside the front door, his arm across Julien's shoulders to help him remain upright.

His face was waxy pale, his eyes sunken. His left arm hung at his side, his sleeve soaked in dark red. Blood ran down his fingers, dripping onto the floor. A puddle rapidly formed on the black and white marble squares.

No one could lose blood like that and live.

Not for long.

As she met Fox's gaze, the look in his eyes said he knew it, too.

Chapter Nine

ဢ

"My God, he is killed." Anne paled and swayed forward.

Ari caught her and pulled her back before the older woman pitched headlong down the stairs. Forcing her to sit against the wall, Ari squatted before her, tapping her cheeks. "Fox is not dead, Anne, but he needs our help. I have not time to take care of you, too. Can you help me with Fox?"

Anne nodded, jerkily.

Casting a quick glance below, her heart leapt into her throat. Fox had fallen to his knees. Julien's hold on him looked to be all that kept him from falling on his face. As chatelaine of *Château Nuage,* taking care of the ill and injured had been her domain. She had helped treat her first injured man, a servant who had broken his leg, when she was twelve years old. And she had seen this type of heavy blood loss before. Dolpho's face, pale as a death's head, flashed her mind's eye. Dolpho had died.

She knew she must get Fox's bleeding stopped, if he was to be saved.

If it was not already too late.

No!

Not this time!

She drew in a deep breath, willing herself to think clearly, or she would be of no use to Fox. Her thoughts went back to *Château Nuage,* when Dr. Keiss had been there for a prolonged visit and a scullery maid had driven a knife deep into her thigh. As Ari tried to remember everything he had done, she rose to her feet and told Anne, "Find clean sheets. At least two. And you must find Mrs. Coventree and send her to me with them. Tell the cook to put a large kettle to boil. Oh, and soap. Not fancy milled, but good, strong lye, like what is used for the laundry. Have someone bring the hot water and soap to Fox's bedchamber and turn down the covers. Do you understand, Anne?"

Using the wall for support, Anne got to her feet. "Coventree, sheets, to you. Kettle, soap, bedchamber."

"Go down the servants' stairs and hold onto the railing. Now hurry." Ari was halfway down the stairs to the hall as she said the last.

No, Fox could not die, Ari told herself. He was too strong and vital. From the moment she'd first met him in the hall after awakening at Stonerose, the force of his personality had challenged her as no man's had before. She'd never known anyone like him.

And if she did not act quickly, he would be lost.

Fox was now unconscious on the floor and Ari fell to her knees beside him. "Help get his coat off. I must see the wound," She commanded Julien and tugged frantically at the blood-soaked sleeve, aware that with every beat of his heart, his life's blood was draining away.

"Let me." Julien produced a knife from a sheath at his belt and sliced up the sleeve, right across the chest to the buttonholes. "It's a knife wound. I tried to stop the bleeding, but couldn't. We were attacked near the manor, just at the edge of the wood, or he would have never made it home."

Attacked? A dozen questions rose in her mind, but now was not the time for questions.

After Ari peeled the coat and shirt back, Julien cut the cloth strip tying the saturated pad against Fox's shoulder. Ari lifted it, and blood spurted from a two-inch gash in his upper pectoral. Grabbing the muscle, she pressed the wound closed with her bare hands, holding as tightly as she could.

With little effect.

"What do you think?" Julien's tone was grim.

"*Dieu*. To be right there, it is only a small artery, but it is determined. Quickly, cut off his shirt and give it to me. I need something to press against the wound, or he is lost."

Julien sliced through the other side of the coat and down the sleeve and did the same to the shirt beneath. He pulled what was left of the shirt from Fox and thrust it into her hands.

Ari pressed it to the wound with all her might, rising on her knees to put her weight on it. All the while, she said silent prayers. The pasty hue of Fox's skin showed he could not stand to lose much more, but hot blood still seeped between her fingers, nudging a dark memory to life.

Looking down at him, her stomach knotted.

Not again.

Remembered horror surrounded her in a dizzy swirl—lightning flashes skittering across a hell-black sky, cold sheets of rain washing over her, Dolpho's life's blood warm between her fingers. Like Fox's now. She'd said desperate prayers then too. Unanswered prayers.

"No, you will not die!" she shouted.

Julien looked at her in silent approbation.

"Here, Milady. The sheets you asked for." Mrs. Coventree huffed as she bustled down the stairs, her round face creased with concern.

"Julien, go get one and tear it into strips, please. Use your knife," Ari instructed.

Meeting the housekeeper in the middle of the great hall, Julien took the hem of a sheet as she held it and cut through the linen and unfolded the cloth and tore it in one swift movement.

"Should I ride for the doctor, Milady?" a footman asked.

Ari glanced about her and was surprised to see most of the staff gathered in stunned silence. She hadn't been aware of anyone entering the hall. "*Non*. There is not time. Besides, the doctor is a great fool. Bring me a lamp—a lighted lamp—and a letter opener. Or a long, thin knife." She looked up at the housekeeper. "Mrs. Coventree, do you have bascillicum powder?"

"Yes, Milady. I have the powder in the stillroom." The housekeeper hurried away, right behind the footman.

"My gram usually handles these things for people on the estate, but she's off at me sister's in Dartmouth," a familiar voice said above her.

Glancing up, Ari found the maid, Molly Bailey, wringing her hands in distress. "Not to worry, Molly. We will take care of what needs to be done." Ari wished she felt as confident as she'd tried to sound. "Please, find Lady Anne. Tell her to prepare his lordship's bed. You, Thigpen," she directed her attention to the footman next to Molly, "see that a fire is laid in your lord's chamber."

Both hurried away.

Julien placed several clean pads of cloth beside Fox's head, and held one at the ready. Ari nodded to him and tossed the soaked shirt aside. Julien pressed the new cloth to the wound.

"You want the lamp and the knife to cauterize?" he asked.

"*Oui*. I do not wish to. The chances of infection are increased. But I must stop this bleeding."

Julien answered in perfect French, surprising her. "Fox asked me not to alarm the staff. Do not say anything about the attack I told you of."

Ari was curious, but did not pursue it. There were more imperative things on her mind. She said in English, "The wound looks clean. It should not kill him, if the bleeding can be stopped. It needs to drain as it heals, and it will not if we burn so much it closes completely. We will try to sear only where the artery is severed."

Looking at her with respect, Julien grinned, his white teeth flashing in his shark's smile. "I'd think I'd rather have you than some sawbones. Nicer to look at anyway."

"You are not amusing."

The footman returned with the lamp and a long, pointed knife.

"Excellent. Put it there, where I can reach it. Then get ready to help us hold him. He's very strong. Hold his arm tightly when I tell you." Looking around, she saw only Littleburn was left unoccupied. The maid stared, her eyes wide in her round face. "Give the knife to Littleburn."

"Yes, Milady." After thrusting the knife into the maid's grasp, the footman knelt beside Fox.

"Littleburn, remove the globe from the lamp and heat the knife blade in the flame. Concentrate on the tip."

The maid blinked at Ari but didn't move.

"Do it now!"

As if coming out of a trance, the maid rushed to kneel by the lamp. Using her apron as a potholder, she lifted the lamp globe off and thrust the knife tip into the flame.

Fox groaned as he regained consciousness. The footman caught his bloodied arm as he tried to lift it.

"Hold still. As still as you can," Ari urged him.

"Cold." His teeth chattered and he clamped his jaws shut.

"I know you are cold. Look at me." Ari brushed the hair from his forehead and cupped his cheek, trying to smile confidently. "You must hold still, or this bleeding will not be stopped. Do you understand?"

His mouth a tight, white line, he nodded. With his chest exposed and smeared with blood, Fox looked so vulnerable — could this be the same man who had held her pinned against the wall just yesterday? Or who had held her tenderly in his arms two nights before?

Mrs. Coventree hurried toward them, her face, red, and her breath, rasping. "Here it is the powder…in the tin."

"Thank you." Ari took it from her, opened it, and set it behind her, out of the way.

"The bleeding isn't slowing." Julien looked grim.

"I know," Ari answered in French. "It will not do to let the others see how worried we are." Then she continued in English, "When I tell you, take the pad away and open the wound. It may bleed more, but don't be alarmed. We must cauterize it."

"When you are ready." Julien looked almost as pale as Fox.

Feeling far from ready, Ari gazed at the man pinioned on the floor. Her hands shook so badly, she was afraid she would fail. What if this didn't work? A glance at Littleburn showed the maid dutifully holding the knife blade in the flame. The tip glowed and was changing from red to white.

It was time to act.

Ari prayed for the strength to do what must be done and laid her hand on his forehead. It felt cold and moist. Not a good sign.

"Fox?"

"I'm ready," he said between gritted teeth. His gray eyes were steady, though he shivered.

"Hold his arms tightly." Ari glanced from the footman to Julien, assuring herself both were ready.

"Can I help, Milady?" the housekeeper asked.

"Yes. Hold his legs. Sit on them if you have to. He must not move."

"That won't be necessary," Fox said as Mrs. Coventree grasped his ankles.

"Good. But we will hold you, just in case. This will burn like hell's own fire," Ari assured him cheerfully. Inwardly, she cringed. A hot, sick feeling rose in her throat at what she was about to do. But there was no choice. The waxy pallor of his skin grew more pronounced with his every heartbeat.

"You needn't seem so pleased about it," he grumbled. His gaze held hers, warm, penetrating, seeming to read her uncertainty. "You'll do fine," he whispered.

Ari forced a smile, warmed by his concern for her when it was his life's blood that was draining away. "As will you. I will have nothing less. Here. You must bite on this." He allowed Ari to place a folded strip of cloth in his mouth. Holding his gaze, Ari sat back on her heels. "Littleburn, turn the knife so I can grasp the handle, but continue to hold it in the flame."

"Yes, Milady."

Glancing at Julien, Ari nodded. The stable master tossed the blood-soaked pad he'd been holding against the wound aside and grasped the flesh of Fox's upper shoulder at either end of the gash. Pressing inward, he made the wound gape. Fox sucked a harsh breath through clenched teeth, the muscles bunching at the hinge of his jaw.

Ari grasped the knife handle with one hand and forced a clean cloth into the gash with the other, drying it out as best she could. At the same time that she removed the cloth, she touched the white-hot knife to the side of the wound. A wisp of smoke curled upward, carrying with it the horrible scent of scorched flesh and burned blood.

Fox groaned and his head arched back against the hard floor, the tendons and veins in his throat standing out.

After dumping a liberal amount of the powder into and around the wound, Ari wiped the area with a clean pad. Her heart sang as no more blood gushed out.

He trembled with pain.

"Still. Still. You must not tense up so. You might force the bleeding to start again." Tears wet her cheeks, but Ari smiled as she looked into his eyes, confident that he would not bleed to death. "And this is such a little prick of a wound, you shall be embarrassed to death if you die from it," she assured him.

* * * * *

"Bascillicum powder. Nothing but bascillicum powder?" Lady Anne wrung her hands as she paced by the foot of Fox's bed, darting anxious glances at her brother. "How about a nice poultice of lye and sheep fat?"

Ari smiled at Fox's disgruntled look. "Sounds interesting." She gently wiped his face with a damp cloth. Bringing the cloth around the angle of his jaw, she admired the strong curve.

His gray eyes narrowed, Fox said, "I'm too weak to resist such evils. You must defend me against Anne's nostrums."

"Only if you take mine without question." Ari's gaze went to the clean white bandage tied across his chest and shoulder, checking for any telltale red.

"I think I might. If I have you to look at while I swallow. 'Twould make anything palatable."

Blushing, Ari busied herself dipping the cloth into the basin of cool water. Since her debut in Vienna, she had been the recipient of many compliments, some by very silver-tongued courtiers. This compliment warmed her as no other had.

Silly heart, she scolded her wayward organ, stop fluttering so. He is only a man.

Dynamic, vital, a man like no other you have known. A man who might be dead, now, her heart reminded her with a stab of pain.

The feeling of emptiness the thought brought was disquieting. How ironic that she had once sought his death, and now the thought of almost losing him hurt her so.

"I have an excellent extract of myrrh gum in my valise I could get." Anne paused at the foot of the massive four-poster, a hopeful expression lighting her face.

Fox shot a distressed look at Ari.

Wiping the other side of his face, Ari smiled. Holding his gaze, she said, "I thought that myrrh was for an inflamed bowel."

"Oh, yes, I think you're right." Anne resumed pacing.

"I think a good shot of brandy would be medicinal under the circumstances," Fox suggested.

"And, pray, what are the circumstances?" Anne demanded. "Forgive me if I seem insensitive to your weakened state, but it does not help my peace of mind when you won't even tell us what befell you."

Sighing, Fox grumbled, "You tax my waning strength but, if you must have it, I will tell you. Julien and I were exploring the creek that borders my property with an eye to clearing the woodland and making it productive. Julien had ridden a distance ahead when I spotted a rabbit in a snare. When I dismounted to investigate, the poacher surprised me. The fellow had a knife."

The tale left much to doubt, he knew, but it would have to suffice. He couldn't very well tell Anne and Pallas that he and Julien had lain in wait above Goat's Head promontory and watched a meeting between Dandelion and two French officers. The French had been warier than Fox thought, sending men out to skirt the area. He and Julien had been spotted, but had gotten away.

Or so he'd thought.

They'd been ambushed by four French marines at the edge of the park, within sight of the manor. They had been fortunate that the Frenchmen had wanted to take care of them quietly and not draw attention. Julien and he would now be dead if the four had used guns instead of knives. He'd been fortunate also to have Julien fighting beside him. Both of them had learned to fight with knives at the side of their cousin, Tecumseh, when Fox and Julien had gone to the Ohio Valley as teenagers to find their grandmother's people, the Shawnee.

"The fellow got away?" Anne's eyes were wide.

"Not to worry. He probably thought I was a game warden come to haul him in front of a magistrate. He wasn't one of my people, and he was only interested in escape," Fox assured his sister.

"He will not bother us at Stonerose, Anne, with these stout footmen about. I believe one of them used to be a boxer," Ari said reassuringly.

"I suppose you are right, Pallas. But when I think what might have happened...just like my husband and older son." Anne caught her breath on a sob.

"Anne, don't overset yourself on my account." Fox tried to rise.

Pressing him back against the mattress, Ari commanded, "Be still. I will sit on your chest if you move again."

Looking stunned, Fox lay meekly back on the pillows, his brows riding upward. "Yes, ma'am."

"Anne, his color is not good. I will not have you distressing him." Ari looked sternly at the older woman, who nodded contritely. "Now, tell me, what may we give him to strengthen his blood?"

"A decoction of yellow dock?" Anne asked uncertainly.

"Yes. That sounds like just the ticket," Ari agreed. "If you wish, you may add honey and lemon to make it pleasant to the taste."

"I'll be back in a thrice." Anne bustled toward the door, only to stop cold. "Oh, but I am remiss in my duties as chaperone. Although to treat a wounded man, it is permissible to expose the wound, but you, Pallas, should not be in here alone with him in his undressed state."

Glancing at the wedding band on her finger, Ari said, "If I am a widow, I believe it is not too improper to give aid to a wounded man."

Anne pursued her lips as if considering. "No, I suppose that makes a difference, but you are young and pretty, and it would still be improper for you to be alone with my brother. I'll send a maid to keep you company."

Fox said, "Anne, bring Julien with you when you come back."

Nodding, she left.

As Ari wiped the strong column of his throat, she was aware of Fox's gaze on her face. And she was very much aware when his gaze moved lower, to the cleavage revealed by the low neckline of the gown.

She felt another blush bloom on her cheeks.

"This was a new gown, wasn't it?" he asked. "It's ruined."

Looking down, she privately agreed. There were spots of blood on the bodice and a larger stain on the second tier of the skirt. "It is of no import."

"Anne needn't worry about propriety. My body isn't up to improper." His gaze dipped into her cleavage again. "Which is most disturbing from where I lie."

"It is only the blood loss," Ari told him, trying not to blush. "You will have plenty of improper thoughts in a couple of days."

"That is heartening."

"In a week, you shall be well on your way to licentious behavior."

"I shall try to justify your faith in me."

Smiling, Ari rinsed the cloth again. His skin was still pallid, and his hand cold. But, if his wound didn't reopen, she was certain he'd live. The thought made her want to shout with joy.

He is not for you, her practical side warned. He had a title and position in society, which he would enhance with whomever he married.

She reminded herself sternly that she was a refugee and a baker's granddaughter. Her title was empty, carrying no fortune or position with it. And even when she had been heir to the château and a modest fortune, no nobleman had wanted to take her to wife. She had learned her lessons well.

When she turned back to the bed, Fox caught her hand, his gaze intense.

"Thank you."

She nodded.

Taking the cloth from her hand, he tossed it aside, then twined his fingers with hers. "If you still have plans to do away with me, you missed a prime opportunity, you know. Without your help, I'd not be alive."

"You are being overly dramatic."

"Dramatic? We both know you saved my life." His voice was a weak whisper.

Ari parted her lips to protest, then drew in a sharp breath as Fox slid his thumb across the back of her hand.

His lids drooped, his eyes becoming a smoky gray beneath their heavy lashes. "You are like no other woman I've ever known. Wise, filled with humor and a zest for living that sweeps others along. But your smiles are often sad. Who are you sad about? And who are you?"

Caught unawares, Ari blurted, "Who are you?"

He smiled. There was no humor in it. "Yes. Why should I expect you to part with your secrets when I'm unwilling to reveal mine?"

"I truly do not know what you want." She pulled her hand away.

"The truth." The words came out as a sigh.

Meeting his gaze levelly, she said, "The truth? When you said the name Dolpho, I saw a handsome, dark-haired man with laughing, dark eyes. And I know…he is dead." She looked away. "I can tell you no more than that."

"You remember nothing else?"

Remaining silent, Ari let him think that was the case. Though how long she could fool him, she was not certain. One thing she was convinced of, the Earl Grandquest was playing his own deep games. Who had stabbed him and why? No poacher had inflicted that wound.

Fox Grandquest was much more than he seemed. How could she bare her soul to him when the more she learned about this man, the deeper the mystery surrounding him became?

With a final glance at the white bandage, Ari pulled the covers up to his throat. "Rest. Cook is bringing up beef broth. That will help keep you warm. I'll watch over you as you rest."

Fox closed his eyes, though she sensed he was not asleep. She built up the fire and sat staring into the flames as she turned her situation over in her head.

After a time, a perfunctory knock sounded and the stable master pushed open the door. Anne preceded him into the room, carrying a tray with teapot and cups. She sat the tray on a table and went to Fox's bedside. Popping a hand on his forehead, she asked Fox a multitude of questions as she assured herself he was not about to pass the veil.

After glancing at the man on the bed, Julien came straight to where Ari sat. He'd washed and changed out of his blood-smeared clothing, and his silvery hair was pulled back in a queue. Dressed in a clean coat and breeches, though it was still the rough clothing of a stablemaster, he took her hand and kissed it as gallantly as any nobleman had ever done.

"You have balls the size of a bull's."

"I beg your pardon." Ari snatched her hand away.

He grinned cheekily, then his black eyes became serious. "Without your skill, Fox would be dead. I have never been in that situation before. Never cauterized a wound or seen it done. You didn't flinch, but did what was necessary. I owe you a debt too great to repay. If ever you have need of anything, I place myself at your disposal. You have only to send for Julien Fox."

"What do you mean? What debt could you owe me?"

"You saved my brother's life."

Chapter Ten

ဆ

Anne turned and stared at the young man with striking, silver hair. "*Julien Fox*...of course. I should have guessed," she said enigmatically.

A corner of Fox's mouth lifted. "You will find something of a family resemblance."

Looking from one man to the other, Ari declared, "Yes, there is a resemblance, in bone structure and skin tone, but I feel all at sea. How can he be your brother? From what I know of the House of Grandquest, Fox, you are the youngest of ten. Julien is younger than you."

"Not by far. A couple of years," Fox said hoarsely, his fatigue telling.

"I will tell you how they can be brothers. One of them is a bastard — which is not a bad thing, all things considered," Anne said, bringing up her *pince nez* and staring at Julien.

"Well put." Julien grinned, unabashed.

Anne dropped the eyeglasses and let them dangle. A wordless communication seemed to pass between Fox's two siblings, then Anne asked, "Why are you living above the stables? You must move your things into the manor, of course. You are one of the family, after all."

She looked uncertain about the latter.

"I hope you'll understand, the stables are where I want to be and no one must know who I am. I've 'gone to ground' at the moment. Explanations would be awkward."

"I see." Anne was clearly relieved at his refusal.

Ari guessed his refusal saved Anne from being obliged to make awkward explanations of her own about Julien to friends and neighbors.

Turning to Ari, Julien said sincerely, "Remember, if you need anything, anything at all, call on me. I am a man of my word, and I'll not forget what you've done."

* * * * *

Ari closed the door to her room, feeling physically and emotionally drained. Under Anne's watchful eye, Fox was resting peacefully. Ari planned to get a nap and then spell Anne.

Fox had almost died.

The thought struck like a brick. Had Ari not been there, had she escaped sooner, she knew with terrible certainty Fox would have bled to death.

Fate?

Shaking her head, she went to the corner of the room, picked up the cork from the floor, and stuck it into the peephole. Every day she found it on the floor. She had ceased to wonder who was playing this rude game with her.

Placing a tin thimble atop it, she was certain that whoever it was wouldn't peep into her bedchamber as she slept. The thimble would fall if the cork was pushed out in the night, and the noise would awaken her.

After banking the fire, she put on her nightgown and glanced at the ruined gown she'd been wearing and tossed it aside. The gown mattered not a whit. Barring infection, Fox was going to be all right.

She hugged herself. He would live. And breathe.

And love?

No.

Venturing down that avenue of thought would be dangerous to her already fragile peace of mind.

Blinking wearily, Ari lifted the lap desk from the bed, where she had left it. She'd hidden her letter to Stubby within it, in the middle of the other sheets.

"If you need anything…" Julien's words came back to her. Had he meant it? Was he a man of his word? If he was, she could swear him to silence and have him post the letter to Stubby. As she put the desk on a table, atop various pieces of the walking dress she had basted together, she turned the possibility over in her mind. He would do it. His offer had been sincere.

And she did have to leave, she reminded herself again. Fox had figured out who she was, though not quite her true identity. It was just a matter of time before he had proof.

What would he do then? She didn't believe he'd turn her over to a magistrate, but someone else might.

Feelings were strong against the French. Napoleon's wars had claimed many British sons. She had no proof that she was innocent, and in this time of hatred, her accent alone might well convict her.

Ari admitted to herself that she didn't want to leave Stonerose. Oddly, she was coming to feel at home here. Anne was warm and kind. Fox was as compelling as he was dangerous. He occupied her thoughts far more than was wise.

Her going might disturb Anne for a short time, but both Fox and Anne would go on with their lives after she was gone. She would soon be forgotten, she assured herself, wondering why the thought made her feel empty.

All the more reason to leave as soon as possible! Tomorrow. She would go to the stables tomorrow and ask Julien's help. Then, after Fox was out of danger, she'd have Julien post the letter. Soon she'd be on her way back to London and she could start anew. Anything was possible, she had only to decide which way she wanted to go and what she wanted to do with the rest of her life.

Or rather, anything was possible except remaining here.

Opening the desk, she flipped through the stack of rough sketches where she'd hidden the letter. Finding it at the back of them, she frowned, an odd feeling creeping down her spine. She could have sworn she'd hidden it in the middle of the stack...

Drawing it out, Ari unfolded it and cold washed through her. Stubby's name was circled. Scrawled in a spidery hand across the bottom of the letter were the words, *Don't trust him!*

The paper trembled and she dropped it as though it burned her. Her hand to her throat, she stared at it. Who had done this? Why? Who at Stonerose would even know Lord Stubbins? Perhaps Anne? Maybe Fox? Could either of them be responsible?

Retrieving the letter from the floor, she studied it again. The words were wavy and uncertain, almost unreadable. The penmanship looked to be by a very old or frail hand. That deepened the mystery — there was no one at Stonerose so old or frail.

Moving to the fireplace, she dropped the letter onto the ashes she'd heaped over the last coals. It bent and curled with the heat and blackened and burst into flame.

One thing was certain. Someone had thrown a big, hairy spider into the soup pot.

Now what was she to do?

* * * * *

"Oh, piddle. I had forgotten all about the supper party I planned for next Friday night." Anne tilted her head back, sighting through her eyeglasses at a sheet of blue vellum paper. "Now here's Mrs. Wallingford accepting and hinting that I should extend the invitation to her houseguest, a young lord named Myre. Fox, I'll have to send one of your footmen around with our apologies before everyone sends acceptances."

"A supper party?" Ari asked, pausing with scissors poised above Fox's bandage. It had only been three days since he was wounded, but he would not be kept abed. He sat in a chair drawn up before the French windows in his bedroom, his dressing gown open in front to expose his bandage. The morning sun pouring through the open drapes bathed him in a golden glow. And he managed to look lordly, even though he was pale and his hair tousled.

Fox frowned at his sister, a line forming between his eagle-wing brows. "I remember you mentioning having a party, but I didn't realize you were carrying through with the plan."

"I thought I had told you, dear. Didn't I? Well, it's a moot point, now. We must cancel." Anne sat down in a chair beside the wide desk and drew paper and pen to her.

"Why should you cancel?"

Looking over the top of the glasses clipped onto her nose, Anne fixed Fox with a stern look. "Even though it isn't for a fortnight, you, my dear nodcock, will still be far too weak."

"I think I will be capable of eating supper. I'll chew very slowly."

As she tried to position the scissors to snip the cloth wrapped around his wide chest, Ari said in exasperation, "Do hold still, or you shall have a second stab wound." Ignoring his raised brow, she cut through the binding and then the second strip around his shoulder. Her gaze was drawn to his well-defined pectorals. Ridged abdominal muscles were stacked underneath. The absence of chest hair intrigued her. All the men she'd seen without shirts as she had tended injuries at *Château Nuage* had hairy chests. In London, she'd seen shirtless men digging ditches. Every man had a furring of hair, and she'd been drawn to think all men were hairy of chest. And some hairy of back.

Fox was different. Only one thin line of dark hair appeared beneath his navel and disappeared beneath the waistband of his doeskin pants. As she peeled away the cloth, his skin was warm to her touch. She wanted to trail her fingers over his chest and explore the smooth texture of his skin. The color fascinated her, though his body wasn't quite as bronze as his face.

He watched her from beneath half-lowered lids, his eyes warm and dark and amused, and she realized she was taking far too long with the simple task. To her dismay, Ari felt her cheeks growing warm.

Two plus two is four. I will not blush.

Briskly, she finished unwrapping the strip of cloth and tossed it aside and peeled away the inner pad. She found the two-inch wound pink and healing.

"Anne, the cut is mending. I do not think Fox will turn up his toes if he goes down to supper. He needs to do as much as feels comfortable for him, to aid him in recovering his strength."

"And by now everyone will have heard of my mishap. Rumors will run rampant if you cancel, Anne."

"I cannot like it. But if you insist..." With a final, disapproving glance, Anne lifted another letter. "If you grow too fatigued I suppose you may retire early," she muttered.

After saturating a clean cloth with turpentine, Ari began cleaning the wound. His nipple puckered when touched by the damp cloth, just as her own did when touched by cold. She stared at it, fascinated.

"Is something wrong?"

Fox's deep, smooth voice drew her gaze to his face. "No. I was just, ah, inspecting the wound."

"I see."

She felt his gaze still on her, but refused to glance at him. Feeling a telltale flush again creeping into her cheeks, she threw down the cloth and took a clean pad from the ready stack on a nearby table. *Four plus four is eight — how does he overset me so easily?*

"Is there much pain?"

"Anne's willow bark decoction has done a marvelous job of relieving it." Turning to his sister, he said, "Thank you for your care."

Anne smiled her pleasure. "I am happy I could help in some small way. 'Tis Pallas we owe the greatest thanks. Without her efforts…"

Humbled, Ari didn't know quite what to say.

"Indeed." Fox agreed and frowned as he peered through the window. "Is that Geoffrey in the maze? Where are his coat and cap?"

"No coat? Where is he?" Anne rose and hurried to the window.

Ari turned, but saw no one in the maze. Turning back to Fox, she caught a twinkle in his eyes.

"He just disappeared into the heart of it. I may be mistaken about who it is." Fox paused. "And that cough he had is nothing, I'm certain."

Shaking her head at his mendacity, Ari readied the pad to put on the wound by dampening it with turpentine so it would not stick to the healing flesh. She needed to finish changing the dressing and escape, before her pulse beat increased tempo again and her shaking hands gave her away.

Resolving to remain indifferent was easily done, she decided. But being this close to his exposed chest made maintaining an indifferent attitude remarkably hard.

"Geoffrey has been coughing? Oh, dear." Anne frowned.

"I have heard no coughing, Anne. I am sure Fox exaggerates."

"But Geoffrey has such a delicate constitution. I'd better see if he is indeed outdoors without his coat." She moved toward the door.

As the door closed behind Anne, Ari frowned at Fox. "That was not nice, sending your sister on a wild-goose hunt."

Fox laughed, his eyes crinkling at the corners. Suddenly, he looked years younger. "Chase. Wild-goose chase."

His laughter reached into her heart, lightening it. Shrugging, she firmly scolded herself for her reaction, and for noticing the way a dark lock of hair fell onto his forehead. What did it matter that he could look boyish, or like a stone god? He could be nothing to her, she reminded herself.

"Hunt, chase—it matters not. But that you would be so unkind as to lie to Anne is unconscionable."

"I didn't lie. Look." Fox pointed to the window, where Geoffrey could be seen at the heart of the maze, sporting neither coat nor cap.

"Oh."

"And he was coughing last week." His eyes twinkled again. "I caught the little thief with one of my cigars."

Ari made a long production of replacing the cork in the turpentine bottle. "I was wrong. Pray forgive me."

Fox's gaze again had that quality of seeing too deeply, as though he was trying to look into her soul. She turned away, unwilling to bear his scrutiny.

"Your apology is not necessary. I did aim to be alone with you. I want to thank you." His voice was a warm rasp. "I'm aware that I owe you my life."

Her heartbeat became erratic. She felt as though the organ had moved, taking up residence in her throat. Ari swallowed. "You have thanked me. And as I told you, you would have been too embarrassed to die of anything so trifling."

After sprinkling the pad with a liberal amount of bascillicum powder, she lightly pressed it to the wound and reached for a rolled linen strip to bind it with. Fox caught her hand. She frowned at it. Why was he always doing that?

His big hand caressed her smaller one, and a thrill ran through her from the point of contact down to her toes.

"What are you doing?" she asked, striving to sound normal, just as if all the world hadn't spun crazily at his touch.

"You have been unusually solemn. It disturbs me."

Still holding the pad in place, Ari frowned as met his gaze. "Then you are too easily disturbed."

"Your eyes are as deep as the sky. They give little away. I find myself often wondering what you are thinking."

At his question, her gaze moved to his lips. She'd been thinking of the way they felt on hers, and wondering if she dared kiss him again. The lines bracketing his mouth deepened as he smiled.

"Ah. We are of like minds."

Catching her behind the neck, he drew her down and touched his lips lightly to hers, like the caress of a butterfly's wings.

Warmth streaked through her. Oh, this was beyond unfair! How could he play havoc with her emotions when he was too weak to stand?

She broke the kiss. "Pray, stop."

"Do you really wish me to?"

Sighing, she shook her head. "*Non*. That is not what I want."

"What do you want?"

She again met his gaze. "The stars. Orion, the dark-haired hunter. Unobtainable in the night sky. Above my touch," she whispered the last, her heart constricting a little at the admission.

"Not above your touch. You are an equal to any man." He stroked her cheek. "But you are confusing myths. Artemis slew Orion, not the wise Pallas Athena," he said huskily, using both of the goddess's names.

"I am not wise." Closing her eyes, she sighed and moved closer, unable to resist. She touched his chest, exploring the warm, smooth texture of his skin beneath his robe and marveling at the hard muscle beneath it. Her fingers grazed his flat, male nipple, and his sharp intake of breath as it drew into a tight nub excited her. "I am not wise. If I was wise, I would have left when Anne left."

Wrapping his arms around her, when she would have moved away, Fox rested his cheek against her. "Don't be afraid. I only want to hold you. Or do you feel you're betraying Prince Rudolpho's memory just by being this intimate?"

Pallas pulled away. The cool air meeting his bare skin where she'd been pressing against him emphasized the loss of contact.

Fox shook his head. "Forgive me. I shouldn't have asked. It doesn't matter." Not long ago, she'd told him she couldn't remember being with another man—why was he trying to make her remember her past lover?

"Such things always matter. The need to know arcs like lightning in your eyes." She smiled sadly. "And I will tell you the truth. I do not remember ever truly loving another man." When had she become so adept at paring the truth into such a fine lie?

"I do believe you. Again, I ask that you forget I asked."

Her fine eyes flashed with emotion. "Some things are wrought in stone. They cannot be changed. I would like to thank you for not telling your sister that you suspect I am—was—the prince's light-o'-love. That would place me beyond the pale, and she should feel betrayed for having granted me her friendship."

"I said it doesn't matter."

She looked down at the cloth pad she still gripped in her hand, as though wondering how it came there, then threw it down. "I think it would be best if Thigpen handles all future dressings. There seems to be no infection, and as long as the wound continues to heal, I need not see it."

"This isn't the end of it," Fox promised. He wouldn't allow it to be. Tenderness filled him as tears pooled in her eyes, and he reached for her again.

He clenched his hand as she bolted for the door.

When would she trust him?

But then, why should she?

* * * * *

"I want to ride. Which horse shall I take?" Ari asked. After flying to her room and getting her old cloak, she had gone to the stables. She wanted to feel the power of an animal beneath her. She needed to feel the freedom of racing the wind.

A short-legged groom hurried to keep up as she paced beside the long row of loose boxes. "I don' know what you be looking for, Miss."

"Something sound. This one is sickle-hocked," she said of a bay mare. "That one is ewe-necked, as well as toed-out," she pronounced of the next animal. "The dappled gelding is too small—is he part Shetland? I thought his lordship kept a fine stable."

"He does. These be left over from the old lord. The earl's brother what died."

Longing to get away, to be alone, Ari spied what she was looking for. "That one, please," she said pointing across the aisle at a sleek black.

"Oh, not that 'un, Miss."

"Why not?" She was growing impatient.

"That gelding is his lordship's horse." Julien came up beside her. "A stubborn beast. After it threw the former earl, breaking his neck, his lordship gave orders that no one besides himself should ride it."

"Then which horse may I ride? If I do not get a horse soon, I might scream."

"She'll ride Courser. Fetch a sidesaddle," Julien told the groom. "And have Willie saddle the gray gelding for me."

"I do not need an escort," she told Julien sharply, her fists clenched.

He took her arm and led her toward a beautiful dun hunter. "If I hadn't made a vow to myself to be nice to you, I'd tell you just what you do need." His eyes gleamed wickedly beneath eagle-wings brows. In that moment the resemblance to his brother was striking. "And I bet you're a...bruising rider." His suggestive tone said his meaning had nothing to do with horses.

"And if I had not made a vow to be kind to you, I would show you bruises." Ari narrowed her eyes.

Holding up his hands in mock surrender, Julien took a quick step back, but he grinned unabashed.

Unable to resist his charm, she smiled too. Then was dismayed as tears welled in her eyes, blurring her vision.

She turned away, looking down the long aisle. A dust mote swirled in a ray of morning light prying under a shutter. There were always currents, movements, eddies at work, she thought watching it. Always unseen activity beneath the surface.

"What's wrong?"

Ari sighed. What was wrong? Nothing. She had someone peeping into her room and going through her things. Stubby had been her hope of leaving. Now, someone, perhaps the same someone who peeped, had made her afraid to trust Stubby. And Fox. Fox made her senses swim, made her dream of things she knew were impossible. Even if they were not impossible, Fox was not what he seemed.

She had to get away before she went insane. But not before Fox was fully healed. She would not leave him until she knew he was well.

She could not do that.

"My shoes hurt," she said on a sigh.

A dark winged brow rode upward, skeptically. "I see." Going down on one knee, he lifted her skirt.

Aghast, Ari glared down at the top of his silvery head. "I do not believe this. What are you doing?" She snatched her skirt from his grasp.

"My, you do have big feet." He sat back on his heels.

"It is not polite to comment on a lady's extremities," she said tartly. "And they are not big. I am very tall, so they must be...adequate."

"And I have never pretended to be polite. It's much too boring." Julien dusted his hands as he stood. "Well, only when it suits my purposes," he amended with a wink. "Did you get those shoes from some housemaid? They look bloody uncomfortable. And you can't ride in those—there's no protection from the stirrup strap. Even with a sidesaddle, your ankle will be rubbed raw."

She might have told him she had ridden in even less substantial footwear, remembering the one slipper she'd been wearing when she'd ridden to Dartmouth. But her ankle had indeed been rubbed raw, then. "Please. It does not matter. Have you never just needed to be free?"

"I understand," he said seriously. "And I think I have a solution. Young Geoffrey was in the stable yesterday, and his boots might fit you. I'll go rip them from the little urchin's feet, if you but say the word, Milady."

Ari felt a smile spread over her face. "You are brilliant. I am certain he will have extra boots with him." Starting for the door, she said, "I shall ask him if I may use them."

"The horses are almost ready. Wait but a moment and we may ride back to the manor house."

A few minutes later, as they rode side by side along the path skirting the barren rose garden, a movement drew Ari's gaze to the window of her bedchamber. Abruptly, she reined in her mount. Shading her eyes, she squinted, trying to see past the glare of the morning sun on the glass. Just for an instant, she'd seen a man, ramrod thin, with a shock of black hair. *Mon Dieu*, she'd thought…

"What's wrong?" Julien reined his horse to a halt. "You look like you've seen a ghost."

Ari's gaze snapped to his. "*Cher bon Dieu*, how did you know?"

Julien frowned, "How did I know *what*?"

Without answering, Ari put her heel to her mount's flank, and the horse raced around the corner of the manor. At the side entrance, she pulled the reins, dismounting even before the horse had stopped and tossing him the reins. Running inside, she bolted up a narrow servant's stairs, nearly oversetting Littleburn, who was carrying down an armload of dirty linens and bath sheets.

Once upstairs, Ari shoved open the door to her room. Bailey stood frozen on the opposite side of the bare bed, a sheet stretched in her hands as though she had been just about to spread it over the mattress, the covers humped carelessly on the floor.

Her heart beating in her throat, Ari looked around the four corners of the chamber. "Where is he? Where is the man who was in the window?

"Where?"

Chapter Eleven

ઈ

"Who, Milady?" Bailey blinked at her.

"The man I saw, just now, in the window."

Bailey's gaze darted around the room. "You had a vision, Milady?"

There was an odd look in the little maid's eyes. Ari shook her head. "No, I thought—"

She clamped her teeth together. Bailey would certainly think her daft if she admitted the truth. Drawing in a deep breath, she wondered if perhaps she was seeing things. The maid still eyed her apprehensively.

She gave her a reassuring smile. "It is my mistake. Let me help you with the sheet. It is far bigger than you are."

"No, Milady." As Ari started forward, the maid took a step back, sheet still spread in her outstretched arms. Her expression bordered on terror and she almost tripped over the pink satin coverlet she'd left carelessly piled on the floor.

Halting, Ari frowned. Obviously, her odd behavior had poor Bailey thinking her ready for Bedlam. "As you like."

"Is something wrong?" Julien said, catching up to Ari in the doorway. "You bolted away as though Satan, himself, was on your heels."

"Nonsense. He was riding beside me all the time."

Ari closed the door and left the maid to her work. At his frown, she said, "It is nothing. I suspect someone has been going through my things. I thought I saw a man standing in the window, and so rushed up here to confront him. However, it was only the maid changing the bed linens.

"Now, I shall find Geoffrey and beg a pair of boots, then meet you below."

Later, as she and Julien gave their mounts free rein and the horses raced across a stubbled winter field, Ari knew what she'd been missing—freedom. Riding reminded her of carefree days when she and Dolpho would race across the Alpine meadows of their homeland. Julien stayed slightly back, as any good groom might. She was grateful that he did not talk, but left her alone with her thoughts.

After that first ride, he brought her a mount around every morning after breakfast and accompanied her as she rode over the estate.

* * * * *

"Come, I have something to show you!" Excitement lit Anne's eyes as she motioned to Ari to join her by the foot of the stairs.

"What is it?" Just back from her morning ride, Ari removed the riding hat and gloves Anne had insisted on lending her along with Geoffrey's boots—which had proven a little too wide, but comfortable.

"Just come. Do hurry."

Apprehension touched her heart. Ari practically threw the hat and gloves at a waiting footman, and quickly shrugged off her cloak. "Tell me, is it Fox? Has he developed fever?"

"Fox? Oh no. No fever. This is something marvelous." Anne seized her hand and rushed her up the stairs, not pausing until they had reached Ari's bedchamber. "And just in time for the dinner party! I have been watching for your return so I could see the look on your face when you see this." She pushed the door open. "Just look."

Ari paused in the doorway, stunned at the finery spread over the bed. Day dresses, walking dresses, evening gowns— garments of every sort and in a multitude of colors were there.

"I do not believe it." Moving to the bed, she stared in consternation.

"There's more, Milady." Bailey beamed happily.

Noticing the maid by the foot of the bed, Ari turned and blinked. "More?"

"Yes, Milady." Bailey moved to the settee and made a sweeping gesture with her arm. It was piled high with underthings of all imaginable types. "All these. And there are shoes—"

"Shoes?" Ari said in wonder, seeing rows of slippers by the bed. There were shoes to match everything. All looked butter-soft and wonderfully comfortable.

"And reticules, bonnets, parasols. And just look here, Milady." Bailey rushed to a wingback chair and lifted a pelisse of emerald green velvet trimmed in ermine. "I've never seen anything so fine."

"It is very fine, of course." Ari fingered a day dress of fawn merino trimmed with a grosgrain ribbon of the same color.

"You aren't pleased," Anne said, eyeing her in concern.

"No, truly, this is all very nice. Did...did you tell Fox to order it?"

"This was all ordered before I arrived, and, since I knew nothing of your existence, I couldn't very well have prevailed upon my brother to do this for you, could I? It is all his generosity."

"I see."

Anne frowned. "Is it that the dresses are drab? Is that what displeases you? The pelisse will do well enough, but these other things are bare of frills and ruffles. And the colors. I don't know what he could have been thinking—the colors are not at all bright and cheery enough. Fox should have commissioned some reds and bright pinks. Perhaps something in fuchsia. I told Fox he should have consulted me before placing the orders. Well, all is not lost. I have a great many brooches I could lend you. We shall contrive to frill them up, my dear. We shall sew on yards of lace and ribbons and bows. What do you think?"

"No." Ari shot her a horrified look. Realizing her *faux pas,* she amended, "I mean, I like these subdued colors. I fear my hair is as cheery as a crackling fire, so bright fabrics rather go to war with it. And these clean lines should suit my height perfectly. But, Anne, I cannot accept them."

"And why not?" Fox asked from the doorway.

He was dressed in the buff breeches he'd been wearing earlier that morning, and a white cambric shirt and simple dove gray waistcoat. A coat of bottle green superfine was draped over his left shoulder and his arm was held in a sling.

"Because it is too fine a gift, of course. I cannot accept all this." Ari clenched her hands in the folds of her skirt.

"It offends your pride?" he asked, drawing closer.

Aware of Anne's and the maid's interested stares, Ari said stiffly, "I do not mean to seem ungrateful, but I would rather not discuss it."

"Oh, but we will," he assured her, holding her gaze. "Anne, Bailey, leave us."

Anne looked uncertain. "Fox, I don't think—"

"Close the damned door when you leave."

Spurred by his dark tone, the two women scurried from the room. He moved closer to Ari. "Now, what is wrong?"

"*Sangre de Christo.* What is wrong, you ask." Ari gave him a fulminating look.

"Are you upset because you'd rather choose clothes for yourself?" He looked honestly puzzled.

Ari clenched her teeth and closed her eyes, seeking vainly for the peace of mind she had found on her brisk ride through the manor's parkland. Did he even realize how he was treating her?

"You believe I was Prince Dolpho's kept woman, but I find I have not the heart nor mind of one. I cannot accept expensive gifts like this. You know quite well that it would not be proper. Indeed, you would not offer it to me if you considered me a decent woman."

"You think I am trying to buy you?"

"I do not know what to think."

She turned but Fox caught her hand. "I ordered these things weeks ago, when I was convinced you were Peterson's wife."

"You did?" Ari looked at the gowns heaped on the bed and the truth of his statement was obvious. Of course they had been ordered weeks before. This finery could not have been sewn overnight.

"Yes. I've never thought of you as a woman of easy virtue, even after I discovered you were with Prince Dragonetti." He made circles over the back of her hand with his thumb. "Would that you were of easier virtue," he murmured.

"Oh." She looked at her hand. She wanted to pull it from his grasp, but what he was doing felt so nice. Surely, such a little pleasure could not hurt anything.

Fox tugged, and she found herself drawn against his chest. "I have made no secret of the fact I want you. I understand how you misinterpreted my gift." Thick, black lashes shielded his eyes. He touched the wedding band circling her finger. "Part of the reason for these gowns is I wanted to see you in beautiful clothes. But know this, whatever you are, or whatever you have been, you are an honorable woman. I have never imagined you as less."

"Pray do not speak of things you do not know," she implored him. Trapped by the web of deceit she had woven, Ari thought miserably that an honorable woman would hardly continue with the charade she was embroiled in. But what could she do? She was still wanted by the Crown.

"I don't know with certainty, but I do have a good idea. You may not remember who you were before, but your personality shows who you are inside. When I first saw you in

Dartmouth, with your hair floating out on the wind and determination like steel in your eyes, I thought you were magnificent. You looked like a Valkyrie, a fierce warrior spirit. And I wanted you even then.

"After the militia attacked, you could have hidden yourself away, left the area, left England, but you believed me responsible. You told me you asked only the pleasure of seeing me in hell when you got there and would have counted your life well spent if you could have avenged Dragonetti's death." He shook his head. "He was the luckiest of men."

Ari swallowed as the sting of her lies became almost unbearable. This man had taken her in, seen that her wounds were treated, and honored her as if she was a guest and not the madwoman who tried to blow his head off. Now, she had unjustly accused him of trying to buy her favors—and if she was honest with herself, she would admit it was because she wanted him as she'd never wanted another man.

Whenever she saw him, desire started building inside her. At night, she had lain awake, remembering his kisses and reliving the thrill of them until a gnawing emptiness made it hard to find sleep.

"I cannot accept these. Please, you have done so much—too much. I can accept no more."

She turned toward the door, and he caught her arm. "Pallas, wait. I—" A wave of dizziness swept over him and he grabbed the bedpost. "Damnation." His face was suddenly etched in harsh lines and there was a pallor underlying his skin.

"*Madre de Dios.* Are you all right?" She took his right arm, draping it over her shoulders to support him as she guided him to sit on her bed. "You are doing too much. You should still be abed."

Several phrases in rapid, unintelligible Italian, then German followed the statement. Fox assumed all to be assessments of his lack of judgment. Even though his head spun as if he were riding a whirligig, her concern was heady. The caring in her eyes warmed a place in his heart.

Was she capable of feeling for him the depth of emotion she had felt for the prince?

Could he be happy with less?

Her sky blue eyes regarded him solemnly. "You are likely to cause your shoulder to bleed if you overdo it."

"But I have lascivious behavior I need to be about—you assured me I should be up to it in a few days, remember?" He tried to ignore the sick lurch in his stomach.

"When I said that, I thought you would conduct it in bed," she replied tartly.

He smiled wickedly. Catching her wrist, he pulled her down. She ended up on her back with pale gold tulle puffing around her head like an iridescent cloud. Or a halo, he mused. Tendrils had escaped from her severe coronet of braids and corkscrewed beside her flushed cheeks.

Being careful of his injured shoulder, Fox pinned her with his thigh across her legs and caught a handful of the gold material, sliding it across her flushed cheek, rubbing it back and forth. "I knew this color would look magnificent on you."

"Please." She wet her lips, drawing his gaze to them.

"Please what?" He cupped her breast through her gown and kneaded gently.

Eyes widening, she caught her breath. "Please."

Unable to wait longer, he kissed her. Her soft lips parted beneath his, inviting him to explore the sweet cavern of her mouth. When her tongue met his he groaned his need into her mouth and deepened the kiss. Probing her mouth relentlessly, dueling with her tongue, he felt her surrender. Catching her soft moans in his mouth, he sighed as Pallas cupped his face, arching against him and pressing her breasts more tightly against his chest, telling him that her need matched his.

"I want to see you." He tugged at her neckline as he kissed a path from her temple to her throat.

"Yes."

"I want to caress your breasts."

She arched again and moaned softly. "Please."

"And kiss them."

"Oh, yes." She lay back, panting, watching him through half-closed eyes.

He fought to pull the neckline lower, hampered by the sling on his arm. "Damn, the gown is too tight."

"It will have to be unhooked in the back."

"Unhooked?" Dizziness swept over him again, nausea close behind. He rolled onto his back, a wicked curse spewing from his lips.

Propping on her elbow, Pallas looked confused. "Are you all right?"

Her lips were swollen. He wanted nothing more than to pull her atop him and kiss her senseless. Then let her straddle him and ride him until they were both senseless.

"No, hell, I am not all right, or you'd be well on your way to being ravished by now."

"Oh. *Oh!*" Her cheeks became a delightful shade of pink. She stood, her breasts like ripe oranges, half exposed in the square neckline of her gown. "I cannot believe—I mean, I do not usually act... *Oh, my.*" She straightened her gown an instant before Anne barged through the door, brimming with righteous indignation.

"I can't countenance it. This is not...is not... Fox, what is wrong?"

He gave his sister a darkling glance. "I think I've overextended myself."

* * * * *

163

A garland of lemons and apples interwoven with evergreen boughs stretched across the massive mantle. Small pyramids of fruit and nuts were spaced along the table, where they could be enjoyed between courses. Greenery and red bows were draped around the painting of the first earl Grandquest that hung above the marble mantel.

Anne had done a splendid job. Catching his sister's eye, Fox lifted his wineglass slightly in a private salute. From her position at the other end of the long cherrywood table, Anne smiled and inclined her head in acknowledgment.

He hadn't believed that his sister could pull it off. Foisting the acquaintance of an unknown quantity such as Pallas on rural English gentry was no mean feat. But as Anne had vowed, the cream of the district was seated in his dining room, a tribute to Anne's social acumen. When he'd voiced his doubts, his sister had laughed and assured him that everyone would come out of curiosity, if for no other reason.

Fox admitted to himself Anne had been right. Before dinner had been announced, he had turned aside several discreet questions about Pallas. Everyone was plainly fascinated with her.

Especially the men.

And why not? She was easily the most beautiful, vivacious woman he'd ever known. Seated midway down the long table, between him and Anne, she looked ethereal, a creature of mists and starlight. Surely not of this same dingy world he inhabited.

Ari's dark auburn hair was caught up in a Grecian knot and careless curls framed her face and spilled over her bare shoulder. Her high-waisted gown of midnight blue velvet had puffed sleeves off her shoulders, displaying her graceful neck. Silver spangles covered the bodice and skirt and edged the low neckline. A collar of paste diamonds encircled her neck. Other diamonds dangling at her ears and scattered in her hair added to the illusion that she was more than flesh and blood.

Fox decided it was best not to dwell on the attention the gentlemen were paying Pallas, but he promised himself that he would teach young Myre subtlety if that young rakehell dipped his gaze into her cleavage one more time.

His sister was in her element. Gowned in a gunmetal gray dress, which Pallas had prevailed upon her to wear, Anne looked beautiful. The gown was barren of ruffles and frills and had but one small brooch pinned to the bodice. Pearls at her ears and a strand around her neck were Anne's only other adornments.

Fox was aware of the frequent glances she sent down the table to Sir Leonard Dent, a widower seated on Fox's right. Sir Leonard's estate bordered Stonerose on the north, and Anne had surprised Fox that afternoon by speculating on how nice it would be if she married Sir Leonard and lived on a neighboring estate.

Draining his claret, Fox signaled the footman to refill it.

"This variety seems particularly resistant to spotted rot, though we've not had a wet enough winter in which to test it." Anne's attention fell on barren soil as Sir Leonard expounded on the virtues of a new variety of winter wheat he was trying on his estate's home farm.

"Perhaps the weather will oblige and turn warm and wet." Ignoring the compote filled with trifle setting before him, Fox damned spotted rot and took another sip of wine. His interest at the moment was wholly focused on the ephemeral creature with the flame of deep auburn hair holding court midway down the long table. Myre had leaned close to her, whispering something into her ear that made her smile, all the while treating himself to the view down her neckline.

Fox decided he would thrash him.

Sir Leonard smiled, flashing uneven white teeth. "You've been preoccupied all evening, Fox." Sir Leonard's gaze swung to Pallas. "I must say, I can see why. She is lovely. More than lovely. She has young Myre captivated."

Arching a brow, Fox said, "She is a bit nicer to look at than you, Leonard."

"Tell me," Sir Leonard lowered his voice, "is it true? Did she try to take your head off with a blunderbuss on the Dartmouth quay?"

Feeling himself suddenly the focus of interest of all those sitting within hearing, Fox sipped his claret and set his glass down carefully. "Anne and I have a wager about who will hear the most bizarre rumor about Pallas. This one may make me the winner."

"You must know the neighborhood has been abuzz for weeks. I suppose the rest of the story has no merit either." Sir Leonard leaned close, so only Fox could hear. "That she was stark naked as she aimed the gun."

What drivel was being circulated about Pallas? A twinge in his injured muscle made Fox aware he had clenched his fists. Forcing a laugh, he said, "I can't believe anyone of sense would repeat such an absurdity."

Sir Leonard nodded. "So it is untrue. Why are all the best stories fabrications?" As Pallas' light laughter floated to them, Sir Leonard looked thoughtful. "I don't suppose you are going to enlighten us with the truth."

"As a gentleman, I cannot."

A smirk twisted Sir Leonard's mouth, tilting his pencil-thin blond mustache beneath his long nose. "Of course, as a...gentleman."

Fox held very still. The facts of his birth were well known in a society that thrived on gossip. His maternal grandfather, a wealthy, Boston merchant, had been a staunch loyalist, supporting the Crown when the American colonies rebelled. When the man's daughter, Fox's mother, fell in love and became pregnant by Jules Fox, a rebel leader and a man of mixed race, she was beaten and forced to marriage to Earl Grandquest a general in Cornwallis' army.

A sophisticated man, the old earl had taken it in stride when six months after their marriage his wife had given birth to a healthy son. After all, she had been his third wife and he had nine older children, five of them sons—an heir and four spares. Fox carried the Grandquest name, and despite the odds, eventually inherited the title. But he had borne the stigma of bastardy all his life.

Now, he was surprised to find the old wound still tender.

Sir Leonard said nothing, merely flicking an imaginary speck from his ruffled cuff before lifting his wineglass.

"Judith tells me you've just returned from London Town, Sir Leonard. What is the word from Whitehall?" asked Mrs. Applegate, seated on Sir Leonard's other side. "I have so little word from Ronald," she said, naming her younger son who was with Wellington on the Peninsula.

"We are still at the mercy of French spies, madam. And if they aren't stopped, they may be England's undoing."

Everyone was suddenly silent, and turned to Sir Leonard. Seeming to enjoy the attention, Sir Leonard sat up straight, his gaze sweeping around the table, lingering on Pallas. He went on, "A fleet of privateers was waiting to intercept our last supply convoy. No match for our frigate escort, of course, but light and maneuverable, and well able to inflict damage in a running fight. They were well informed, too, concentrating their attack on the *Titan II*, which carried a store of powder and shot for Wellington's troops. The *Titan* was lost with all hands and those much needed supplies."

"My word," George Wallingford exclaimed.

Mrs. Applegate shook her head, the feather on her turban bobbing in the light of the chandelier. "What are we to do?"

Judith Bastrop, Sir Leonard's twin sister, leaned toward the older woman, an action that set Judith's ample bosom on the table and threatened to spill it from her low-cut gown, like melons rolling from a toppled basket. "French spies run tame here in Devon, too. Under our very noses. Perhaps," she shot a look at Pallas, "even eating at the same tables." Drawing herself up stiffly, she fanned as she met Fox's gaze, a challenge glinting in her eyes.

Damnation, he wouldn't allow the harridan to slander Pallas. He wouldn't have her marked as a pariah simply because she had a French accent.

The silence grew thick. The assembled guests watched Fox and Pallas, awaiting their reactions.

Fox turned to Pallas and was surprised to see she didn't look upset in the slightest. Instead, she sat tall and straight, one elegant brow lifted as she watched Judith with the same fine disdain with which a lioness might study a bleating sheep. She showed more breeding than anyone at the table, Fox thought proudly, even Sir Leonard and his sister, who were fond of pointing out their family could be traced back to William the Conqueror.

So it begins. Ari put down her fork, her stomach clenching. She was careful to keep her features schooled so none of her apprehension would show. However, she was alive to every nuance of expression around the table. When Anne had persisted in the madness of including her among the guests, Ari had known there would be awkward questions. There was nothing for it but to brazen it out.

Anne rose. "I think it is time for the ladies to leave the gentlemen to their port and cigars."

As the men leapt to their feet, both Lord Myre and the gentleman on her other side, Donald Wallingford, vied for who would pull out Ari's chair. Judith Bastrop struggled alone until a footman came to her aid.

Ari rose. "I am confused." She laid her gloved hand on her bosom, a practiced gesture that drew every male eye to it. "Is it, as you English say, 'bad form' for one to make remarks that might cause one's dining companions discomfort?"

Anne smiled at her. "Why, yes. *Bad form* it is."

"I thought it must be," Ari shrugged, an elegant lift of her shoulder. "But then again, I wondered if I just did not comprehend your English manners."

"Well, I never," Judith Bastrop spluttered in the face of the cool setdown.

Pallas picked up her fan, like a queen lifting her scepter, Fox thought. Before Judith could say more, he lifted his claret glass and tapped it with his fork, drawing everyone's attention. "Ladies, gentlemen, these are dark times. Something very near an accusation of treason has been brought at my table. I would clear the air before we go further, so I ask that you all resume your seats."

When Fox's gray gaze touched her, Ari felt infused with warmth. There was caring that said no harm would come to her. And there was unbending strength, which, when he looked around the table, said he would brook no dissension.

Fox stood taller than every other man at the dining table, even Sir Leonard, though the latter was near the same height. As he waited for his guests to all be seated, he looked every inch an earl, a striking figure in his black eveningwear. His cravat was tied in "the waterfall," an effect Dolpho had often tried in vain to achieve. The starched muslin nestled under his strong chin was starkly white, contrasting with his bronze complexion.

But Ari worried the inside of her lip. Was Fox pale under his tan? The candelabras between them made judging his skin tone difficult. The morning he'd grown dizzy after he'd tumbled her onto her new gowns, he'd had a sickly green cast to his skin. She'd not seen the wound since she gave over its care to Thigpen three days before—something she now much regretted.

Could he be fevered? Was an infection setting in? Fox had been keeping to his bedchamber, though he'd seen a steady stream of people on business involving the estate. Anne complained that he was taxing himself too much, but she had assured Ari that he was healing rapidly.

He must be improved, Ari decided. Tonight, Fox had eschewed a sling. That was a good sign, wasn't it? Or was it only stubborn pride? She had noticed when he moved his arm there was a slight tightening around his mouth, as though he was in pain.

When everyone was reseated, Fox said, "Now, Mrs. Bastrop, you alluded to spies. Please don't be reticent. Tell us plainly where you see a threat."

Judith glared at him. "I will oblige you, sir. My son, Nathan, is a lieutenant of the militia. A few weeks ago, his squadron sought to arrest two very dangerous spies, an Italian prince and the woman he was living with. And *this* a bare seven miles from here. Nathan told me the militia chased them through the night, into the woods and bogs. One of the spies seems to have been grievously wounded."

Judith turned to Ari, a triumphant gleam in her eyes. "I believe you, Miss, were wounded by a bullet when the earl brought you here, which makes one assume that all this about you holding a gun on him in Dartmouth is nonsense."

Though she was careful to keep her expression neutral, Ari was startled by the fact that it was so close between Stonerose and the cottage she and Dolpho had rented. Of course, the bogs made the area almost impassable, except by a small boat on the creek, which ran through it…

The same wide creek that ran below the hill on which Stonerose was situated? Why had that not occurred to her before?

Judith continued to stare at her. Ari flicked her fingers at the woman, as though waving away an annoying insect. "I do not remember ever being in Dartmouth. I do not remember anything of it," she said truthfully. Those memories had never returned.

"Lord Grandquest, what have you to say to that?" Judith asked triumphantly.

Fox sipped his wine, then set his glass down, one winged brow rising as he regarded the woman. "She has…amnesia."

A chuckle went around the table as tension eased. Judith's cheeks became pink.

"Seriously, I know of the militia's misguided attack on Prince Dragonetti and the woman staying at the cottage with him. The militia was fed false information, leading to that attack. The truth is the prince had been working for England, trying to discover the principals involved in the ring smuggling secrets out of the country and using our area of the coast to make their runs. He should have been given a medal as a hero—instead he gave his life and is now being defamed."

"How do you know the raid was a mistake?" Sir Leonard asked.

"Because I supposedly supplied the information which led to the warrant for the prince's arrest. I was in Dartmouth at the time and never sent such a letter to Captain Phips."

"Then the militia murdered an innocent man," Lord Myre said grimly.

"There was evidence found in the cottage that the prince was, indeed, guilty of spying," Judith snapped. "I know I should not reveal what you've told me in private, Leonard, but I feel compelled to defend the truth. And," she said with a dramatic pause, "Nathan *saw this woman*. He said she was very tall and had red hair."

Fox regarded Judith levelly. "The 'evidence' to which you're referring was, I believe, some details of troop movements from two years ago, before Wellington was driven back to Portugal. It smells of a red herring, placed in the cottage after the militia attacked."

"I beg to differ, Lord Grandquest," Mr. Wallingford interjected. "But it is well known that the prince was a close friend of Viscount Stubbins—Mrs. Wallingford is a devoted reader of the society pages in *The Times*."

"Yes, I never fail to peruse them," Mrs. Wallingford agreed.

"What does any of this have to do with Lord Stubbins?" A sinking feeling moved through Ari's stomach.

"Why, the viscount was a spy. He shot himself after details of Wellington's proposed spring campaign were discovered in his possession. It is common knowledge that he and the prince were good friends. Needless to say, the Earl of Meadowbridge, his father, was forced to resign as vice-secretary of the War Ministry."

"*Mon Dieu.*" Ari crumpled her napkin in her lap. The words scrawled on her letter to Stubby came back to her. *Don't trust him.*

She remembered Stubby laughing, joking, never serious. Now he was dead. A traitor! And Dolpho. Stubby might have been the one who betrayed them to Dandelion, who caused the militia to attack them at the cottage. Cold washed through her. "This was in *The Times*, did you say?"

Mrs. Wallingford nodded. "Oh, yes, all the details."

Ari wondered just what the newspaper had reported. Had others been named? Stubby must have been a pawn. A willing pawn, it seemed, but still only a pawn. Dandelion was the chess master, outthinking the best minds in England, like Dolpho and Lord Blaine.

Feeling someone's gaze upon her, Ari looked up and found Fox watching her closely.

"Did you know the viscount?" Lord Myre called her attention away from Fox. The young lord's eyes gleamed as they dipped to her cleavage and rose again to her face.

"Lord Dobbins?" Ari shook her head. "*Non.* But I am very sorry for any father so betrayed by his son. Why would any English lord do such a thing?"

Even as she asked the question, she remembered Stubby had been an avid gambler, usually short of money. However, sometimes he'd been amazingly full in the pocket.

"Stubbins," Sir Leonard corrected. "As to why, I'm sure I can't say. Selling out his own country is the lowest thing a man could do, in my opinion."

"Perhaps the viscount befriended the prince to spy on him as he worked for military intelligence. But I am certain that the prince was an honorable man." Fox drained his glass.

Ari studied her hands, letting Fox's word warm her.

When the ladies again rose to leave the table, Ari excused herself, as per Anne's instructions, saying she was going to her room to fetch a shawl. Anne had told Ari she must give her twenty minutes alone with the ladies and Ari's acceptance would be assured.

Ari didn't like it, but obeyed.

When she returned with her new shawl of white merino shot with silver threads, all eyes turned to her as she entered, and all gazes were sympathetic. Save for Judith's.

Feeling as if she'd just walked into a play and didn't know her lines, Ari noted Anne's smug look and felt her brows rising in wonder. However easily she'd been accepted by the gentlemen, before dinner the ladies had been, at best, wary. Just what fustian had Anne told them during her absence?

Anne took her position at the tea table. She glanced at Ari. "Black, one sugar, I believe."

"Yes, thank you." Glancing around uncertainly, Ari started toward Anne.

"Here, let me...Pallas." The Wallingford's daughter, Mary, took the cup from Anne and brought it to Ari, smiling.

"Thank you." She accepted it and found a seat on an Irish triple chair, the middle seat of which was turned backward. During dinner, Mary had been decidedly cool toward her and had spent a great deal of energy making calf eyes at Lord Myre. Whatever had Anne said to bring about this change?

"Are you comfortable? Would you like a footstool?" Mrs. Applegate asked, her feather bobbing earnestly.

"No. Thank you, ma'am. I am fine." Ari shot another curious glance at Anne. Only Judith, standing behind Anne, still looked hostile, speculation written on her broad features.

Anne continued serving tea. "Mary, could we prevail upon you to favor us with a selection at the pianoforte? You were practicing in your family's music room yesterday when I called on your mother, and I was transported as I listened."

Blushing happily, Mary seated herself at the instrument and after a moment's indecision, began playing a lively minuet. Mrs. Applegate settled her matronly girth into the seat at the other end of the triple chair from Ari and tapped her fan against her gloved palm in time with the music.

When the gentlemen rejoined them, Ari watched for Fox, but neither he nor Sir Leonard appeared.

Mary switched to a Scottish air. Snapping open her fan, Mrs. Applegate murmured to Ari, "A little too obvious, don't you think? Lord Myre is, of course, of Scot's blood."

Lord Myre seemed oblivious to Mary's tribute as he bantered with Anne and Judith.

As Mrs. Applegate seemed to be waiting for Ari to remark, she ventured, "I shouldn't presume, but Lord Myre seems worldly beyond his years, and Mary is such a young girl. They hardly seem to suit."

"Oh, my dear, they are perfectly suited. Wallingford has a fortune and social aspirations—his father is the most disgusting Cit, you know. Myre has a title and needs a fortune. What could be a better, more convenient arrangement?"

Mrs. Applegate's callous statement reminded Ari sharply of the taint of trade in her own background, but she refused to feel belittled. "So the Wallingfords will barter their daughter for connection to a title. What of love?"

Folding her fan, Mrs. Applegate looked at Ari with a great deal more sympathy than Ari thought her question should merit. "Oh, my dear, when one is young, one only thinks of love. But life is much too uncertain to marry for it." The older lady shook her head, her feather bobbing. "Even where there is a grand passion, it often comes to tragedy, now doesn't it?"

"I am not certain what you are talking about." Ari glanced again at Anne, wondering yet again what Anne had concocted.

"Oh, nothing. Nothing. Just rambling in my dotage, dear."

Pausing to smile or speak to each, Lord Myre worked his way through the ladies, moving toward Ari all the while. No, she could not endure Lord Myre again, with his shallow sallies and his greedy eyes.

Before he could draw near, Ari rose, murmuring something to Mrs. Applegate about a headache. Avoiding Myre, she circled around the room to where Anne was serving tea to the gentlemen and kissed Anne's cheek. "It has been a lovely evening. Thank you for including me. I have a slight headache, so I will go up to my room now. Would you make my excuses?"

"A headache?" Anne frowned and popped her hand on Ari's forehead. "Oh, pooh, I can feel nothing through this glove."

"I will ask your maid for some of your white willow bark decoction, if you would not mind," Ari told her soothingly.

Anne's expression brightened. "Certainly. Good night, dear. I hope you feel better by morning." With a glance around, she added in a whisper, "Leaving now will create greater mystery in your wake. You'll be besieged with invitations."

"I shall owe you my success." Ari smiled, but her only true concern at the moment was the news that Stubby was dead. Thinking of his betrayal and how it had almost caused her to shoot Fox made her truly feel ill.

Escaping the drawing room, Ari went down the marbled hall in the opposite direction from the stairs, to Fox's study. Fox had *The Times* delivered from London, though it was always several days old when it arrived. She guessed she would find a stack of past issues in his study.

However, she didn't expect to find the two men who rose abruptly as she entered.

Fox looked tired and drawn. There was a tightness around his mouth, which could have been caused by pain. Ari was immediately concerned.

Smiling urbanely, Sir Leonard looked her over like he was inspecting a hunting mare. "Come in, my dear. We have almost concluded the business we were discussing."

Drawing herself up stiffly, Ari closed the door behind her and returned Sir Leonard's appraisal, looking him up and down from the toes of his buckled shoes to his thinning blonde locks. "I find such familiarity offensive, sir. I have barely made your acquaintance. I am certainly not 'your dear'."

"Now see here—"

"The lady finds your familiarity offensive. An apology is in order, Leonard," Fox said quietly.

Sir Leonard looked at him incredulously. Seeing that the earl was serious, Sir Leonard spread his hands, his expression changing all at once from outrage to contrition.

So rapid was the change that Ari was reminded of a chameleon lizard she had once seen in an exhibition in London.

"Certainly. No offense was intended, I assure you. It is just what does one call so lovely a young lady when she has no name?" His lips parted in a smile, but there was no smile in his eyes.

"Pallas. As you were told when we were introduced before dinner." Ari decided that he was as officious as his twin sister.

His smile faded. "Pallas." He bowed stiffly.

"You wanted something?" Fox asked, his expression unreadable.

"Yes. Ah…" She could hardly tell him she wanted to read about Lord Stubbins' death. "But what was it? I have forgotten now what drew me here. If you will excuse me, I will leave you gentlemen to your business."

What had she been after, Fox wondered, as the door closed behind her?

Sir Leonard demanded, "What are you going to do about her now that you know who she is?"

"I have listened to you make suppositions and accusations. You have offered no evidence."

"And I tell you, Grandquest, that woman is the Comtesse D'Ambois."

Chapter Twelve

🐾

Ari peeked out of her bedchamber. Down the hall, the faint light still glowed beneath Fox's door. Good. He was still awake. In the hours since she had left the study, she had come to a decision. It was time for the truth. All of it. After she told him everything, she felt certain Fox would understand why she must leave Stonerose.

It was the only logical course.

So why did the thought make her heart feel too heavy to beat properly?

Stiffening her spine, she reminded herself that there was no choice. No matter what farradiddle Anne had concocted about her, it was only a matter of time before whatever lie it was came unraveled. She might even be exposed as the woman the Crown was looking for. If that happened, Anne and Fox would face repercussions for having befriended her.

And she also wanted to assure herself that Fox's wound was healing properly with one last look before she went. Gathering up the kettle she'd taken from the kitchen and the basket, in which she'd placed supplies, she made her way down the hallway to his bedchamber and knocked softly.

Fox really had looked tense and strained in the study. She should never have relinquished the care of his shoulder to Thigpen. What could a footman know of such things? Probably even less than Dr. Kilpatrick, who thought all ills could be cured by bleeding or purging. Fox answered the knock. Pallas had been in his mind since he'd bid the last guest goodbye. Still, as he swung the door wide, he was surprised to find her standing there, as though summoned by his thoughts.

Her glorious hair was loose and flowing over her shoulders. Light from the candlestick on the side table painted it with shimmering burgundy highlights. A woolen shawl covered her shoulders, but as she entered the room and moved toward the fire, the light from the flames showed through the skirt of her nightgown, outlining her form in golden light.

Watching the motion of her hips moving, Fox felt himself stiffening. Whoever she was, whatever she'd done, she had but to appear and hot desire for her shot through him.

He closed the door.

Turning, Ari's gaze was drawn to his wide chest, visible in the deep vee in his Chinese red dressing gown. The firelight kissed his skin with bronze, gold, and shadows, outlining his muscles. Looking at it made her want to push the garment wider and smooth her hands over his flesh, to explore the contours and muscles. He still wore his black satin knee breeches, though his stockings and his shoes had been discarded. Funny, she had not noticed before how muscular his calves were.

Giving herself a mental shake, she set the basket on a low table and placed the kettle on the hearth, deciding it would be best if she got on with what had brought her here and stopped looking at his body like a child looking at a bakery window.

First his wound, and then her confession.

For after her confession, he might not let her touch him.

She drew in a deep breath. "I have been worried. This evening, you looked as though you were in pain. Are you?"

"I am experiencing a certain...discomfort." He moved closer.

"Sit down. I may be able to help you."

Ignoring her request for him to sit, Fox moved to her and cupped her cheek, brushing his thumb across her full bottom lip. As she gasped softly, he felt heat leap into his manhood. "I'm certain you may help."

Her eyes became dark blue and liquid. She caught his hand and pressed it against her cheek in a way that touched his heart, then planted a kiss in the hollow of his palm in a way that set his body afire.

He reached for the ends of her shawl.

"What are you doing?" Bemused, Ari stared up at Fox as he untied the knot holding it. Looking at her from under half-lowered lids, he didn't answer. When he tossed the woolen wrap aside and started undoing the buttons down the front of her nightrail, she understood. "No. That is not why I came here." She caught at his hands.

"Then why did you?" He brushed her fingers aside and continued.

"To tend your shoulder."

"No. That isn't the reason." He continued unbuttoning.

"No?"

"That could have waited until morning."

"I am very concerned about it. I have seen how tense you are. You have been in pain all evening."

"If my wound was all that brought you here, then you would have had Anne come with you. You aren't an innocent." He paused, his gaze meeting hers. "Pallas."

"Am I not an innocent?" Ari barely registered the odd emphasis he placed on her temporary name. As Fox worked the tiny buttons loose, the backs of his fingers grazed her breasts, and she caught her breath, losing interest in what he might be hinting at.

He stilled at her reaction and deliberately brushed her nipple through the thick flannel, sending a hot jolt deep down inside her.

"No. You aren't. You didn't come here out of concern." His face was saturnine in the glow of the fire as he rapidly finished the line of tiny buttons and pushed the gown off her shoulders. Her gown caught at the crooks of her arms, and her breasts were bared to his gaze—gloriously round and ever-so-slightly tip-tilted, the satin globes were crested by brown nipples, which puckered in the cool air.

"You are beautiful," the words were a sigh.

A thrill ran through her at the sheer desire twisting his features.

No, to give in, to make love to this man—*Dieu*, that *would* be madness. The maddest thing a Mad Benoit ever did.

The hot ache that sprang to life between her thighs argued that it would not be so very mad.

Wetting her lips, she forced herself to remember what had really brought her to his room. She must tell him. Everything. "Listen, you are right. There is another reason I came alone, at night. But it is not what you think."

"It's not important why you are here." Fox cupped her breasts in his callused palms. "Let us enjoy the fact that you are."

"Oh, *merde*." As he gently kneaded her breasts, she arched against him, clutching at his robe. "Yes. Yes, it is important. But— *Ahhh*." Her head fell back as she moaned deep in her throat. It was damned hard to think of anything but his hands on her breasts.

"Why?" He caught her nipples between his thumbs and forefingers, working an ancient magic on her body. Her breath rasped between her moist, parted lips and the changing patterns of her pleasure were visible on her face. The sight of her growing aroused worked a magic of its own on him. "Why is it important?" he whispered roughly.

"Because—" She opened her eyes and caught his hands. "Because I want to tell you the truth."

Remembering what Sir Leonard Dent had told him, Fox looked into her eyes and knew the last thing he wanted at this moment was to know the whole of her relationship with Prince Dragonetti.

Maybe, it was the last thing he ever wanted to know.

"Don't talk." He pulled her tightly against him, letting her feel his arousal.

Her hands on his chest, she pushed as far back as his arms would allow and shook her head. "I must tell you. Then, you will understand why I have done much of what I have done."

Fox pressed his erection harder into her softness. "This is the only truth between us." He moved against her. "Feel the truth?"

She groaned, and he kissed the tender skin of her jawline and sucked lightly on her earlobe. As she shivered, he growled deep in his throat, "I understand all I need to know, Sweeting. I understand that you like this."

Catching her nipple again, Fox tweaked it lightly as she gasped her pleasure. "And I think you'll like this." Bending, he laved the sensitive peak with his tongue. He felt her fingers in his hair, pressing him to her breast.

Chuckling at her eagerness, he nipped the taut bud with his teeth. She arched and shuddered, moaning softly as he continued the assault.

"You do like that, don't you?"

"Yes. Yes. It is…this is as nothing I've ever experienced before."

At her words, hot blood surged in his loins. It could be that the prince had never aroused her fully or brought her to climax.

"That is all the truth I need to hear. And this is all the truth I need to feel." Taking her hand, he kissed the palm, then brought it between them. Pressing it to the front of his satin knee breeches, he guided her fingers over the hard length of his shaft.

Her eyes were wide and luminous. "It is longer than my hand."

He laughed softly and she moved her hand up and down the length of it, and it was his turn to gasp. "God, yes. Like that. Touch me, Sweeting."

Fox found her mouth, plunging his tongue inside again and again, thrusting with his body in rhythm to her strokes. Closing his eyes, he was certain that he'd never felt anything as sensual as her fingers wrapped around his manhood, stroking him through the satin material.

But he hadn't been inside her yet.

At the thought, a jolt of need shot through him and a tingling ache began. God, he'd wanted her so long, so badly, it might end before it started. His every muscle rigid, he fought for control as he caught her hand, stilling her strokes.

"Be still or I shall disgrace myself."

"I can feel the heat of you through the satin," she said in wonder. "And you are so big—" Her eyes grew uncertain.

Tenderness wrapped around his heart. Bringing her hand to his mouth again, he kissed her palm once more, then sucked her fingers, one at a time, all the while watching the passion showing in her heavy-lidded eyes. "I want to see you."

Slowly, he pushed her nightgown the rest of the way down her arms and watched as it slid down her body and puddled at her feet.

Her skin was soft beige, splashed with honeyed shadows by the firelight, shadows that defined her narrow waist and the soft flare of her hips. Her legs were long and well-shaped. A thatch of curls the color of a new copper penny nestled at the apex of her thighs.

"You are a goddess."

He knelt, pressing his face to the softness of her stomach, Fox slid his hands over her rounded buttocks and down her long legs, wanting to touch every inch of her, to memorize the warm satin feel of her skin, her smell—lavender and woman. Memories to sustain him through the long time ahead. Time without her.

His fingers found the puckered scar from the bullet wound on her thigh and he kissed the imperfection.

"Fox," Ari tugged his arms, urging him to rise. "I want to see you, too," she said in a rush, before she was overcome by shyness.

He obediently stood, and she slipped his dressing gown from his shoulders, marveling at how wide they were, how the bunched muscles felt beneath her hand. The white bandage stood out starkly against his darker skin. She combed her fingers through his hair and smoothed her hands over his smooth chest, avoiding the white linen strip tied around it.

"Is your wound healing?" How could she have forgotten about what had brought her here in the first place? It seemed Fox was right. That was not the real reason she had come.

"Yes."

"You are certain? I mean, there is no redness or, or a bad smell?"

"Are you trying to cool my ardor?"

"I am not," she returned, blushing for no reason she could name.

"No. My shoulder is healing. There is nothing that will prevent me from loving you." His gray eyes glimmered darkly. "Except that you've left my breeches buttoned."

Biting her lip, Ari turned her attention to undoing the buttons. Swiftly, before she could think about what she was doing, she pushed his breeches down his lean hips and muscular thighs, drawing a sharp breath as his shaft sprang free. Long, rigid, the same light tea color as the rest of him, it was as magnificent as the rest of him.

Ari stared, fascinated by the forbidden sight. A virtual forest of black, straight hair was at the base of his shaft. And she had been right about his balls. No little chestnuts, these.

Fox stepped out of the breeches, then caught her hand and drew her to him until their bodies touched. "You look unsure. Don't be."

Looking down to where her pale breasts were pressed against his darker chest, Ari mused that he was a perfect contrast to her, darkness to light, fire to shadow. Her nipples tingled at the contact with his skin and warmth washed through her, pooling between her thighs.

Fox smoothed his rough hands down her back and over her buttocks, cupping them and pressing her closer to his erection. "Tell me what you want," he murmured near her ear.

"You," she said simply, knowing as the words left her lips it wasn't true. She wanted more. She wanted for this night to be only the first. To spend a lifetime in his arms.

But those things could not be hers. So, she would snatch this little happiness while she could, and then later, she would have this memory to hug to her heart.

"Only you." She sighed.

He pulled back, the look in his eyes growing soft. "I wanted you the first moment I saw you aboard *The Dancer*, even as you aimed a pistol at my heart." As he spoke, he smoothed his hands up and down her back, creating a fission.

"Were you mad?" Ari closed her eyes. His touch warmed her, relaxing her, and at the same time, filling her with anticipation of where those strong hands might venture next.

"You were magnificent. Standing there in only a nightgown, and that torn and covered with blood, your wonderful hair floating on the wind. But there was steel in your eyes. You had come to find justice. Or make it. I admired your courage. Admired you, even as I wondered which of my sins had found me out."

And I envied the man that you'd loved so dearly you would have died to avenge him.

Growing restless, she turned her face up to him and parted her lips for a kiss. As his mouth claimed hers, Ari knew Fox was right. Here was truth. The only truth that mattered — the feelings that flamed between them.

Cupping his face between her palms, she gave herself up to the narrow reality of this man, this instant, sighing as the world spun away.

He kissed his way down her neck to her collarbone, pausing to lave his tongue into the hollow before moving on. Then cupping her breast, Fox brought her nipple to his mouth.

As he suckled, pleasure washed through her and need. Her head fell back. "When you do that, I feel so strange."

Slipping his hand between her thighs, cupping her nether lips, Fox found her hot and moist and ready. He parted her nest of curls and touched the tiny nub hidden there, rubbing gently as he continued to suckle her breast.

Gripping his shoulders, Ari cried out, wondering what was happening to her. She would explode, she was sure of it.

Quitting his delicious torture of her nipple, Fox straightened, watching her face as he teased the tight bud of her passion.

"Do you experience more than one orgasm?" He wanted to believe he was right in his earlier guess—that she hadn't experienced the true wonder of loving a man.

Her eyes opened and she wet her lips. "I…have yet to experience one."

His face went still. Growling deep in his chest, he promised, "You're about to."

"How can you know?"

"I'm going to make certain of it." His mouth found hers again, and she believed him.

This was the sweetest pleasure she'd ever experienced. Ari clung helplessly to him as his fingers worked magic. His fingers and mouth left her shuddering and helpless as they worked their magic.

And wanting more.

Hot, liquid need was building inside her.

This was the Benoit madness, she realized. The taint of madness all Benoits seemed to bear. Her ancestors had proven it time and again, throwing away reputations and fortunes, even their lives, for love. This was why her grandfather had abducted one of the Hapsburg princesses. Why Ari's own father had married a baker's daughter and, when the love of his life died, he'd stepped off a balcony and plunged a thousand feet to his death, unable to conceive of life without her.

The Benoits did not just fall in love, they were consumed by it.

At last, Ari understood. Too late.

Fox pulled away and taking her hand, guided her to the bed.

"Lay back, Sweeting."

She obeyed. After she'd lain back on the bed, he spread her legs and knelt between them. Firelight gilded his wide shoulders, his dark hair. His face was shadowed but his gray eyes gleamed as he smoothed his palms over her thighs, spreading them wider.

Fox combed his fingers through the moist curls. "Ah, Sweet, you're beautiful here, too." He positioned her legs over his shoulders and slipped his hands beneath her, cupping her buttocks.

As she felt his warm breath on her most private parts, a tiny prick of alarm rang in her head. "Fox, what—"

He thrust his tongue into the heart of her, tasting her musky warmth. She was hot inside, the lips of her womanhood swelling, inviting him to do more. He thrust his tongue into her again and again, lapping at her juices, exploring the soft folds as deep as he could reach.

Gasping, Ari gripped the sheet, transported to a different plane. Heat coiled deep within her, building, growing tighter and heavier. What was this wondrous feeling? This possession? She had thought herself sophisticated, that she knew about sex. She *had* delivered babies, after all. But as she experienced this wild possession, she knew now she had not understood at all. *Mon Dieu*, this was why there were so very many babies born!

Fox groaned into her hot sheath as she pulled his head closer, urged him to stroke his tongue deeper. The vibration of it sent wild pleasure coursing through her. He pressed his mouth hard against her hot opening, stroking his tongue as far inside her hot, musky folds as he could reach, then he pulled back and laved her clitoris.

Ari bolted half-upright as pleasure convulsed her middle. "*Mon Dieu!* What did you do?"

Fox circled her tight sheath with his tongue and then stroked and suckled her clitoris.

Gasping, she touched where his tongue had just played, finding the sensitive nub.

His eyes gleamed darkly as he watched her fingers. "Play with it, Sweeting."

She obeyed, amazed as her own finger sent pleasure shocks through her. She had known that this little nub was sensitive, that sometimes when she rode a horse it caused a sweet ache. She had had no inkling of the possibilities. Dipping his head again, Fox licked her clitoris while she touched it at the same time, sending unbelievable waves of pleasure through her.

His assault made her a creature of carnal need. She was certain she had to have more. And just as certain more pleasure would be more than she could bear.

When the first pleasure convulsion took her, Fox took over for her, pressing his thumb to the sensitive nub as he raised his head and watched her face. Wave after wave crashed over her and through her, stealing her breath and lifting her to a place where there was only sensation.

He continued to massage the sensitive nub with his fingers until the last shudder left her. Then, smiling, he lay down beside her and he cradled her to him. He kissed her forehead. "Now, you have experienced orgasm. How did you like it, Sweeting?"

She touched his cheek with shaky fingers. "I never knew —"

Running out of words, she turned into his embrace and kissed him, finding a musky taste on his lips and tongue. Realizing it was her own juices she tasted made heat surge through her again. She pressed closer, deepening the kiss, and the still hard shaft of his desire was like a brand against her abdomen. As she continued her kisses, she slid her hand between them and stroked the length of his shaft.

He tore his mouth from hers. "Pray, don't," he said thickly. "You aren't ready for more, not yet."

Feeling a renewed quickening at his words, Ari licked his lips. "I might be."

There was still an emptiness inside her that hadn't been filled. She sensed that the warm steel and velvet she held was the answer to her need. It would give her something more even than the glorious sensations she had just experienced. "I want to feel you inside me." Still holding his member, she felt him leap at her words.

Rising above her, he parted her thighs with his knee.

Instinctively, she widened her legs as she felt the tip of his shaft touch her center. She drew in a shaky breath as heat and need again coursed through her.

Holding his weight on his arms, he looked deeply into the blue pools of her eyes as his shaft eased into her a little. God, she was wonderfully tight. Never had he wanted a woman so intensely. Never had a woman so thoroughly fired his blood. His hard cock urged him to drive into her tightness, but he held himself in check, watching her expression of wonder as he possessed her slowly, inch by creamy inch.

Dark and half-closed, her eyes reflected her wonder. Her breath rasped between her parted lips, and he couldn't resist her mouth, kissing her as he thrust deeper still...and met an unexpected barrier. Freezing, Fox stared down at her. Every muscle in his body screamed for him to thrust harder, to sever the thin wall and take what she offered.

His brain screamed that she had lied. Again.

Lost in a perfect dream, Ari struggled to grasp what was happening as he suddenly broke off the kiss and held rigidly.

"You're a virgin!"

"I know."

"Damnation!"

She felt him pulling out. Whimpering with need, Ari caught his shoulders, wrapping her legs around his narrow waist in invitation. "Do not stop. Please."

"I told you, I wouldn't hurt you." The words were gravel. His arms trembled as he held himself over her. His features were twisted with the battle he waged within himself.

"I need you inside me." Ari tilted her pelvis, surprised to feel him slip deeper. She bit her lip as sensations sparkled through her. "Nothing has ever felt so right. Nothing, *Mon Dieu!* Not even…before with your tongue…and lips."

Catching a ragged breath, she thrust upward again, this time pressing onward as she felt a tiny stab of pain.

Fox's face twisted in stark lines. It was the face of a man at war with himself.

Losing the battle, he moved inside her.

"Please — yes!" Ari caught her breath as he moved again. Suddenly, he was fully, gloriously sheathed inside her. She scarcely absorbed the sensation before he pulled almost all the way out, then filled her again. "Oh, yes. Please. *Please.*"

Her cries became wild and intelligible as, with strong, sure strokes, Fox brought them both to shattering climax. She clung to him as they exploded together.

Afterward, Fox rolled onto his back and cradled Ari, stroking the damp tendrils of hair from her forehead. "Are you all right?"

She smiled. "I am perfect."

Thick lashes drooped and closed. Her head was cradled at the hollow of his uninjured shoulder, her hand on his chest, fingers splayed against his skin. Kissing her temple, he tasted her salty perspiration. He felt an incredible tenderness well up inside him.

Followed closely by boiling anger.

A virgin.

She had deceived him yet again.

"Then we need to talk, *Comtesse.*"

Chapter Thirteen

ରେ

She was perfectly still for the space of a heartbeat. Then, thick sable lashes fluttered and opened. Ari sat up, drawing the sheet around her protectively, her blue eyes wary in the uncertain light cast by the fire.

"How long have you known?"

His anger grew. "More to the point, *how long have you*?"

"Fox, I wanted to tell you before…" She made a vague gesture that encompassed the bed.

"How long?"

"Almost from the beginning," she admitted softly, scooting farther away from him, and wincing slightly as she did.

Guilt stabbed his conscience as he saw her look of pain. He'd taken her maidenhead—and she'd given it freely.

Did that mean anything? That he could trust anything she said? He started to reach out to her, but let his hand drop. "So, all this pretty nonsense about not remembering Dartmouth, or who you are, was deception."

"No. I do not remember Dartmouth, or trying to harm you. That is the truth. When I awoke, Kilpatrick kept asking me questions about Dartmouth, but I could not answer—I still could not answer them if you asked. When he suggested I had a memory loss, I thought it might buy me time to get away."

Once again, looking into his eyes, Ari thought of moonstones. Hard. Cold. Without compassion.

Where was the tender lover who had carried her to the stars just a few moments before? Where was the caring she'd felt in his touch, in how he'd held her? It had been an act, part of his seduction of her, she thought bitterly. Yes, and she had been all too eager to be seduced.

Hot tears threatened but she blinked them back, refusing to let them fall.

"You've made me into the greatest fool in creation." He got off the bed.

"I was afraid for my life. I thought you a—" Realizing what she was about to say, she clamped her teeth together.

"What?" he demanded, leaning nearer, pinning her with cold gray eyes. "What did you think?"

"I thought you a murderer," she said quietly. "Dolpho and I traced Dandelion's trail from Whitehall to Devon. You are active in Whitehall and Devon. Dolpho had forged contacts with the smugglers who are forced to be unwilling pawns in Dandelion's games. All evidence pointed to you, though Dolpho was unconvinced, I was certain. Then, the militia—"

She shook her head. The memory made her tremble. "*Mon Dieu*. They came with the storm." She closed her eyes, drawing in a deep breath as she relived the confusion and fear of armed men breaking down the door, angry shouts, the thunder of musket fire, and jagged lightning splitting the night as though hurled by an avenging God.

"Dolpho…by the cliff's edge, I tried to stop the bleeding. I tried, I tried. His life's blood ran between my fingers. I could not stop it." Reliving the terror on top of her hurt was too much. Tears wet her cheeks, and she swiped at them angrily. "He begged me to find you. He made me promise. I thought he was naming you as his murderer."

"You thought I was Dandelion?"

"I thought you a murderer. See, we had managed to take a horse and were almost away. But there was a tall man with a gun by the lane. I saw him in the lightning flashes as he fired." Ari caught Fox's hand, willing him to understand. "You were the one we had concluded Dandelion to be. I thought the killer was you. As I was trying to stop his bleeding, Dolpho said your name. I thought he had recognized you, had gotten a better look than I had. So, I swore to him that I would find you and…and *that* is all I remember before I awoke at Stonerose."

Fox was quiet for a space, her pain touching his heart against his will. "You awoke, injured, vulnerable in what you believed to be the lair of a murderer—you must have been terrified."

"I was *not* pleased."

"I can understand your actions in that situation. It's why you've continued with the farce that puzzles me. You could have left."

Ari smiled bitterly. "While Toby and Ben were watching me, I plotted to do just that, but I was hampered because I was still healing. Before I could leave, you returned. I soon realized your concern for my wellbeing was real, not a ruse. And that your actions were at odds with who and what I thought you were."

His face darkening again, Fox said, "After you knew I wasn't a French spy, you still continued with the farce. Even after I guessed you were the woman from the cottage—*why*? Couldn't you trust me?"

"No."

Fox sucked in a harsh breath. "I see."

"I take leave to doubt it." Ari told him. She still couldn't tell him all of it. If what she believed was true, then she had more than herself to consider, now. She hugged the warm hope to her heart.

Smoothing the sheet between them, she said, "I am without family in England, without money, and wanted by the Crown as a spy. I still might find myself dancing on a gibbet. I thought to protect my neck and family name from the scandal."

"Your family name? If avoiding scandal was so important, what were you doing in the wilds of Devon looking for a French spy?"

Ari glowered. "There is no point in talking to you."

"Which means you have no answer."

"I was in disguise when—"

A precipitous knock, then a groaning of unoiled hinges cut her off. Ari put her hand to her mouth as a panel beside the fireplace opened inward. "*Madre de Dios,*" she whispered through her fingers.

Julien stepped through the opening. His clothes were dirty and ripped, and there was a bloody cut at his temple and a purplish bruise around his right eye. Looking from Fox to Ari, he whistled softly, then frowned and touched his split lip.

"What the bloody hell is the meaning of this?" Fox stood.

"Sorry to intrude. I heard your voices and knew who you were entertaining, Fox, but I had no idea you were, ah, entertaining." Julien's gaze moved to Ari, one dark winged brow, so much like his brother's, rising.

"Damn." Wincing again, he touched the cut on his forehead and stared at the blood on his fingers. "Bloody sod used a belaying pin."

Having Julien burst in and witness her shame was beyond enough. Wishing she could just sink into the mattress and disappear, Ari clutched the sheet more tightly about herself as she felt a blush suffuse her whole body. It had been mortifying enough that Fox had made love to her then turned on her in anger, when she'd only wanted—

What?

What had she expected? An avowal of undying love? No, that would have been beyond the realm of possibility. Perhaps just tenderness and then she could have pretended that he cared. Tenderness would not have been too much to expect, would it?

Feeling fresh tears threaten, she stiffened her spine. She'd been thoroughly disabused of her illusions, but she still had her pride. She would not cry again.

Fox's expression was thunderous as he started at his brother. "Turn around, or I'll bloody well turn you around."

Grinning lopsidedly, Julien complied. "I don't blame you for being upset, but this really couldn't wait, not even for rapture."

Fox grabbed his dressing gown from the floor and put it on and brought Ari her nightgown. "I am sorry," he told her, the look in his eyes sincere.

Summoning her dignity, she ignored him and pulled the gown over her head. Standing, she began to work the tiny buttons closed.

"Your fingers are shaking. Here."

"*Non*." As he reached for the buttons, she turned, avoiding his help. How dare he, to point out that her fingers were shaking—he was beyond unspeakable!

When half the buttons were done, Ari gave up and moved around Fox. She snatched up her slippers and shawl, barely pausing to don them before heading to the door and escape.

Fox stepped into her path. "This isn't finished, Pal— *Arielle*."

Lifting her chin, she squared her shoulders. "Do not make so much of it, Fox. I was only satisfying my curiosity."

Stunned, he stared at the door after she'd closed it behind her.

Julien picked up the iron kettle from the hearth, touched the side and shook his hand. He splashed the water into the basin atop a low bureau, grabbed a cloth from the basket Ari had left and wet it. "Ah, that feels better," he said, pressing the cloth to his split lip.

"Why are you here?" His hands clenched at his sides, Fox glowered at his brother.

"She's an incredible woman, you know. I owe her a debt for saving your miserable life. So, if you're only toying with her, I'll have to take it upon myself to—"

"Talk. You wouldn't have come in secret at this hour if it wasn't important. That's the only reason I haven't given in to the urge to punch you in your other eye."

Julien chuckled, then sobered. "You're right. I would not have come. Deveril from High Hill Farm came down to the stable at noontime and told Billy Freeman the French schooner had signaled just before dawn. Now, it was only a few days ago that the French ship came, when you and I surprised Dandelion as he was meeting with the French colonel. It's unlikely the ship would have been back this soon. Also, fog was as thick as cotton wool this morning before dawn, so I took leave to doubt that Deveril could have seen a signal lantern from the Channel. So we trussed him up like a Christmas goose and left him in the tack room."

"A trap?" asked Fox, finally able to pull his mind away from the hurt in Pallas' blue eyes.

Not Pallas. Comtesse D'Ambois. He would do well to remember that.

"Yes." After rinsing the cloth, Julien applied it to his eye. "A trap. But we were the ones to spring it." He grinned, then winced again. "Damn." He touched the cloth to the split on his lip again.

"I daresay you will live," Fox told him. "What happened?"

Julien told him of how they had paddled the boats to the mouth of the creek to Gemscove, they'd found an impressment gang waiting instead of their friendly French smugglers. A British naval schooner was sitting in the waters off nearby Goat's Head. Because he'd suspected a trap, Julien was prepared with two boats filled with armed men. After a brief fight, the Jack Tars had taken to their boats.

"The only casualty was Billy, who suffered a broken leg. I left him in his grandmother's cottage with a dose of laudanum and his two younger brothers and I came to tell you what transpired. Now the laudanum should have had time to take hold, I must go back and see that leg set properly."

"I will make inquiries and find out what I can about who arranged this, but I have little hope of uncovering anything." Fox removed a key from a large ring and gave it to Julien. "Here. One floor below is the study. There is a derringer in the right drawer of the desk. Take it, and keep it with you. I feel this is just the beginning. When Dandelion finds out he hasn't gotten rid of the smugglers who can testify as to how he's been operating, we may expect something more from him. Put the word out, no more smuggling and every man stay close to home."

"Fox, smuggling is a way of life here. It's not likely the men involved will pay attention to your edict, even though you are their lord."

"Aye, you are right. With England's Corn Laws, who can blame them?" Fox knew on some less prosperous estates, smuggling often meant the difference in men feeding their families and seeing them hungry. "Just tell the men the earl hopes that there will be no 'midnight enterprises' until Dandelion is brought to justice. They have not liked being used by the spy and now he has turned on them, trying to have them impressed. I think they will agree to it."

Julien nodded. "Be careful, yourself. One attempt has been made on your life. There could be another." He paused. "I want to know something. You called her 'Arielle'. Have you given our goddess of wisdom a new name?"

"Her old one. Arielle Benoit, Comtesse D'Ambois."

"Ah." Understanding spread over Julien's features. "How long have you known?"

"She has known from the first. A connection of the Hapsburgs, and a noblewoman in her own right." Fox tried to keep his expression bland, but bitterness crept into his voice.

"Are you angry because she knew and spun you a Banbury tale? Or because she's of noble birth?" Julien asked.

"This is none of your—"

"Ah, but I made her my concern when she saved your miserable life." He shot Fox a challenging look. "And I hope you don't believe that nonsense about curiosity. A woman of her mettle doesn't give the gift lightly." Julien moved to the bed and tossed back the covers. A smear of blood against the whiteness of the rumpled sheet gave silent testimony to what had transpired.

His black brows drew downward, and he leveled an angry gaze at Fox. "I heard you arguing. That's why I thought nothing of entering uninvited. My God, man, if she had given me such a gift, I would have held her tenderly afterward and reassured her of my caring. You took her in disfavor because, by accidents of birth, she's nobility and you're a cuckolded earl's bastard son."

Long after Julien had gone, Fox stood with his hand propped on the mantle, staring into the dying flames. His brother was right. She had given herself freely, not using her body to bargain, though in truth, her future was far from certain.

And he'd been a perfect ass.

* * * * *

Chilled by more than the cool air of the hall, Ari hugged her shawl about her as she returned to her room. How could he act so cold? After what they had shared—had it meant nothing to him? Was it only lust that he'd felt for her?

Of course it was. She'd been a fool to imagine it was more.

After slipping inside her room, she closed the door. But as she turned the key in the lock, the skin on the back of her neck prickled. Someone was there, behind her. She was certain.

Ari started to turn, but a hand clamped over her mouth and dragged her backward against a hard chest. Making angry noises, she struggled wildly.

"For God's sake, *Cara*, do not scream," a familiar voice hissed by her ear.

Every muscle in her body went still, except her heart. It tried to leap from her chest in joy.

The hand was removed from her mouth.

"You are dead," Ari whispered, afraid to believe.

"Not bloody likely."

Ari spun around and threw her arms around her cousin's neck. "*Cher bon Dieu.* I held you as you breathed your last." Tears sprang to her eyes.

Someone lit a candle. Ari was vaguely aware it was the maid, Molly Bailey, but her joy at the miracle she was hugging overshadowed all else. Dolpho, alive! The idea he might be had begun to niggle at her after she found her letter to Stubby written over, but she hadn't dared to hope. Not really.

"I am not a ghost, *Cara.*"

"I do not believe it. Let me look at you." She took a half step back. As she looked him over, her joy was suddenly tempered with concern. He was thin. Too thin. And as pale as the old white shirt that floated about him. He might have been a stick scarecrow in a farmer's field. Only the spark in his sherry brown eyes remained of the old, insouciant Dolpho. Ari cupped his face between her palms.

"Where? How—*merde!*" Tears choked off her questions. After the humiliation and disappointment she'd just endured, finding Dolpho alive was soothing balm to her lacerated heart.

She was no longer alone.

Dolpho grinned. "I thought it time to come out of the wall."

"So, it was you." She hit him, her tears flowing harder, then she hugged him wildly. "It was you pushing the cork out of the wall. Scribbling on my letter. I thought I was losing my mind."

He looked contrite. "I have been very bored. I thought the note would give you a clue. But you always were a little slow on the uptake."

"When I saw my note to Stubby, I did not know what to think. It was as though you reached out from the grave to protect me—but the handwriting was only a scrawl. Not yours at all."

"I did take a ball in the shoulder not long ago. Makes writing a bit difficult."

"I wanted to tell you, Milady." Bailey stepped forward. "But Rudy said it would be for the best not to. See, we didn't rightly know if 'e'd get better or not for the longest time, what with 'is shoulder getting right infected an' all. It took all of me Gram's skill to bring 'im through. And then you didn't seem to know who you were anyway, so there didn't seem any point. When I told Rudy you couldn't remember yer own name or anything, 'e was right worried about you. 'E insisted on coming 'ere so 'e could watch over you, though Gram was sure it would do 'im in."

"You stayed in the wall?" Ari turned to him.

"And a very warm little nook I had, with the chimney going into the crawl space providing heat. Molly would bring me food, or I'd go down to the kitchen at night. Besides keeping an eye on you, I didn't want to stay at the Freemans' any longer than I had to. It placed them in danger of arrest. You know, Ari, that we are wanted by the Crown?"

"I know."

"After reading the letter what you wrote to some viscount, Rudy finally guessed you were 'umming it, Milady—and a right good job of it you did, too. I was sure you'd lost your memory."

Catching the maid's work-roughened hand, Ari squeezed it. "Thank you for taking care of him. I can never repay you for what you've done."

"Oh, but it was me pleasure, Milady. Besides, you've always been kind to me." Molly looked at Dolpho, who smiled warmly, causing the little maid to blush. "And I don't think of it as needin' repayin'."

"You are too kind, my sweet." Dolpho pulled the maid close and kissed the top of Molly's mobcap.

Ari was struck by the intimacy of the gesture, but there were too many other things to ponder right now to give the act any thought. "But how did you get here to Stonerose?" she demanded of Dolpho. "You must know I would not have left you, I would never have left you, if I had known you were still alive." Ari crammed her knuckles in her mouth as she realized what she'd done, leaving him alone to die.

Dolpho sighed. "Forgive me. That is why I had to deceive you. I knew if I did not, you would be foolish and stay. Making you believe I was dead was the only way I could protect you. It was all I could do for you.

"And what did you do after my sacrifice?" he asked incredulously. "You try to shoot a peer of the realm. What brought about such madness?"

It seemed the night for explaining her actions. "I thought it was Grandquest by the lane, the man who shot you. I know now I was wrong."

"Ah." Understanding glinting in his eyes, Dolpho shook his head. Then his gaze darkened as he looked her up and down. "And where have you been tonight?"

Aware of her disarray, Ari clutched her shawl together over her half-buttoned gown and squared her shoulders. "That is none of your business."

"What has Grandquest done?" he demanded.

She stamped her foot. "What I do is my own concern."

Dolpho shook his head. "I could see he had designs on you, but I thought you were too wise to be seduced by the blackguard. I will call him out."

"And you are a fine one to talk. The intimacy between you two is obvious," Ari said, looking from him to the housemaid. "Dolpho, how could you? Bailey is hardly more than a child."

"I beg pardon, Milady, but I am full-growed, though a mite short, to be sure. Nineteen years old, I am, and married the last four years past," Molly asserted. "Though I never lived much with my Tommy, 'im being a soldier and all. 'E was with Wellington on the Peninsula, until 'e was listed as 'missing' last spring. Anyway, to answer you, it was me brother, Bill, who found Rudy. Bill, 'e's one of the 'gentlemen' if you know what I mean." Molly shot Ari an uncertain look, as though wondering how much she should tell.

"Billy was my contact with the smugglers," Dolpho supplied. "When the militia was searching for us, they disrupted Billy and his friends, who were busy bringing some very fine French brandy ashore. As Bill was running away, he came across me."

"When Billy recognized Rudy, he brought him to our Gram's."

Dolpho's arm circled Molly's shoulders and gave the girl an affectionate hug. "Her grandmother is a 'Wise Woman,' knowledgeable about the local herbs and plants—but we will talk more about this later. Now, I need for you to help me repay Billy's kindness. He has a broken leg and needs your help."

Molly said, "Gram would 'andle it in a thrice, but she's visiting me sister in Cornwall. Sally's first is nigh due and it's a great comfort to 'ave Gram there."

"Is the bone sticking out?" Ari asked in dread. Such breaks almost always had to be amputated. She wasn't up to that. "And has anyone gone for Dr. Kilpatrick?" Going to the wardrobe, Ari dug out her patched maid's dress and old brown cloak.

"No, me brother who came to fetch me said the bone's not showing, thank goodness. But 'tis swelling and in sore need of being set before it gets any worse. I'd do it, only I never had the stomach to learn Gram's ways," Molly said, worry puckering her brow. "As for the doctor, Billy won't 'ave the man near 'im. Not since the doctor shaved old Mrs. Greenpear's 'ead and put a 'ot mustard plaster on it to treat the palsy, and 'er three-and-eighty!"

"Smart man, your brother. Molly, if you would not mind, help me to dress? Dolpho, wait in the wall. I shall be ready in a moment."

Chapter Fourteen

ఌ

A knocking at her door awakened her and Ari forced her eyes open. "One moment, *s'il vous plait*."

Propping on an elbow, she sleepily caught the bed curtains and jerked them open. Yawning, squinting into the still dark room, she saw by the light filtering around the drapes drawn over the windows it was well past dawn. She yawned again, wanting to roll over and go back to sleep, until she remembered why she was so tired. What she and Fox had shared had been the most beautiful moments of her life.

And what had happened afterward had been dark and devastating.

But her hurt was soothed somewhat by the discovery that Dolpho was alive. Rolling onto her back, Ari hugged her pillow and smiled up at the canopy. Her cousin was alive, and she wasn't completely alone anymore. That knowledge was balm for her battered heart.

There had been some tense moments last night at the Freeman cottage, where she and Dolpho were confronted by Julien. But all had worked out well when she'd reminded Julien of his pledge to aid her. He hadn't liked it, but he'd agreed to keep the fact that Dolpho was alive a secret. Then working together, she and Julien had set Billy Freeman's leg.

Keeping Dolpho a secret was the only logical course. She'd told Julien what Sir Leonard had said at dinner about damning evidence being found in the cottage—evidence that she assured Julien was false—and Julien had understood. After the real spy was caught, they could return to their lives.

Ari ran her fingers through her tangled hair, wondering why she hadn't braided it before bed. Another memory surfaced — Fox, kissing the strands. Warmth surged within her as she remembered him naked and beautiful, remembered the way the long, sinewy muscles of his back and shoulders had felt under her hands, the tightness of his buttocks, his powerful thighs.

His shaft filling her.

He'd taught her of love. As they'd merged, all her being had focused on that one perfect moment. She bit her lip, echoes of their passion chasing through her, making her breasts tingle and a warm heaviness settle deep inside.

It had seemed perfect. It had seemed more than a merging of bodies, but a blending of souls.

But that had been an illusion.

Naïve, that was what she was. Naïve as a schoolroom miss. She had confused his desire for caring. Oh yes, she had yielded readily, greedy for the fulfillment he had brought her. She could not regret it, she realized in surprise. How could she regret the most perfect thing she'd ever experienced in her life, even though it had been illusion?

But now she was wiser, she fully understood the dangerous power a man wielded over a woman. The power to seduce. The power Fox had wielded over her.

She'd only come to her senses when he'd called her by her name.

And how had he learned her name, when only Dolpho and a French agent had known it?

No, she would not tease herself with that, not now. Fox was not Dandelion. There was some other explanation of how he'd learned who she was.

The knock sounded again. "Milady, it be important."

Reluctantly, Ari got out of bed and opened the door.

The maid, Littleburn, bobbed apologetically, her face creased in concern. "Pardon, Milady, but the earl, he sent me to get you. It's his wound—he said tell you it's suddenly very bad."

"His wound?" Ari put her hand to her throat. "Yes. Yes, of course. Please go to the kitchen and bring a kettle of boiling water and a cup of salt. Oh, and a fork. Let me see, is that all? Yes. Yes, hurry."

The maid scurried away.

Going to the dressing table, Ari found a brush and began working the tangles from her hair. *Merde*. She should have taken care of his shoulder last night instead of his male needs. If she had, he would not be ill this morning.

Fear made her hurry with her toilette. Ari donned the same patched maid's dress she'd worn the night before. When Littleburn returned with a kettle, Ari was watching for her. "Come. Hurry."

"Please wait up, Milady," the maid begged as Ari's long strides made her rush to keep up. "The water will spill."

Fox's door was open. As Ari entered the bedchamber, she found him gazing out of the window, his face somber. The Chinese red dressing gown was draped over his shoulders. His posture was tense—from pain? Ari wondered, alarm tightening her throat.

"I trust you slept well," Fox said without turning. His voice was ragged.

The pulse hammering in her throat increased its speed. "Please sit, Fox."

He glanced at her and complied, seating himself in the wing-backed chair where she had last dressed his shoulder.

Ari found her basket where she'd left it the night before and moved it to a small table beside his chair. As she snipped the band of cloth at the top of his shoulder, he stared through the window where a blanket of white pressed against the glass.

Her hands shook as she cut off the dressing. "You are in pain?"

"I do hurt."

As Ari peeled away the dressing, her dread increased with each layer she opened. When at last it was uncovered, she stared at his wound uncomprehendingly. The cut was pink and closing.

"This does not look infected. I do not see how it would cause you such pain." She searched his face and was caught by the unexpected need in his eyes.

"The pain isn't from that wound, but one nearer the heart," he said softly. "I fear one that is self-inflicted."

Looking away, Ari blinked back tears of relief. The shoulder wasn't infected at all, but healing well. He was in no danger.

Relief was quickly replaced by anger. Oblivious to the presence of the maid, she declared, "I have a strong urge to hit you for frightening me so."

"Please, no." A light flared deep in his eyes and he smiled. "The last time you did, my jaw was sore for a week." He touched her hand, taking the old dressing from her fingers and tossing it in a basin Littleburn had placed on the floor for the purpose.

A thrill skittered up Ari's arm from the point where his fingers made brief contact with hers. The scent of his shaving soap was faint and tantalizing. She tried to ignore both. "I do not remember punching your lordship."

"Fox. Don't we know each other too well now for there to be formality between us?"

The deep timbre of his voice vibrated through her, bringing a flood of warm memories. Yes, she knew him well. She had stood with him, flesh to flesh, her nipples pressing against his warm chest. She had felt the thrill of his big hands cupping her breasts, his fingers dark against her lighter skin. She had seen the wonder in his eyes as he sheathed himself in her, again and again.

Ari sucked in a sharp breath as echoes of sensation coursed through her stomach and heat pooled low in her abdomen. *Mon Dieu*, he did that so easily. It would not do to let him know *how* easily.

Biting her lip, she schooled her face into a mask of indifference. "I came to tend your wound. Not to discuss how well we know one another." She draped his dressing gown over his left shoulder and across his wide chest, with well-defined pectorals, covering as much as possible from her view, while leaving his injured shoulder free.

The memory of smoothing the red silk dressing gown from his body, discovering the texture of his warm bronze skin came to her unbidden. Putting her mind firmly on the task at hand, she poured the steaming water from the kettle into the basin and added a large amount of salt.

"Would you pretend we have shared nothing of importance?" Fox asked in French. "What are you afraid of?"

"So, you do speak French. I wondered," she said in the same language.

"We have things to talk about, and using French is the only way to have privacy." He glanced at the maid hovering at Ari's elbow. "I wish to apologize. My behavior was bad." His face grew grim. "I was an ass."

Ari shrugged, biting the inside of her lip again. What he said had hurt. But it had returned her to her senses. "I can understand your anger, but not that you didn't let me explain when I had come here to tell you everything. Where did you learn my real name?" Using the fork, she carefully dipped a pad of cloth into the steaming basin, then held it, letting the excess water drip back into the pan.

"I was afraid of what you would say."

She was aware that he didn't answer her question. "That seems a feeble reason."

"I thought you would tell me you were in love with Dragonetti."

Ari studied his face, lean and starkly sculpted, almost harsh in its beauty. Strength was in the set of his jaw and the steadiness of his gaze. Afraid? Ha. She doubted he'd ever been afraid in his life. "I do love Dolpho," she said at length.

Fox was perfectly still for the space of a heartbeat, the muscles bunching at the hinge of his jaw. He looked away. "I see."

"No, you do not. I love him as you love Anne. As a brother. Dolpho and I grew up together. *Château Nuage* was a lonely place. Dolpho, my cousin, was also my only friend."

When the pad had cooled enough, Ari wrung the excess water from it. "This is going to sting," she said, switching to English. "But I am happy to see the cut is healing well. I should not have to tend it again." She met his gaze, making her meaning clear.

"I think I shall need your care for a very long time," he assured her, speaking in French.

Be still, you foolish heart. It beat as though it would fly from her chest. Her fingers trembled as she pressed the hot cloth to his shoulder. She hoped he would not notice.

What he wants is a mistress. Nothing more. Even if there should be love– The thought was too terrible to finish. Far better that he should only desire her, than to love her. To have him love her would be unbearable.

"There is so much about you I want to know." His voice was deep and soft. "Tell me about St. Cyr. What was your life there like?"

Ari shrugged, keeping her gaze focused on what she was doing. "There is not a great deal to tell. The château is very isolated, especially when the deep snows of winter shut it off from the world. There was little to do but learn. So, I attended classes with Dolpho. *Grandpere* saw to it that Dolpho was educated as befitted a prince, certain he would someday regain his throne. He had seven tutors and other instructors who taught fencing and boxing. There was even one from Greece who taught us wrestling using the whole body. That was what I demonstrated to your brother." Ari smiled as she remembered Julien's expression, until her gaze met Fox's. There was an intensity there, a hunger that was unnerving.

She dipped the pad again and focused on his wound as she held it to his shoulder. "I learned everything I could about everything. *Grandpere* had many learned friends, professors, intellectuals. Whenever some would stay at the château — it was convenient to those traveling between France and Austria — I would sit and listen to them talk for hours, discussing philosophy, art, history."

"An exotic life." He imagined her as a young girl in pinafores and braids, sitting in on classes in Latin and Algebra, her quick mind soaking everything up.

Somehow, it was a lonely picture.

He understood now the sense of loss that must have overwhelmed her at Dragonetti's death. And he felt a surge of relief that the prince had been a friend, not a lover. "Did anyone warn you that society looks down on intelligent women?"

"How do you feel about them?" Ari had decided a long time ago that she didn't care a whit if society looked askance at her for her brains. She was already looked down upon her for the taint of shop in her background and the streak of madness in the Benoit line. So, she had pleased herself and learned all she could.

"I find one very intelligent woman more captivating than I could ever have imagined." He caught her gaze, his eyes dark and intense. "I want to take my time and unravel the mystery which is Arielle, to discover all her secrets, what makes her smile, what brings tears to those lovely eyes."

She looked away, stoically holding the pad to his shoulder. Gazing at her averted face, Fox wondered again about her words from the night before, as he'd wondered countless times during the sleepless night.

"I was curious."

Was Julien right? Had her pride caused her to say that? Or did she view what they had shared as part of her education?

"Where did you learn your healing skills?" he asked, unwilling to dwell on the possibility. Fox frowned as he noticed a streak of dust and cobwebs on the skirt of her dress. More mysteries. Where would she have gotten that? It looked as if she had been in the tunnels.

Ari soaked the cloth again, then wrung it out and reapplied it, never meeting his eyes. "My mother and father both died when I was quite young. I took on the role of chatelaine at an early age." Her voice was emotionless. "I helped our old housekeeper tend the sick and injured. When she retired, the new housekeeper had little knowledge, so she helped me—I was about twelve. The château was very isolated, as I have said. If someone was sick or there was an accident, it had to be dealt with, so I learned all I could about stillroom skills. I did not want someone to die because I lacked the knowledge to help them.

"When *Grandpere* saw I had an interest in medicine, he invited his friend, Dr. Keiss, retired from the University of Munich, to stay at the château one summer. Dr. Keiss taught me much about the inside workings of the body. A brilliant man, he did not believe in bleeding at all, and only used leeches to treat blackened eyes and bruises.

"During the time he was at the château, a scullery maid had an accident with a knife, driving it far into her thigh and the bleeding would not be stemmed. I knew nothing about cauterizing. The poor girl would have bled to death but for Dr. Keiss. He showed me the technique for cauterizing the artery without sealing the wound. So you really have Dr. Keiss to thank for your life."

"Thank you." Fox smiled. "After your being so long a mystery, your open sharing of your life is like having the lid to a treasure box opened and seeing the wonders within."

Ari fumbled in her basket for the tin of bascillicum powder as she gathered her thoughts. How could he say she was a mystery when he'd known who she was? Clutching the tin, she demanded, "How did you know my name?"

He was silent for a moment. "I'm not at liberty to say."

"I see." She felt he was hiding something.

Silly goose, she admonished herself, he's hiding nothing of import. Just a contact he does not want to reveal.

Like Stubby?

The thought chilled her and she pushed it away. No, not Stubby. Fox was not a murderer. Not a French spy.

After applying bascillicum powder, she said in English, "Littleburn, you may wrap the wound."

As Ari turned to leave, Fox caught her arm.

"Don't."

The word vibrated from deep in his chest.

Ari looked down at his fingers circling her wrist below the frayed cuff of her dress. How easy it would be to lie to herself, to believe he felt more for her than desire. But that would not make it true.

Keeping her expression neutral, she asked in French, "What?"

He answered in the same language. "Do not put this wall between us. If you are honest, you won't deny your feelings. If there's nothing else," he said, an edge of bitterness lacing his words, "there's passion."

Something like pain flashed in her lovely eyes, gone too quickly to decipher. It was replaced by a hot spark of anger.

"If you were honest, you would tell me how you know my name. As for passion, passion is not enough."

She pulled free of his grasp and left.

Fox damned the presence of the maid. It had prevented him from pulling Ari down on his lap and kissing her until she gave in to all the feelings she was hiding.

Strangely, he agreed with her — passion was not enough.

But it was a damned good place to start.

Chapter Fifteen

ဢ

Ari closed the door of her bedchamber and leaned against it. How had Fox known her name?

As suspicions, like serpents, raised their heads, she wanted to throw herself across her bed and weep. But that would bring no answers.

Drawing in a deep breath, she moved to the wardrobe and chose a day dress and tossed it onto the bed. After stripping off her gray maid's garb, she poured water into the washbasin and performed her morning ablutions. A slight soreness at the apex of her thighs reminded her sharply of the wonder she had found in Fox's arms...

Illusion.

All illusion.

When he'd taken her to his bed, he thought her Dolpho's mistress—had he not admitted as much by his surprise when he found she was a virgin?

But how did he know my name?

Slipping the dress over her head, she decided to go back to Fox's room and demand answers. If she did not, her suspicions would grow and fester. It was past time for games. She was sick to death of this subterfuge.

A light knock sounded at the door. "It's Coventree, Milady."

"Enter, please."

Ari struggled to do up the back fastenings of the day dress as the maid entered. Seeing Ari's difficulty, Coventree set the silver salver she carried down on the bedside table. There was a crested card upon it. "'Ere, let me, Milady."

"What have you there?" Ari turned and gave her access to the back of the garment.

As the maid did up the row of tiny hooks, she said, "Lord Myre sent up 'is card, Milady. 'E's waiting in the drawing room, and he begs the pleasure of your company."

"Lord Myre?" Ari frowned as she remembered the man's interest in her bosom the evening before. "Ah, I should have known he would." It would soon be time for her to meet Geoffrey for the chess game she had agreed to, and she intended to speak with Fox first. Before she had time to change her mind.

"Pray tell Lord Myre I am indisposed."

"Very good, Milady."

After Coventree left, Ari tidied her hair then donned a light shawl. As she studied her reflection in the cheval glass, she stuck out her tongue. Her image mocked her, doing the same.

"Pudding heart." *Merde.* It was one thing to make a resolution about boldly demanding answers. But suddenly she was not at all certain she wanted to know.

"Pudding heart, indeed," she murmured again as she closed her door. Gathering up her courage, she went to Fox's bedchamber. She would find answers. Or at least, have all her questions out in the open.

Her hand on the door latch, Ari paused outside his door as she heard voices within.

"What do you mean, Deveril's gone? How?" Low and angry, Fox's voice came to her through the stout mahogany door.

"It's bloody apparent what I mean. He's gone. I went to the tack room to give him food and water, and he was gone. The ropes I used to bind him were on the floor. Someone had cut him loose."

That was Julien, she realized.

"Someone cut him free."

"That's bloody apparent, too," Julien said dryly. "I put the stable lads to searching for him before I came to tell you."

"We must find him before he has a chance to give the game away."

"We will find him and alive," Julien said darkly. "I want to know who he's been taking orders from."

Ari jerked her hand away from the latch as though burned. Who was this Deveril? Why had Julien held him bound? What game was Fox worried about this Deveril giving away?

Non. Non. It could not be.

An ill feeling rose in her throat, but she shook her head, denying the obvious possibility. As silently as she could, she hurried back down the hallway, intent on finding answers.

The first step was to find out as much as she could about Stubby's death. Downstairs in Fox's study, she quietly closed the door behind her and searched through the stack of newspapers on the desk. She found several articles concerning Stubby's disgrace and then suicide. Shaking her head as she put the last down, Ari could hardly credit that Stubby had betrayed them. He had seemed so warm and genuine. But she had the scar on her thigh as proof, did she not?

And if she had been fooled by Stubby, might she not be fooled by Fox?

Non. She would not believe it.

But the kernel of doubt that had taken root as she listened to Fox and Julien just moments before now became a fist clenching her insides.

Non. Think. Think. You must prove Fox's innocence…

Or his guilt, a little voice whispered.

Pulling open a drawer, she quickly searched its contents, finding nothing of import. Most of the papers were receipts from workmen and tradesmen concerning the estate.

See, there's nothing here, because Fox is not a spy, she told herself.

The next drawer yielded a piece of folded vellum, the red wax seal on which was broken. The seal was still recognizable as Fox's crest. Ari unfolded it and read, and her fingers shook. Cold washed through her as she reread the Earl Grandquest's orders to Captain Phips to arrest her and Dolpho as French agents.

"There you are, my dear," said a cultured male voice at her back. "I thought it was you I saw flit past the parlor doors."

Her heart leaping into her throat, Ari gasped and stuffed the vellum into her bodice and spun around.

Looking smug, Lord Myre closed the door and strode nearer. He was every inch a dandy, with shirt points reaching nearly to his cheekbones and an elaborately tied cravat under his rather weak chin. Tight pantaloons left little to one's imagination, as though he was proud to display what he had.

"I believe, sir, I sent word by the maid that I would not see you this morning." Ari drew herself up.

"Seeing to Grandquest's needs, were you?" Myre stopped far closer to her than was proper.

She would have stepped back, but was trapped by the desk. "You are rude."

The young man grinned, unabashed. "I have to hand it to Grandquest — he has cheek. Putting his mistress up in his house, then bringing in his sister to give the hum a semblance of propriety." He chuckled, his gaze on her bosom. "Of course, I didn't believe that farradiddle Lady Anne invented for a moment. It's obvious you were the prince's whore, and now he is gone and you have turned to Grandquest for protection." He touched her breast.

Ari slapped his face, the smack resounding loudly.

"By God!" Myre grabbed her neckline and jerked her to him.

"This is beyond enough!" Shoving with all her might, Ari sent the young lord sailing back into the bookshelves. He hit it with a solid and very satisfying *thump.*

"Why you…" His face red, he started for her again, but the bookshelves behind him swung open with a shriek of unoiled hinges, drawing him to look back.

"Good God." Ashen faced, Myre leapt aside as a body tumbled out.

Ari put her hand over her mouth.

* * * * *

A circle of onlookers waited, their faces grim. Fox nodded and Julien turned the body over, and suddenly all the air seemed to have been sucked from the room.

Ari put her hand to her throat. A gaping gash crossed the man's neck. Blood saturated the front of his coat, soaked the forearm of one sleeve, and stained his hand. The other fist was clenched. A hot, sick feeling rose in her chest and she looked away.

"Deveril," Julien said, drawing her attention back to the body.

"This is the man you were looking for?" As soon as the words left her mouth, Ari realized her mistake. She shouldn't have known they were looking for someone. Meeting Fox's gaze and seeing the accusation there, she cried, "I am not a murderer!" She sank back on the edge of the desk, her legs too unsteady to hold her weight. "I am not."

"No one has suggested you killed this man. To suggest a lady such as yourself could look a man in the eyes and pull a trigger, or drive a knife home, would be absurd, wouldn't it?" His tone was soft, but his fists were clenched.

Ari understood that he spoke for the benefit of Lord Myre and the servants present.

"Thigpen," without taking his gaze from hers, Fox addressed the footman, "escort Lord Myre to the parlor and see that he has brandy and send someone for the constable."

"Cleese," Fox commanded the other footman, "close the door and stand guard outside it until the authorities arrive. Let no one enter."

Pale and shaking, Lord Myre left. The door closed behind him and the servants. Only Ari and Julien and Fox remained. Fox turned to Ari, his face a bronze mask except for the white lines of strain bracketing his mouth. "How did you know we were looking for this man?"

"You would not believe me."

"That, at least, is the truth." The bronze mask cracked, revealing his pain. "Why did you kill him? To silence him, to keep him from betraying you?"

"I did not kill him. Or anyone."

"Enough." He moved closer as he spoke. "I'll have the truth."

Squaring her shoulders, she stood ramrod straight. "I did not kill him."

"Fox, this man has been dead for some time. He's going stiff. She didn't kill him." Julien rose, holding something up to the light. "This was in his hand. It's a copy of your signet ring seal."

"There was dust and cobwebs on the skirt of the dress she wore this morning. She had been in the tunnels. She could have cut Deveril free then and cut his throat."

"No." Ari trembled, hating the look in his eyes.

Ignoring her protest, Fox took the stamp from Julien and held it beside the ring he wore on his finger. "No doubt, this was used to seal the fake letter from me to the militia captain. A seal is easy enough to copy."

"False letter? How is it false?" Unconsciously, Ari touched her bodice where the damning letter rested. The parchment crackled, sounding loud as thunder in the quiet of the small study.

Merde!

"What have you there?" Fox held out his hand.

"Nothing." She shook her head.

He caught her neckline and reached into her bodice, drawing out the parchment sheet. His frown deepened as he looked it over.

"Is this what you were looking for last night? Dent and I must have inconvenienced you by being here in the study."

"No. I was not searching for that."

"What were you after, then?" he asked darkly. "Weren't this letter and Deveril the last two links that had to be gotten rid of before you were safe? I've never thought the prince was the spy. If he had been, all activity would have stopped at his death. And it bloody well hasn't. There was another courier murdered last week. By God, now I understand why the murders and espionage continues. It has been you, all along, orchestrating it even while under my roof."

"No." Her vision swam with unshed tears, but she forbade them to fall.

Catching her shoulders, he stared at her, shaking his head, and then his hands turned gentle, caressing. *"Why?"*

Daring to look up, Ari saw hopelessness in his eyes matching that which she felt.

"Why?

"If I was this villain, why would I have written a letter to Captain Phips ordering my own execution? Why would I have gone to Dartmouth to find you, believing you were the one who sent them to kill us?"

Fox straightened, obviously unable to argue with the logic of what she'd said.

"I am not a murderer...and neither are you!" Hope bloomed within her at the realization. Fox had not killed Deveril. His and Julien's early conversation was proof of that. He'd had no notion of where this man was.

Someone who feared exposure had murdered him.

"*Mon Dieu*, I feel as if a thousand stone weight has been lifted from my heart. It is not you. It is not you!" She hugged him fiercely.

"Stop it." His voice was a rasp. "No more of your games."

"You're wrong," Julien said. "She did not kill him."

"Wrong?" Fox looked at his brother. "Where would she get that smear of dust and cobwebs except in the tunnels?"

"It was a gray dress she was wearing, wasn't it?" As Fox nodded, Julien expelled a gusty breath. "Then, yes, Ari was in the tunnels last night. She went with Molly Bailey to the Freeman's cottage and helped me set Bill's leg. I escorted her back myself, through the tunnels."

Hope lighting his eyes, Fox touched Ari's cheek, smoothing a path across it. Voices rose in argument beyond the door, one of them the well-modulated tones of Lady Anne. Moving to open it, he told Julien, "Take Ari to her room, then try to trace Deveril's path before the authorities arrive."

Julien nodded. "I wonder why he came here? He could have disappeared once he was free."

Fox paused, his hand on the door handle. "We might never know." He went out to talk to Lady Anne.

Julien held out his arm. "Milady?"

Feeling suddenly weak, Ari leaned on his strength and they left the study. Much too distraught to endure Anne's questions, she was grateful, as she passed them in the hall, when Fox caught Anne's arm and told his sister to let Ari rest.

"Thank you for coming to my defense," she said as she and Julien climbed the stairs.

"If you prove me wrong, I'll place the noose around your pretty neck with my own two hands."

Ari was taken aback. "Your faith in me is not misplaced."

Julien was silent until he had opened her door and surveyed her room, then nodded to her that it was all right to enter. "Deveril was killed by someone inside the manor.

Frankly, I trust no one completely, save Fox. And there is the matter of just how you knew who Deveril was and that we were looking for him." He folded his arms, waiting for an answer.

"I listened at the door of Fox's bedchamber when you and he were talking. A bad habit." She shrugged. "I plan to give it up for Lent. But, no, the poor man was not killed inside the manor."

"What do you mean?"

"You saw the same things I did. The gash was long, but not deep. The jugular was probably nicked, but not severed." Sitting on her bed, Ari twisted her hands together, her stomach going queasy again as she recalled the grisly details. "Do you remember how blood covered the front of his clothes, but there was only a little on the floor behind the bookcase? I feel certain he was attacked elsewhere and came in the manor seeking help, but died before he could find it."

"Dandelion," Julien said.

"Dandelion," Ari echoed. "If the letter to the militia captain is a forgery, then he neatly took care of the threat from Dolpho and cast suspicion on Fox. Brilliant." Something teased her about the name, Dandelion. Ari shook her head, at a loss, too exhausted by the day's events to focus properly.

Julien looked thoughtful as he moved to the door. "Lock this when I'm gone."

"Thank you for keeping your silence about Dolpho. I am grateful that you are a man of your word."

Julien paused at the door. There was a disturbing light in his ebony eyes. "Don't be too grateful. It occurs to me that, although I'm certain you didn't kill Deveril, Dragonetti had every opportunity, didn't he? What Fox said made me think — if the prince was the spy, all activity should have stopped when he died. But Dragonetti isn't dead, is he?"

Cold washed through her. "*Non*. You saw him last night. He is far from well. You could not believe he is guilty."

"He wheezed like a consumptive and looked as though a strong wind would blow him away. Yes, that gives me pause to think he could not overpower a strong man like Deveril. And the man we observed wading through the marshes the night before Fox was stabbed was tall and athletic. And he was also hooded. Also, there was no blood in the tack room, just the severed ropes we had bound Deveril with."

"As I told Fox, if Dolpho is the traitor, who then set the militia on us in the cottage? We did not betray ourselves."

"Deveril might have done that. He had the fake stamp."

"Deveril?" She placed her fingers at her temples and rubbed in small circles. "You are giving me a headache. If Dolpho was the spy, why would Deveril betray us? Deveril was working for the spy."

Julien shrugged. "Deveril may have been trying to break free of Dandelion's hold."

"That is all speculation. You are not going to tell your brother about Dolpho with so little hard facts—say that you will not!"

"I gave you my word. I have never broken it. But if I find further evidence pointing to the prince, I will have no choice. This murderer must be stopped."

After Julien left, Ari locked the door. Then she moved a heavy wingback chair in front of the hidden door by the fireplace. It seemed everyone in Devonshire knew about Stonerose's passages.

She sat down upon the chair, exhausted. What a coil. Suspicion had come full circle. Unless she could find evidence of the real spy, Dolpho was at risk.

Only one thing gave her reason to rejoice, Fox was not the murderer.

* * * * *

Later that day, Ari stared out the window of the parlor. The fog had hung on all day and was now growing ever thicker. The clipped scrollwork design at the opening of the yew hedge maze thirty feet away was barely discernible. The men tramping about the gardens and the manor had finally gone. Lads from the stable had been brought in to scrub the study. Anne had told her there had been mention of calling in the Bow Street Runners to investigate, but the sheriff of the district had taken umbrage and the plan had been abandoned.

Ari had visited the Freeman cottage to fill Dolpho in on the events. News of the murder had beaten her there. Dolpho sat brooding and quiet throughout her visit. When questioned, Molly had blushed and confessed that Dolpho was with her the whole night and morning.

But how much weight would Molly's word carry if Dolpho was put on trial? Little, Ari feared.

"Beg pardon, Milady."

She turned and found Molly, who had accompanied Ari back to the manor, just inside the door. In her starched apron and mobcap, Molly was the very picture of a proper maid.

"The earl's requested to see you in your bedchamber." Her voice dropped and she glanced over her shoulder as she continued, "He's 'aving all the passages closed and the secret doors nailed shut. Thank God, the prince is gone from 'ere."

Fox stood by the fireplace as Ari entered. She tried to ignore the warm leap of her heart as he looked up from the flames and met her gaze. "You wished to see me?"

"Yes." He felt a tightening in his chest as he watched her move toward him, her carriage regal. Something warm wrapped itself around his heart when she smiled. God help him, it was the same whenever she came into a room.

Her gaze went to the large space revealed through the open wall panel.

"Someone has been living in there." Thinking of some man hiding, watching Ari as she dressed or slept filled him with impotent fury. "If I ever find out who..." He left the sentence unfinished.

"You will what?"

She looked up at him, her eyes wide and luminous. He had the strangest feeling she hid a smile.

"Never mind what. Why aren't you upset? This might have been anyone."

"Yes," she agreed. "It might have been anyone. A murderous fiend or a guardian angel."

She watched in silence as Cleese removed a flint and tinderbox, several candles, a tin canteen of the type used by soldiers, and three empty wine bottles. Then the footman swung the wall panel shut and began to nail it closed.

"We will secure the loose paneling we found in the hall also. Whoever was hiding here worked it free of the moldings and was using it as an access to the rest of the house. It seems I should have taken Geoffrey's tale of a ghost disappearing into the wall more seriously."

"Hmmm. After all that wine, I can see why he loosened the hall panel. He probably required access to the privy." Ari smiled.

There was nothing in her attitude to indicate she'd discovered a murdered man only a short time before. Fox studied her sparkling eyes, unwilling to dwell at the moment on why she wasn't more upset at this new discovery.

"Forgive me. I should have listened to you when you told me you had the feeling of being watched." Catching a tendril of burgundy-auburn hair that had escaped from her coronet, he smoothed it behind her ear and brushed her cheek. Her skin was warm velvet.

"Yes, you should have."

"I am learning not to take what you say lightly. If I underestimate you, it's because I've had no standard to measure you by." He took her hand, and turned it over, running his thumb over the light calluses on her fingers—how would a noblewoman acquire calloused hands? "I'm sorry for the accusations I made earlier. Trust doesn't come easily for me. And you've not been exactly forthright. But I shall endeavor to give you my trust from here on."

"Oh, you dare not trust me," she cautioned, her eyes gleaming. "That would be foolish, indeed."

Almost as foolish as loving you would be. He stared at her coral-pink lips, the words echoing loudly in his mind. God help him, he cared too much already. He knew his pledge to trust her was given because he was desperate to believe her innocent.

But what if he was wrong?

The knife and signs of a struggle Julien found in the entrance of the tunnel by the creek showed Deveril had not been attacked in the manor, but she could have killed the man in the tunnel.

No, he didn't want to believe that....

Discovering Dandelion could reach at will into his household and do murder had tilted his world, made it very unsteady. The old feelings of rage and helplessness he'd endured when he was a boy resurfaced. Everyone he loved was at risk. And he was more frightened than he'd ever been when Henry had been laying into him with a cane.

"My lord, I think I do trust you. Just a little. But not in all things."

Her lids drooped and her eyes darkened, drawing him into their depths, caressing him. As the footman banged another nail into the wall, Fox cursed the man's presence, wishing he could take her right here, right now. Back her against the wall, lift her skirts, and possess her totally and completely — and perhaps that would lift the dark thing that had suddenly perched in his soul.

"Anne will be beside herself. I must go reassure her again that we are not all to be murdered in our beds." Holding her gaze, he added softly, "Tonight..."

Her gaze dropped to his bronzed hand engulfing her own, apricot roses bloomed on her cheeks. She pulled free and hurried away.

Leaving him with his doubts as he went to find Anne.

* * * * *

The big clock in the great hall below bonged eleven times. As it ceased, the house was quiet again. Oppressively quiet. Ari curled up in the wingback chair, staring into the dying fire. The grisly discovery in the study had placed a pall over the household as thick as the fog that had persisted over the garden all day. As the tones of the clock died away, it was as though the house held its breath, waiting for what would happen next.

Her thoughts were going in circles, and all circles came back to Dandelion. She tried to focus her mind on the spy, on fitting the pieces of the puzzle together. There was a key there, somewhere. She sensed it…but whatever it was eluded her.

And Fox kept slipping unbidden into her mind.

"Tonight," he had said.

Did he think, now that they had been together, she was his for the taking?

What they'd once shared had been magical, and deliciously carnal and satisfying, just to leave her hungry all over again. The Benoit madness. Oh yes, she craved being with him again, being flesh to flesh, feeling him fill her, as an addict craved opium. To love was to be possessed.

But her season in Vienna came to mind. It had taught her who she really was in the eyes of society. Ari remembered the hot humiliation she'd felt when she'd let the baron, whom she fancied herself in love with, into the rooms she and Dolpho had rented, believing he was seeking to be alone with her in order to propose. He was smooth and experienced, and his kisses had excited her. When his hands had wandered to her bodice, she had been entranced by the feelings he engendered.

Until his drunken friends grew impatient and pounded on the door. They'd asked if he was finished yet and was he going to be a good sport and give them a turn.

Von Bohr had laughed at her outrage and told her she surely couldn't have had expectations of marriage—no nobleman in his right mind would align himself with one of the Mad Benoits. Turning her to the cheval glass, he commanded her to look—she was pretty enough, but tall as an Amazon, drenched in shop, and a raging bluestocking in the bargain. What gentleman would want her for a wife? He went on to say that he would choose a wife whose background was impeccable and who never wanted to discuss politics or science, and who'd never pretend an understanding of either. A wife he could be proud of.

Using the heel of her hand, she'd broken his arrogant nose.

The last log on the fire burned through, broke into two pieces, and fell off the andirons. An unburned end rolled down onto the glowing embers and a new blaze sprang to life. Remembering Fox's touch on her cheek made tenderness well inside her. And remembering the promise in his gray eyes as he'd told her "tonight" made her shivery and warm at the same time.

Non, she told herself firmly. She must not let him in—she was not glancing at the door in anticipation.

But when a light knock sounded, it was anticipation that skittered through her.

She opened it with trembling fingers.

Fox stood in the dark hall. He wore only a white shirt, which was half-unbuttoned, exposing his chest, and leather breeches that fit his slim hips like a glove. His face was cast in shadows as he held out his hand.

"Come."

Chapter Sixteen

∞

"*Non*. No." Ari took a step back. If she did not end this now, where would it end? With her ensconced in a house in St. John's Wood, like the other mistresses of the *Ton*?

His eyes gleamed like liquid silver. "Then I will come in." He stepped inside and closed the door firmly behind him.

Slowly, his gaze moved from her ankles upward. He lingered on the flare of her hips and the swell of her breasts.

"You are not welcome in my room." Ari placed her hand on her heart, annoyed that it had doubled its tempo under his perusal. He had touched her with no more than his eyes. Did she have no control at all where this man was concerned?

The answer was an obvious "No". The Benoit madness was in her blood, urging her to seize the moment.

He searched her face. "Are you afraid?"

The question caught her off guard. "I am not afraid. Not of you." It was the truth. She feared her own emotions where this man was concerned.

She did not believe he would hurt her. Not on purpose.

"You weren't afraid when you showed me your fire last night. Why are you now?" Fox wrapped her in his arms, and slid his hands gently over her shoulders and down her back, bringing her body fully against his. "You seduced me so thoroughly, though I realized you weren't terribly experienced, I never guessed I was your first. Forgive me. I should have been more gentle."

"Is that why you grew angry that I was a virgin?" The memory of him moving within her turned her insides into aching heat.

"I was angry because I am a fool. I thought you something, and you proved me wrong—as you have done every time I think I have you figured out." The scent of lavender filled his nostrils and he buried his face in her hair, finding it freshly washed and still damp. The tresses felt cool to the heated skin of his cheeks. "What we shared was perfect. The most perfect thing I've ever known."

Ari considered this. So, she had not been the only one awed by what they'd shared. She hugged the knowledge to her heart. It warmed her. But she couldn't let the knowledge weaken her resolve.

His hands were doing too good a job of that!

Beneath his stroking hands, Fox gradually felt her relax and press closer. She felt so right against him, her soft curves fit perfectly against his hardness. He murmured, "Why are you afraid now? What has changed?"

"I did not understand the danger then. Now, it is all I see." She pushed at his chest until he released her and went to stand before the fire, rubbing her arms as if suddenly cold.

"Danger?" Fox stood behind her, near but not touching. That she would be arrested because of Anne's story about her? As if he could let that happen…

"You will not understand. You are a man. It is natural for you to conquer, but I…I do not like being out of control, a puppet to another's will." Ari drew in a deep breath, achingly aware of his closeness. When in his arms, she felt so cared for. Cherished. And therein lay the real danger. Of needing Fox too much.

His passion was real, but his tenderness was just part of his lovemaking, not love. She didn't doubt him—he'd said their lovemaking was special to him—but no matter that, he hadn't given his heart.

He didn't trust her enough for that.

If it was only just his lovemaking she craved. Ari sighed. "Now, I know what it means to be seduced. Powerless. You fill me with need so hot I can think of nothing else. *Non*, I cannot think at all!"

"Maybe it would be best if neither of us think." Pulling her back against him, he pressed the hardness of his erection into her softness.

"I must touch you." His voice was a throaty rasp near her ear. His big hands gently cupped her breasts, kneading and stroking, and her nipples hardened under his clever fingers. "You think I somehow have more choice than you do, that I can resist this heat between us. Yes, I could resist you but, first, I would have to resist breathing."

He caught her nipples and gently squeezed through the cotton muslin of her nightgown. She arched back, showing her pleasure.

"All day, even with all that's happened, hot memories of what we shared has filled my mind, making it difficult for me to concentrate on anything else. I understand you were merely curious. Aroused and wanting to know what happened between a man and woman. I understand. But, Ari—"

"No." Ari twisted around in his arms and placed her fingers on his lips. "Oh, no. I was hurt when I said that stupid thing. You were angry because I lied to you about knowing who I am, and I—"

He silenced her with his lips, a gentle tasting of her mouth and bent his head and rested his forehead against hers. "I was wrong to lash out at you. I regretted it the instant those words left my lips, and I would have told you so…but my brother has exquisitely bad timing."

"Yes, that he does." Ari gazed into his eyes. The flames of the fire were mirrored in their dark gray depths. What she saw there made her shudder, and she circled his waist with her arms. Fitting her head beneath his chin, she pressed her cheek to his chest. Feelings roiled within her. Dark and unknown. She had a strong urge to turn and run. But she knew with helpless certainty she wouldn't.

He wrapped his arms around her, drawing her even closer. *Mon Dieu*, and her desire for him…

She was powerless, again. Unable to resist the need to be one with this man. Mad as any of the Benoits before her. An addict—and after just one taste.

"Is that all you are afraid of? That you will lose control?" he asked, his voice, a soft rumble in his chest beneath her ear.

"I want you so much, I am afraid I will disappear. Be swallowed up by my own need, and nothing else will ever matter again. I don't like being out of control. Weak."

"You aren't weak." Fox slid his hands down her back and cupped her buttocks through the thin cotton barrier of her gown. When he'd seen Deveril's body, when his gut had wrenched in the belief that this woman had killed a man, a chasm had opened up at his feet and his whole world had teetered on the edge, ready to tumble in. When it came to this woman, he was certain of only one thing—she was not who or what she seemed. She was smart enough and strong-willed enough and cunning enough to be the lynchpin of the French spy ring. And, God help him, there was more evidence that said she was than said she wasn't.

All that had saved his sanity was remembering her wonder as they'd joined, her enthusiastic responses to his touch, his lovemaking, and her wonder and untutored caresses as she explored his body.

He had introduced her to passion.

"It's your strength I find the most beautiful thing about you. It's your strength that fires my blood, makes me stand in my pants every time you walk into a room. And, at times today, the strength of passion we shared last night was all I could be certain of," he said honestly.

"This cannot be wise."

"Not at all wise." Fox framed her face between his hands and turned it up so that she was forced to meet his gaze. The intelligence gleaming in her expressive eyes, the satin of her skin, her sweet breath—these things and a thousand others combined to strip him of his ability to resist making love to her.

"No." She shook her head as she read his intent in his eyes.

"Yes." He held her gaze, lowering his mouth to hers with deliberate slowness. He needed to feel it, that he held this power over her, at least. Her body hadn't lied when he thrust into her, feeling her heat, her muscles convulse around him.

"No—" she said again. The syllable was lost in his mouth as his lips melded against hers, hot, knowing, sending quivers of reactions between her thighs. Fox thrust his tongue deep inside her mouth, stroking it in and out, in a rhythm as old as time. Moaning, she met it with her own, toying with it, tasting, stroking, matching its carnal dance.

Ari breathed deeply, savoring the faint smell of bay rum mixed with that scent that was particularly his own. Needing more than the kiss, she pulled away and found the strong column of his throat, nipping it lightly, tasting his skin, as she ran her hands over his shoulders, loving his heat and hardness and the sheer size of his body. He made her feel small and fragile. He made her feel complete, and, at the same time, as though she could never be complete without him.

Oh, Fox was dangerous! He made her forget that her life and all she held dear was perched on a knife's edge. Dandelion was still at work and no nearer to being unmasked than before. He'd killed a man practically within the manor. No doubt, his intent had been for her to be blamed. As she nearly was.

The cambric of Fox's shirt came between her and the warm skin she wanted to explore. With a feminine growl of frustration, she tugged at it, impatient to have it off.

His hands shaking, Fox jerked the shirt free of his breeches. Without regard for the carved bone buttons or the finely stitched buttonholes, Ari ripped it open and stripped it from his shoulders, leaving his warm bronze skin exposed to her hands and mouth. Kneading. Touching. Tasting. She felt she couldn't get enough, and Fox stood still, enjoying it as she had her way.

As she wrapped her arms around him, she pressed her breasts tightly to his naked flesh and lightly raked his spine with her nails.

"Damn." Every muscle rigid, Fox sucked in his breath. Ari tilted her head back, her gaze, passion-drugged but curious. Watching him closely, she again raked the shallow valley in the middle of his back. Again Fox went rigid, his expression so intense she couldn't tell if he was caught in the throes of pleasure or if he was in terrible pain.

"Witch. For a novice, you have learned quickly." Holding her chin, he stroked the satin of her bottom lip with his thumb, watching her eyes darken.

"Then you like it when I touch you?"

"I bloody well like it."

A small smile twitched her lips. Sly blue lights gleamed in her eyes and she bent her head and surprised him again, applying her lips and tongue and teeth to the skin below the linen bandage crossing his chest.

Watching her, her mouth moving over his torso, Fox was frozen by what she was doing to him. Until her hand found his erection. As Ari stroked him through the leather pants, his blood became liquid fire.

"God's blood." Gripping her shoulders, he wanted to pull her more tightly against him, encouraging the exquisite torture.

He needed to push her away, before he lost all control. How could she fire his blood so, when they'd been together only the night before?

A savage ache beneath her stroking fingers urged him to put her down onto the bed and take her swift and hard.

No.

For all her boldness, she was surely tender from their lovemaking last night.

And continuing to give Ari her way was a small return for her exquisite gift. In giving herself to him, she had given him her trust. At least, for that moment in time.

Her mouth moved to his flat male nipple. She grazed it with her teeth and sucked it, her hand continuing to stroke and squeeze.

"Enough." He caught her hands, forcing her up against his chest, quelling her wild assault. "Hold still." It was a dark plea.

His every muscle seemed tensed, his face twisted into hard lines. Ari felt power. Feminine power. Heady and primitive, it surged through her and she smiled.

An imp whispered in her ear, and she swiveled her hips against his arousal. "Or what?"

He held rigid for the space of a heartbeat, silver lightning in his eyes. It struck her. Searing her. Arcing a path of liquid heat through her, turning her molten and quivering to her very core.

His breath left him all at once, as if he'd been holding it through some crisis. Then catching her nightgown at the collar, he ripped the buttons through the buttonholes, much as she had done with his shirt.

"Or this."

Her breasts tingled madly as the cool air hit them, the peaks, already tight coral buds. Fox's breeches followed her gown to the floor and his penis stood, taut and ready.

Suddenly Ari found herself beneath him, her legs spread by his thighs. Her hands were held above her head as his weight and heat and hardness pressed her down into the mattress.

Shifting her wrists into one hand, he freed the other and touched her breast, cupping it, kneading it. She arched helplessly against him. As his fingers found the coral bud and flicked it, she bucked and writhed, moaning for him to enter her.

Unable to delay a moment longer, he released her hands and positioned himself at her opening. Slowly, inch by hot, creamy inch, he pressed inside. Her muscles tightened, quivering and caressing him as if she welcomed him home.

Ari clung to him as he moved. She sighed when he was fully sheathed and wiggled her hips. Fox slipped his hands beneath her and tilted her hips to better advantage. Suddenly, he was even deeper.

And moving.

Writhing and whimpering, she urged him deeper, harder, faster. Lightning sizzled over her skin, and though her, then again, shooting sparkling pleasure through her core.

As her fingers dug into his buttocks, he held himself up on stiffened forearms, his satyr's face, dark above her, and he watched her pleasure. He swiveled his hips in another deep thrust, and suddenly she was falling through blackness, then lifted up on his next thrust to become a shooting star.

"Sweeting. Yes. Hold nothing back." His voice came to her from far away.

After one last surge into her, his release came, hot and hard. A pleasure more intense than he'd ever known possessed him, convulsed him, consumed him.

Arielle wound her arms around his neck and drew him down to her. She became his only point of reference as he was lost in her exploding heat.

* * * * *

When Fox opened his eyes, the fire had died to faint embers and the room had grown chilled. A stub of a candle spluttered on the bedside table, giving off uncertain light. It was enough to show Ari half-draped over him, her head pillowed on his good shoulder and her glorious hair spilling over his chest. Tenderness filled him as he remembered the power of their lovemaking. Nothing in his life had ever been as perfect.

And perhaps nothing ever would be again.

Secrets clung to her like the scent of lavender, pooled in her cerulean eyes. Secrets, which he knew instinctively were dangerous, or she would not keep them from him at this stage of the game.

But what? What was so terrible she could not tell him?

Fox gently stroked her hair. Her body was pale against his dusky bronze skin, her warmth pillowed against him. He asked himself, wasn't that part of what fascinated him, her mystery? The danger he sensed? She had laughed and assured him he dare not trust her. Had that been a deeper warning than he knew?

His head didn't trust her. Only his heart.

Careful not to wake her, he caught the satin coverlet and flipped it over them, watching her sleep until the candle sputtered out.

* * * * *

"So sorry to disturb you, Milady. I knocked twice but—" Molly Bailey stopped short. One hand on the door handle, the other moved slowly to her mouth, her eyes rounding.

Awakened abruptly by the maid's intrusion, Ari sat bolt upright. Cool air hit her naked breasts, and she looked down in surprise and jerked the covers up to her chin.

And then she realized she was not alone.

Sprawled beside her, his naked back exposed from the waist upward, his dark head cradled on his arm, was the Earl of Grandquest.

"Merde."

His face was turned away from Molly. Twitching the covers over his head, Ari congratulated herself on her ingenuity in preserving his identity.

Fox came awake, rolled onto his back and sat up. His dark hair was tousled, his bronze chest, completely exposed except for the bandage crossing it.

All male and magnificent.

Looking at him, Ari forgave herself her weakness. And Fox had shown her that she had power over him. The knowledge was heady, and she hugged it to her heart.

Eyeing Molly darkly, Fox ran splayed fingers through his hair. "Bloody hell."

"I'm ever so sorry, My lord. Milady. I really didn't — ought not 'ave — oh, 'cor me. But I really shouldn't ought to 'ave come in 'ere a'fore you called permission." She backed for the door.

"Do not leave." Ari frantically motioned her inside. "But, pray, close the door."

As the maid obeyed, Ari berated herself. A glance at the drawn drapes showed sunlight prying between the panels. How could she have slept through the night in Fox's arms? And without even drawing the bed curtains.

It had been surprisingly easy, she realized, looking at the appealingly disgruntled man beside her. She'd never slept more soundly. Except for being awakened by kisses sometime in the small hours, when Fox had made love to her again.

She put her hand to her cheek. "Molly, you must tell no one."

Wringing her hands together, the maid nodded energetically, the wide ruffle of her mobcap flipping up and down. "Of course not, Milady. But what about Lady Anne?"

"Anne?" Fox asked, and shook his head, not understanding. "What about Anne?"

"Lady Anne is in such a taking, My lord. She's been turning the estate upside down, she 'as, looking for your lordship, ever since she went to your room early this morning and your lordship's bed 'adn't been slept in. 'Erself is on 'er way up 'ere, now."

"Bloody hell!" Fox said, this time with more feeling. Flipping the covers back, he swung his long legs off the bed.

Emitting a high-pitched squeak, Molly spun around and faced the door. "May I be excused, Milady?" Her tone was desperate.

"*Non*. Not yet." Ari said.

As Fox bent and snatched his breeches from the floor. Ari was treated to an excellent view of his taut derrière and well-muscled thighs. But this was not the time to dwell on such marvels.

Hopping out of bed, she grabbed her gown. Fox yanked his breeches on without bothering with stockings or smallclothes. She snatched both from the floor and tossed them into the bottom of the armoire, slamming the door and catching her nightgown in the process.

"Damn." Ari yanked the door open again and jerked the gown free.

When she turned back around, Fox caught her to him and gave her a swift, hard kiss that took her breath.

"It occurs to me I picked a poor time to have the secret passage nailed shut."

His eyes held a light that she'd not seen before. As he released her and shrugged into his shirt, he smiled wryly, and years fell away leaving the cold, noble Lord Grandquest looking boyish.

Recovering from her musings, Ari fumbled with her nightgown, looking for the hem so she might slip it on. "Molly, you must check the hallway and make certain no one will see Fox leave."

"Yes, Milady." Molly flew through the door, obviously glad to escape.

Ari pushed her head through the neck opening just as Molly rushed back in. "Lady Anne is on the main stairway, My lord. What am I to do?"

"Lock the door." Ari pushed her hair out of her eyes and vainly tried to close the nightgown.

"Where are my boots?" Fox muttered, looking under the edge of the bed.

"You did not wear any— Why does this thing refuse to be buttoned?"

Fox caught the edges of the offending garment. "You have it on inside out."

Tears of frustration welling in her eyes, Ari murmured terrible things about all nightgowns ever created.

"Sweeting," Fox caught her face in his hands and forced her to look up from her frantic efforts. "Don't fret. What is the worst that could happen? That Anne should find we've been together?"

"Yes." Ari glared at him. "You are a man. How could you understand? Such things only enhance your reputation. But I am not a man." Anne was the only female friend she'd ever had, and now Anne would lose all respect for her. An empty place formed at the pit of Ari's stomach as she imagined the look on Anne's face when she found Fox in her bedchamber.

Chuckling, Fox said, "It should be a stickier situation were you a man, I think— Ouch." He rubbed his arm where Ari punched him.

"How can you take this lightly?" She was near tears.

"My dear, don't worry," he said seriously. "If we are discovered, I will do the gentlemanly thing and marry you."

"Oh, Milady." The maid clasped her hands and beamed her approbation, reminding Ari abruptly of her presence.

"Do not post the banns yet, Molly." Ari looked at Fox, hurt.

"What, Milady?" The maid looked from one to the other.

Fox frowned. "Likewise, if you find yourself with child, I will do my duty—"

"How honorable, My lord," Ari cut him off. She looked away and blinked rapidly. "However, such noble self-sacrifice will not be necessary. I would not have you."

"What do you mean, you'll not have me?" Fox stared at her. Stiff and regal, she turned and stared back at him, obviously offended by his offer.

A loud knock at the door preceded Anne's voice. "Pallas? Oh, pooh. I mean Arielle. You know, it's much too bad of you to make me learn a new name just when I'd gotten used to the old one—Ari, are you awake, dear? You must wake up. I'm frantic. Fox is missing, and I know he has been murdered, like that poor man in the study. Like my poor Bobby and John were murdered. I cannot bear it if it has happened to Fox, too. Oh, do let me in."

"She cannot find you here. Get into the armoire," Ari hissed at Fox. She jerked open the carved door and a rainbow of gowns frothed out, barring his way.

"Ari?" The cry was high-pitched and had a desperate edge. The door handle rattled. "Ari, are you murdered, too?"

"Anne, I am not murdered. One moment," Ari called loudly.

"There's no time to fold 'im into the clothespress—down behind the bed," Molly whispered.

"She'll see him," Ari whispered back.

"Not if 'e lays flat-like, and you drop the coverlet over 'im. It's yards and yards big—'e'll look like a wrinkle." Molly winked.

Understanding dawned as Ari remembered the day she thought she'd seen Dolpho standing in the window and when she came upstairs, he had disappeared. "I see." She snatched up the coverlet and turned to Fox.

He was staring at her. "You want me to hide?" he asked incredulously.

"Now, if you please. Down," Ari whispered urgently, giving him an encouraging shove.

Glowering, he stretched out beside the pedestal bed, there being no room to get beneath it. Ari flung the pink satin over his prone form and puddled it artfully. Then she grabbed a gown from the armoire, held it in front of her, nodding to Molly.

The maid opened the door.

Anne rushed into the room in a flurry of canary-yellow ruffles that made the older woman look consumptive. The frown between her brows added to the effect.

"Anne, can this not wait? I am not dressed," Ari cried.

"I am sorry. But Fox has not been home all night." Anne began to pace. "His bed is untouched, and Thigpen says he hasn't seen Fox since ten last evening. Julien knows nothing. No horses are missing. I must send for the constable!"

"No, please do not."

Anne turned in mid-pace to stare.

"I mean, I am certain he would not wish you to do that."

"But, he isn't in the manor and after that terrible business yesterday in the parlor…"

"You are overreacting, and who can blame you after yesterday, but you must think before you act. Have you considered all possibilities? A woman, perhaps? He is a young and virile man, *n'est pas?*"

Anne's gaze widened with Ari's meaning. She resumed pacing, but in a much less agitated manner. "You think he is with a woman? Do you know where he is?"

"How could I know? But a tryst might offer a reasonable explanation for his absence—one that he wouldn't want exposed. That is the first thing that occurred to me." Ari shrugged. "But I am of French extraction."

"Oh, I had not thought of an *affaire de coeur*. Oh, I hope it's not that vile Lady Judith. She makes no secret of her desire for him. No delicacy, that woman."

"Judith? I do not think so. Your brother, he has impeccable tastes," Ari said, a trace of smugness in her tone.

Anne sighed. "You're convinced he is safe?"

"I feel very strongly that he is. If you will wait in the breakfast room for me, I'll be down in a thrice, I promise. We will sort this thing out, and without embarrassing your brother by bringing in the constable."

There was much Ari needed to talk to Anne about, anyway. Anne putting it about that Ari had been Dolpho's wife had thrown a great rub into things. Ari still hadn't a clue how she was to get out of that tangle once the real spy was caught and Dolpho could again take a place in London society.

"Oh, it is really too bad of Fox if he has put us to this worry for some tryst." Anne grumbled. Pausing in the doorway, she looked back with a frown. "But do tell me, before I go, why are you about to don a ball gown?"

Ari looked down at the gold tulle she was clutching to her bosom. "I felt like dancing?"

Raising a delicate brow, Anne looked at her askance for an instant, then laughed. "Oh, I see. You are quizzing me." She closed the door, not waiting for a logical explanation.

Dropping the ball gown on the bed, Ari released a sigh and met Molly's admiring gaze.

"What a 'um, Milady."

Fox rose and tossed the coverlet atop the ball gown. "Indeed. You deceive well, don't you?"

The words were softly spoken, but the atmosphere of the room changed, as though a storm cloud covered the sun. Without looking at the maid, he commanded her, "Wait outside, please, Molly."

Bobbing a curtsey, Molly instantly obeyed.

"I did not lie to your sister." Ari searched his expression for a sign of the warmth she'd seen there earlier. Seeing none, she rubbed her arms.

"That is your genius, isn't it? 'How could I know? A tryst might offer a reasonable explanation.' You deceive so thoroughly. Listening to you tell Anne everything, and nothing, brought to mind a dozen conversations with you where I know now you did the same with me. You seldom lie outright, but you deceive so damned well."

"You know why I deceived you. If Deveril's murder did nothing else, it should have brought home to you that my situation here has been deadly serious. I was uncertain whom to trust."

"Do I?" He caught her hand, trying not to be distracted by her breasts, half-visible in the deep vee of her still open nightgown. She had been honest in her passion, at least. Her body didn't lie.

He longed to ask her why she'd thrown his proposal back in his face, but pride forbade him. He had a good idea.

"*Little bastard!*" Henry 's shrill voice came to Fox over the years, reminding him of all the reasons a comtesse would look askance at his offer. "*The result of the heated coupling between that bitch Father married and some colonial cur — you'll go to the stable, where bastards belong.*"

"Are you still?"

"What do you mean? Am I what?" She was completely aware of his touch and wanted nothing so much as to be in his arms, feeling protected. Cherished. She wanted this sudden stranger to go away and for the tender lover of last night to return.

But, devoid of warmth, his face might have been cast in bronze.

"Uncertain whom to trust? Are you?" His tone was as dark.

She wet her lips. "No. I know now that I can trust you. I think my heart always knew, but my mind, it was slow to accept the truth."

"Then stop deceiving me."

"I am not —"

"Yes." His voice was a low hiss. "When you suspected someone was watching you through this peephole, I took it lightly." He had thought one of the servants guilty, but this wasn't some footman's doing. "And now that we find proof that you were right all along — and I am upset, you aren't. Why? What's changed since?" He pulled her to him. With his thumb beneath her chin, he tilted her head back and searched her face, his gray gaze demanding honesty. "Trust me. Tell me whom you are protecting?"

Like a kite suddenly without wind, Ari fell back to Earth. "*Dieu*. Every time I relax and think I can be completely honest with you, holding nothing back, something happens to remind me I cannot."

"That is what I thought." He turned away.

Ari caught his arm, willing him to understand. "I trust you. But some secrets are not my own."

Removing her hand, he said, "And that, Comtesse, is why I don't trust you. You warned me against it only yesterday, didn't you? After considering it, I think it excellent advice."

After he was gone, she stared at the closed door. Having to choose between Fox and Dolpho was so unfair. Because Dolpho was ill and vulnerable, she'd had no choice but to protect him. His welfare might depend on her discretion.

Although she was convinced Fox wasn't the spy, she was equally convinced that one of his close associates was. Someone had told Fox her name. It had to be Dandelion. Or someone working for the spy.

Until Dandelion was caught and hanged, no one she cared for would be safe.

* * * * *

"No, no, I don't believe Fox mentioned who told him your name. However, it was too bad of him and you to go on with the hum so long! To think, I had you married to your cousin." Anne chuckled, slathering a piece of toast with fig preserves. "Well, that at least was a piece of brilliance. I am sorry your cousin is no longer with us, but now you may play the merry widow with no harm to your reputation. They will all believe you are 'the red-haired woman' at any length, no matter what you say."

"No, I cannot." Ari shook her head emphatically.

"Why?" Anne waited expectantly, the toast halfway to her mouth. "Why on earth are you so firm about it? Your cousin is dead, and since he was deposed, there is no moral conflict over inheritance."

Sighing at Anne's stubbornness, Ari was glad they were alone in the breakfast room. She had to convince Anne not to persist in spreading it about that she, Ari, had been married to Dolpho.

"Because…he was like a brother. He watched out for me, defended my honor…"

Anne's smile was sympathetic. "The prince protected you while he lived. It stands to reason he'd want you to have the protection of his name now that he is no longer here, doesn't it?"

"Yes," Ari conceded. She lifted her cup, frowning as she stared out the window. The day beyond the panes was as gray and foggy as yesterday. She had the strong urge to unburden herself. Telling all seemed like it might be the only way to convince Fox's sister to abandon the tale she'd fabricated.

But Ari dared not take the chance of telling all. Anne loved sharing gossip. She might inadvertently make a slip that would place Dolpho's life in danger.

While Ari was lost in thought, Anne eyed the new widow speculatively. A faint, crescent-shaped mark marred the side of Ari's neck. A passion mark—she wasn't so old she'd forgotten what one looked like. What a hum. Had Ari and Fox truly thought she would not recognize the shape of a foot sticking out beyond the bed, even hidden by the coverlet?

"Tell me," Anne asked casually, "are you a virgin?"

Ari choked on her coffee and spilled it on the table as she rattled the cup into its saucer. "What?"

"Are you a—"

"I heard a'right the first time."

"Well, then, why did you ask—"

"Shock." Aware that her cheeks were burning, Ari fortified herself with a deep breath. Meeting the older woman's gaze levelly, she said, "No. I am not a virgin."

"Then being a widow will save awkward questions when we see you safely married, won't it?" Anne smiled happily.

Staring at her friend as if she had sprouted another head, Ari said slowly, "It seems it would. Were I to be married. I have no desire to—"

"Of course, you do. And being your cousin's widow is just the ticket." Anne cut her off. "After all, the prince can't have any objections. And society will forgive a widow much." She nodded wisely, her air of one who knew. "A widow who is a princess may be as eccentric as she likes. There's nothing the high sticklers like so well or toady to so noxiously as someone who is their social superior. We'll have an unparalleled success."

"What will be a success?" Fox asked, entering the breakfast room. He wore buff colored breeches that fit his muscular thighs like a glove, and a coat of brown superfine.

"Ari in society, Fox. Ari will set society aflame. I've decided we should leave right away. Christmas in town will be dull, but we must start planning our season and introducing Ari around. Anyway, you can't expect us to remain here with a murderer running loose. I didn't sleep at all last night. And my nerves weren't helped this morning when I thought you missing."

Letting Anne's last remark pass without comment, Fox's gray gaze touched Ari briefly, his expression remaining impassive but for a slight tightening of his jaw. "I think she has all the makings for a social success. Lineage. Hauteur. She'll have the beasts of Almacks eating from her hand."

"There is no reason for sarcasm." Ari felt the sting of tears behind her lids, and chided herself for letting him have the power to hurt her.

Frowning, he asked, "What sarcasm? I have every confidence you'll be the toast of London."

Anne waved her marmalade knife dismissively. "Fox wouldn't know about the Mad Benoits, dear. He has spent most of his life in America making money. Anyway, none of the great families in Europe are without a touch of madness. Why, we had a great grandfather who liked to dress like Queen Anne." She added a swirl in her marmalade. "I was named for him, you know."

"He was a relative of yours, Anne. But thanks to my dubious lineage, he was no blood relation of mine." Fox stared at Ari, as if expecting some reaction.

Lost in her own misery, she didn't notice.

"That is to your advantage, then, brother!" Anne exclaimed.

With a disbelieving glance at Anne, he said, "Actually, it's good that you wish to go to town. I came down to tell you to pack. I have to go to London, and until this business is settled, I want you both with me, where you'll be safe."

"Good." Anne beamed. "I can be ready within the hour. I'll leave my maid to pack the bulk of my and Geoffrey's things and bring them later. Ari can have Bailey handle hers."

"As you have social aspirations, Comtesse, this will serve well. There will be holiday parties to attend." He looked remote.

"I have no desire to enter society." Glaring at him, Ari threw her napkin across her uneaten porridge.

"Oh, pish. You'll love it." Taking a bite of her toast, Anne looked from one to the other as she chewed daintily.

Chapter Seventeen

Mayfair, London

ဆ

"Black?" Anne tilted her head, sighting through her *pince nez*. Behind her, the drapes of the small family parlor of her Belgravia townhouse had been opened and the watery light of the London morning filtered in. She dropped the eyeglasses and they disappeared amid the puce ruffles running rife over her bosom. "Half-mourning I could understand. So many marriages are of convenience, no one thinks twice if a widow doesn't put on sack cloth and ashes."

"Since I am not going into society, it does not matter." Ari shrugged and turned before the cheval glass mirror, viewing the hem of her new black merino, making certain it hung properly on all sides.

"And that is much too bad of you. I should have had such fun introducing you to society."

Ari caught the older woman's hands and said sincerely, "I am sorry I cannot lend myself to your fun. I hope you will understand that I do not wish to live another lie."

"Yes, I suppose I do. A shame. With your hair, black looks *magnifique* on you. You should have had all the gentlemen at your feet in a fortnight."

"I do not care to be tripping over gentlemen. It could be tedious, not to mention dangerous — I might fall and do myself an injury. Besides, *mon ami*, I am not looking for a husband." Ari smoothed a wrinkle from the gored skirt and tugged the short, fitted jacket until it fit as she thought it ought.

"It is just because Fox is being a dull stick, isn't it? There is no better way to bring a man up to scratch than to be sought after by his peers."

"I am not trying to bring Fox up to scratch. And I would not like society. I know it of a certainty."

"Why on earth should you say that?"

"Because I have been into society in Vienna, and I was thoroughly snubbed." Ari met Anne's gaze in the mirror. "Did you know my maternal grandfather was an American? He had a bakery shop in a city called Philadelphia. Between that and the madness thought to taint the Benoit line—why else would a comte marry a baker's daughter if he was not mad? And then there was the unfortunate incident with my grandfather abducting one of the Hapsburg princesses—I gave Austrian society quite a lot of entertainment. I could not enter a room without society matrons whispering behind their fans."

Anne's face was wreathed in sympathy and she shook her head. "Oh, you poor dear. I had no idea. You and poor Fox have suffered much that was beyond your control."

Ari wondered why such a large stone replaced her heart whenever she heard Fox's name? It wasn't as if he was pining away for her. Since escorting them to London and depositing them at Anne's townhouse, he had not sought her out at all.

And just *how* had Fox suffered?

Do not ask. Do not ask! How can you stop longing for him if you insist on discussing him at every opportunity?

Despite her advice to herself, she could not resist. "Why do you say that? How does Fox suffer?" She bit her lip, afraid more might spill out. *Mon Dieu, have you no will?*

No. None.

"All of London knows he was a spurious heir. And even before he faced London gossips, I'm afraid the scars my brother Henry inflicted run deep—he treated Fox not like a younger brother but like a hated misfit, making him live above the stables, beating him." Anne brushed a tear from her pale lashes.

"It has made Fox often rigid, freezing out people before they offer a slight to him, I suppose."

Ari had learned of Fox's past from Ben. Taken with what Anne said, it made her wonder, with Fox's background, why should he look askance at hers?

Unless he wanted a wife with impeccable breeding, one who would lend him the consequence he felt he lacked?

Turning away to hide her rioting feelings, Ari leaned close to the glass and adjusted the high-collared white lace fichu she'd added to her round neckline. It was just the right touch, softening the severe lines of the gown. With her auburn curls caught up in a simple twist, she thought she looked her best.

Not that it mattered. She would probably not see Fox, and he was the only man she cared to impress. *And that was beyond foolish. Indeed, she was Eve's daughter!*

"I have scarcely seen him since we came to London," Anne said as if reading Ari's thoughts. "It was too inconsiderate of the American ambassador to arrive in town practically at the same time we did and start placing demands on his time. These colonials have no sense of station." She made a moue of disapprobation, obviously forgetting both Ari's and Fox's colonial connections.

"Fox is *liaison* between the United States Embassy and Whitehall. No doubt the duties that keep him busy are very important," Ari said, wishing she really believed it. Perhaps it was wise of him to stay away. Meeting his gaze over the breakfast table and remembering their lovemaking would be beyond awkward.

Warmth surged within her at the thought.

A light knock preceded a maid wearing a stiffly starched apron and stiffer expression. "Beg pardon, Lady Anne, but there are visitors. Lady Eelston and Miss Wellard await you in the front parlor."

"I will be down directly." Pausing at the door, Anne said, "You will pardon me for abandoning you?"

"Of course. Geoffrey and I are going to the Pantheon Bazaar. I promised to help him shop for the perfect Christmas gift for you." But first, Ari planned to call on the Earl of Meadowbridge, Stubby's father. She was determined to make good use of her time in London to clear Dolpho's name. And if she was going to unmask Dandelion, Stubby's father was the logical place to start.

"Splendid. I do so like the brooch I saw at the little jewelry maker's shop near the middle of the street. You can't mistake the brooch—it is formed of paste diamonds in the shape of Tower Bridge. If you point it out to Geoffrey, I shall steer Fox to a new parasol to match that new walking dress of yours."

"No, Anne. He sent me that lovely muff when we arrived in London as an early Christmas present."

"He did that because I told him how your hands froze as we went to church. It upset him greatly to hear it."

Ari smiled, but doubted Fox had been greatly upset. After Anne was gone, she stared at the door, wondering if the ache to be near Fox would ever subside? Should she have played her cards differently? If she insisted, he would still do the gentlemanly thing and marry her—he had said as much. He was passionate. He desired her body. Perhaps that would have been enough. She would know the joy of waking each morning in his arms. Was she a fool to want more, to want his love?

No. Ari wrapped her arms about herself and knew she couldn't accept less than love. She had hungered so long to be loved and cherished, a hunger she could never remember being without. A hunger, not for the offhand, brotherly affection Dolpho showed her, but to be the center of someone's world.

Of Fox's world.

The Benoit madness? Yes, this had to be it. Had it always been a part of her, though she only now realized it? Of course, the seed was there, just waiting to grow. Why else would having Fox love her be so important to her? Why else would she need him so much? If he could just love her and need her as she did him…

Scarcely could she remember her father and mother, but she did remember laughter and low conversations. They'd been so consumed by each other, they'd been almost oblivious to all else. Even their small daughter. After her mother died of a lung fever, her father had stepped off the balcony of *Château Nuage*. It was a sheer drop, hundreds of feet, to the valley below.

Her grandfather had been distant, preoccupied by his scientific studies — into which he'd retreated after his Hapsburg princess had died in childbed before the age of thirty.

Her father and her grandfather had both known an all-consuming love. They had been unable to go on normally after that love was taken away.

In Fox's arms, she had barely tasted what such a love might be like. But that was enough to understand the Benoit madness.

She should count herself lucky if Fox never again sought her out, she told herself. If she escaped with only this ache in her heart, before he became the center of her world…

* * * * *

"So, you're saying *potpourri* really means *rotten pot*. That's funny. The potpourri Mother makes smells nice. She uses rose petals and lavender." As the hired carriage hit a bump, Geoffrey grabbed his low-crowned beaver.

Ari held onto the edge of the seat. Beyond the low roof, the driver's imaginative curses sounded above the clip-clop of the horse's hooves. Outside the window, the West End lay under a thin blanket of snow, which had fallen last night and was already going gray from soot drifting down from the innumerable chimneys of the city.

"Yes, but think about the word and you will see. In French, pot means pot, and does not the verb *pourir* mean *rot*? The word is taken from a Spanish dish, *olla podrida*, where meat and other things are put into a pot and left for a few days before cooking.

The French borrowed the dish from the Spanish, and the name somehow came to mean 'a bit of this and that'."

"I thought words were words. I didn't know they changed." Geoffrey made a face. "I hope Mother's chef doesn't find that recipe for rotten pot."

"I do also." Ari smiled. Dull tutors and public schoolmasters had drubbed all Geoffrey's enthusiasm for learning out of him. She hoped to rekindle the boy's interest in applying himself to his studies.

As Geoffrey looked out the open window, a thoughtful frown puckered his expressive features. The fashionable townhouses passed by at a sedate pace. There were few doorknockers in place, to indicate where a family was in residence. Many of those houses also had evergreen wreaths on the doors and their windows were alight.

"What about *bankrupt*?" he asked. "It's something about benches, isn't it?"

Nodding, Ari said, "*Bank* is indeed from *bancus*, Latin meaning 'bench'."

"I'm a fair hand at Latin," he said brightly. "Is *rupt* from *ruptus*?"

"Yes, the same Latin root as *rupture*. Do you see how knowing Latin gives clues to many languages?" Ari felt encouraged.

"I hadn't thought about Latin that way."

"Now, if you will put your mind to the secret behind the word *dandelion* and figure it out, I will be very grateful. I have been racking my brain."

Geoffrey nodded wisely. "That's what that spy fellow calls himself, isn't it? I heard Uncle Fox talking."

"Yes, that is the name he uses," Ari said as they pulled to a stop before the Earl of Meadowbridge's townhouse in Grosvenor Square. While Geoffrey waited for her in the parlor, a somber butler showed her into the study and took her bonnet and pelisse. The entire household was hushed, as if grief had stolen all life from it. Ari moved to a high, glass-fronted case and was reading the names of leather-bound books filling it when Lord Meadowbridge joined her.

"Comtesse? Or is it Princess? I noted you signed your letter with the former." Gaunt and stooped, the earl offered her his pale, thin hand.

Taking it, Ari made a deep curtsy. He helped her arise, surprising Ari with his strength. She said, "Comtesse, please. It was good of you to see me. I hesitated to intrude on your solitude, but I believe it important."

"Nonsense, child." There was shrewd speculation in his watery blue eyes as well as the pain of grief.

"But you wonder why I am here."

"Yes, I wonder." He smiled. "Sit, please." He motioned her to a comfortable looking chair and waited until she was seated before he took one near it. "You speak frankly. I find that refreshing in a female. I shall speak frankly, too. I am happy you came. It offers me the opportunity to say how grieved I am by the actions of my son. They have cost you much. You were married to Dragonetti, I hear."

"Thank you." Ari sighed and played with strings of her reticule. "I had hoped the rumor of our marriage would not find its way to London. I will be truly frank. No, Dolpho and I were not wed. Our relationship was as brother and sister, although we are only cousins. With little money to sustain us and no other relations to turn to, we lived in the same house to economize, and I enjoyed helping him in his work.

"Dolpho and I were living in the cottage near Little Braxton and I was pretending to be his wife as we traced the route Dandelion was using to get information out of the country. Dolpho had learned that certain smugglers were involved and they were helping him, but that is as far as we got. My marriage to the prince is Lady Brickington's invention in an effort to save my reputation."

"Indeed." The earl looked thoughtful. "The prince was like a second son to me, and I knew of his work. Given the prince's reputation, society would never believe your protestations of a brotherly relationship. Lady Brickington is a wise woman. You might do well to heed her advice. If I can do anything to aid you, you have only to ask."

"Thank you, sir." Ari added dryly, "I pray you won't regret the offer. Between the English authorities and French spies, I feel far from secure."

"You are right. Though I've resigned my position in the War Ministry, I've used my contacts in Whitehall to see that no formal allegations were put forth against the prince. Those nodcocks had it in their heads that the prince was the lynchpin of this business, until another courier was killed in Dover. His throat sliced, as is Dandelion's trademark. The prince, being dead, is obviously not responsible for this one, so the authorities have been convinced to look elsewhere."

"Another courier." Ari touched her throat, feeling ill.

"And my contacts tell me that the information he was carrying will do great harm to our men fighting on the Peninsula this winter. I would the prince had named this madman, if he had an idea of who it is."

"He did not know who the spy is, though I believe the spy thought he did and so shot him." As Ari regarded Lord Meadowbridge, an idea took shape. "I saw the man who shot Dolpho that night when the militia came riding down on us. I *do* know who it is."

Inwardly she cringed. A streak of madness in the Benoit line? Ha. It was as wide as a bloody turnpike. Only a madwoman would set herself up as the target of this killer.

The earl sat straighter. "By Heaven, you saw him? Let's have his name then. To see that cutthroat dealt with is my fondest desire."

"*Non.* I will keep it to myself until I have proof. Soon, I will have it and I will tell the authorities. And that brings me to why

I've come. I know it is a great intrusion, but if you would allow me to go through Stubby's papers and other possessions, I believe I may find something confirming the name I suspect."

Later, as her and Geoffrey's hired carriage arrived at Anne's townhouse, she saw Julien driving Fox's town coach around to the mews. Fox was home! She could tell him what course she had started and what she'd discovered.

And then, perhaps the rift between them would start to heal.

Once inside, Geoffrey rushed up the stairs, excitedly calling for the servants to come fetch the paper-wrapped parcels from the hackney. As she untied the ribbons of her bonnet, Ari hurried into the parlor. "Where is the earl?"

A maid looked up from dusting the furniture. "In the library, Milady. But he's not—"

"Thank you." Without waiting to hear more, Ari opened the mahogany door to the library and paused on the threshold. Fox stood by the mantle, focused on the glass of brandy in his hand. His cravat was a snowy fall at his throat, contrasting with his tea-colored skin. Tall and dark, impeccably tailored in his cutaway coat and pantaloons, he looked every inch the London gentleman. He turned to her, his brows drawing together in a frown.

"Countess, this is *not* a good time."

At his cool tone, something tightened in her chest. Ari resolutely pushed her feelings aside and stepped into the room. "I wish to speak with you and I do not give a fig about 'good time'. I spent a very productive afternoon, going through Stubby's personal accounts, and I know— *Oh.*"

The last as she moved farther into the room, and she saw Fox was not alone. There were three other gentleman with him, only one of whom she recognized—Sir Leonard Dent.

"This is not a good time," he repeated darkly.

Searching his expression, she ached to see warmth. There was none.

"Nonsense, Grandquest. This is an excellent time. Pray introduce us," said a very white-haired gentleman. He was dressed in an old-fashioned frock coat and knee breeches. Beside him, a younger man with a sharp face was dressed in an unfashionable wool coat and breeches. Sir Leonard Dent was the third man. He rose from a wingback chair on the other side of the fireplace and bowed slightly.

"I am acquainted with the countess. Or I should say, *princess?* I collect you have regained your memory, now, Your Highness."

Dent was one name that had appeared many times on Stubby's ledger. At first, Stubby had lost large amounts to him. Later, Dent had paid larger winnings to Stubby, almost as though on a schedule. Dent was tall enough to be the man who shot Dolpho, Ari thought. But beyond that it was impossible to tell. If only she'd gotten a better look and had recognized the man, as she'd told Lord Meadowbridge she had.

"Sir Leonard." Ari gave him the slightest of nods. There was a strange tension in the room. Was it due to her presence?

"Princess Ari," Fox said, his lips held a mocking twist, "Let me make you acquainted with Lord Blaine and Mr. Higgins."

Both men bowed.

She nodded to both, as though they were equal to each other. "Lord Blaine, I feel I know you through Dolpho—Prince Dragonetti."

"Princess, I am sorry for your loss." His voice was raspy, but his gaze was shrewd.

"I prefer my own title, Comtesse D'Ambois."

"Of course, Comtesse." Lord Blaine bowed again.

"Stubby?" Dent asked. "Comtesse, did you mean Viscount Lynching? Please, go on. You were saying?" He touched the breast of his cutaway coat.

"I was saying…" Should she? Ari hesitated. Her plan had seemed logical when she conceived it, but the man she sought was a murderer.

However, Dolpho would continue to be suspect, perhaps even charged if they didn't unmask the true villain. If she was careful, there was no reason her plan shouldn't succeed.

Not glancing at Fox, although her every fiber was completely aware of him, she took a deep breath and plunged onward. "Yes, Sir Leonard. Stubby was an avid gambler. I have a theory that whoever this spy is, he was someone who gained a hold over Stubby through his gaming, perhaps, holding large debts. Lord Meadowbridge was kind enough to allow me to go over Stubby's personal accounts and—"

"Comtesse, this is not the time to discuss such things. I pray you will excuse us," Fox interrupted, his stance rigid. The look in his eyes beseeched her.

"Nonsense, Grandquest. If the Comtesse can shed light on this matter, she should speak up now." Lord Blaine smiled encouragingly at her.

It was a lion's smile. With his wrinkled brow and snow-white hair, a very old lion, to be sure, but a lion, nonetheless. A prickle of unease slipped down Ari's spine.

"After all," Blaine continued, "we are all deeply involved in the search for this spy."

"Yes." One blond eyebrow rode upward as Sir Leonard eyed her with an odd intensity. "Countess, have you discovered who this Dandelion might be?"

Dangerous. Behind his smooth manners, she sensed Dent could be ruthless. Why had she not seen it before? "I thought you only a clerk in the Foreign Office, Sir Leonard. I fail to see how you are involved."

His face went livid, then mottled color stained his cheeks, contrasting with his thick, yellow side-whiskers. "It is not for you to question what my involvement might be. If you have information, reveal—"

"Dent, enough." Fox's voice was low and steely.

"Yes, Dent. There's no need for rudeness," Lord Blaine said. "Grandquest, what can be your objection to this woman talking?"

"I have my reasons." Fox's gaze never left hers.

"I suspect yer reasons might be some'ot we just were talking about, yer lordship," the man named Higgins spoke up.

Ari glanced at him. There was shrewd intelligence in his face, also. She asked him, "Which was…?"

Higgins bowed. "Beg pardon, Milady, but 'at's private."

"You are from Bow Street, one of the famous Runners?" she surmised.

Higgins looked surprised and bowed again. "The very same, Comtesse."

Ari digested this piece of information. So someone was being investigated. Fox? One glance at his tense expression seemed to confirm it. No wonder he'd been concerned with what she might say. She dared not say anything that could be taken against him.

She could, however, further set up herself. Dent was the spy. She was certain of it. And if she could goad him into an unwise move, she would have proof.

"I will tell you what I know, Lord Blaine." She flicked a brief glance at Dent, who stood still as a statue. "The proof of who Dandelion is lies in Stubby's personal ledger."

"We have already examined that ledger."

"But you did not know what you were looking for. I will tell you, but first I want Dolpho exonerated. I have heard the rumors. They blacken his name. We worked for the English cause, and Dolpho gave…" She brought a black-edged handkerchief out of her sleeve and held it to her mouth, shaking, as if unable to go on.

Fox grasped her shoulders and guided her to a chair.

"Thank you," she whispered and closed her eyes tightly.

Lord Blaine spoke, "I will see the prince's name is exonerated. In light of recent events, it is obvious he wasn't Dandelion. Then we will talk again and you will tell me what you suspect."

She nodded, afterward the door opened and closed. When she looked up, only Fox and Sir Leonard were still in the room.

"I find your show of grief an amazing change from the merry woman who could not even remember her own name," Sir Leonard drawled and helped himself to brandy from the decanter on a low table.

Ari shrugged and tucked her handkerchief back into her sleeve. "Like your show of manners, it is at times useful."

Sir Leonard stiffened. He seemed to wrestle with his self-control, before shrugging and raising the snifter to his lips.

"What in hell are you about, Ari?" Fox stared at her as though he'd never seen her before.

"Clearing Dolpho's name. Although he served England, the English are content to vilify him simply because he was not one of them," she told Fox angrily.

"You don't have anything for Blaine, do you?" Sir Leonard guessed.

She felt the weight of Sir Leonard's gaze on her, and rose before facing him, unwilling to give him the advantage of looking down on her. Ari opened her mouth to assure him that she did, indeed, have some interesting information regarding money, which Stubby owed to him. But some instinct warned her direct confrontation was not the way. She shook her head. "Perhaps I wished to see Dolpho exonerated, and so I misled Lord Blaine a little."

"But you did go through Stubby's ledger and papers? Bow Street has already searched everything, of course." Sir Leonard seemed terribly intent on her answer.

Another uncomfortable feeling crawled down her spine. Shrugging, Ari opted for yet another role. Adventuress. "Stubby and Dolpho gambled often. I was looking for any money he might have owed to Dolpho. I found nothing. A pity. If Blaine had offered me money, I would have told him about the man I saw shoot Dolpho. The same man who is one of many listed in Stubby's ledger." Her gaze met Dent's meaningfully. The look in his eyes was hard, like slate, and she lost the courage to say more.

"Fox, if you will pardon me?" She started for the door.

"No you don't." Fox caught her wrist. "You aren't leaving. Dent, excuse us." His voice was as cold as the north wind singing through the crags on Mount St. Cyr. His eyes were the bleak gray of the sooty London sky.

Dent set his snifter down and left.

After he had gone, Fox's touched gentled and he caressed her arm. "*Why?*"

Her eyes, fringed by sable lashes, wide and luminous, held no trace of guilt. No hint of lies. Achingly blue, they made him think of Caribbean waters and soft breezes, a life far away from subterfuge and espionage, wars, divided loyalties. And murder. Looking into her eyes, he could believe her as innocent as a babe.

But not an hour before, Lord Blaine had laid a letter from Napoleon in his hand, a letter taken from the cottage near Little Braxton commending the Comtesse D'Ambois for her good work and assuring her of a handsome reward for her service to the empire.

Chapter Eighteen

ഓ

Fox shook his head. No, it couldn't be true. Could it?

She tried very hard to kill you in Dartmouth. She lies as easily as most young ladies flirt. Even now, you don't know what she's holding back…

Fox had to admit that Ari could be the spy.

"I do not understand." Ari looked up him. A faint, apricot blush colored her cheeks. Her lips were a darker apricot, moist and parted.

Fox clenched his fists. God's blood, he wanted to wind his fingers through her hair and bring her mouth to his. Kiss her until they were transported to that place where passion would make him forget all he knew and suspected about her.

"You are looking at me very strangely. Why were those men here? Are you…are you in trouble?" She tried to pull her hands free, but he held them tightly.

"I am in no trouble."

"You are frightening me." She tugged again.

"Just be still, Sweeting." Cupping the back of her head, Fox angled her mouth to receive his kiss.

"No." She turned her face away. "Do not kiss me. For a week you've been avoiding me, as if we've never shared anything. I have my pride."

"Avoiding you was the only way I could keep my hands off you. Just let me hold you, Sweeting." Wrapping his arms around her shoulders, he pulled her against his length and rested his chin atop her head.

The allure of being held by him was impossible to resist. Just resting her cheek against his wide shoulder could not be so wrong, could it? In his arms, she felt so protected and cherished. She closed her eyes, savoring that illusion. "Nature shows there will be no child," she said at length. "You need not worry about being forced to wed me."

"A pity."

Did she imagine his sigh? "You cannot mean that." Ari pulled back to look at him. "You cannot wish to have been forced to wed one of the Mad Benoits. All of London would have laughed."

"All of London be damned." Fox shook his head. She was the most amazing, vibrant, intelligent woman he'd ever known. Even as he'd stayed away, he'd been planning his assault, anticipating breaking through her objections and convincing her to be his wife. He'd imagined their loving would bear fruit and she would be forced to wed him. That, with time, she would come to love him, too. Silly imaginings, better suited to a schoolboy than a grown man.

Then Lord Blaine had laid the letter in his hand and all the world had turned to dust and crumbled. The evidence was irrefutable.

Fox had suspected she was involved, but he'd never imagined his beautiful Arielle could be at the root of the madness. Could be responsible for the murders.

But even as his heart denied it, in his mind the pieces fell into place. It was Ari. She was smart enough and cunning enough to orchestrate the spy network, even though he'd argued when Dent had said the very same thing.

Arielle was Dandelion.

She would hang.

It was only a matter of time before she was arrested. Indeed, he didn't understand why Lord Blaine hadn't had her arrested when she came into the room.

"You are trembling," she said, looking up at him, frowning.

"Quiet, Sweeting. It is nothing." Fox pulled her more tightly against him again and stroked her back and shoulders.

As Ari again rested her cheek against his shoulder, fear touched her heart. Something was terribly, terribly amiss. There had been tension in the air when she came into the library. The suspicion that Fox was in trouble again nagged her.

Ari pressed closer and listened to his heart beating strong and sure beneath her ear. Faint scents of tobacco and bay rum surrounded her as his hands stroked her shoulders and back, soothing her. Until, for no reason she could name, she remembered that Fox had once been her and Dolpho's prime suspect as Dandelion.

To suspect him had been ridiculous, had it not?

"Lord Bellmore is giving a masked ball tomorrow night — Christmas Eve. I received an invitation weeks ago. Lord Blaine came to say he hoped I would attend to aid in security."

"Why would Lord Blaine request your help to secure a masked ball?"

"Russia's alliance with Napoleon is falling apart. The Czar is sending a letter for the Prime Minister in hope of starting negotiations for a new alliance. It will be given to the Prime Minister under cover of the ball. Blaine wants all his operatives there to ensure all goes well. If Dandelion should intercept this, it could have far-reaching consequences."

Fox stroked her hair. The bait was placed. If she was Dandelion, she would not be able to resist trying to intercept the packet.

"I should think the Czar would be anxious. But why not go through the Russian Embassy?" Ari asked. This was not what she wanted to know, but she accepted that Fox was not ready to talk about whatever the real problem was. It was the way of men, she supposed.

"There have been incidents in the past. The Czar doesn't trust his own people."

"I see. Is there more news from Russia?" If she kept him talking of other things, he might eventually open up. It had often worked with Dolpho.

"Nothing of consequence."

Fox felt a loss as Ari pulled out of his arms. Watching her move to the hearth, his heart grew impossibly heavier. Most women would be worrying over what to wear or how to obtain a costume at this late date. The Comtesse D'Ambois was concerned with getting more information. Didn't she realize that her actions were telling? Or did she think him such a fool he could not see the truth?

She held out her fingers to the flames. "Fox, back in Devon someone told you my name. Who was it? I asked before and you would not say, and, to be truthful I did not pursue it because I still had doubts about where your loyalties lay. Inside, I was afraid…well, now that does not signify. But I must tell you, in all of England, only Lord Stubbins knew my real name, and he was the one who betrayed Dolpho and me to Dandelion. Do you see what that means? I believe whoever named me to you is connected with the spy. Or perhaps, he is the spy. It was Dent, was it not?"

Taken aback as she guessed right, Fox moved beside her. "Yes, it was Dent. But that doesn't mean he is a spy. There were papers found in the cottage revealing your identity. I've seen them. They were turned over to Dent's father, Lord Cowling, the magistrate of the district. Dent brought them to Lord Blaine."

Ari turned, one eyebrow rising. "I see. Damning papers, I take it?"

"Very."

She shook her head. "I should not be surprised. After he got the militia to do his bidding, it is only logical that Dandelion should have planted some 'evidence' to make the attack look justified and throw the authorities further off his scent."

Fox held perfectly still. Hope was like shaft of sunlight prying into his shadowed soul. What she said was logical. The letter could have been forged, the emperor's seal and all, just as his own seal had been forged on the note to the militia captain.

He pushed aside the knowledge that she could just as easily be guilty and let hope of her innocence warm his heart. He asked hoarsely, "Do you know how beautiful you are?"

"What are you—"

His fingers on her lips silenced her. Then he stroked her hair, her face. "Beautiful." He planted quick kisses at the corner of her eyes, her mouth and his mouth claimed hers.

Ari tried to hold rigid. But the fire behind his kiss kindled an answering fire within her. Her concerns for the future melted away. And her bruised pride from their past encounters was shoved aside. There was only this perfect moment, only Fox's lips and hands and strong body. She pretended nothing else existed. And it was easy to pretend.

Fox's mouth moved to her throat, tasting her skin. "I want you," he whispered between love bites.

Her eyes flew open, the spell broken. "No. Please."

His mouth charted a fiery path from her neck to her breasts, nipping her skin through her clothes, murmuring his need, until he went down on one knee and started lifting her hem.

Ari found the will to push him away. "No!" Trembling, she held him at arm's length. "No. I am a fool to love someone who only wants me to warm his bed."

Fox went still, looking up at her. "Please, don't say you love me."

"Do not worry." She turned away to hide the tears in her eyes. "I ask nothing of you. Nothing. Nothing at all."

As she sailed through the door, her head high, Fox felt his gut clench. This was another game. It had to be. She was playing to his feelings for her in case she needed his help in her schemes.

But what if she did love him? Could he see her hang?

Could he see her hang, even if she did not?

Just take her away. Sail away, leave England forever. You owe these people nothing.

That wasn't true. Though he wanted to hate this island where he'd spent an unhappy childhood, England had been calling him all the time he'd spent abroad. The people at Stonerose, his tenants, needed him to manage the estate properly, to overcome the years of neglect from his brothers and restore the land. They were his responsibility. To his surprise, he had a place in the community and in society. No one seemed to look askance at him.

He belonged to England.

And he owed Peterson the promise he'd made as that young man died in his arms. Fox had sworn to find Dandelion and to see him hanged.

Or her.

* * * * *

"I must talk to you," Julien whispered as he moved beside Ari in the parlor.

The room was festooned with ribbons and greenery. Ginger men arranged by the wassail bowl awaited big-eyed children. A cheer went up from the assembled servants and their families as Anne placed the last decoration, a *papier-mâché* angel atop the evergreen tree that everyone had just helped to decorate.

"And I must talk to you. I have placed myself in danger," Ari told him.

Frowning, Julien noticed her unconsciously twisting her hands together. "How so?"

"Come." As the servants lined up to received a cup of wassail ladled by Lady Anne assisted by Geoffrey, Ari led Julien to a secluded corner. "I have put it about that I know who the spy is."

Julien looked sardonically amused. "There are many who will believe you, I'm certain."

"I am tired of this villain leading us a merry dance. If Dolpho should surface now, he would probably be clapped in irons. But since all think Dolpho is dead, they have finally turned their eyes elsewhere. These English are having a difficult time accepting that one of their own is guilty."

"That is more true than you think."

Picking up on his odd inflection, she asked, "What do you mean?"

He hesitated, glancing about as if making certain they were not overheard. "The favored suspect now is the very beautiful and intelligent Comtesse D'Ambois."

Ari touched her hand to her throat. "You cannot be serious. Lord Meadowbridge said nothing of this."

"I am indeed serious. Servants often know as much as their masters. Lord Blaine's driver described the evidence found against you in the cottage, a letter from old Bony, himself, thanking the Comtesse for her service to France and assuring her of huge future rewards."

"I cannot believe…" Ari sat down and put her hands to her cheeks, feeling a prick of moisture in her eyes. "The French destroyed my life, stole my inheritance and murdered my grandfather—how could anyone believe I would work for them?"

"Quite easily," Julien assured her dryly. "Ari, I've made some arrangements. If you seem in immediate danger of being charged, I will see that you are smuggled out of the country at once."

Ari studied his determined features and knew here was someone she could trust with her life. She steadfastly ignored the look of longing in his eyes. It disturbed her to be the cause of his pain, but there was nothing she could do. If her heart was not already given…

"Thank you. I pray fleeing will not be necessary." Drawing in a deep breath, she released it slowly to calm her fluttering nerves. "And thank you for believing in me. It seems your brother does not."

Fox had to know of this, she realized with a sinking feeling. That was the real reason for Lord Blaine's visit. Julien knelt on one knee beside her. "Then my brother is a fool. If a woman like you cared for me, I'd sweep her away from harm and all governments and their games be damned."

"But I have given him much reason to doubt me." She sighed. "Thank you for being a friend." Ari touched Julien's cheek and smiled, then stood.

Standing, he executed a smart bow. "As always, I am at your service." Then added in an undertone, a wicked glint lighting his eyes, "The world has too few truly beautiful, tall, long-legged women for even one to be at risk of dangling from a rope."

"Rogue." She smiled.

As he moved away, Ari was grateful that she had at least one friend in a world that seemed increasingly allied against her.

Two friends, she amended, as Anne caught Julien's sleeve and thrust a steaming cup of wassail into his hands. Ari had thought herself so clever putting it about that she knew who the spy was and hinting that money was what she wanted. It had seemed a simple matter of waiting for an offer and tracing it to its source.

Dandelion wasn't worried about her little games, it seemed. He was playing a game of his own. What could she do now? Wait until she was charged and hope to escape?

Non. She would clear herself and Dolpho, too. If Fox had baited a trap for Dandelion and no one guessed it was a trap, then the spy would be there.

And so would she.

But first she needed to protect Anne from the consequences of being her friend.

* * * * *

"You can't be serious in this?" Anne took a gown from atop the stack on the bed and returned it to the wardrobe. "This is Christmas Eve. You can't mean to remove yourself to those cold rooms on Carson Street with no one to keep you company, no companion. And living alone in a rented room will place you quite beyond the pale."

"There are reasons I must leave that I cannot explain. And the rent on the rooms has been paid for several months, so it is the logical place to go. As to a companion…there are reasons I should not have one at this time. But not to worry. I shall keep to myself. No one will know I am unchaperoned." Ari pulled the gown out of the wardrobe and returned it to the stack she was arranging atop a sheet. There had been a new fall of snow the night before. Outside the windows, the morning sun ricocheted off a world that was dazzlingly white. It was easily the brightest day Ari had ever seen in London. The sunshine seemed to mock the sleepless night she'd spent.

"I insist you stay until after the twelve days. We light the Yule Log tonight."

"I have promised Geoffrey I would be here for that. I will bring my things and then return for the ceremony."

"Oh, do tell me what is wrong?" Anne caught her shoulders, searching her face. "Both you and Fox look like death warmed over this morning. Has he done something, Ari?"

"No." Only made her fall in love with him. He could not be held accountable for her silly heart. "It is not him, exactly. It is…" She shrugged. "Too difficult to explain."

"Have you told him how you feel?" Anne asked frankly.

Taken aback, Ari stared at her friend. "Is it so obvious? Am I making a cake of myself?"

"No. But I was not born yesterday."

Ari shook her head. "I can honestly say that both Fox and I are caught in a situation that is beyond our control. That situation is why it is necessary for me to move out of this house."

"You are terrifying me," Anne said seriously.

"I will be fine, I assure you." Whether she succeeded in catching Dandelion, or had to flee England, she would be fine, Ari thought ruefully. She had Julien's word on that.

Only her heart would not be fine. But there seemed little help for that.

Geoffrey bounded into the room. "Julien sent me up to tell you the coach is waiting—do you really have to go? I want you to meet my new tutor. He's ever so much nicer than the masters at school."

"It is best that Ari leaves," Fox said from the doorway, his expression as cold as his tone.

Hearing him say it hurt. Keeping her face averted, Ari added another gown on the stack on the bed.

"Why, Uncle Fox?" Geoffrey demanded.

"Yes, tell us why." Anne demanded, sounding much like Geoffrey. "Ari speaks in riddles."

Fox looked at his sister, his expression unsoftening. "No, Anne."

Anne stamped her foot. "You both are as close-mouthed as clams. Very well, go if you must, Ari, but know that you are welcome here anytime." She gave Ari a quick hug and left the room, dabbing at her eyes with her handkerchief.

"Carry the bandboxes, please, Geoffrey," Fox directed. "You may go with Julien and help Ari, if you wish."

Ari said, "Send in that tallest footman, please, Fox, if you will. I don't want the hems of these gowns to be dragged on the floor." All too aware that she was alone with Fox, she made a show of arranging the gowns just so and flipped the edges of the sheet over them and tied the corners, making a drape.

"I will carry them. None of Anne's footmen are as tall as your shoulder."

Squaring her shoulders, she looked into his eyes. "Have no fear that I shall ever again make you feel awkward by telling you that I love you."

His face grew impossibly colder, his eyes, the color of the granite crags on Mount St. Cyr. "I know you are leaving to protect Anne and Geoffrey. In view of what you told Blaine and Dent yesterday, I think it wise."

She shrugged. "I thought you had missed the nuances of what I said to Dent. You did not seem overly concerned."

"Anyone could see what you were about," Fox told her, darkly. "I went through that ledger myself with the same thing in mind. On it, Dent seems the most likely go-between, doesn't he? And you hinted to Dent that you could be bribed not to talk about your suspicions. As no large packets of money have arrived, I'd say that gambit went awry."

"You think I am in no danger then?"

"Oh, yes, I think you've placed your bloody neck on a chopping block. I'd like to haul you to Curzon Street myself and sit on you to make certain you'd stay safe and don't dream up other coils. But duty calls me elsewhere, so I'll arrange for men to watch your flat. It may take a while for them to arrive, so sit tight and go nowhere until I send word that it is safe." Picking up the bundle of gowns, he turned on his heel and left the room.

Head high, Ari sailed past him and down the stairs. Once she was seated in the coach, Fox wordlessly transferred the gowns to her lap and stepped back. A footman put up the steps and closed the door. After, he tapped on the side of the carriage and it started forward.

"What's wrong?" Geoffrey was seated across from her in a mélange of bandboxes.

Ari dabbed her eyes with her handkerchief and tucked it back into her sleeve and gave him an uncertain smile. "My heart is bruised, if not broken. But I shall survive."

"Uncle Fox." Twisting his mouth to one side, Geoffrey nodded wisely. "Mother says you two will make a match."

Taken aback, Ari shook her head. "I take leave to doubt it." As an afterthought, she added, "No doubt, your mother is usually wise in these matters, but in this case there is much going on of which she is not aware."

"Oh." Geoffrey frowned, seeming distressed by this bit of intelligence. "I do think it would be ever so nice if you were to marry Uncle Fox, you know. So does Mother. I heard her tell her friend, Dotty. That is why she is so keen on seeing you accepted into society."

Ari's eyes grew moist again. "Your mother is a special friend."

"Are you going to be a watering pot?"

"I am sorry. I think I am."

Geoffrey fished inside his coat and brought out a folded note. "Here. I wasn't going to give this to you, but maybe it will pluck up your spirits."

"What is it?"

He shrugged as Ari took it from him. "I dunno. A boy dressed in ragged clothes ran up to me as I was climbing into the coach and gave it to me. Said it was for the 'Countess' from some gentleman who was 'bang up to the mark'. I'm sorry I wasn't going to give it to you, but I figured it was from an admirer and so…"

"You did not want Fox to have competition?"

Geoffrey looked unhappy. "But the way Uncle Fox was staring at you, all thundery and not saying a word, he'd deserve it if you'd find some duke and throw him over."

"Indeed, he would." Ari smiled. "Geoffrey, you have made me feel much better."

She broke the simple wax splotch sealing the note and her smile faded as she read the contents.

"Are you going after a duke, then?" Geoffrey asked as she refolded it.

"No," Ari said, and thought, *I am going after a spy.*

Chapter Nineteen

80

"No."

Kneeling by the hearth, Julien hung his head and shook it slightly. Still in his heavy driving coat and tricorn, he reminded Ari of a bull refusing to move under the herdsman's prodding.

"You will not lend your support? As you like then." Ari whipped a Holland cover off a chair. Dust boiled into the musty air and she sneezed. Old and worn, the furniture looked no better without the covers. The flat didn't offer the feeling of sanctuary she'd hoped to find there. Dark and dismal, everywhere she looked, the image of Fox's cold, gray eyes was before her. Did he, too, believe she was the spy? Was that why he'd been so eager to distance himself and Anne from her? Chilled from more than the cold, she went on to the next cover, plucked it off, and sneezed again. "Then I shall have no choice but to go alone."

"No. A meeting with a murderer in an isolated area of Hyde Park? A maggot has gotten into your idea pot. If I must tie you, you will not go." The newspaper in the fireplace took flame from the tinder, and Julien nestled pieces of coal atop it.

"If I were you, I should not try to bind me."

Grinning, Julien gave her a lecherous look, one eagle's wing brow rising in challenge. "Oh, I wouldn't *try*. And if you struggle, well, that will only make it more interesting." He winked, as if she could possibly miss his meaning. "Who knows, you might like being bound. Some women find it very…satisfying."

Ari stalked away.

Geoffrey pushed through the door, laden with the last of the bandboxes. "I left the footman to watch the coach and keep the impudent stealers away," he said, naming those thieves who cut open the back of coaches and stole the seats. "And why should a woman find it satisfying to be trussed up?" he asked, his eyes barely peeping over the largest box.

Rising, Julien brushed off his knees. "I shall tell you in a couple of years, Viscount."

"Please, place those in the first bedchamber with the other things, Geoffrey." Glaring at Fox's brother, Ari added, "Pay no attention to Julien."

"Look daggers at me all you wish. I am not so big a fool as to be swayed by a pretty pair of peepers. What time is this meeting supposed to be?"

"Four, today, is the time," Ari lied. It was at one. She knew the meeting might be designed to lure her into a trap that would throw more suspicion on her. She wanted to go without lawmen, in case that was Dandelion's plan. "If you will bring the rest of my things, then you may accompany me."

"I'll have a word with Fox about sending someone in your stead. You'll see, it's the wisest course."

Ari sighed dramatically. "I suppose you are right."

"You are far too complacent."

"And you are far too suspicious."

Uncomfortable under his scrutiny, Ari went into the kitchen and opened the door to the stove. Shoveling old ashes into a bucket, she readied it for a fire. It was patterned after the style the American, Mr. Franklin, had designed, and she had often thought it a shame it was not in the parlor. The cast iron threw off a great deal more heat than the fireplace, which seemed to send most of its warmth up the chimney.

Ari reflected how empty the flat would seem now that she was alone. She had the unhappy feeling that she would be spending a great deal of time alone. As she considered her life over the past few months, she had to admit she'd lived up to the reputation of the Mad Benoits, and even surpassed their exploits. No wonder Fox had said what he did — *"Don't say you love me."*

It still stung that he'd thrown her declaration back in her face. Yesterday afternoon, she had been confused by his manner. But this morning, his coldness had made his feelings clear enough.

Ari furiously cleaned the stove, taking shovelful after shovelful of cold ashes out. When she was finished, she threw the small shovel atop the bucket and reached for the coalscuttle.

"Here. Let me," Julien said, entering the room. Kneeling, he placed the last bit of kindling in then added a few pieces of coal on the grate atop it. "There's not much to get it going." He drew out his flint and tinderbox. "Give me the lamp. We'll make certain it catches."

She handed him the lamp, and he opened the well and splashed the coal with oil.

"I could use some newspaper to light this with." Julien looked at her expectantly.

Ari glanced about. She pulled the note Geoffrey had given her out of her sleeve. "Use this."

He took it from her and twisted it before he struck his flint. The spark caught in the tinder and he stuck a corner of the twisted note to the small flame. When it caught, he quickly placed it beneath the kindling and that flamed. Some of the coal was burning. "We could use a bit more coal, here."

"I shall fetch the other scuttle."

As Ari left the kitchen, Julien pinched out the flame on the note and smoothed it out. After reading it, he shook his head and tucked it inside his coat.

When she returned, he added more coal to the flame. "Devious devil, choosing teatime for a meeting. All the civilized world will be sipping Earl Grey and eating scones."

"A veritable fiend," Ari agreed, wondering at his statement.

Once the fire was set, Julien straightened and looked around. "There is no food in this place, I take it?"

"Not a crumb."

"It's hardly a day to go to the greengrocer's. I'll fetch some bread and cheese when I come back with the rest of your things."

"Would you wait and come back around three? If I'm not to go to the park, I would like to join Geoffrey and Anne for tea. Afterward, they are lighting the Yule Log. It is Christmas Eve, you know."

"So you've decided to be sensible, have you?"

"I always strive to be sensible, though you would not know it from the results." Julien gave her a narrow look, and Ari had the feeling he didn't believe her. But it was no matter. By three, she would have been to the park and back. If all went well.

"I'll be here at three, then." He touched the brim of his hat, like a proper servant, and left.

After Julien and Geoffrey were gone, Ari went to the hearth and dislodged two stones. Reaching into the hollow beneath, she drew out a box containing Dolpho's matched dueling pistols and a small pouch of coins.

* * * * *

Ari looked out the open window of the hackney carriage at the sturdy, middle-class houses lining the narrow street. A coal seller's dray plodding ahead of them slowed their progress until it turned into an alley. As they turned onto Kensington Road, the wider thoroughfare edging the park, the carriage horse picked up speed in response to the driver's clucking and snapping the reins.

The clopping hooves rather matched the tempo of her heart, Ari reflected. Drawing in a deep breath, she felt the reassurance of the weight in her lap and turned her attention to the scenery. There was much more traffic here, both carriages and drays, even an occasional rider, though the latter was in the minority in this frosty weather.

One horseman caught her eye as he passed the carriage at what Ari considered a reckless pace given the treacherous condition of the icy cobbles. She frowned. It was Fox, swathed in a heavy outer coat, his curly brimmed beaver anchored with a gray muffler which hid half his face. But it was Fox. She recognized the tall black he was mounted on. Another man rode on the other side of him on a nondescript bay.

A knock sounded atop the carriage and the driver lifted the speaking hatch. "Are you certain it be the Park Lane Gate you be wantin', ma'am? We'll be at the south gate off Kensington in a thrice. Much nicer pathways there be at the south side."

"No. Park Lane, please."

Ari leaned out of the window. She saw the tall black and Fox disappear into the south gate of the park.

Coincidence. She leaned back against the worn seat cushions. He was just out exercising his gelding. Nothing more. What else could bring him to the park?

Ari thrust her hand into the rabbit fur muff Fox had given her. As the hackney rolled on, she cradled the barrel of the dueling pistol she'd hidden there with one hand and grasped the butt in the other. Holding it didn't bring the same comfort it had before she'd seen Fox.

It is coincidence, just coincidence, that he is going toward the park, too. That is all, she told herself. Perhaps, he found her missing from the flat and was looking for her.

Outside the wrought iron gate off Park Lane, a group of children, bundled up in a ragbag assortment of mufflers and knit hats and ill-fitting coats, skipped in a circle, arms linked, as they sang out their joy of the season:

"Christmas is a comin',
the goose is getting fat!
Please put a penny in

the old man's hat!
If you've not a penny,
a ha' penny will do.
If you've not a ha'pence,
God bless you!"

Laughing and shrieking, they collapsed in the snow. Two girls began to make snow angels. A boy got to his knees and began packing a snowball, only to take a hit broadside before he had his missile formed to his satisfaction. He launched it anyway, amid much teasing as it came apart, dusting his intended victim with fine, white powder. Their laughter formed moisture clouds in the crisp air.

As the carriage rolled slowly through the gates, Ari smiled as she watched their play, the weight of a dueling pistol in her lap adding an odd contrast to the carefree scene. Her smile faded as a memory teased the back of her mind and gave her a strong feeling of *déjà vu*. Children had laughed before as she'd held a gun. It was cold then, too. Somewhere…Dartmouth? A faint memory of laughing children, more ragged than these, surfaced. She'd been on her way to confront Dandelion then. *The same as now.*

And she'd found Fox…

A feeling of foreboding slipped down her spine. Ari told herself she was being silly.

The driver lowered the steps and helped her down. "Six pence, Mum."

Ari dropped a shilling onto his gloved palm. "Do you have children?"

"Yes, ma'am. Two little ones. A boy and a girl." There was fatherly pride in his eyes, which crinkled at the corners from a lifetime of squinting into the sun.

"Do you love them both? Even the girl?"

He seemed taken aback by the question. "Yes, ma'am. I love one as much as the other. More dear than me own life's blood, they are."

"Buy them a licorice for Christmas and hug them every day, so they will never doubt it."

His eyes lit as another shilling joined the first. "Yes, ma'am. I surely will." The money disappeared inside his heavy coat.

"There will be two more like those if you will wait here until I return."

The small man nodded and tightened the muffler anchoring his hat to his head. His quick, jerky movements reminded Ari of a bantam rooster.

"I 'spect, as it's bleedin' cold, ma'am, you won't be longish?"

"I 'spect you have it right." Turning, Ari started in the direction indicated in the note.

Her half-boots crunched through the crust of the untrammeled snow. The park glistened, pristine white under its dazzling new shroud. Except for the tiny, double-footed marks from a sparrow, no footprints marred her path. All was still and quiet, the only noise coming from the streets beyond the park walls.

Too quiet.

Was there someone waiting by the largest oak, as the note stated? Or had she been led on a wild-goose hunt? The man she was to meet with might have come into the park from a different direction, she reasoned, so that she would not have seen his prints.

But, if that was the case, who might have come with him?

Her steps slowing, Ari made her way through an aisle of head-high rhododendrons. The evergreen branches bowed under burdens of white, and her serviceable gray cloak brushed the sides, causing small avalanches. The aisle was, no doubt, designed for spring lovers stealing moments of privacy. As Ari entered the shadows under the trees, she imagined more sinister uses for the hidden lane, and she felt the back of her neck prickle.

If you are to be this cowardly, you should not have bothered to come! *Mon Dieu*, if you quake at a dark path, what will you do if you find the fiend, Dandelion?

She knew it had been unwise to come, still, there were so few leads, she had had to chance this one. And she was armed, she reminded herself.

The narrow aisle opened onto a meadow, at the center of which was a small pond, now frozen over. As she stepped from the rhododendrons, Ari expelled a pent-up breath and looked around. The big oak stood on the far side of the pond, but there was no one beneath it. Deciding to wait, in case the man who'd sent her the note should show up, she started toward it.

A flock of starlings jumped into the air amid a thrumming of wings.

"*Merde!*" Ari stopped, a gloved hand to her throat as she waited for her heart to stop its dreadful thudding. "Do not be so pudding-hearted," she said in self-disgust. "A fine adventuress you make!"

"Eh? 'Puddin' 'earted,' she says." A man chuckled. "Do you taste as sweet as a figgy puddin'?" asked a guttural voice behind her. "Oi'll bet you do."

Whirling about, she found a giant of a man. His steps as quiet as a cat's, he had followed her through the shrubbery. As he looked her up and down, a smile stretched his thick lips, revealing rotting teeth.

Praying her fear wouldn't show, Ari stiffened her spine and raised a haughty brow. "Is a taste worth your life?" she asked as she cocked the still hidden pistol.

"Whadda you mean, Ducks?" The big man stopped and eyed her narrowly. "You ain't no fire ship, are you?" He took a threatening step nearer.

Ari pointed the hidden pistol in his direction. Suddenly, she was grabbed from behind, her arms jerked back until her elbows touched together. Crying out in pain, she felt her knees buckling.

"He means do you have the French pox, my dear." The voice by her ear was garbled, disguised. It sounded like rocks grating in a gristmill.

Pain seared her arms and shoulders in white-hot waves. Desperately, she tried to maintain her hold on the gun, but it slipped from her fingers.

"Ah, a pistol was hidden inside. A shame, now the priming will be wet," the man behind her sneered.

Ari groaned in frustration, and she struggled to break his vise-like hold. Then all fear left her. The faint scent of bay rum clung to her assailant.

And she knew she was dead. She hoped she was dead. God could not be so cruel as to make her go on living.

"*Fox?*" The word was a disbelieving whisper.

The tall man behind her stilled and growled in the fake voice, "Surprised to find the Earl Grandquest here? You came here expecting hush money from Dent, didn't you?"

"Yes, I expected Dent, damn you. How could you, Fox…" The knot in her throat tightened, but she kept her tears at bay. She would not give Fox Grandquest the satisfaction of seeing how thoroughly he'd fooled her. Or how his betrayal was tearing out her heart. "*Why?*"

"Quite simple, my dear. I'm tired of your interfering ways." To the thug, he said, "Do her and let's be out of here."

"After Oi taste her figgy puddin', Oi'll do her. Not before. Come here, Ducks." The man reached for Ari with one hand, a knife glinted in the other.

The man behind her hissed, "I will not be disobeyed. Get on with it!"

"Now, listen here," the thug leveled a menacing look at the man, raising the knife meaningfully. "Oi'll do it, only in me own sweet—"

Ari kicked upward with all her strength, feeling the toe of her sturdy boot drive deep into the softness between his legs.

His eyes bulging, he bent double. A croaking sound grated from his throat. Ari landed another hard kick in his soft gut, and he sailed backwards.

Her arms were wrenched cruelly back. A red haze of pain rose before her eyes, and she sucked in her breath.

"Where did you learn those wicked tricks?" he growled in her ear. When she didn't answer, he wrenched her arms back further.

Unable to stand, she sank to her knees. He loosened his hold, but her relief was short-lived. A fist caught her on the temple, and the snowy ground rushed up.

The cold snow on her face revived her. Ari rolled to where her muff lay, the pistol half-buried in the snow. She caught the muff clumsily, the abuse of her arms left her fingers feeling numb, useless. She felt like shouting with joy as she managed to pull the pistol free.

The ruffian was on his hands and knees, vomiting.

"Get to your feet, you stupid arse." The tall man kicked him in the ribs.

Ari shook her head, trying to get rid of the ringing in her ears.

The thug rose on his knees, again. "Oi'll have yer ballocks fer me breakfast, yer rum cove!"

Although her vision swam, Ari recognized the flash as the tall man picked up the knife from where it had fallen in the snow. He caught the ruffian under the chin with the blade, and terror and surprise twisted the ruffian's features as a terrible gurgling sound issued from his throat. He fell on his face. The snow immediately turned crimson around his head.

Bile rose in Ari's throat.

Bloody knife in hand, the tall man took a step toward her. His face was swathed in a gray muffler, except for his eyes, just visible between the muffler and the brim of his tall beaver hat. Were they gray eyes? She squinted, but her vision blurred and she shook her head to clear it.

"I am next, I take it." On her knees, Ari raised her pistol, blinking rapidly, trying to clear her vision. She remembered Fox's soft touches and tender words.

How could she have been so deceived?

"It won't fire, my dear. The snow will have wet the priming." Again, the voice was disguised, no more than a harsh hiss.

"You cannot be certain." A prickle of tears made her vision swim even more. She blinked furiously, but the world remained a blur. "The most ironic thing is, I sent a letter to Lady Anne to be given to Mr. Higgins of the Runners should something happen to me. In it, Fox, I named Leonard Dent as my murderer."

The tall man stopped dead. "That's ironic, indeed."

Ari blinked and tried to see his eyes—but his face was a blur.

"Come nearer, and we shall see if this pistol fires or not." If it did, his death would serve justice. If it did not, her death could only ease the pain ripping at her heart. *Cher Bon Dieu*, how could she have been so wrong?

"I think not." He took a step back. "It occurs to me that I've spent a great deal of effort to throw suspicion your way. Why should I kill you?" He tossed the bloody knife in the snow beside her and turned.

"Hold! I will shoot."

"Who are you trying to convince, my dear?" He strode away.

Tears streaming down her face, Ari lowered the gun.

* * * * *

Holding a cool cloth to her temple, Ari unhooked the chain and turned the key. Resplendent in the Grandquest livery of green and gold beneath his driving coat, Julien stood on the landing.

"I left the chaise in the mews behind the building. There's an armed man wandering about there. Another one is in the hall. The rest of your things are in the chaise, but they should be safe until I fetch them." He took in her state of dishabille and frowned. "Lady Anne is expecting you for tea."

Ari swung the door wide and stood back to allow him entry. "Thank you for coming to fetch me. But I do not think I shall be joining Anne and Geoffrey after all. Please, tell them I have the headache."

In truth, she could not bear to see Fox again, not after seeing him wield that knife. There was much unanswered in her mind, much which did not make sense. How he had managed to carry off his spying she could not guess. Sometimes it seemed he had had to be in two places at once. But she could not dispute his guilt. She had the admission from his own lips.

Julien set the basket he was carrying on a nearby table and gently grasped her chin, turning her face to the fading light issuing through a high window. "I'll just wager you do have a headache. Who did this?" One winged brow rose as he looked into her eyes, demanding answers.

Pulling away, Ari hugged her wrapper and shawl more tightly about her. Her walking dress was spread over a chair by the fire to dry. It had been a dismal ride back from the park in wet clothes. "You do not want to know," Ari told him. "I hope you brought tea with the food. I feel my insides are so frozen, I may never feel warm again."

"I did bring tea. Sit and I'll brew it." Julien guided her to a chair. "Your hands are icy. What have you—"

Understanding dawned in his sherry brown eyes. "You went to the park anyway, didn't you, nodcock?" At her nod, he said, "I knew you would, why else would you tell me the wrong time to throw me off." At Ari's questioning look, he admitted, "I read the note."

Ari flushed guiltily. "I am sorry that I lied to you. I should have heeded your advice."

"I told Fox what you were about and he said he would stop you. What happened?"

Red snow flashed in her mind's eye. *Mon Dieu*, that confirmed it. She shook her head. "You do not want to know."

"Yes, I do. But first I'll put the kettle on." Julien disappeared into the kitchen and soon the clanking of the kettle lid and splashing of water could be heard. He came back into the parlor and sat on a footstool before her chair. "Now, while we wait on the kettle, I'll hear what happened."

"I was prepared for one man. There were two. One of them is still there. Dead." Ari drew in a deep breath and tried to school her features not to show the bleakness she felt inside. As she explained what had happened, she carefully left out the most disturbing fact of all. How could she tell Julien his brother was a killer?

"After going to a great deal of trouble to lure you there, why didn't he kill you?"

"I honestly do not know. After he...he killed the ruffian, he turned for me. And I told him of the letter I sent to Anne, to be given to Bow Street if I did not return. I told him that in it I named Dent as my killer."

"Well, there you have it, then. It was Dent and he didn't want Lady Anne giving that letter to the Runners. Which means I better get back and tell Fox all of this. And keep an eye on Anne and Geoffrey, just in case Dent tries to recover the letter."

Ari said nothing, wishing she could believe it was Dent. After Julien fetched the rest of her things, she locked the door behind him.

The aroma of freshly baked bread rising from the basket Julien had brought assaulted her and started her stomach roiling. She should eat something, she knew. But she could not imagine ever being hungry again. She took the food basket and the tea things into the kitchen and placed the cups and saucers into the pan she used to wash up.

A heavy thumping on the door drew her back to the parlor. As she opened the door a crack, she felt all the blood drain from her face. Standing on the landing in a greatcoat and top hat with a gray muffler swathed about his neck, was Fox Grandquest. "Open the door."

"*Non.*" Ari pushed it closed.

The door flew inward under his kick, and Fox stalked inside.

Ari backed away. Where was the guard? she thought frantically. Then she realized he was in Fox's pay.

Fox tossed something on the card table. Ari recognized her rabbit fur muff—she had dropped it in the park.

"You should be more careful with the presents I give you."

Chapter Twenty

ॐ

"Stay away." Ari hated the quaver in her voice. It told of the fear she knew must show in her face. In his tall beaver hat and caped greatcoat, Fox looked impossibly big and just as dangerous as he had in the park.

"You're afraid." His brows drew downward. "You should be."

As he came nearer, Ari backed away, staring at the gray muffler around his neck. "Stay away. *Dieu*, why have you come? To torture me further? You must know you destroyed me in the park."

"What game are you playing now? You talk in riddles. But you admit you were in the park." Again Fox stepped nearer, and Ari backed away. In a sudden move, he caught her wrist and pulled her against him. "My God, what have you done, Ari?" His voice was ragged.

"Let me go!"

His hands smoothed over her back, pressing her to him so tightly it seemed he wanted to absorb her whole into himself. *"What have you done..."* Slipping his hands beneath the wrapper, he started to smooth it from her shoulders.

"No!" Ari caught his wrists.

Fox paid no attention to her feeble attempts to stop him. Without thinking of what he was doing, he brushed her hands away and stripped off her wrapper, leaving her dressed only in the flannel gown beneath. Her glorious hair was unbound, tumbling about her shoulders and down her back. He buried his face in it and closed his eyes, inhaling the faint scent of lavender.

Here, as her body pressed against his, with her scent filling his mind, he could pretend that she wasn't a murderess.

She tried to pull away. "Fox—"

He placed his fingers on her lips and frowned. "What is this?" Grasping her chin, he turned her face so he could inspect the purpling bruise on her temple.

"Well you know what it is," she said in a dark whisper.

"Did...did the man you killed do this to you?" Dared he believe she had acted in self-defense? Was there a logical explanation to her actions?

Stiffening her spine, Ari glared up at him. He could only murder her once. And death would be a release from this terrible pain eating her heart. "How can you be so cruel? You know well that you hit me with your fist."

"Don't play this game!"

"What game? You hit me. In the park. And then you...then you killed that man." She put her fingers to her lips to stop their trembling.

Fox stilled. What she said fit the marks in the snow he'd come across with Higgins. Higgins had pointed out that there were only large footprints near the murdered man, not her smaller ones.

"When you were hit, did you fall down?"

"You know it! You know that I did. "

"And the other man, he walked away, toward the west?"

Ari pounded his chest with her fists. *"Stop this, stop this!"*

"Why did he kill him?"

"You—are you trying to drive me mad?" Tears scalded her cheeks. "You killed him because you told him to kill me and he did not obey. *You!*"

"Kill you?" His face was stark as he grasped her hands, pulling her against him, stopping her assault. "Why didn't he kill you?"

"The brigand wanted to rape me first, so I drove the toe of my boot into his soft parts and put it out of his mind. You were angry that he did not obey instantly."

"Why did the second man not kill you himself?"

"He said...*you* said...you had gone to too much bother to throw suspicion on me to kill me." How had his arms come to be wrapped around her? And why did they feel so right? *Dieu*. She *had* lost her reason.

Ari stilled and sniffled. "That does not make sense, does it? Why did you let me live?"

"Ari, it was not I."

It was not he. Her heart leapt, but she shook her head, unable to nurture hope that might prove false. "Do not lie. Do not torture me so. I *saw* you. You hit me."

"I spoke to you?"

"Yes." She looked at him in surprise. "No. Your voice, you made it different. Disguised it."

"I tell you, Sweeting, it was not I. Did you see him clearly?"

"No. He came on me from behind. I saw him only after he hit me. My vision, it was not clear then. But he was wearing a dark gray coat and top hat. A muffler, this color, covered his face." Her voice grew bleak. "The smell of bay rum clung to him. That is why I was certain it was you. You always smell faintly of that scent. You do so now."

"Half the ton would have been dressed like this today and bay rum is a popular hair pomade."

"He was very tall. As tall as you." Ari broke away, afraid to surrender her disbelief.

Fox tossed his greatcoat on the settee. His hat and muffler followed. Catching her hand, he pulled her against his chest. "Forget governments and loyalties, whatever yours are. Believe in me, in this moment." He smoothed her hair from her face.

"I....do. I am a fool for it, but I do believe in you." She tried to pull away but he held her tightly. She asked bitterly, "And you, do you believe so completely in me?"

"You have never been honest."

"No. That is true." Ari sighed. "Not even now."

She thought of Dolpho. "No. Some secrets still aren't mine." Tears blurred her vision as she looked up at Fox. "When I thought you the murderer, my world was ended. I was dead. Hold me. Let me know that all will be well."

"All well? My God, you could have been the one lying in the snow, your throat cut." Fox crushed her against him, kissing her hair, her neck. His mouth found hers and melded to it as he pulled her nightgown up.

Grasping her around her waist, he lifted her. "Wrap your legs around me, Sweeting."

Ari obeyed, needing to be nearer. She knew she could never be close enough. She kissed him as he walked, holding her. The hardness of his arousal rubbed her most sensitive parts, even though his pantaloons were between them, and her blood took flame. She hugged him more tightly.

Fox set her on the game table. Quickly, he tugged off his cutaway coat. Ari ripped his waistcoat and lawn shirt open, taking no care for the buttons. She wanted only to taste him, to smell his scent, to touch him, to fill her senses with him and forget the fear she'd known.

He caught her head and tilted it back and kissed her swiftly and laid her back and pushed her nightgown up over her breasts. Positioning his erection at her moist entrance, he held her hips immobile and thrust into her softness. "Never, never again...take such a chance. Ah, Sweeting." Pulling almost all the way out, he slammed into her again, harder. "I should never have let you out of my sight." His voice was a ragged whisper.

Ari clung to him as he filled her—*Fox was not a murderer.* Whimpering, she tilted her hips to receive his next thrust even more deeply, desperately needing to feel him inside her.

"Deeper," she whispered, hoarsely. "Harder, *please*—I need to feel all of you," she whispered, catching his shoulders and trying to draw him down so that their bodies touched.

He refused to bend to her pull. Instead, he lifted first one of her knees, and then the other over his shoulders and pulled her to the very edge of the table. Thrusting into her, he filled her more than she'd ever dreamed possible, stretching her completely. "That's right, Sweeting, take all of me." He thrust again, then ground against her.

He was so far inside her, the sweet, throbbing ache that began to build in her seemed like it went impossibly deep. Ari scratched at his shoulders, wanting, needing to feel his body on hers. "My breasts...they are on fire..."

He cupped her breasts, his big hands dark against her pale skin. Tweaking her nipples and kneading her breasts, he thrust into her hard again and again, filling her completely. Pleasure so intense she could not bear it convulsed her insides, consuming her, rushing through her body and taking her to a plane far beyond.

Afterward, Ari opened her eyes, and found Fox watching her with incredible tenderness lighting his face. A tenderness she had not seen before. She realized he had never allowed himself to show it. Looking down, she saw he was still sheathed inside her, and new ripples of sensation shot through her body.

She touched his face, and Fox kissed her palm, his gray eyes, soft.

"Never, never take a chance like that again. Never do such a mad thing."

Ari felt all the joy drain from her. She wriggled her bottom and they were no longer joined. She scrambled away, sat up and tried to straighten her nightgown. "But what might you expect from one of the Mad Benoits?"

Understanding knit his brows. "A poor choice of words, Ari. No more."

"But apt." She smiled humorlessly.

"Here, Sweeting." Though she protested and tried to pull away, Fox took her in his arms, smoothing her hair. "Your family doesn't suffer from madness, Ari, but from too much courage. Would that more had such depth of conviction."

Gathering her up, he carried her to a wingback chair near the hearth. Sitting with her, he tucked her head against his shoulder. "Now, you will tell me why you went to the park alone. You deliberately told Julien the wrong time. If he had not read the note, I would have never known what you planned. I rushed here to the flat, but you were already gone. At the park, I got there minutes after you." The ruffian's body was still warm. "Why did you place yourself at risk?"

"Why did I have to? You were treating me like three-day-old fish. I asked for Julien's help, but he would not lend it. He said to stay out of it and tell you. I am not some milk-and-water miss who cannot handle my own affairs." *Oh, what a terrible liar I am — this pride almost cost me my life!*

"I am not deceived this time. You're not naïve. You had a reason for doing this ma — unwise thing."

"I had a gun."

"Ah, then why did you not use it? I didn't hear a shot, or I might have found the meeting place sooner."

Ari did not answer.

His voice softened, "What you said earlier — for some reason, you didn't shoot because you thought it was me."

"My powder was wet," she said crossly.

"I should learn not to think too highly of myself. And I should think more highly of you, though I know you're still not telling all. When Julien gave me the note and told me you were to meet with the spy, I thought it was all a red herring to throw Bow Street off the real scent — your own."

"You believed that?"

"It isn't so hard. Far easier to believe than an intelligent woman going alone to meet with a murderer."

"My course seemed logical at the time. I thought, at worse, it was a trap to shift more suspicion on me. At best, I would find the spy."

"Shift suspicion onto you is exactly what you have done. It was obvious that a woman was involved in that business in the park."

"Also…" Ari paused, biting her thumbnail as she cuddled against him. The time had come, she decided, when she must bind up her wary heart and place her trust in him. He was not Count von Bohr. He'd never told her lies, trying to get under her skirts. She sighed.

"Also, Dolpho is alive, though injured and still far from well. I have been protecting him, or else he might have been hanged by now. I thought if I could unmask the real spy, it would clear Dolpho from suspicion."

"Ah. So you've come to trust me with that, at last."

Ari was aghast. "You knew. How?"

Fox chuckled, the sound rumbling pleasantly beneath her ear. Being in his arms made her feel small and protected.

"Stonerose is mine. There is little that happens there that doesn't find its way to my attention. I saw a young man splitting oak for firewood outside Granny Freeman's cottage the morning we left for London. He was obviously in great pain as he wielded the axe, and after two swings, he had to rest. He was the person staying inside your bedchamber wall, was he not?"

Ari nodded. She sat up and met his gaze levelly. "How did you get my muff? Didn't Higgins want it as evidence?"

"I feel certain he would have, if he had seen it. It was almost buried in the snow. As he was examining the body, I pulled it out and recognized it. In a moment of madness, I tucked it inside my coat."

He wrapped her in his arms and pulled her against his shoulder once more. "You aren't afraid anymore. You no longer believe it was me."

Ari sighed. "I must be mad. You have made me disbelieve my own senses. You, and the fact that it is not logical that Dandelion lured me there to kill me and left me alive. I told him I had left a letter with Lady Anne to be given to Mr. Higgins if I did not return. I see now that that saved me."

"What does this letter say?"

"It says Dent, whom I have always suspected, is the murderer. I thought it was you I was speaking to, but when I said that the letter named *Dent*, the man backed away."

"That's what Geoffrey meant," Fox said suddenly. "Geoffrey said to tell you *Dandelion* came from old French—*dent de leon,* or *lion's tooth*."

"The name *Leonard* means lion and *Dent*, tooth. Of course." Ari straightened. "We must find Dent at once!"

"We?" The thunder was in his eyes. "*We* must do nothing. You will never place yourself at risk again."

"But, Fox, the masque tonight—Dent will try to intercept the message from the Czar."

"But you will not be there."

"And *why* will I not?"

"Because, I think, we must get you to Anne's townhouse to watch out for her. The letter you sent her might have placed her in jeopardy."

Ari rested her head against his shoulder and sighed. Fox smiled into her hair as he sensed her surrender to a greater duty. At least this time, he would succeed in keeping her safe.

Chapter Twenty-One

଼ଓ

"Anne, I am so sorry. I could cut off my tongue for having mentioned the letter. I would never have placed you in danger on purpose." Ari shook her head. "It was so stupid of me not to see, to even think that that evil man could have been Fox. In truth, my heart knew better, but my brain shouted it down."

"I have you and Julien in here, and those two nice men Fox sent are watching the outside of the house. I feel quite safe. All is forgiven, my dear. When I think what you went through…"

Anne gave a delicate shudder and linked her arm through Ari's as they strolled down the hall toward the parlor.

"Your friendship is very special to me. You know, I've never had a female friend before."

"Oh, pooh." Anne blushed and gave Ari a quick hug. "The truth is, I was likely to expire from the tediums before I met you." She added with a twinkle, "Now there's seldom a dull moment."

Ari smiled. "Thank you."

"Well," Anne declared, flustered, "the staff will be waiting."

As they continued on to the parlor, Ari peered into dark corners and behind statuary, the weight of the small pistol Julien had given her heavy in her pocket.

Because Ari couldn't identify him as the man in the park, Fox said there was not enough evidence to bring charges against Dent. Nevertheless, he'd been certain the spy would be unable to resist the bait of the Russian packet. He was also certain the villain would try for it at Lord Balmore's ball.

All this would be over soon, and Ari was glad. The events of the last few weeks had quite sated her thirst for adventure.

Anne led the way into the parlor, where the household was gathered expectantly. Drifting to a quiet corner, Ari watched as Anne greeted her people, accepting their good wishes for the season and expressing the same to them. Everyone was in good cheer, in part because it was Christmas Eve and in part, Ari suspected, due to the wassail bowl, which was nearly empty.

Geoffrey offered Ari a cup of the warm spiced wine.

"Thank you. Look at you, my friend." Ari took the cup and whirled her forefinger, indicating he should spin around for her inspection.

Grinning broadly, Geoffrey complied. He was dressed for the festivities in a new cutaway coat and pantaloons, a cravat beneath his chin tied in the simple style in which Fox wore his. The lad's face was scrubbed until his nose and chin had shiny patches and every hair on his head was plastered into order.

"Ain't it bang up to the mark? Uncle Fox gave me the new clothes for Christmas. His own tailor did them up," Geoffrey said proudly.

Fox had been a good influence on the lad, Ari decided. There was little about him that resembled the whining child she'd met a month before. "You are a very handsome young man. Alas, I can see you will break a thousand hearts." Ari winked, and Geoffrey blushed a fiery red.

A cheer went up as the Yule Log was carried in by two stout grooms. The two grunted as they positioned it on the andirons. It filled most of the fireplace. That done, Julien made a great show of setting kindling beneath it, then touched a lit taper to the kindling. A more exuberant cheer went up as both kindling and log took flame at once.

"It's considered bad luck if the log is hard to light or if it goes out," Geoffrey told her. "So I soaked it with coal oil."

"Handsome and clever," Ari amended.

"Where's Uncle Fox?"

"Fox will not be joining us." She lowered her voice conspiratorially. "I think he is making sure the trap for the spy is properly set, now that, thanks to you, we know for certain who it is."

Geoffrey blushed again. "I've been called 'smart' and 'wise' more today than my whole life put together. This afternoon when he brought you home, Uncle Fox thanked me for unraveling the puzzle about who Dandelion is. He also told me I'm smart." Geoffrey squared his shoulders, proudly. "And he asked me to help you and Julien keep an eye on Mum, just in case Dent comes for that letter."

Ari set her cup down and, ignoring his protests, caught Geoffrey in a tight hug and kissed his cheek. "Your help may have saved England many lives. *Joyeaux Noel, mon ami.*"

He blushed again, stuttered that he was happy to save the country, and escaped into the crowd gathering around the pianoforte.

Anne sat down to the keyboard and began a rousing rendition of "Good King Wenceslas". One brave housemaid started singing the old carol and was soon joined by others.

Julien moved to stand beside her, an old cricket bat held at his side. "Another conquest?"

"No. Merely a Christmas hug."

"Do I get one?" His tone was wickedly teasing, but there was longing his eyes.

Uncomfortable, Ari shifted her gaze to the group at the pianoforte. A couple of the younger maids kept making calf's eyes at Julien and wandering under the mistletoe *kissing ball* tied to the chandelier. "If you wish."

As Julien grinned and opened his arms wide, Ari pointed to the girls, who tittered and blushed.

"You are cruel, Comtesse." Nonetheless, Julien gave the pair of maids a lecherous wink, sending them into giggling fits.

"Have you talked to all the servants?" she asked, putting their talk on a less dangerous level.

"Yes, as I told you earlier." He sighed. "You always avoid my gambits."

"Why do you waste your charm on a woman whose heart is given?"

"Why is the sweetest apple on the tree the one just out of reach?"

"But if you cannot taste it, how do you know it is sweetest?" Ari saw by his dancing eyes she had somehow made a mistake. "Cease," she cried, putting her fingers on his lips to stop whatever impudent words were about to tumble out.

He caught her fingers and kissed them.

Ari snatched her hand back. "Be serious!"

"Serious?" Julien sobered and ran his finger along the back of a lyre-backed chair. "Seriously, this—"

A crash of breaking glass sounded from somewhere in the depths of the house.

The noise in the parlor slowed and stopped, like a music box winding down. Ari caught his arm and met his gaze in wordless communication. A smaller crash followed the first, and Julien picked up his bat, from the corner where he'd propped it.

Catching Anne's eye, Ari nodded and mouthed, "Play."

Anne hit a chord, then began to sing, "Gentle Mary Laid Her Babe".

As everyone gradually joined in the old carol, Julien moved into the hall, hiding his bat behind him.

Ari was on his heels. Her hand in her pocket, she held the butt of the pistol to keep it from banging against her thigh as she walked.

"I wonder if there'll be more snow tomorrow?" Julien motioned her to continue talking.

"I do not think so. Is that all you have?" She indicated the bat.

He lifted his long-tailed, livery waistcoat and showed her the butt of a pistol thrust into the waistband of his breeches.

"There is the danger I shall blow my brains out as I pull it out." He grinned.

Ari laughed out loud. "Half the world would mourn — that is, the half that is female."

The wavering light from the sconces along the wall showed her joke brought only a flicker of a smile to his lips, quickly gone. "I will be leaving next week, when the *Sun Dancer* sails. That's the other ship in the Fox shipping fleet. A third is under construction in Boston."

Ari stopped and turned to him. "I don't know what to say. I—"

A slight scuffling sound caught their attention.

Julien pointed to the kitchen and mouthed, "Stay behind me."

She nodded, her heart pounding.

In the narrow hallway leading to the kitchen, they heard more rattling sounds, coming from the butler's pantry. Julien drew the pistol from his waistband. Flattened against the wall, Ari held her breath. Using the cricket bat, he pushed open the door.

Candlelight spilled out, along with a strong smell of gin and low, off-key singing.

Julien dared a quick peep within and lowered his gun.

Seeing Julien's posture relax, Ari looked around the doorframe. Anne's normally very proper butler half-sat, half-reclined against the wall. A stool overturned between his naked legs showed the source of the biggest crash. The bottle of gin cradled lovingly in both hands showed the reason.

"Damme, but the thing threw me." He gave them a slack-jawed smile.

"We can't have that, now can we, G'vnor." Julien stuck his pistol back into his waistband. Pushing Ari back, he said, "He's not wearing breeches. I'll get him up the servant's stairs and to bed."

"I shall go tell Anne all is well."

Hurrying back along the hall, Ari's heart beat much lighter than it had going down it. It was unlikely Dent would trouble himself over a letter filled with supposition, she decided. They were all being overly cautious. Jumping at shadows.

As she neared the study, Ari paused and listened to Anne's clear soprano singing "What Child is This?" A chill touched her, and she realized an icy draft was flowing through the open door of the study.

It had been closed when she and Julien passed it a few moments before.

The sound of a cock being ratcheted back froze her blood.

"Come in. I've been waiting for you." The voice issued from the darkened room, as cold as the winter air flowing in the open casement window.

Panic thrummed through her veins. Julien would be halfway up the backstairs by now, too far away to help her. To cry out would bring Geoffrey and Anne's useless footmen. Someone would be hurt.

Seeing no other option, Ari moved quickly into the shadowy room lit only by the moonlight streaming in through the open window curtains. She hoped fervently that there was not enough light to show the weight of the pistol pulling at her skirt pocket. "What do you want—*oh, my!*"

The last as she kicked a chair to cover the sound of her thumbing back the cock. "Who put that chair there? I have broken my toe!"

"Close the door and be quiet, or I'll break your bloody neck."

Ari did as she was told and blinked. As her eyes adjusted, she spotted Dent in the shadows behind the desk. He held not one pistol, but two.

"Do exactly as I say. As you can see, if you cut up stiff I have one bullet for you and one for whichever of your friends comes to see what is wrong. Now, what are you hiding in your pocket?"

Ari ground her teeth. She could turn the barrel upward and fire through her pocket. But there would be little chance of hitting her target. Then Geoffrey would come rushing in—*no.* She could not risk it.

She placed her pistol on the desk between them. "You came for the letter."

"Letter? Ah, yes. What kept me from getting rid of you in the park. I knew you were bound to realize your mistake in thinking me Grandquest," Dent chuckled. He uncocked one gun and stuck it into his waistband, picked up the letter, slipped it into an inside coat pocket, and he picked up her gun. "I thank you for reminding me of the second reason I came."

Swallowing past the growing knot in her throat, Ari asked, "If you are here for more than the letter, what is it?"

"To plant evidence, of course. Very damning, too. The key to Wellington's old message code is now locked in the second drawer." Dent chuckled. "You see, it was long ago decided that Grandquest should be named as Dandelion. Then you appeared and proved troublesome, so we began to throw suspicion on you. You'll be found to be his accomplice. Perhaps, the reason for his downfall. Delilah to his Sampson, as it were. I can hear the speculation now."

"You will not ruin Fox. He has already gone to Lord Blaine with your identity."

"Yes, I know." Dent seemed unconcerned. "Grandquest has been filling Lord Blaine's ear with how Leonard Dent is the same as *dent de leon*—Dandelion. Pity, he never considered that dandelions often have more than one head. Some heads are yellow, and—"

"Some are white," Ari finished. Her knees threatened to buckle as the meaning sank home. Fox. He was in a trap!

Dent circled the desk and thrust the barrel of a pistol into her ribs. "Through the window. Now."

Chapter Twenty-Two

~

The cavernous ballroom at Balmore House glittered with the light of a thousand candles refracted by faceted crystals dangling beneath the many chandeliers. The effect was reflected again and again with the many floor-to-ceiling mirrors on every wall, in imitation of the Hall of Mirrors at the *Palace at Versailles*. The ball had scarcely begun. Only a few costumed couples came together in the steps of a country dance. A few more gathered around the edges of the parquet dance floor.

Fox's position, half-hidden by the potted greenery screening the orchestra alcove, afforded an excellent view of the anteroom door, behind which a Russian courier waited for Spencer Percival, the Prime Minister. The courier was protected by two of the king's Hussars.

Garbed in a concealing black domino and mask, Fox knew he was unlikely to be recognized or approached by acquaintances. That left him free to concentrate on the matter at hand, watching for Dent. Even in costume, Dent's height should give him away.

And after tonight, Ari should be free of suspicion. Then he could turn his attention to wooing her properly. Remembering the fire of their lovemaking that afternoon, he felt a surge of warmth in his loins. *Improperly* had its advantages, too.

Watching the anteroom door, Fox was again possessed by the feeling he'd overlooked something, something vitally important. But what? Like the cold permeating the nearby wall of French windows, an odd sense of urgency crept through him. Crossing his arms over his chest, he leaned a shoulder against the gold flocked wallpaper, trying to ignore the feeling. But he had a strong urge to abandon his post and ride back to Anne's townhouse to assure himself all was well.

That was madness. Here was where he could help Ari. If they could capture Dent in the act of trying to steal the diplomatic packet, Ari would be freed of suspicion.

Then what was wrong? What piece to the puzzle was still missing...*what?*

He thought back over the last few months. Obviously, Dent killed Deveril. Fox had no idea if Dent was in town when Peterson was murdered, but he could easily find out. However, last week when the courier was murdered in Dover, Fox had seen Dent playing cards at White's Club.

Of course, Dent had underlings, like the thug in the park. Perhaps more than underlings. An accomplice.

The night of Anne's dinner party, Dent had said, "This Dandelion often seemed to be in two places at once."

Remembering the statement, Fox realized there'd been a certain smugness in the man's tone. Damn! He should have seen it sooner. He was looking for more than one man. Something else that had bothered Fox was Lord Stubbins' role in it all. Fox could accept that Stubbins had used his father, Meadowbridge, to gain knowledge of what was happening in the War Ministry. But reliable sources had informed Fox that the aging Meadowbridge had been little more than a figurehead in his department for many years. The old lord would have been privy to little that was truly secret.

Dandelion's sources seemed better informed. Certainly Dent's minor position in the Foreign Ministry would never make him privy to such sensitive information, such as who the vital couriers were and what routes they traveled.

The orchestra finished a lively country dance and paused. The sudden silence was broken by the tinkling of small bells. Fox looked up as Lord Blaine approached. Dressed in the black and white diamonds of a harlequin clown, the jingling bells were on the pointed toes of Blaine's shoes.

"Relax, Grandquest." He motioned to the footman bearing a tray. "You look in need of warming. Here." He lifted a snifter from the tray, and gave it to Fox, smiling.

"To your health." Taking another glass, Blaine raised it in a toast.

"And yours." Fox matched the salute, then sipped the liquor. He frowned. A faintly bitter taste lingered on his tongue.

"Drink up. Now that we have the who of it figured out, all will soon be over."

"Let us hope so."

Lord Blaine pulled a key from the pocket of his waistcoat. "Come with me. I'm in the mood to play Father Christmas. One glass should not dull our young Hussars' senses overmuch, I think."

As Blaine took the tray from the footman and disappeared into the anteroom, Fox followed, closing the door and locking it behind them. Two young Hussars in bright red uniforms stood guard over a Russian, whose coat was bedecked with enough braid work and medals to decorate a whole regiment of the King's Lifeguards.

Watching the older man play congenial host, Fox wondered if Christmas had had a softening effect on the old lord. Blaine was normally a dour man, not one likely to trouble himself over the comfort of two young soldiers he didn't know. But Blaine was being more than congenial, proposing toasts to their health and making small talk.

Palming the snifter to warm it, Fox swirled the liquor. An odd smell, almost indistinguishable from the heavy scent of the brandy, caught his attention. Lifting the glass to the light of a wall sconce, he found tiny flecks of white swirling about the bottom.

And he noticed his lips and tongue were growing numb.

Blaine was eyeing him speculatively. Blaine, the piece to the puzzle that had been missing.

"Stop. Don't drink that." Fox knocked the glass out of the first soldier's hand—too late. It was almost empty. Feeling as if he moved through deep water, Fox reached beneath his domino and drew out the pistol he'd hidden there.

Pointing the gun at Blaine, he said, "The brandy is poisoned."

The second soldier pointed a bayoneted rifle at Fox. "Put down the gun."

As though his hands were not working properly, the first soldier grabbed for his rifle, but dropped it. "What the…?" His speech was thick. He cast a surprised look at the glass rolling across an Aubusson rug and sank to his knees, then sprawled on the floor.

"I said put down the gun." Menacingly, the soldier placed the point of the bayonet against Fox's chest.

Seeing no other option, Fox uncocked the pistol and let it fall. "Think man. I am not the one who gave you drugged wine."

Moving to his fallen comrade, the Hussar shook him. "Freddy?"

In a surprisingly fast movement for a man his age, Blaine picked up the fallen rifle and drove the bayonet into the soldier's back. Yanking it out, he stabbed at Fox.

Catching the end of the barrel, Fox forced it aside. "Grab him!" he shouted at the Russian courier, who sat astride a chair, one arm propped on the back.

A mildly interested look crossed the man's flat features as he watched the proceedings. The Russian drained his glass, tossed it in the nearby fireplace, and pulled a pistol from his waistband. Cocking it, he pointed it at Fox. "You let go, yes?"

"Point that bloody thing at him." Fox wrenched the rifle away from Blaine and stood holding it by the barrel, looking at the Russian in disbelief. "He just killed your guard."

"*Nyet*. Lord Blaine told me the guards were untrustworthy, and of a plan to steal the Czar's letter." He hitched the courier pouch a little higher on his shoulder.

"Shoot, you fool," Blaine cried.

Fox kicked the pistol away and stood holding the rifle barrel. "Don't let either of us have a weapon then," he challenged.

"I like that." The Russian smiled. "Now, put down rifle. I think both of you will wait for the Prime Minister." After throwing the rifle on the floor, Fox met the big man's gaze levelly.

"The brandy was drugged. You saw the soldier fall after he drank it."

"Yes. Blaine told me he would drug the untrustworthy soldiers."

"He put the drug into your glass, too." Fox couldn't know this, but it stood to reason.

"Nyet."

"Then why are your lips growing numb?"

The big man blinked in surprise and scowled at Blaine. "My mouth feels very strange…"

"Pay him no heed," Blaine declared. "He is trying to confuse you."

"Am I?" Fox shook his head. His vision was growing fuzzy. "Or is he?"

"Silence. We'll wait for the Prime Minister. I will give him the packet."

Fox mentally measured the distance to the rifle on the floor. If the Russian succumbed to the drug, could he reach the pistol, before Blaine could get to the rifles?

"The harlequin costume of black and white seems appropriate for a double agent. Why, Blaine?"

"Money. I've never been a wealthy man. I've given many years in the service of England and have little to show for it. France shows its appreciation of my special talents."

"You admit it. You aren't afraid our friend here will take it amiss?"

"He won't take anything amiss in a very short time," Blaine said.

Aware that Blaine was right, that the Russian was fading, he tensed. As the big man slipped from the chair, Fox grabbed the gun from the floor and cocked it before Blaine could get to a rifle.

"Hold."

Blaine shrugged. "And how much longer do you think you'll be conscious? I put enough opium in that brandy to drug ten men, plus foxglove to speed its effects. It's useless to fight it."

"So, if I lose consciousness, you will take the letter and secrete it somewhere."

"Yes, I'll hide the letter. And you too. You will be dead, of course. All will conclude you grabbed the missive and disappeared with it, admitting before you left that you are the spy and the Comtesse, your accomplice. To my shocked horror. But then, it will be confirmed when a search of Lady Brickingham's house is made and a military code key is found."

"Code key?" Fox shook his head. He had to stay conscious. He had to keep Ari free of suspicion.

"Oh, not the new one. It would be stupid to let Whitehall know the French have broken their new code. The old one. Still, it should be sufficient."

A tapping sounded at one of the French windows. Then glass shattered and someone undid the lock. The curtains billowed inward as it was opened.

"Come out slowly." Fox divided his attention between Blaine and the unknown entity behind the curtains.

Ari emerged from the draperies. Fox felt his heart leap into his throat. Her long hair was loose and tangled, her gown torn on the sleeve, her wrists were bound before her. She looked frightened. Leonard Dent appeared behind her, and he held a gun to her back.

"Fox." The look in her eyes beseeched him to help her. Then her gaze went to the men sprawled on the floor and she paled. "*Dieu*." She bent to check the nearest soldier, but Dent yanked her hair, hauling her erect.

"Let me go. These men, they need help."

"Be still, Comtesse, or I will blow your head from your shoulders."

Fox held himself in check, very much aware that the odds were against them. There were two men with all their facilities against one, half-drugged. If he gave in to his anger, it could cost Ari her life.

Blaine took a step forward. "About time, Dent. Now get the courier's pouch and slit these soldiers' throats."

"Stand where you are, Blaine, or you are a dead man. Dent, release the Comtesse." Fox braced his legs, putting his back against the wall to help him remain upright.

Dent laughed and curled a forearm beneath her chin. "I'll wager I care less for Blaine than you do for this pretty piece."

Ari struggled to free herself. Fox prayed his fear for her wouldn't further cloud his thinking. It was nearly impossible to stand by and watch her struggle with Dent. When Dent pressed the gun to her temple, she held still. But, uncowed, she called Dent a bastard in five languages, before he tightened his hold on her neck, choking off further speech.

Blaine said laconically, "Grandquest had my special brandy. He is on his last legs."

"And what if the prime minister should arrive before those legs give way?" Dent asked.

"He's not due for another thirty minutes." Shrugging, Blaine said, "Shoot Grandquest and the comtesse now if you've no taste for waiting. We shall say we have foiled their attempt to steal the Czar's letter. Perhaps, in the confusion, I can take charge of the packet, and I'll have time to read the letter, anyway."

"Shoot Grandquest? An excellent idea." Dent swung the gun toward Fox. Before he could pull the trigger, Ari dealt him a hard kick to the shin with the heel of her shoe, and stomped his instep, then drove an elbow into his groin. Gasping, Dent loosened his hold, and Ari wrenched free.

"Bitch!" He swung his pistol toward her.

Fox fired and dove for the Russian's pistol on the floor and pointed it at Blaine before the old lord could grab the other rifle. "Hold!" Acrid blue smoke from the gunpowder filled the air. In the next room, the orchestra ground to a halt, like a music box that had been dropped and broken.

Surprise masked Dent's features and a round circle on his forehead leaked blood. He fell against Ari, and she pushed him away.

"Get Dent's other gun and hold it on Lord Blaine," Fox commanded.

Nodding, she yanked the little pistol Julien had given her from Dent's waistband and held it on Blaine.

Fox dared a glance at her. "Are you all right?"

The door rattled as someone tried it. Shouts for someone to unlock it came from the other side.

"You'd better take your lady and run," Blaine calmly advised. "Suspicion is already high against the two of you. All I need say is how I found you attempting to steal the Czar's letter and no one will question that I speak the truth. You are an outsider, Grandquest." His lip curled in a show of distaste. The harlequin's costume lent absurdity to the gesture.

"After all the men you have killed, you expect Fox to let you go? I shall shoot you myself," Ari snapped, cocking the pistol.

Blaine shrugged. "I think they will have the door open in a few moments. We'll see who is believed."

"Oi think Oi'd like to hear more of what the earl has to say about it." Higgins came through the drapes. Two more men were behind him.

"Thank you, ma'am," he said, taking the gun from Ari. "And thanks for the tip to keep our peepers on Lady Brickingham's house, My lord." At Higgins' nod, the two men bracketed Lord Blaine and started searching him for weapons, despite his vehement protests.

Fox moved toward Ari. Swaying, he caught her to him. "Are you all right? Did he hurt you?" He touched her lips with his own.

"I am fine, but for this rope." She held her bound hands up.

"Is Anne all right? Geoffrey?" Fox asked as he clumsily untied her.

"All are well," Ari assured him. Once her hands were free, she framed his face and searched his eyes, alarmed at how dilated the pupils were. "Are you? What did he give you?"

"Opium and foxglove. But I barely tasted it. I think my head is already starting to clear." He nodded at the soldiers. "They had a great deal more."

Ari knelt by them, testing each one's pulse. "This man is dead, but the other needs a doctor at once." She moved on to the Russian. "He is a little stronger, but in danger also. They must have their stomachs purged."

Higgins nodded to one of his men. "Open the door, but let no one in. Ask the lady of the house to provide a purgative—most households have Puke on hand for emergencies. And have her send a footman for a doctor."

As the man left, Higgins prodded Dent's body with the toe of his shoe. "This cove slipped in Lady Anne's house without us none the wiser, but when they raised a hue and cry after the countess, we followed the tracks in the snow in the alley and saw him bundlin' the lady into his carriage. He had quite a job of it, too. The comtesse can hold her own," the Runner said in an admiring tone. "We followed to see where he took her."

Higgins nodded at Fox. "Oi'll handle it from here, My lord. Now, if you'd like to take your lady away, a'fore the circus starts when we open the door... Oi'll be 'round tomorrow to talk to the two of you, My lord."

"Thank you." Fox held onto Ari as they made their way through the open window into the crisp night.

Once safely away, Ari looked up into his face, trying to see his eyes in the moonlight. "You need a doctor, also."

He unhooked the cape to his costume and swung it around her shoulders, covering her. "I will be fine now that you are safe." He kissed her forehead.

Her eyes misted. "Never make me worry like that again!"

"Why would you worry?" Fox smiled.

"You talk too much. Here. Lean on me. I am strong." Giving him her shoulder for support, she led him through the dark garden.

"Yes, you are strong. Have I told you how much I love your strength?" He tucked her head against his shoulder as they stumbled along between silent hedges.

"Is this the opium talking?"

"What if it is?"

"I will have to lay in a supply."

Fox chuckled. "You could make me laugh at my own funeral. I love your wit, Ari. And your mind. You suspected Dent immediately, didn't you?"

"It is the opium talking. No gentleman loves a woman who is smarter than he is."

"I said nothing about *smarter*." Fox breathed deeply of the crisp air, his head clearing more and more. "Equal, perhaps."

Ari sighed. "Surely you must think my actions are not those of a lady. I could change," she offered tentatively. "Become more *proper*. You need a proper wife to secure your position in society."

"Propriety would drive me mad."

"Speaking of madness —" she began.

"I told you, the Benoits aren't mad at all. They give their all for what they believe. They love true and with all their being. If loving like that is a form of madness, then it is a glorious one. If you loved me that intensely, I'd count myself the luckiest man on Earth. Because that's the way I love you, Ari."

"You love me?" She looked up at him. "I am so tall —"

"You are just right."

"And so educated —"

"I abhor willful ignorance."

"Do you really love me? In spite of my flaws?" Her eyes glistened in the half-light.

"No, nodcock. Because of your supposed flaws. You are the most fascinating person I have ever known, and I love you just as you are. I will spend the rest of my life loving you."

"Oh, Fox. Yes, it is madness." She wiped her eyes. "And no madder Benoit ever lived than I. Mad to fall in love with you so completely, I never want to be separated from you. Completely mad but it is a glorious madness, is it not?"

"A glorious madness," he agreed, then kissed her, because he could not wait one second longer.

Epilogue

🔊

Wind filled the great, triangle sails, popping the canvas taut, and it boomed like a cannon shot. The schooner's rigging creaked as the ship sliced through the waves, driven before the freshening wind.

Braced against the angling deck, Prince Rudolpho stood at the starboard rail, looking back at England. Drawing in a deep breath of the clean, salt air, he exhaled it in a cloud, which was whipped away immediately. The day was cold and clear, and the chalk cliffs of Dover were a startling white beyond the blue, blue water. Looking back at England, he had never felt so free.

"What are you thinkin', love?"

Rudy looked around. Wrapped in a thick woolen cloak, Molly made her way across the tilting deck and joined him at the rail. He wrapped his arm around her and looked back at the receding land. By staying *dead* and letting everyone believe Ari was his widow, as Lady Anne had put about, Ari's reputation would be saved. She could marry Grandquest and take her rightful place in society. Though Ari had argued against it, Dolpho had insisted it was what he wanted.

And it was.

"I'm thinking I'm content. More content than I can ever remember being." He kissed the dark curls on Molly's forehead.

"Ye've no regrets?" She looked up at him, her brown eyes shadowed by concern. Enunciating her words carefully, she continued, "You were born to privilege. Mayhap, it'll be greater hardship than ye've bargained for to be just plain *Rudy Dragon*."

"*Rudy Dragon* is exactly who I want to be. I've never had a choice but to act the part to which I was born. Never before, that is. Now that Ari is supposed to be my widow, by disappearing, I can protect her."

"I worry that you'll miss the life you've known." Molly bit her full bottom lip.

"What you mean is, will I grow tired of you?" She nodded shyly and he hugged her tighter. "Never, my love. But what of you? You've left your family and all you've ever known behind. Any regrets?"

"No. I'll be with you as long as you'll have me." Molly tilted her face up, love shining in her eyes.

"There is one thing that would make me happier."

"What be—*is* that?" Molly asked, correcting herself.

"If you'd consent to let the ship's captain make us husband and wife."

Feeling her nod against his chest, Rudy smiled into her hair and planted a kiss in it and tucked her head under his chin and watched the coast of England recede. Rudy again thought that Ari had done him the greatest of favors. By leaving Prince Rudolpho behind, for the first time in his life, he was completely free. Free to be whomever he chose. Free to love whomever he would.

"We will have a good life, you will see."

Why an electronic book?

We live in the Information Age — an exciting time in the history of human civilization, in which technology rules supreme and continues to progress in leaps and bounds every minute of every day. For a multitude of reasons, more and more avid literary fans are opting to purchase e-books instead of paper books. The question from those not yet initiated into the world of electronic reading is simply: *Why?*

1. ***Price.*** An electronic title at Ellora's Cave Publishing and Cerridwen Press runs anywhere from 40% to 75% less than the cover price of the exact same title in paperback format. Why? Basic mathematics and cost. It is less expensive to publish an e-book (no paper and printing, no warehousing and shipping) than it is to publish a paperback, so the savings are passed along to the consumer.

2. ***Space.*** Running out of room in your house for your books? That is one worry you will never have with electronic books. For a low one-time cost, you can purchase a handheld device specifically designed for e-reading. Many e-readers have large, convenient screens for viewing. Better yet, hundreds of titles can be stored within your new library — on a single microchip. There are a variety of e-readers from different manufacturers. You can also read e-books on your PC or laptop computer. (Please note that Ellora's

Cave does not endorse any specific brands. You can check our websites at www.ellorascave.com or www.cerridwenpress.com for information we make available to new consumers.)

3. *Mobility*. Because your new e-library consists of only a microchip within a small, easily transportable e-reader, your entire cache of books can be taken with you wherever you go.

4. ***Personal Viewing Preferences.*** Are the words you are currently reading too small? Too large? Too... ANNOYING? Paperback books cannot be modified according to personal preferences, but e-books can.

5. ***Instant Gratification.*** Is it the middle of the night and all the bookstores near you are closed? Are you tired of waiting days, sometimes weeks, for bookstores to ship the novels you bought? Ellora's Cave Publishing sells instantaneous downloads twenty-four hours a day, seven days a week, every day of the year. Our webstore is never closed. Our e-book delivery system is 100% automated, meaning your order is filled as soon as you pay for it.

Those are a few of the top reasons why electronic books are replacing paperbacks for many avid readers.

As always, Ellora's Cave and Cerridwen Press welcome your questions and comments. We invite you to email us at Comments@ellorascave.com or write to us directly at Ellora's Cave Publishing Inc., 1056 Home Avenue, Akron, OH 44310-3502.

Cerridwen Press

Cerridwen, the Celtic goddess of
wisdom, was the muse who brought
inspiration to storytellers and those in
the creative arts.

Cerridwen Press encompasses the best
and most innovative stories in all
genres of today's fiction.

Visit our website and discover the
newest titles by talented authors who
still get inspired — much like the
ancient storytellers did...

once upon a time.

www.cerridwenpress.com